Kalyna's *song*

Kalyna's
song

LISA GREKUL

COTEAU BOOKS
WWW.COTEAUBOOKS.COM

This is a work of fiction. Names, characters, places, and incidents either are the product of the author's imagination or are used fictitiously. Any resemblance to actual persons, living or dead, is coincidental.

Edited by Geoffrey Ursell.
Cover and book design by Duncan Campbell.
Cover photo by Simon Watson, The Image Bank/Getty Images.
Author photo by Janis O'Neill.
Printed and bound in Canada by Gauvin Press.

National Library of Canada Cataloguing in Publication

Grekul, Lisa, 1972-
Kalyna's song / Lisa Grekul.

ISBN 1-55050-225-5

I. Title.
PS8563.R446K34 2003   C813'.6   C2003-910496-6
PZ7.G73KA 2003

    2   3   4   5   6   7   8   9   10

401-2206 Dewdney Ave.
Regina, Saskatchewan
Canada   S4R 1H3

Available in the US and Canada from:
Fitzhenry & Whiteside
195 Allstate Parkway
Markham, Ontario
Canada   L3R 4T8

This publication has been funded in part by the Ukrainian Canadian Foundation of Taras Shevchenko, with the assistance of the Ukrainian Canadian Congress, Saskatchewan Provincial Council.

The publisher gratefully acknowledges the financial assistance of the Saskatchewan Arts Board, the Canada Council for the Arts, the Government of Canada through the Book Publishing Industry Development Program (BPIDP), the Government of Saskatchewan, through the Cultural Industries Development Fund, and the City of Regina Arts Commission, for its publishing program.

For Auntie Sophie,
and in memory of
Auntie Jean and Uncle Sam.

PROLOGUE

Swaziland

1990

When I board the plane in Manzini, the sky is about to burst. For the first time in months, there are clouds, dark grey and heavy with rain. The drought is almost over. You can feel it in the air, see it in the faces of the people milling around the airport. They're ready for the rain. They know that it's coming.

I want rain before I go, so that when my plane rises and veers west I can look down on the countryside and watch it come to life again. When I arrived in Swaziland, almost a year ago, everything was green and lush. Humid enough that my T-shirt stuck to my back the moment I stepped onto the tarmac. So different from the winter that I left behind in Alberta. Mom and Dad tell me that they're having a cold, dry December. These days, the temperature in St. Paul is minus twenty, minus twenty-five, with hardly any snow. They're bringing my winter coat with them to the airport in Edmonton, and my felt-lined winter boots. I don't want to think about stepping into that deep freeze. I'm not ready to leave.

Of course, I can't change my mind now. Even if I could, I'd only gain a few more days — a few weeks, at the most — in Africa. Sooner or later, I'd have to make my way back to Canada. Students who go to United World Colleges on scholarship are required to return to their home countries once they've finished their studies. We're supposed to teach people about what we learned, living together with other students from around the world, from all different races and religions. I'm supposed to spread the word about peace and love. Like a missionary, but without the Bible.

Maybe I will, eventually. First, though, I have to get through the funeral. Then I have to decide what I'm going to do with myself at home. My plans have changed so much over the past few days, over the past twenty-four hours, I feel like I'm in a tailspin. After final exams and graduation, I was going to backpack around South Africa with Rosa. My flight home was booked for mid-January, not late-December. And I wasn't going to stay in Canada. Not for long, anyway. I was going to bend the UWC rules – stay home for a while, then leave again. I have all the application forms for universities in Johannesburg and Cape Town. Rosa and I both wrote away for them. We were planning to meet again.

As the plane starts easing down the runway, I lean my forehead on the window, pressing my nose against the glass. Within minutes, we're airborne. I keep my eyes on the ground, trying to memorize everything that I see. The hangars around the tarmac, the other airplanes. The car park outside the airport, and the road that leads from the airport to Manzini. I thought that I might see the college one last time, but the clouds are too low and too thick. After awhile, I can't see much of anything.

Then a flight attendant appears at my side, to see if I'd like a drink. I ask for some tissues. My supply of Kleenex has run out.

At least I don't have to sing at the funeral. I can sit in a pew like everybody else, and I don't have to bite my bottom lip to stop myself from breaking down. For as long as I can remember, since I was a little kid, my family has made me sing at birthdays, anniversaries, retirement parties. At weddings and prayer services. I'm not allowed to sing at funerals, though. Not funerals that are held in the Orthodox church, at least. In the Orthodox church, only the priest can sing, and the cantor, and the choir that sits in the loft above the congregation. It's just as well. There are no instruments in the Orthodox church, so even if I could sing – even if I wanted

2

to sing – I wouldn't be able to accompany myself on the piano or the guitar. And I don't like to sing a cappella.

But I can't say it doesn't bother me that I won't be singing at my cousin's funeral. Kalyna loved my singing, more than anyone else. At family gatherings, whenever I stood up in front of the crowd, she made sure that she was in the front row, up close to the microphone. She knew all the words to the songs that I sang, especially the Ukrainian songs. Sometimes she sang along with me, clapping and swaying in time to the music. The truth is, I should be singing at her funeral. She would want it that way.

The problem is that she'd also want her funeral to be in the Orthodox church.

My parents hardly ever took Sophie, Wes, and me to their church, the church that they grew up in, and I'm glad. Szypenitz church is dark and musty. In the summer, it's stifling hot; in the winter, you can see your breath. It always smells bad, though. Like mothballs and incense. Father Zubritsky is crazy about incense. His services go on forever, and by the time he's finished the church is hazy with smoke. I'm not looking forward to the incense at Kalyna's funeral. Just thinking about it makes me dizzy, and sick to my stomach.

Yet, for some reason, Kalyna liked being in church. I used to watch her at weddings, the way she listened to Father Zubritsky, her eyes fixed on him. It's strange how well-behaved my cousin was in church, how at home she felt there. But then Kalyna wasn't like other people.

Mom and Dad say that Kalyna used to be normal, when she was growing up, and even after she got married, for the first few years. I never knew her then. Auntie Mary, Kalyna's mom, is my mother's oldest sister. In fact, Auntie Mary is almost twenty years older than my mother. When Kalyna was born, my mom was seven years old. So Kalyna was more like a cousin to Mom than a niece; more like an aunt to me, really, than a cousin.

Except that she never acted like an aunt. Most of the time, she acted like a little kid. We had to babysit her, basically, because she'd wander away if no one was watching. For a long time, I was embarrassed to be around her, and scared, too, of what she might say or do in front of other people. Kalyna used to wear silly outfits. Clothes that didn't match, plastic flowers in her hair. Cheap rubber flip-flops and shiny costume jewelry. You couldn't count on her to follow a conversation properly because she was constantly drifting in and out of her own crazy world. Sometimes she'd forget where she was, and who she was with. Out of the blue, she'd ask, "Who are you? What's your name?"

I used to remind her that we have the same name. Kalyna and Colleen. Hers is the Ukrainian version of mine; mine, the English version of hers.

We *had* the same name. Past tense.

In the future, though, no matter what happens – no matter where I go, or what I do – when I think about my time in Africa, I'll always think about Kalyna. Before I left Edmonton, bound for Swaziland, she was the last person to say goodbye to me in the airport. Now I'm coming home to say goodbye to her.

The plane touches down in Johannesburg right on time. Once I get through passport control, I'll head straight for the British Airways departure gate. Then I'll leave Africa behind me. Not just Swaziland, but all of Africa.

Standing in line at the security check, I sift through my backpack, making sure that my passport is with me, my visa to get into and out of Jan Smuts Airport, my plane ticket. All of my important papers are tucked into my book.

I bought the book in Paris, on a stopover during my trip to Swaziland. It's a book filled with blank pages, like a diary. My plan was to write in it all year and then give it to my parents, and my sister and brother, so that they could see what it was like for me at the college. But I only wrote in it during my flights to Swaziland, and for a few weeks after I arrived. After that, I got too busy. I couldn't keep up. Flipping through the book now, I'm embarrassed. I wrote everything in code, to hide my words from Siya, the Swazi guy who was sitting next to me on the planes from Paris to Johannesburg, Johannesburg to Manzini. And I wrote such silly things. I can't show it to anyone, least of all my family. Mom and Dad would laugh. Sophie and Wes would howl. I'm tempted to tear out all the pages that I've written on.

But I have a better plan.

Yesterday, after I heard the news about Kalyna, I went down to the music room at school. I was supposed to be finishing my final project of the year, my essay on Ukrainian folk music. Instead, though, I got to thinking about Kalyna's funeral, and my friend Rosa, and my old piano teacher, Sister Maria. And I started to write a song for all of them. The song should go in my book, I think. When I get home, I'll paste it onto the pages that I filled with my writing. So the writing will always be there, underneath the music, only no one will be able to see it. That's how the song works, after all. In layers. One voice on top of another voice on top of another. If you dig deep enough, there's an embryo of a melody at the centre of it all that ties the song together.

In a way, the embryo is me, and as the melody changes and grows, it tells my story, better than words. I don't know if Kalyna would understand the song, but maybe that doesn't matter. She'd like it anyway. She'd love it.

She'd probably sing along.

PART I

Dauphin

ONE

The festival in Dauphin, Manitoba, begins with a parade of competitors from across the country. Our dance club has known about it for months. It's like the opening ceremonies of the Olympics. All of the festival dancers, singers, and instrumentalists gather at noon on the steps of City Hall. There are official welcome speeches and opening remarks, and then the whole crowd marches toward the festival grounds. Dance groups walk together, carrying flags and banners to identify themselves, and where they're from. Our mothers have worked for weeks sewing an enormous blue banner on which they have stitched our dance club's name – in English and Ukrainian – with white thread. The banner says

Desna – Дисна
St. Paul, Alberta

Our MLA gave us one hundred and twenty miniature Alberta flags. At eleven-thirty, with each of us waving two tiny Alberta flags, the Babiuk twins holding each side of the banner, we're a sea of blue. A proud sea of Alberta blue.

One of our chaperones, Mrs. Demkiw, had the idea to come early – to make sure we got a good spot in the parade, near the front. She insisted that we arrive at City Hall before noon. By twelve-thirty, though, when no other dancers have arrived, we're starting to get nervous. Mr. Demkiw runs up the steps to City Hall. There are festival posters pinned up on either side of the doors to City Hall. *Join Us in Dauphin for Canada's National Ukrainian Festival, August 1-6, 1984.* But the doors are locked. The dancers, all in full costume, get restless. It's hot in Manitoba – hot and humid. The girls waste no time peeling off their velvet vests and headpieces. Their noses bead with sweat, their makeup runs in the heat of the midday sun. The Babiuk twins develop matching wet stains under their arms. My little brother Wes whines to Mom that he's thirsty. If I were a bit younger, I'd whine too. My cousin Kalyna is the only one who doesn't look wilted in the heat. For once in her life, she's dressed just right for the occasion – short shorts, and a cotton halter top.

All of the adults are worried – the Demkiws, the Farynas, the Yuzkos, and my parents. While the men gather to discuss the situation, rubbing the sweat from their foreheads with handkerchiefs, the women try to find shade for the dancers under various trees around City Hall. The chaperones decide that we'll wait until one o'clock and then reassess the situation. Tammy and Tanya Yuzko and my older sister Sophie say that they're going to die, over and over again. Tammy and Sophie are both fifteen. They're always together. Tanya and I are best friends too. Even though we're two years younger than our sisters, and in different dance groups – they're Seniors, we're Intermediates – we all hang around together at dance competitions and performances.

"I'm going to die of sunstroke," says Tanya.

"I'm dying already," says Tammy.

"Colleen," says Sophie, "this is worse than death."

I chose not to wear a costume today because I'm not actually dancing in the festival. At a pre-Dauphin dance rehearsal, I injured my knee. I'm still competing – in the singing competition – but, technically, I'm not part of *Desna*. Mom entered me in the Women's Vocal Solo Category. I'm on my own here.

But I feel sorry for the dancers. Most of them, anyway. Carla Senko, one of the girls in my dance group — who is also in my class at school — looks as though she's about to faint from the heat. I take some pleasure in watching her suffer. We don't get along. We've never been friends. Carla is a bully and a boss. A know-it-all. She's pushy and mean — and still, somehow, the most popular girl at school and in Ukrainian dancing. If Carla drops from sunstroke, I might just smile and look the other way. *Boh ne be bu kom,* as my mother would say. God doesn't hit with a stick.

At a quarter to one, one of the guys from the Senior group marches over to the chaperones and says, "If you don't get us out of here, we're hitchhiking home."

That's when the parade of dancers arrives. Out of nowhere. They descend on us like a thundercloud, like a hailstorm. Like a plague of locusts. The *Volya* dancers from Saskatoon, *Trembita* from Sudbury. They come dancing and singing. Vancouver's *Dazhboh* Ensemble, Kamloops' *Skomorokhy* Ensemble. Hordes of them, hundreds of them, smiling and laughing. *Sopilka, Kateryna, Vesna,* and *Dumy.* All the Ukrainian dance groups from every corner of the country. The parade started as it always starts, at the festival grounds. The participating dancers marched as they always march, *toward* City Hall. The Demkiws misunderstood. They got their wires crossed. Everyone else got it right except us. We're the laughingstock of the festival.

There isn't time, though, to dwell on our mistake. Our first dance group competes at three o'clock on the mainstage. We have to collect ourselves. Regroup. The chaperones call us together for a pep talk before the competition begins. They tell us to hold our heads high. So we missed the parade. So what? The dancing is what matters.

By three o'clock, the festival grounds are alive with people — dancers milling around in groups, all in full costume, old people with walkers and canes, the odd wheelchair. Moms and Dads, little kids, babies. A few teenagers holding hands. They all carry festival programs with them; some carry umbrellas to shield themselves from the sun. Most of the competition is held on stages under tents, but sometimes there isn't room under the tarp for the whole audience. Mothers spread sunscreen on the arms and legs of their children.

As I make my way toward the stage to watch our first dance group compete, the Senior Girls, I hear applause in the distance, a voice making an announcement over a loudspeaker. Two old women sell *pyrohy* and *kolbasa* from inside a trailer that's been converted into a portable kitchen; polka music blares from a ghetto blaster beside their grill. The sign over their trailer says *Baba's Best.* Seven dollars for a half-dozen *pyrohy,* a chunk of sausage, and a pop. There's a long lineup outside the window of the trailer.

My parents are sitting in the bleachers with Wes and Kalyna. Sophie is offstage with the other Senior Girls, all in *Lemko* costume, all waiting for their music to begin. I don't want to sit next to Kalyna, but she's saved a seat for me, so I have no choice. Wes doesn't mind Kalyna because he's too young to know that there is something wrong with her. Sophie and I know the truth, though. Kalyna is weird. We never know how to talk to her, what kinds of things we should say. There's no way to predict what planet Kalyna is on; she randomly selects the stuff she talks about. Now that I'm sitting next to her, I want to move. I'm scared of her. She might drool, or touch me.

A few minutes after I sit down, the adjudicators announce that our Senior Girls' *Lemko* Ribbon Dance has been disqualified. The judges say that the *Lemko* costumes are inauthentic. The girls aren't even allowed to compete. There is some confusion offstage as the adjudicators talk privately to our dancers and parent chaperones, the Demkiws and the Farynas. Mrs. Demkiw and Mrs. Faryna put their arms around some of the girls to comfort them. Mr. Demkiw shakes his head while he listens to the judges. Mr. Faryna storms away. Sophie looks out into the crowd, trying to find our faces. Kalyna signals to her by waving her arms wildly over her head.

Later in the day, our Intermediate Girls' *Bukovynian* Wedding Dance comes in fourth. The girls – girls I dance with all the time – stand side by side onstage, holding hands while they listen to the adjudicator's comments. Some of them look as though they're about to cry. I admit, I'm not upset to see Carla Senko being criticized onstage along with the other dancers. I've hardly spoken to her since she dropped my mother's Ukrainian class to sign up for French. I don't mind seeing her lose. In fact, I enjoy it. But my heart aches for the other girls. I dance with them every week. They're my friends, and I don't want to see them humiliated like this, with the whole world watching. A few of our dancers in the audience boo when the medals are presented.

After the competition ends for the day, on our way back to our motorhome at the campsite, Mom and Dad whisper to each other about the judging. I walk behind them with my sister Sophie, and the Yuzko girls, Tammy and Tanya. We can't understand it. No one in our dance club has ever taken less than silver away from competition, and we've competed a lot, at festivals in Hafford and in Vegreville.

Then, on the second day of competition, our Senior Boys' *Hutsul* Dance takes bronze, and our Senior Group's *Hopak* comes in last in its category. Something is wrong. The dancers are devastated, the chaperones livid. On the second evening of the festival, the Demkiws and Farynas walk over from their campsite to our campsite for an emergency meeting. All of the adults slip into the Yuzko motorhome, locking the door behind them.

Maybe they needed to have an emergency meeting sooner. Sitting in lawn chairs at the Yuzko campsite, Tammy, Tanya, Sophie and I can hear drinks being poured inside the motorhome. The men say, *"Dai Bozhe."* There is quiet conversation and some laughter. But after a few minutes, Mrs. Demkiw starts raising her voice. Tammy and Tanya look at each other, Sophie raises her eyebrows.

Mrs. Demkiw yells, "Inauthentic costumes? Kevin Kowalchuk is a good instructor. He did six months of research in Ukraine. In

Ukraine! Six months in Ukraine and they're going to tell me our costumes are inauthentic?"

Mrs. Demkiw is head of the *Desna* Costume Committee. She must feel responsible.

"This is discrimination!" she hollers. "Did you notice how many Manitoba groups took gold today? It's because we're from Alberta. It's *discrimination!*"

Then Mr. Faryna starts up. "I never trusted that Kowalchuk, never from day one. I even told my wife. I told Freda. I told her there'd be trouble with him. I know Kowalchuks from way back, I went to school with Kowalchuks. You know what they are? Goddamn *Poles* is what they are. Our kids have been dancing in goddamn *Polish* costumes because their instructor is a goddamn *Pole!*"

I don't like what Mr. Faryna is saying about our dance instructor. It's not fair. Kevin isn't even here to defend himself. Someone should remind Mr. Faryna that Kevin is on tour right now – in Ukraine – with *Cheremosh,* the professional group he belongs to. That's why he couldn't be with us in Dauphin. Right this very minute, Kevin is in Ukraine.

After Mr. Faryna has had his say, Mrs. Demkiw pipes up again. She says that Mr. Faryna doesn't know what the hell he's talking about. Then *Mrs.* Faryna joins in, defending her husband and calling down Mrs. Demkiw. I hear Dad trying to break in, trying to calm everybody down. He suggests that maybe the competition is a bit stiffer here in Dauphin than at other festivals. It is the National Festival, after all. For the first time ever, our dancers are coming up against the best in the country.

Mr. Faryna bangs his fist on the motorhome table. "We *are* the best in the goddamn country!"

The inside of the Yuzko's motorhome becomes quiet for a moment. We can hear the murmuring of voices, the clinking of glasses.

Not a moment later, the door opens. It's Dad asking us to fetch his bottle of Lemon Hart rum.

"And pour yourselves a little shot," he says, winking. Sometimes Dad puts a tablespoon of rum into our Cokes. "You're going to have your work cut out for you, Colleen. You'll show them who's best in the country."

Dad's words echo in my ears as I sip my rum and Coke. Tanya, Tammy, and Sophie all give me dirty looks.

There are still hard feelings between us. The fact is, their trip to Dauphin was ruined long before it even began, and I ruined it. Our parents were never planning to come to Dauphin. Sophie, the Yuzko girls, and I were going to Dauphin in the fancy Greyhound with all of the other dancers, and it was going to be one big party. But three weeks before we were scheduled to leave, after I hurt my knee, the plans changed. Mom and Dad came up with the idea that I go to Dauphin anyway; that I enter the vocal competition. I sing in Ukrainian all the time – at family weddings, anniversaries, birthday parties – so it made sense. Why not sing in Dauphin? Since non-dancers aren't allowed to travel with dancers on the bus, Mom and Dad decided to take the whole family in our motorhome. Why not make a holiday of it? There was no stopping them. Why not invite the Yuzkos to travel with us in a caravan? John Yuzko – J.Y. – is Dad's best friend. Dad and J.Y. teach at the same school; they bought identical motorhomes three years ago. And then the final straw. Why not bring along my cousin Kalyna, give Auntie Mary and Uncle Andy a little break from watching her?

You're going to have your work cut out for you, Colleen. You'll show them who's best in the country.

The more I think about it, the more I realize that Dad is right. I start to see the gravity of the situation. Tanya, Tammy, and Sophie might not see it, but if things continue the way they are going, if the dancers continue to lose, then I have to win. Not for my own sake. For the sake of the group, for the sake of the team. For the glory of *Desna*. My gold medal will prove that we are good, authentic Ukrainians after all. I'll mend the wounds of the

Costume Committee. Sophie, Tammy, and Tanya will forgive me
for ruining their trip. They'll see that it was all worthwhile in the
end.

In my head, I go over the introduction to my song, the words
of my song, the guitar chords of my accompaniment. I compete
on the sixth and final day of the festival.

But I'm not just competing.

I am going to do battle with the best this country has to offer.

TWO

The next morning, Day Three, shortly after we've had breakfast, I excuse myself from the group. Everyone from *Desna* is heading over to the mainstage to watch our Senior Boys do their *Zaporozhian Kozak* Character Dance. I tell Mom and Dad that I'm not feeling well – a touch of sunstroke probably – and that I'd like to rest. But I'm not going to sleep, and I'm not feeling sick. In fact, I've never felt better. A lot is riding on my performance now, and I have to rise to the occasion. My plan this morning is to dress in my *Podillian* costume, a bright white, two-piece fitted suit, embroidered with burgundy thread, with matching burgundy boots and a white satin pillbox hat. I'm going to walk around the festival grounds in costume, taking deep breaths. Taking in the spirit of the competition. This will get me in the right mood, help me psych up for what's to come.

My *Podillian* costume is new. It's never been worn. Our dance group has just started learning the *Podillian* Polka. According to our instructor, Kevin, no Ukrainian dance club in the country has ever done a *Podillian* dance.

Poltava is the norm. At Ukrainian festivals in Vegreville and Hafford, *Poltava* is everywhere. Girls in velvet vests, boys in baggy pants. Spins, acrobatics, it's *passé*. On occasion, we've seen a *Transcarpathian* dance, and *Lemko* is gaining in popularity. For a while, *Hutsul* was in vogue – leather moccasins instead of boots, personalized sheepskin vests. Boys performed *Hutsul* dances with wooden axes. One year in Veg, an all-male dance group from Canmore danced the *Hutsul Arkan* around a fake fire – charred logs, orange crepe paper, Christmas tree bulbs – to replicate the ambiance of the Carpathian mountains. Then the *Hutsul* trend caught on, and the *Hutsul* costumes of dancers from every dance club started to look the same because all of the mothers took the same *Hutsul*-vest-making seminar in Saskatoon. I know. My mother made three.

Once I've put the finishing touches on my *Podillian* costume, once I've tied up my hair, and covered my head in a hair-net, and then pinned the hat to my hairnet, I make my way from the campground to the festival grounds. It's a short walk, but the sun is rising and there is no breeze. I feel sweat form on my nose, on my back, under my blouse and vest. I probably won't walk for long. I don't want to stink up my clothes for the competition. The *Podillian* costume can't be washed in a normal washing machine, like other costumes. It's dry clean only.

I buy a pop from *Baba's Best* because I can't afford to get dehydrated before the competition. I might lose my voice. Ice-cold orange pop. I hold the can to my cheek, to my forehead. Then I open it and take one long drink. As I'm walking away from the trailer, I close my eyes, taking the odd sip, taking in the sound and the smell of the place. Maybe I'll chat with a few strangers, get to know the people. If members of the audience recognize me on stage, they'll cheer extra-hard. Which can only help my chances of winning.

And then, halfway between *Baba's Best* and the outdoor toilets, I'm knocked over. Knocked right off my feet, orange pop spilling down the front of my body. Down my brand new, pure white *Podillian* vest.

"Damn!" says a guy in black jeans and an embroidered shirt.

He doesn't help me up, but I think that he's noticed the orange pop stain on my bright white *Podillian* vest. Or maybe he's noticed the grass stains on the back of my bright white *Podillian* skirt. He feels bad, since he is the reason that my costume is ruined.

"Damn!" he says, again, and then, *"Shit!"*

"I know. These stains won't wash out."

"Wash *out?* I just lost two tapes! Some asshole swiped two of my tapes!"

"Who *cares* about your tapes? My whole costume is ruined, and I'm competing in three days."

"So wash it."

"It can't *be* washed!"

"Not my problem," he says, with a shrug. "I'm out twenty bucks."

"Here," I say, handing him a twenty-dollar bill. "Now your problem is solved. How about mine?"

He glares at me for a moment, then storms away, stuffing the twenty-dollar bill in his pocket as he goes.

For the next few minutes, I don't move. I can't move. I'm stunned. He wasn't supposed to take my money. I only have forty dollars in total to spend at the festival. I was just trying to make a point: that, whereas he could be compensated for his loss, my costume has been ruined. There's no compensation for that. But he just walked away. The jerk just walked away. With my money.

Now my costume is a mess, and Mom is going to kill me if I don't clean it up before she gets back from watching the dancing.

It's got to come clean. I've got all of *Desna* relying on me, and I can't disappoint them. Back in the motorhome, I try a bit of Perfex on the stained part of my vest. The vest is white, after all, and Perfex is just bleach. The orange pop stain begins to fade. The more Perfex I apply, the more it fades, until the vest looks perfectly new. I sigh, relieved. Next, the grass stain on the skirt. Not so easy, as it covers the part of my skirt that's embroidered. I can't use bleach on the burgundy embroidery. Can I?

I do a little test on my vest. A tiny drop of Perfex on a tiny burgundy stitch. Nothing happens, no change in colour. I drop a tiny drop more. Still nothing.

The fabric of the skirt, though, is slightly different from the fabric of the vest. The Costume Committee couldn't get enough of either fabric, so they used both. And on the fabric of my skirt, the Perfex spreads. It didn't spread like this on the fabric of my vest. As it spreads, the burgundy embroidery starts to bleed burgundy onto the white part of the skirt. It bleeds quickly, the dye from the embroidery changing colour, from deep red to bright purple. I rinse and rinse, and scrub. I take hand soap to it, dish soap. My heart races. An sos pad. Anything to get the dye out of the fabric.

My family arrives at the motorhome for lunch as I am scrubbing, furiously, in the motorhome bathroom, and crying, my tears mingling with the reddish-purple water in the sink.

Sophie finds me first. She lets out a gasp as she steps into the motorhome. Then, not a split second later, my mother arrives. When she sees what I'm doing, she shrieks. Mom and Sophie both wonder why I tried to bleach my costume. Why didn't I wait? We could have taken it to the dry cleaners in Dauphin.

I didn't think of that. I was scared. I panicked.

But there's no time for explanations, not right now. Sophie and Mom kick into emergency mode, grabbing the skirt from me and discussing what should be done. Meanwhile, I throw myself onto the bunk over the motorhome dashboard, crying my heart out over the ruined costume. Wes crawls up after me, putting his hand on my back.

"Don't worry, C'lleen," he says. "Mom will fix it. She can fix *anything.*"

Of course, Mom can't fix my skirt. It's wrecked. And since I didn't bother to bring another costume, I've got to wear it in the vocal competition. Mom is an angel. She doesn't scold me. No harsh words at all. Eventually, once she's determined that there's no hope for the skirt, she joins Wes and me on the motorhome bunk.

"It's all right, honey," says Mom. "Accidents happen. When we get home, we'll get a whole new skirt made. Okay? Don't fret about it. Don't worry yourself."

Mom doesn't understand the seriousness of the situation, though, and there's no use trying to explain it to her. Performers from the *Podillia* region are supposed to be regal and aristocratic. Kevin said that when we put on our *Podillian* costumes, we're supposed to keep our upper bodies stiff, our arms rigid; shoulders back, chin up. How can I keep my chin up knowing that I'm the only *Podillian* to get onstage with a bright purple bum? How can I put my shoulders back knowing that the fate of *Desna* is sealed? All because of me. I'm their last chance, and I screwed up.

I just can't stop crying. I'm going to fail the whole group. And on top of everything else, I've given twenty dollars to the jerk who did this to me.

I tell Mom and Sophie about him, once I've calmed down enough to speak. The way he ploughed into me and swore at me and walked away, my money in his pocket, without so much as a "thank you" or an "I'm sorry." Sophie calls him a coward. Mom says that I should go out right now and find him. Give him a piece of mind. Get my twenty dollars back.

"The girls will go with you," says Mom. "Sophie, Tammy, and Tanya. All four of you – go! Stand up to that bully!"

But I insist on going alone. I got into this mess, I'll get out of it. On my own. I put my damp, ruined costume back on, so that I can show him what he's done. "See?" I'll say, pointing to the stains. "See what you've done?"

I find him in the musicians' area of the festival grounds, in a tent filled with weird instruments – Ukrainian instruments that I've heard about but never seen before. There are several men playing *banduras,* upright stringed instruments with dozens of strings. Like a cross between a guitar and a harp. Another guy blows into a *trembita,* a long, thin horn, something like the horns that they play in the Swiss alps. His face turns bright red when he blows. An old, grey-haired, prune-faced man plays sweet, high-pitched tunes on his *sopilka*. Which is basically a wooden flute. Beside him, another old man turns the handle on a box, making the saddest sound I've ever heard, almost like a bagpipe. I don't know what his instrument is called. I can't even figure out how the sound is made. At the far end of the tent, I spot the guy who knocked me over. He's playing a *tsymbaly*, a hammer dulcimer. Cassette tapes are on display beside him.

When he see me coming, he stops playing. This is it, then. My moment of reckoning. I'm going to speak calmly – no yelling or swearing – but I'm going to get my point across nonetheless. I want my money back and I want an apology.

The guy speaks first.

"You're that girl, right? The one from this morning? Look, I'm sorry. I got kind of riled up by that prick who stole my tapes. I'm really sorry. I don't make much money at these things, you know, so every tape counts."

"Yeah, well."

I catch myself stammering. I notice for the first time that he's cute.

"You gave me some money," he says, standing up, reaching into the pocket of his jeans.

His jeans are snug in the hips and crotch.

"Here." He hands me the twenty-dollar bill. "I'm not taking your money."

"Oh, but you did. You *did* take my money. And if I hadn't found you, you'd still *have* my money."

"No, no. I looked for you. Honest. I checked out all the competition tents. You said you were dancing but I couldn't –"

"Singing," I say, lifting my skirt so that he can see the tensor bandage around my knee. "I'm singing, not dancing. I wanted to dance but, well. You know. It didn't work out."

"Oh," he says. "Wow. That sucks."

There is a moment of awkward silence between us.

"Maybe you'd like to take a couple of my tapes? Free. No charge. You can just have them. I mean — I don't know if you'd be interested. It's me playing the *tsym* — uh — dulcimer. I don't know if you like, you know, *tsym* — dulcimer music."

"It's okay," I say. "I know what a *tsymbaly* is. Yeah, sure. *Tsymbaly* music is okay, I guess."

He hands me two tapes.

"Have a listen," he says. "Tell me what you think."

I take the tapes away, and my twenty dollars. And when I get back to the campground, everyone is waiting to hear what's happened — Mom and Dad, Sophie and Wes, Kalyna, the Yuzkos. While I've been gone, they've obviously been talking about the incident. So I wave the twenty-dollar bill as I walk into our campsite, and they all cheer and whistle. They want to hear all about it, what I said, what he said. I promise to tell. But first I lock myself into the motorhome bathroom to look at his tapes.

His name is Corey Bespalko. On the back of his cassettes, it says that he's from Brandon, Manitoba, and that he was born in 1967. Which makes him seventeen. Four years older than me. On the cover of the first cassette is an outdated photograph of him. He looks thirteen, fourteen at the most; skinny and pimply, with dark growth on his upper lip. He is sitting behind his *tsymbaly* with the name of the album arched across his chest in block letters, *Corey Bespalko Dulcimer Favourites of Yesterday and Today*. All in all, the album looks cheap. When I peer closely under the letters, I can tell that Corey's shirt is a little short in the sleeves, and it isn't really embroidered around the collar. Someone's just sewn on red-and-black tape, the kind of cheap appliqué that's manufactured to look like embroidery. Cheap cheap cheap.

Then I tell myself that maybe it's not his fault. Maybe he has no *Baba* to cross-stitch a shirt for him. Maybe his mother is a practical woman — why invest in a real embroidered shirt for her son when he's going to outgrow it in three months? Maybe he has no mother, no one to tell him that his sleeves are too short, that his appliqué collar is tacky. Maybe he's an orphan, making his living like a gypsy, like an Old Country *kobzar*, playing music in exchange for bread.

For his second album, *Corey Bespalko Ukrainian Dulcimer Favourites,* Corey has gotten hold of a real cross-stitched shirt and he's shaved his upper lip. Otherwise, though, his second album cover looks just like his first. His face is washed out. The angle of the camera makes him look three feet tall and the *tsymbaly* ten feet long.

I keep Corey's tapes – and Corey himself – a secret from my family. After the incident with my skirt, it would be hard to explain to them that he's not so bad after all. That he actually seems pretty nice. They'll tease me if they hear that I've had a change of heart. Boy crazy, they'll say. And anyway, I'm not entirely sure that I've changed my mind about him. It's the *tsymbaly* playing that bothers me. Old men play the *tsymbaly*, not young ones. I've never seen a *tsymbaly* player under the age of sixty. Sophie and the Yuzko girls would probably laugh, call him a geek. Cute, maybe, but definitely a geek.

On Day Four of the festival, I try my best not to think about Corey. I need to concentrate on competing, and on winning. I spend the morning running through my song in the motorhome. I'm singing *"Tsyhanochka,"* and accompanying myself on guitar. I need to practise the accompaniment especially because I'm just a beginner on the guitar. I've been taking piano lessons for seven years, but I've never actually had guitar lessons. I'm teaching myself.

Kalyna wants to stay behind with me – *"Tsyhanochka"* is one of her favourite songs – while the others head out to the festival grounds. Wes begs to stay behind, too, but Mom forces both of them to go so that I can get some practising done.

I don't blame Kalyna or Wes for not wanting to go. I can

hardly stand it myself when, later in the day, I spend some time with the *Desna* group. Our losing streak has continued, and the dancers are all the same – long faces, no spirit. Onstage, they have no energy. We're supposed to smile all the time – *"Zuby!"* Kevin always says, *"Teeth!"* – but the dancers seem to have forgotten. And the chaperones are no better. They don't cheer much or whistle. It seems like they're not even paying attention to what's happening on stage. Everyone is just going through the motions.

Late in the afternoon, I decide to take a walk by myself. I have to, otherwise *Desna's* gloom will rub off on me. They've all lost their competitions, but I still have a chance. The stain, after all, is on the back of my skirt, not the front. Chances are, the judges won't even notice. Not once I've opened my mouth to sing.

I go to Corey's tent. Out of curiosity. I want to hear what he can do.

There are three other girls standing and talking to Corey in the tent. Groupies. They can't be more than eleven, maybe twelve years old. Skinny, runty groupies. *Kids,* I think. How pathetic. And they're throwing themselves at him, too, leaning across his *tsymbaly* in their tight cut-offs and their tight T-shirts. Bras, too. At least one of them has the nerve to wear a bra, as if she needs a bra for her little washboard chest. Corey is letting them all touch his *tsymbaly* hammers, explaining to them how he made his albums. If he sees me, he pretends I'm not there. I wait a few minutes to hear him play, but he keeps chatting with the groupies. After fifteen minutes, I turn to walk out, wondering why I even bothered to come.

As I'm leaving, though, Corey starts to play his *tsymbaly*, and the sound makes me stop. It knocks the wind out of me, as though someone has thrown a punch into my stomach, swung hard and hit me under the ribs. I hear him playing, and then I can't move. He plays as if in slow motion, lifting his hammers over the *tsymbaly*, letting the hammers drop.

I didn't expect this. I only looked at the front of his albums – at his pictures – I didn't pay any attention to his song selections and I didn't even listen to his cassettes. I didn't have to listen. The names of his albums said it all – *Ukrainian Dulcimer Favourites, Dulcimer Favourites of Yesterday and Today*. I expected the old standards – polka music, old time waltzes – the stuff played by all musicians in all Ukrainian bands. The stuff they play on CFCW's *Ukrainian Hour.* "*Nasha* Butterfly," "Spring-time Seven Step," "Stay All Nite Polka," "Red Shawl Tango." I thought I'd feel sorry for him. I thought he wouldn't be very good. I didn't expect this.

He's playing *"Tsyhanochka,"* the song I've chosen to sing in the competition.

He's playing my song.

But he isn't playing it like the *tsymbaly* players on CFCW. Their playing is boring and mechanical and old-fashioned. All of their songs sound the same, even if the time signatures vary, or the tempo. Corey's style is different. He takes the basic melody of *"Tsyhanochka"* and changes it by adding broken chords and arpeggios. Anyone who has ever played *"Tsyhanochka"* knows that it's a three-chord song. Midway through his version of it, though, Corey alters the structure of the song, throwing in complicated chords I've never heard before – not sevenths, major or minor. I'd recognize sevenths. Maybe ninths or thirteenths? The kinds of chords that jazz players use. He's playing a song that I've heard a hundred times before. Yet I feel like I'm hearing it for the first time. I'm amazed. Not just by what he plays, either. The way he plays is like nothing I've ever seen before. He plays with more than his wrists, his hands, his arms. Corey closes his eyes and sways his body over the strings of his *tsymbaly*. As though he's hypnotized by his own music. He presses and unpresses his lips, and turns his head periodically from side to side. The audience doesn't exist for him, I can tell. In the whole world, while he's playing, there's just him and his instrument. Watching him gives me butterflies in my stomach, goosebumps on my arms. I have to look away. I want to *cry*.

The groupies stay for *"Tsyhanochka"* but they talk non-stop through the performance. Of course. They don't know the meaning of the words to the song. They probably don't know that there *are* words to the song. I do. I know there are words. I know all of the Ukrainian words and I even know their English translations. It's a love song. A man, a *kozak,* sings it to his love, his little gypsy. Of all the things Corey could have chosen to play. I'll bet he speaks Ukrainian. I'll bet he knows the words and their meanings.

Over and over again, in the refrain, the *kozak* sings, *"Tsyhanochko moia, morhanochko moia, tsyhanochko morhanochko, chy liubysh ty mene?"* My little gypsy, my girl with the twinkling eyes, gypsy girl, seductive girl, do you love me?

Near the end of the song, she answers, *"Shcho to za bandura, shcho ne khoche hrat? Shcho to za divchyna, shcho ne vmiie kokhat?"* What is a *bandura* that doesn't want to play? What is a girl who cannot love?

Corey must know that I'm watching. I move closer to him and his *tsymbaly,* close enough that I can see the moisture on his nose and above his lips. It's hot in the tent. The hair along the back of his neck is wet, there are wet spots on his shirt, under his arms. He plays and sweats, and I sweat, too, just watching, and I fall in love, right there and then. First with his fingers, the white half-moons rising under his fingernails, then with the white-blond hair on the back of his hands. I fall in love with his wrists, tanned brown, and thin, and with the thick, blue-green veins that run from his knuckles, up his forearms, to his elbows.

After he has played for me, Corey asks me to play for him.

The groupies stop talking.

"I don't know how," I say. "I haven't got a clue. Too many strings. I've never touched a *tsymbaly* before."

As I'm making excuses, Corey takes my hand and seats me behind his *tsymbaly.* The groupies file out of the tent, one by one. I let him slip the hammers into my hands, and then I let him wrap his hands around my hands. Holding my hands in his, we play. Behind me, I can hear Corey breathing and I can feel the rise and fall of his chest. We play a medley of songs. *"I Shumyt," "U horakh karpatakh," "Nasha maty." "Chorni ochky." "Ivanku Ivanku."*

We play and play until Corey takes his hands away and I let the hammers drop onto the *tsymbaly* strings. Neither of us says a word. As I get up to go, sticky behind the knees from sitting so long in this heat, Corey reaches for my hand and pulls me toward him. Over the *tsymbaly*, he kisses me on the lips, just barely, wet and soft. Coming from the other side of the tent, now that our *tsymbaly* music has stopped, I can hear sounds of a *bandura*, soft and slow, plucked like a harp.

Later, lying awake in the dark, in the motorhome beside Sophie, I relive the kiss. My first kiss. I analyze it. I plan for the next kiss, promising myself that I'll do better the second time, be more adventurous. I'll move my lips more, close my eyes, experiment a little with my tongue. Turn my head sideways – first one way, then the other – touch his face with my hands from time to time, like in the movies.

I want to tell Sophie about Corey. In the worst way, I want to tell her. It's not like me to keep secrets from Sophie, I tell her everything. I'd like to wake her up and describe the whole scene – the groupies, me planning to leave the tent, the song. The kiss. I'd like to take her to his tent, to hear him play. Then she'd see first-hand that he's not at all a geek. When he plays, he's anything but a geek. I'd take Tammy and Tanya to the tent, too. All of them. They would understand immediately.

Only I can't do it to them. It wouldn't be fair. Not after they've lost every competition. Not with me about to sing, about to win. They'd be so jealous. I get a gold medal and boyfriend to boot. They get nothing.

So I don't tell.

On Day Five of the festival, I sneak away from the group periodically to watch Corey play. He gives me lessons whenever he can, when the tent isn't too busy. And every once in a while, he steals kisses. I carry mascara and lipstick in my purse to touch up my makeup throughout the day, and I suck on breath mints all day long, just in case. On his breaks, we sit together behind his *tsym-baly*, talking and holding hands. Corey is really Ukrainian, there's no doubt about that. He went to bilingual school and everything. He talks a lot about famous Ukrainian authors, Ukrainian art, Ukrainian music. When we're not together, I plan for the future. Our future.

Next summer, we're dancing in Vegreville at the *Pysanka Festival,* and Corey will be there, too. He'll be playing, instructing, and selling his tapes in a tent – just like he is now. I daydream about Corey moving to Alberta – to Edmonton – one day and about the two of us studying music together. I haven't told him about my plans yet. But I will. I imagine us living together. I decorate the walls of our apartment.

In our bookshelf, we'll keep copies of Ukrainian books like *The Kobza-Player, Sons of the Soil, Men In Sheepskin Coats.* One wall we'll cover with his grandmother's long *Bukovynian* tapestry – a *kylym,* dark green, rust, and gold; underneath it, we'll place Corey's *tsymbaly,* and beside the *tsymbaly,* a *bandura,* which he says that he's going to learn to play eventually. All along our windowsills, we'll put up framed pictures of paintings by William Kurelek. Children playing fox and geese, chasing after a chicken in the snow. Boys playing hockey on a frozen slough. And we'll hang gold Greek Orthodox icons of baby Jesuses and Virgin Marys. Corey is religious and I'm not, but it doesn't matter. Icons are very Ukrainian. We've got to have icons.

On the evening of Day Five, I invite Corey to come hear me sing: tomorrow, two o'clock in the afternoon. Then it will be official. He will officially fall in love with me while I sing *"Tsyhanochka,"* like I fell in love with him when he played it. I'll sing it for him and him alone, with passion in my voice, and longing. *"Tsyhanochko moia, morhanochko moia, tsyhanochko morhanochko, chy liubysh ty mene?"* My little gypsy, my girl with the twinkling eyes, gypsy girl, seductive girl, do you love me?

Yes.

The night before the sixth and final day of the festival, I hardly sleep. I've got too much on my mind. When I perform tomorrow afternoon, Corey will be in the audience. *Desna* will be in there, too. The dancers and the chaperones, plus the Yuzkos, and my family. Afterwards, right after I sing, we're all heading home together, like a wagon train. The Greyhound bus, followed by the two motorhomes. When I think about leaving, I get a lump in my throat. Saying goodbye to Corey is going to be awful.

In the morning, Dad prepares breakfast over the campfire – his famous Saskatchewan Paella. But I have butterflies in my stomach and I can't eat. While the others collect around the picnic table with their paper plates and plastic forks and plastic knives, I'm kneeling at the motorhome toilet. Saskatchewan Paella is just chopped potatoes and onions fried and then topped with fried bacon and fried eggs – all fried a second time and served with toast. The smell of bacon grease wafts into the motorhome through the open windows.

I throw up three times in total. First during breakfast, then again while I'm doing my hair and makeup, and once more as I'm putting on my costume. The third time, my mother catches me lying by the toilet, half-dressed. She wonders if it's a flu. Or maybe it's something that I ate. Sophie intervenes as Mom fishes in her purse for a Gravol to take my nausea away.

"She's just nervous," says Sophie, rubbing my back. "Dry heaves, right? Like always. She'll be fine after she sings. Won't you, Colleen? You'll be fine."

I nod, miserably, my head still in the toilet. I always puke before I sing.

What I'd like to do is spend the morning in Corey's tent, listening to him play once more before I sing, and before we leave Dauphin. Only I'm tired and hungry and hot – it's got to be the hottest day yet – and I don't dare stray far from the motorhome toilet. I spend the morning under the motorhome awning, in the shade, sipping ginger ale while I run through my song. I could sit inside the motorhome, ask Dad to turn on the air conditioning. Only Mom is folding the bedding, and Sophie and Kalyna are washing the dishes. I can't stand to watch what they're doing. Packing up, that is. Preparing to go.

I can't believe that the end of the festival is here. Six days, come and gone, just like that. Corey must be feeling it, too. He's probably downright depressed, playing slow, sad songs on his *tsymbaly*, all in melancholy, minor keys.

Of course, Sophie and the Yuzko girls aren't at all sad to be leaving. They can't wait to get home. Everyone in *Desna* is glad to be leaving, dancers and chaperones alike. The closest we've come to the gold is a silver medal for the Senior Boys' *Poltavsky* Sword Dance. The silver doesn't count for much, though, as there were only two groups competing in that category. So our boys didn't come in second, really. They came in last.

I'm *Desna's* final hope. Without a shadow of a doubt. I'm the last of the group to compete, and our last chance at gold. If I win anything less than gold, then I will have failed them all. My parents will wonder why they bothered with this trip to Manitoba. If I win, though – if I win the *gold* – then *Desna* will save face, and Mom and Dad will see that the trip was all worthwhile.

My legs tremble as I wait in the audience for the competition to begin. Everyone from our group is in the bleachers, ready to applaud when it's my turn to sing. For the first time in days, they seem energetic and excited. The Babiuk twins are holding up the *Desna* banner.

By a quarter to two, the bleachers are filled. Standing room only. The Women's Vocal Solo Category is one of the last competitions before the afternoon Grandstand Show. Everyone has turned out early to watch the singing before they head over to the Grandstand. The front rows are filled with old people – all grey- or white-haired or balding. Little kids run around in front of the stage, mothers run after them. Dads change the film in their cameras. There aren't many dancers left in costume, since most of the competition is over now. They've all changed into street clothes, though some of them leave their medals around their necks. At ten to two, I look into the crowd, searching for Corey. It's early yet. He's still got ten minutes.

I'm the last to sing in my category so I see what I'm up against, my competition. As the other girls perform, my stomach settles a little. One at a time, three girls in black slacks and embroidered blouses go to the mike. All three of them have bad skin and long blonde hair. Stringy blonde hair with brown roots. They look so similar that I think they must be sisters. While they sing, I periodically glance around the crowd looking for Corey. The place is packed. It's possible that I can't see him. Or maybe he's checked the festival program, and he knows that I sing last.

The first of the three is accompanied by an accordion player; she takes the microphone into her hands but holds it near her waist. Even from my place near the front, I can hardly make out a word of her song. The second of the three, taking note of the first singer's mistake, shoves the mike right up against her lips. The action makes the amp squeal. It's painful. I have to cover my ears.

And though the second girl, too, is accompanied by the accordion player, she drifts through six or seven keys in the span of her song. Quite a feat, I think. I search the crowd for Corey, wondering if he's heard her murder the song.

Finally, the third girl takes her turn on stage. Her voice isn't quite as weak as the previous two singers and she manages to stay in the same key as the accordion player. I think I've almost met my match. But then, just as I am prepared to grant that she will take second place at least, she forgets her words. Several awkward seconds pass during which she fidgets uncomfortably, making gestures for the accordion player to keep going while she tries to get her bearings back. It's obviously hopeless. The third singer bursts into tears and runs offstage.

A few minutes later, the announcer calls my name.

"Please welcome our fourth and final competitor in the

Women's Vocal Solo Category – Colleen Lutzak."

Walking onto the stage, I feel sorry for the three girls with their bad skin, their limp hair, their *baba* slacks – Fortrel, I'm sure – and their spiritless performances. I'm still shaky in the knees, and I feel my palms sweat around the fretboard of my guitar. But I have a chance at the gold. I'm sure of it. As long as I sing well, the gold is *mine.*

Instead of my stained *Podillian* costume, I'm wearing Sophie's *Bukovynian* costume – a last minute idea of my mother's, and a brilliant one. It took some pinning to make it fit, but it looks good. I wear my own boots with Sophie's black wool skirt, and her blouse embroidered elaborately on the sleeves with orange and yellow thread. Sophie's vest is made from soft sheepskin leather and black sheepskin wool, so I'm hot. So hot that I can feel sweat trickling down my chest and back, and down the backs of my legs. But the heat, the sweat – it will all seem worth it when I hold up my gold medal, *Desna's* first. I'll hold it up for *Desna*, and I'll hold it up for Corey. To show him that I'm the best.

On stage, my first move is to dismiss the accordion player; my second is to strap on my guitar and do some last minute tuning. And then, before I start to sing, I introduce my song in Ukrainian, something that sets me apart from my competitors. They didn't say a word before they began to sing.

"Ya zaspivaiu sohodni odnu pisniu – 'Tsyhanochka.'"

I say it with energy, with confidence. Is Corey in the crowd, watching me? I can't find him, but then the audience is enormous. I say my introduction to him, wherever he is. I say it knowing that the rest of the performance is just a formality.

Then I give all my heart and soul to *"Tsyhanochka."* I feel my voice filling the stage and the seating area, I feel it soaring over the audience and across the concession stands. People turn from their hot dogs to face the stage. They clap and tap their feet. Old people smile and nod. In the back row, the *Desna* dancers and parents wave; some run up to the stage to take pictures. Mark Babiuk sticks two fingers into his mouth and whistles before I've even finished. At the end of my song, there is applause like I've never heard before. Thunderous applause that goes on for several minutes. Strangers in the crowd stand up and applaud, there are calls for an *encore*. In the front row, the three girls in the Fortrel slacks look glum.

For the awards presentation, all four of us are called onto the stage. It strikes me as particularly cruel. Nobody really wants anything except gold, so two of us are going to be disappointed, and one of us is destined to receive no medal at all.

As the bronze medallist is announced, I applaud with the rest of the audience. It's Louisa Marianych, the second of my three competitors. She tries hard to smile as she accepts her medal, but the disappointment in her eyes is hard to miss. The first of my three competitors gets the silver medal. Lilliana Marianych. So they're sisters after all, I think to myself. Lilliana hardly looks at her silver medal; she turns, instead, to the third sister on the stage.

I look, too, at the Marianych sister who is left onstage, the girl who sang third in the competition. She is looking down at her feet and biting her bottom lip as she shifts her weight from leg to leg. I wish that I could console her, tell her that she's obviously more deserving of a medal than her sisters. She's a much better singer. I'd like to tell the judges. It's not her fault that she forgot her words, she was just nervous.

Just before the gold medal winner is awarded, Louisa and Lilliana Marianych move close to their sister, the girl whose name I don't know; they each grab hold of one of her hands, so that she isn't alone during the final moment of the adjudication, and they take turns whispering in her ear. To comfort her, I think. All three sisters – their arms linked, like one entity – look directly at me as the gold medallist is announced.

It's Lesya Marianych.

The third sister is awarded the gold medal.

Not me, her.

As the adjudicator explains that my pronunciation needs work – I sing with a Canadian accent – I stare straight ahead at the audience. They loved me. They loved my song. I didn't just sing, I entertained them.

The members of *Desna* boo and stomp their feet, drowning out the voice of the adjudicator, and the rest of the crowd joins in. The Marianych sisters tell me that I deserved to win.

"You're so good," they say. "So good."

As I make my way from the stage, toward the *Desna* part of the crowd, a lot of people tell me that I'm good. Good, or great, or wonderful.

"You deserved to win," they say. "It's politics. These competitions are all political. You have a wonderful voice. Just wonderful! Don't take it to heart."

I feel numb.

When I finally reach *Desna*, the chaperones and the dancers are milling around, angry. Everyone is talking about the judging. The wives of Mr. Demkiw and Mr. Faryna try to lead their husbands away from the adjudicators' table, but Mr. Demkiw breaks away from Mrs. Demkiw and swears at the judges in Ukrainian.

"I'm sorry," says Mom, rubbing my back. "We'll have to talk about this later."

"Kalyna's gone *missing*," says Wes. "She's *disappeared*, and we have to *find* her." His eyes are wide, as though an adventure is about to begin.

Mom and Dad aren't alarmed. None of us is the least bit surprised, really. We've come to expect Kalyna's disappearing act. She's always wandering off. It doesn't take much to catch her attention – bright colours, babies, puppies, music. One year during the Klondike Days Parade she followed a bright green 4-H float for two blocks before Uncle Andy caught up with her. Last summer in West Edmonton Mall she got lost for an hour tracking a set of twins being pushed by their mother in a double stroller.

Dad asks Sophie if she's seen any dogs.

Sophie shakes her head, laughing. "Nope, no dogs. But there's music playing all over the festival grounds. Kalyna could be anywhere."

Mom and Dad decide that the best idea is for Mom to look for Kalyna while the rest of us head over to the motorhome. Wes kicks at some gravel on the ground, disappointed that he can't be part of the search party. But Dad explains that the Greyhound and the Yuzkos will be leaving soon. If we split up to look for Kalyna, the whole group will be delayed.

"She was just with us a minute ago," says Dad. "She couldn't have gone far."

I hope, in fact, that Kalyna has gone very far — as far as the Grandstand at the southernmost boundary of the festival grounds. Then Mom will take ages to find her, and our departure will be delayed after all, by half an hour, or more. I need to see Corey once more, to say goodbye.

I tell Dad that I've left my guitar backstage by accident — which is true — and that I'll catch up to them shortly. Which isn't true at all. I need time to find Corey.

I run toward the musicians' tent. I run like crazy, like a mad woman, like I've never run before, weaving through the crowd and bumping into people. It's not easy to run in my boots. They've got two-inch heels that dig into the grass, threatening to slow me down. Once my ankle turns under and I nearly fall. My ankle aches, my heart races, I feel my blouse sticking to my back. But I can't stop. I can almost hear Corey calling out to me with his *tsymbaly*, his hands making the hammers dance over the strings. *"Tsyhanochko moia, morhanochko moia, tsyhanochko morhanochko, chy liubysh ty mene?"*

I know what's happened. It's all clear to me now. Corey came to watch me sing, just like he promised. He showed up in time to catch the whole competition. He watched from beside the stage, where I couldn't see him. So he saw it all. He saw me lose, and he left, disappointed in me.

I stop outside Corey's tent to catch my breath and collect myself. I can hear *tsymbaly* music playing – Corey playing – and it brings a lump to my throat. Already I miss him. I tilt my head back, to keep the tears from spilling onto my cheeks. It doesn't work, so I wipe them with the sleeves of my blouse, leaving blue-black streaks of mascara on my cuffs. A woman in her thirties pushing a baby carriage passes by and, with a look of sympathy, she hands me a Kleenex from her pocket. I blow my nose. I take deep breaths. I pace. And just when I think that I can walk into the tent and face my beloved, he starts to play *"Tsyhanochka." Our* song. I give up. I'm ready to throw myself sobbing onto the grass.

But Corey isn't alone in his tent, he's not alone at his *tsymbaly*. He has seated someone in my place, behind his *tsymbaly*; he's let someone else hold his hammers and he's wrapped his hands around someone else's fingers. It's a girl, smiling and laughing the way I smiled and laughed.

It's Carla Senko.

Together, she and Corey play *"Tsyhanochka,"* my song. For all I know, they could have been playing together all afternoon, right through my performance. I stand and I watch. I watch Corey pull her toward him. I watch him brush his lips against hers. My stomach turns and tears wet my cheeks.

Several minutes pass before I notice Kalyna seated on the other side of the tent, the other side of the *tsymbaly*. I notice her when she starts singing along with the *tsymbaly* music. Kalyna is wearing a white sundress dotted with big, red poppies; beneath the spaghetti straps of her dress, thick beige bra straps are showing. She's pinned a pink, plastic corsage over her right breast and tucked her hair under a bright blue golf hat – a ladies' golf hat, with a thin brim and a white pompom on the top. The pompom jiggles while Kalyna's head bobs up and down, side to side.

I decide to leave the tent. I'll find Mom and tell her that Kalyna is in the musicians' tent. I don't want Corey and Carla to see me like this, mascara running down my face. I don't want them

to see me with Kalyna, either. I don't want them to see that I
know her. I don't want them to see me at all. I just want to disappear, forget that I ever met Corey.

But then, as I am about to walk out of the tent, the *tsymbaly*
music abruptly stops. Corey and Carla exchange looks. He raises
his eyebrows, grinning, and she covers her mouth to stifle a giggle. They are laughing at Kalyna – who keeps singing, loud and
clear, carefully enunciating the Ukrainian words.

Kalyna sings a complete verse before she realizes that her *tsymbaly* accompaniment has ended. For a moment, she looks puzzled.
Then a serious expression washes over her face and she raises her
hands like a conductor, signaling for Corey to continue playing.
Carla laughs out loud. Corey looks away. He's laughing too but I
can see that he's embarrassed, the way most people are embarrassed around Kalyna. Kalyna doesn't understand. She tries again
to get Corey to play, raising her hands to deliver the cue.

I can't let her go on like this. I feel my face flush deep red as
I brush past Corey and Carla, but I have to help Kalyna. I put my
arm gently around her shoulder, leading her out of the tent.

"Who are you?" says Kalyna.

"I'm your cousin. I'm Colleen."

"Me too." She squeezes my hand and laughs. "Me too!"

On our way home from Dauphin, between the Manitoba border and North Battleford, Saskatchewan, it rains non-stop.
Everyone is quiet. Mom sleeps. Sometimes the Yuzko girls ride in
our motorhome, sometimes Sophie rides in theirs. For a while,
they stay in their own motorhomes and talk to each other like
truckers on the CB radio until Dad tells them to stop.

Mostly I sit by our motorhome kitchen table, playing the odd
game of crazy eights with Kalyna and Wes. Kalyna doesn't always
remember the rules, so it isn't easy. And sometimes she makes
up her own rules, and gets angry at Wes and me when we don't

follow them. Eventually, Wes stops playing with us altogether. He plops himself down on the floor and sets out all of his G.I. Joe figures around him. After a while, Kalyna joins him on the floor. Wes is a good sport about it. He lets her borrow three or four of his army men. As he makes the sounds of grenades exploding, airplanes crashing – the sounds of automatic rifle fire and soldiers dying in agony – Kalyna plays house. She makes one soldier the mother, one the father, one the child. I sit beside her on the floor, listening to her make the sound of a baby crying, the soothing sound of a mother's voice.

Then, out of the blue, she gets confused. She can't remember where she is or who I am, so I have to explain things to her.

"I'm your cousin Colleen. Remember? We're going home."

PART II

St. Paul

ONE

My mother says that if I don't learn to sing *"Chaban,"* she'll go to her grave with a broken heart. She says it a few times – over breakfast; when we're in the kitchen making supper; right before bed – but I ignore her. Once, while she's asking me to sing with her, Mom's voice cracks as though she's about to cry. I pretend that it doesn't bother me. I roll my eyes, leave the room.

Usually, when Mom decides that it's time for me to learn a new song, the two of us sit at the piano with her little yellow songbook, *Let's Sing Out In Ukrainian! Zaspivayemo Sobi!* There are more than a hundred songs in the book, complete with music and lyrics. Together, we scan the index until she finds a title that she knows from when she was a girl. Then I sight-read the melody on the piano while she sings along. I can sound out the Cyrillic letters on my own but it's easier if I hear her sing the words. She sings a line and I repeat it until I get the hang of it. Eventually we sing the whole song in unison from beginning to end. Sometimes Mom sings harmony. Her harmony always gives me the shivers.

Things are different, though, since Dauphin. Two weeks ago, after we got home – while we were unpacking the motorhome, actually – I told Mom and Dad that I quit. Simple as that. No more Ukrainian dancing, no more Ukrainian singing.

Now, Mom is doing everything she can to change my mind.

At first, she and Dad both tried to talk me out of quitting Ukrainian dancing. They came up with all sorts of reasons for me to go back in September. I'd miss my friends. Dancing is good exercise. Wouldn't I feel bad not performing at the annual *Pyrohy* Supper and in the Spring Concert? I told them my knee hurts too much – which isn't true. As long as I wear my tensor bandage, my knee feels fine. But the thought of dancing again – in the same group as Carla Senko – makes me sick to my stomach. It's bad enough that I'll have to see her every day once school starts again. The thought of singing is even worse. It would be Dauphin all over again each time I opened my mouth.

Dad said that I'd come around. "Leave it alone," I overheard him tell Mom one night. "Just give her time."

Mom is too impatient to wait, though, and I'm too stubborn to give in.

So she tries bribing me to learn *"Chaban,"* and when that doesn't work she tries other tactics. I find her at the piano one Saturday afternoon with her little yellow songbook open to *"Chaban."* Listening to her hum the tune of *"Chaban,"* seeing her struggle to plunk out the melody with her right hand, I get a lump in my throat. Mom has always wanted to play the piano, but she's never learned how. When Sophie and I started piano lessons with Simone, Mom tried to learn with us. While we practised our beginner pieces, she sat beside us on the piano bench, watching our fingers. Only she couldn't keep up. We learned too fast, and she never got past the first few songs.

I know what she's trying to do. She wants me to feel sorry for her. I'm supposed to just plop down next to her like old times, like nothing has changed. But she wasn't onstage in Dauphin. She doesn't know what it was like. She didn't have to stand there while the adjudicator placed the gold medal around somebody else's neck. She didn't hear Corey playing our song to Carla, or watch Corey kissing Carla, or listen to Carla laughing. I don't care how badly Mom wants me to sing. My singing days are over.

The truth is, everything has changed since Dauphin. Normally, by the end of August, I can't wait for school to start again. Going back to school is a big event in our house. Sophie, Wes, and I get all new school supplies in St. Paul, and new clothes in Edmonton. Mom and Dad get new clothes, too, because they're teachers. They go back to school with us. And then there is the excitement of new homerooms, new textbooks, new workbooks. Catching up with friends about what you did during the summer holidays. For the first time in my life, though, when September rolls around, I want to stay home. What are we going to talk about on the first day of school, the kids who went to Dauphin? How we all lost. How we came home with nothing.

Our whole family drives to school together every morning. We live in the country, which means that Sophie, Wes, and I could take the bus to town, but it doesn't make sense, since Mom and Dad need to drive in anyway. Mom teaches Ukrainian at Glen Avon, the Protestant school for grades one to nine. It's on the west side of St. Paul. Dad teaches English at Regional, the only high school in town, on the east side. Until grade ten, kids in our area go to the Protestant school or the Catholic schools, St. Paul Elementary and Racette Junior High, but eventually everyone ends up at Regional – which is also Catholic, only there are no prayers and you can choose whether or not to take religion there. This year, Sophie is in grade ten, so she goes to Regional with Dad. Wes is in grade six, and I'm in grade eight. We're still at Glen Avon.

Sometimes Dad drives, and keeps the car with him at Regional; sometimes Mom drives. It depends on who has errands to do at lunch. Today, Mom is driving because she has to go to the bank at noon. On the way to school, while everyone else chatters about the first day, I stare out the window of the car, wishing I were somewhere else. Anywhere else. St. Paul seems dingy to me, and worn out. Full of old rusted-out pickup trucks with cracked windshields and big cars with broken mufflers. Before we get to

Regional, we pass the Co-Op Mall – which is just another word for the Co-Op grocery store – and Peavey Mart, where all the farmers shop, and two farm machinery dealerships. We pass the Red Rooster convenience store and gas station; Senecal Tire; Burger Baron. Nothing ever changes in this town. Nothing exciting ever happens here. There aren't any nice places to eat, like in the city, or any real malls. We'll never get a McDonald's. We don't even have a 7-Eleven.

After we drop off Dad and Sophie, and Mom turns the car back onto main street, we drive past the convent and the Catholic church near the centre of town. The cathedral is enormous and brick. It's the most beautiful building in St. Paul – and the tallest, by far. I've never been inside it. The Catholic church is for the kids who go to the Catholic schools. St. Paul Elementary is two blocks east of the cathedral, and Racette is just north of it – right across the street, in fact.

And then, farther down main street, just a few blocks west of the cathedral, are the shabbiest buildings in town, the Donald and the Lavoie. They're both called hotels but everyone knows that they're actually bars. Any time of day you can see drunk Indians staggering out of the doors of the Donald, and drunk rig workers stumbling out of the Lavoie. It's sad, and scary. The post office is right next door to the bars. Mom and Dad never let us kids pick up the mail. At the end of the school day, we wait in the car with the doors locked while they go to our post office box.

The rest of main street isn't much better. There's Al's Topline Tackle, with stuffed deer heads and stuffed fish collecting dust in the window. The Boston Café, Mr. Wong's Chinese restaurant, with faded, handwritten signs advertising the same specials week after week. The bingo hall, three pawnshops, the army surplus store. To get to Mom's parking spot near Glen Avon, we make a left turn at the UFO Landing Pad – St. Paul's big tourist attraction, and the most embarrassing part of town. It's a gigantic, mushroom-shaped slab of suspended concrete with a dozen weather-beaten provincial and territorial flags flying along its back end. The Landing Pad was built in 1967 as our town's Centennial Project. Other towns built curling rinks in 1967; they built hockey arenas, community halls. We built a Landing Pad, so that if aliens were to visit Earth, their first stop would be St. Paul. I hate it. I think it makes the whole town look stupid.

I wear my new plaid miniskirt and my new red shaker knit sweater on the first day of school but, walking through the main doors of Glen Avon, I feel a hundred years old. All the *Desna* dancers look like me – tired and sad and old. When I see their faces in the hallways, it's like I'm back in Dauphin, watching them lose over and over again. Of course, at recess and lunchtime, when they all talk about their summers, nobody mentions the festival. They all want to forget that Dauphin ever happened.

And then it occurs to me that every other first-day-of-school has been the same. I just never noticed it before. Even when we competed and *won* at festivals in Vegreville and Hafford, we never talked about it at school – not to each other, and definitely not to other kids who don't Ukrainian dance. Dancing is like some kind of secret that we all keep. Nobody talks about the practices each week, the costume fittings, our new boots that are specially made in Saskatoon. The *Pyrohy* Supper or the Spring Concert. Some of the boys in my group are planning to audition for *Cheremosh,* the professional dance group in Edmonton that our dance instructor belongs to, but no one ever mentions it around school.

Midway through the first day of school, while I sit with the other girls from Ukrainian dancing, all of us eating lunch together and listening to Carla Senko boast about how she's switched from Ukrainian to French, I realize that we don't talk about *anything* Ukrainian. It's not just dancing, it's everything. I happen to know that Kirstin Paulichuk and Tanya Yuzko go to Camp Kiev's K-Hi every summer for two weeks where they learn about Orthodox church things, and how to speak Ukrainian and do embroidery and make *pysanky.* I also know that Henry Popowich speaks perfect Ukrainian because he lives with his grandparents and they refuse to speak English to him at home. I watched Dad and J.Y. spend half the summer making a *pich,* an outdoor clay oven, in our yard at the farm, so that Mom and Yolande Yuzko could bake bread like in the olden days. But at school none of us says a word about any of it. Not one word.

Glancing over at the Native students in our class, eating their lunch at the other side of the classroom, I wonder if they feel the same way. They must. It must be even worse for them. I've never heard them talk about what it's like to be Native, what it's like living on the reserve. Do they go to powwows in the summer? Do any of them speak Cree at home? There are five Indian reserves around St. Paul – Saddle Lake, Frog Lake, Kehewin, Good Fish, and Fishing Lake – and we have students in our school from almost all of them. It's never occurred to me before but – why isn't there a Cree teacher at our school?

Carla Senko talks non-stop about French class while we eat our lunches. Nobody dares interrupt her because everyone wants to be her best friend. She sits at her desk like a queen bee in her brand-new, jet-black, skin-tight jeans and her pale yellow angora sweater while all the girls giggle and coo at everything she says. Carla says she's quit Ukrainian because it's boring and stupid. All we ever do is learn vocabulary and numbers. In Miss Maximchuk's French class they listen to French rock music and make up plays in French; they learn to play the spoons; and once a month Miss Maximchuk brings in French foods for lunch. Of course Carla knows that my mother is the Ukrainian teacher but she still goes on and on.

When I can't take it anymore, when I get up to leave, Carla says, "No offence, Colleen." As though that makes up for every mean thing she's said.

She's right. I know she's right and that's why I can't fight back. My mother's class *is* boring and nobody likes it, least of all me. I wish she taught something else, anything else, or taught Ukrainian differently. I wish that I didn't have to be the Ukrainian teacher's kid. Mom wishes it, too, because she does her best to forget that I'm in her class.

I've been in Mom's Ukrainian class for four years, since grade four. And for four years, she's completely ignored me. She's ignored me, and I've ignored her. Five times a week for four years we've been in the same classroom, each pretending that the other doesn't exist. I'm afraid that if open my mouth, I'll accidentally call her "Mom" and get teased for it. She's afraid that if she calls on me too much in class, word will get around that she favours me. I have to work twice as hard, three times as hard, as anyone else because Mom marks me harder than any other student. I'm the top of the class but you'd never know it. I never raise my hand, even though I know all the answers.

I try not to blame Mom. I know it's not her fault that every-one hates Ukrainian. She'd rather be teaching something else. There is no such thing as a Ukrainian curriculum or Ukrainian textbooks, so she's had to write her own readers and workbooks, and she doesn't feel qualified to do any of it. She says that she got roped into taking the Ukrainian classes when the school board first decided to offer them because she was the only teacher who had taken a Ukrainian course at university. The principal took away her grade three class and made her do Ukrainian half-time and special ed half-time. Half the reason nobody likes Ukrainian is because we have to sit in the special ed classroom where all the slow kids go for help with reading and math. We feel like a bunch of dummies.

Sometimes, though, I think that if she tried harder Mom could make Ukrainian more fun. At home, we do all kinds of neat Ukrainian things – like singing together, and making *pysanky* at Easter time. She could bring food in like Miss Maximchuk, or we could all go to the home ec room and make *pyrohy*. At the annual Christmas Concert, we could perform dances. All of us take Ukrainian dancing anyway, why not show off for the school?

But I know that Mom won't change her classes, even if I asked her to. Even if I told her that I'll go to my grave with a broken heart. The thing is, my parents don't want us to be too Ukrainian. That's why they never talk to us in Ukrainian, and why they gave us English names. It's partly why they never take us to the Greek Orthodox church they went to when they were growing up. Once in a while, they talk about how they were embarrassed when they were kids at school – because they couldn't speak English properly, and because they ate different foods. Being Ukrainian meant being poor and ignorant. The teachers looked down on them, strapping them when they spoke Ukrainian with other Ukrainian kids. Mom and Dad say that they went to university so that it would be different for us – so that Sophie and I could take piano lessons, and Wes could play hockey. So that we could live in a nice house, and focus on our studies instead of farm chores. So that we'd never be ashamed of where we come from.

The truth is, though, my parents can't forget where they came from – not entirely. They don't want to forget, either. At least that's the way it seems. To each other – to my grandparents, and aunts and uncles – they always talk in Ukrainian. My mom cooks Ukrainian food all the time. Before Sophie was born, Mom and Dad lived in town for awhile but they were never happy there. Dad bought land ten kilometres northeast of St. Paul – land that was partly covered in bush and slough – and worked it like a pioneer, cutting down trees, filling in sloughs. Then he built a house with a big garden next to it, so that he and Mom could live on a farm again, and do everything their parents did. My mother's pride and joy is her garden. She loves to make pickles and jams, pick wild mushrooms, saskatoons, *kalyna* berries. And she makes a point of teaching Sophie and me everything she knows.

In the spring and summer, my dad spends most of his spare time farming the land around our house, taking Wes out on the tractor, and then the swather, and then the combine. He plants wheat, just like his dad did. During the winter, after hunting season is over, Dad goes to auctions, looking for old John Deeres and other farm implements – the kind his dad owned and used. He buys old cream separators, old wringer washing machines, ancient snow machines – anything that reminds him of his childhood on the farm. There's no real profit in Dad's farming. His crops never do well – and, even if they did, he doesn't seed enough land to make money. He keeps three granaries south of the house, in a part of the bush where he cut down trees by hand and made all of us pick roots by hand. But the granaries are empty of wheat and full of Dad's junk. Sometimes, before it freezes in the fall, if Mom needs extra storage space for her vegetables while she's canning, Dad and Wes haul them out to the granaries too.

Although Mom and Dad have never said so, there are rules. Rules that can't be broken. I get it now. I see it so clearly. We never talk about the rules, but we all know them – everyone in our family, everyone in *Desna*, everyone who takes Ukrainian. It's okay to be Ukrainian at home but not at school. At school you act like everyone else. You don't talk about the stuff that goes on at weddings and funerals, at Ukrainian dancing, at festivals. You pretend that you're not Ukrainian. That's just the way it goes.

By the time the news of Dean and Diana's engagement reaches our household – via the BBC, *Baba Babi Cazala,* one *Baba* tells another *Baba* – it's almost Christmas and Mom has stopped trying to convince me to learn *"Chaban,"* or any other Ukrainian song for that matter. Naturally, I'm going to be asked to sing at the wedding, and for the first time ever, I'm going to say no.

At least I think I'm going to say no. Part of me wants to sing, like I always do. It's tradition. Whenever there is a family wedding, the bride and groom ask me to perform. In fact, our whole family gets involved because we're the wedding family. We come as a wedding package. Wes is the ring bearer, Mom is the bridesmaid. In the hall, Sophie plays for me while I sing – mostly in Ukrainian, the odd time in English – and Dad is the MC. We've done this routine for Darlene and Rick, Orysia and Danny, Paul and Kelly, Sonya and Robert. It's always the same. If I don't sing, Dean and Diana's wedding won't feel right.

Dean is my cousin, my rich Auntie Helen and Uncle Dan's son. Diana is the fiancée. The wedding date, May long weekend. At the Hotel Macdonald in Edmonton.

The aunts and uncles aren't altogether happy with the news. The ceremony will take place in the Orthodox church at Szypenitz, which is where the wedding ceremonies in our family always happen, but we've never been to a wedding reception in a ritzy hotel. Plus on the BBC, there is talk of the meal being catered – catered and served rather than buffet-style. Fifty dollars a plate, Uncle Bill has heard, and not one Ukrainian dish on the menu. The bride isn't Ukrainian, apparently. She's an *Angliik*. Not like us. Auntie Rose has it from a reliable source that the flowers will be ordered not from Auntie Pearl – who has a shop in Two Hills and who takes care of the flowers for every family wedding – but from a flower shop on Jasper Avenue. From Auntie Natalka, the first to receive an invitation, comes a report that her son Steve has not been included on the guest list. Auntie Rose calls Auntie Natalka – has she been asked to the Second Day? To the Gift Opening? Auntie Pearl calls Auntie Natalka, Auntie Natalka calls Auntie Marika. Nobody has heard a word about the Second Day. Marika calls my mother, my mother calls Pearl. There is not going to be a Gift Opening. The *Angliiks* are too cheap to feed the guests a second time.

The problem is that Dean and Diana are breaking the rules. Weddings have to be done a certain way and they're doing it all wrong. The bride and groom are supposed to invite the whole family – even distant cousins they haven't seen in years – because otherwise feelings will be hurt. They're supposed to order flowers from Auntie Pearl because her shop has never done very well. She needs the business. And everybody knows that there should be a

Second Day, a Gift Opening, right in the hall where the reception has taken place. The guests eat the leftovers from the wedding supper while the bride and groom open their presents.

This wedding is going to be different and I don't like it anymore than the aunts and uncles. I just might have to change my mind about singing. I might have to say yes when they ask me to sing – to keep at least one wedding tradition alive. In the months leading up to the wedding, I give the matter a lot of thought. It's not an easy decision to make after I've worked so hard to convince Mom that I'm never singing again. I don't like the rules – the rules about not being Ukrainian in some places, and being Ukrainian in others. I don't think they make any sense. But if we can only be ourselves when we're with the family, maybe we should fight for that. Maybe there's a reason to fight. If I don't sing at Dean and Diana's wedding, it would set a precedent for other weddings. Then everything would change.

One month before the wedding, when no one involved in the wedding has called our family, we realize that something's up. We've gotten the invitation, but Dean hasn't called, or Diana. Or Auntie Helen, or Uncle Dan. Not that we expect Dean or Uncle Dan to call – it's usually the women who organize the wedding details. The men just order the booze. Sophie and I think it's weird, and even Mom and Dad are concerned. They should have called by now. Maybe they're behind schedule with their planning; they're waiting until the last minute to ask us. They forgot. It's been cancelled. The wedding's off?

Mom calls Auntie Jean to see if she's heard anything about the wedding plans, then Auntie Jean calls Auntie Helen directly. All the aunts are shocked to hear that Mom isn't going to be a bridesmaid, that Dad isn't going to be MC. That I'm not going to sing. No, the wedding isn't cancelled. But Auntie Helen says that half the marriage ceremony will be conducted in English, and wedding guests must pay cash for their drinks at this wedding.

Conversations on the BBC Hot Line reach a feverish pitch with news of the cash bar. Mom is forced to pull the telephone away from her ear when she calls Auntie Mary. Across the kitchen we can hear the bellowing of Uncle Andy's voice through the receiver.

"Since when? Since *when* do we pay to go to a wedding? Pay to go to a goddamn wedding! Who opened their wallets at my son's wedding? *That* was a wedding. Food, drink, music. That was a *real* wedding, a goddamn real *Ukrainian* wedding. *Nai shliak ta ba trafiv,* goddamn *chewtobachnik.* I'd sooner go to my grave than go to this Englishman-wedding."

But we all go – Uncle Andy included – in suits and dresses, ties and nylons; shoe-polished, powdered, pressed, and high-heeled. Sophie in her orange sundress, me in my lemon miniskirt, bra straps pinned to the shoulders of my blouse.

The road to Szypenitz isn't long – forty, forty-five minutes – but it's boring. More boring than ever because I don't have songs to run through in my head. We drive past St. Bride's, Brosseau, and Duvernay; past the same country stores that sell the usual hard ice cream and fishing bait. As we enter Saddle Lake, there's the same worn, weather-beaten siding on the houses along both sides of the highway that cuts through the reserve. The same mangy dogs and rusty cars with grass growing up through their frames; the same kids playing on the shoulder of the road that leads first to Two Hills, then to Edmonton. After Saddle Lake, we make a sharp turn west toward Hairy Hill, where my parents went to school, then west past the old Szypenitz hall – same old graffiti, *Grad '76, Grad '77* – and on to Szypenitz church, a mile or so down the hill.

As we approach the church, Sophie tries to look on the bright side. She says that this is the first wedding at which we'll actually be able to enjoy ourselves. Usually, we're too nervous to eat the wedding supper. I always throw up before going onstage. This time, Sophie won't have to hold my hair back while I heave into the toilet.

"The fact is," says Sophie, "the aunts always complain about having to make wedding meals at every wedding, every single one. This is their long-awaited, well-earned break. Auntie Natalka hasn't said a word to Steve in six years, ever since he married that divorcee, eight years older than him. What does Auntie Natalka care if Steve's not invited? Plus no one has ever been impressed with Auntie Pearl's flower arrangements. She's cheap with the baby's breath. And, as for the price tags on drinks – we're not old enough anyway."

"You're right," I say, nodding. "Let's forget all the trouble and concentrate on having a good time."

"Let's party on!"

Together, Sophie and I invent a secret party-on signal: the right hand curled into a fist, the right arm thrust up in the air.

In church, of course, it's difficult to make the party-on signal without drawing attention to ourselves, so Sophie nudges me with her elbow and then makes a little horizontal punch with her right fist. We sit on the women's side of the church with Mom while Dad and Wes go to the men's side. I get squeezed into a pew between Sophie and Auntie Rose. Not the best place to be – Auntie Rose's perfume is so strong that it makes my eyes water. Once the incense starts, I'm going to get nauseous.

I should be happy that the ceremony is taking place in the Orthodox church. It's the tradition, after all. It always smells awful, though, in the church, and it's always gloomy. There is a bit of a draft from the open doors, but not enough of a draft to make the air smell fresh. The church at Szypenitz is so old that it doesn't have any lights, just hundreds of tiny candles dripping wax everywhere. I feel sorry for the bride. Organs aren't allowed in the Orthodox church, so she can't even walk down the aisle to the Wedding March. I'd never want to get married in a place like this.

The choir in the balcony above us is what gets the service started. They sound creepy as ever. They don't sing, really, they half-talk and half-cry. If you ask me, the bride looks scared as she walks down the aisle, and I don't blame her. After the choir has done their cry-singing for a while, Father Zubritsky appears in his long, black gown. He comes through the saloon doors at the front of the church. At least they look like saloon doors, the kind that you see in old Westerns. He carries his usual smoking silver ball that hangs on a silver chain. The more he swings the ball and chain, the more the smoke poofs out and up our noses. It stinks. The incense must be rancid. It's like old mothballs, dust, honey, all mixed together. The smell makes me sick to my stomach, just like I thought it would.

Father Zubritsky likes a lot of incense; his ceremonies are always long and mostly in Ukrainian. I've been to other weddings where he officiated so I know what I expect. To pass the time, I flip through the Bible stuck into the little bookshelf attached to the pew in front of me. It's in Ukrainian, but it's got neat shiny paper. I flip through the Bible, rubbing the pages with my fingers.

Auntie Mary gives me a dirty look. She's sitting beside Auntie Rose. It's Mom, Sophie, me, Auntie Rose, Auntie Mary, Auntie Pearl. In the pew behind us are my grown-up cousins, Orysia and Dalia, plus Rick's new wife, Darlene. And in the pew in front of us, Auntie Linda, Auntie Jean, Auntie Marika, Auntie Helen, Auntie Natalka. I find it hard to believe that my aunts come here regularly, by choice. My parents never take us to church. To my aunts, the whole place must seem normal.

My mom has eight sisters, all of whom are much older than she is, and much more old-fashioned. With the exception of Auntie Helen, who lives in Edmonton with her husband, Uncle Dan, the other sisters all live around Two Hills and Hairy Hill. They all married farmers. Besides my mom, Auntie Pearl, who owns the flower shop in Two Hills, is the only sister who isn't a housewife. But my mom is the only girl in the family who doesn't go to church anymore.

After Auntie Mary's dirty look, I try hard to follow what's going on during the ceremony. I just don't understand why Father Zubritsky can't be more cheerful. Why does he have to act like it's a funeral? He talks like the choir sings, half-moaning and half-crying. His favourite phrase seems to be *hospody pomylui* and variations of it – which, Sophie and I joke, must mean *stand up* and *sit down.* We go up, pray silently, pray mumbling, pray out loud. Down. Up. Down, up, down. I try to guess when the ups and downs will come but it's hopeless. I have to watch everyone else for a cue; everyone else seems to watch everyone else.

Who are we all following? It can't be Father Zubritsky because he stands the whole time. It's not the people in front of us. I watch them closely. They follow somebody in front of them. Maybe the ups and downs aren't so bad. At least I have something to think about for the rest of the ceremony. I want to determine who's leading us. Someone in the front row, someone who speaks Ukrainian. Someone who goes to church regularly. Someone who must actually *like* Father Zubritsky.

I think it's my cousin Kalyna.

I watch her carefully. The more I watch, the more convinced I become. It *is* Kalyna. She's leading the whole church. She gets up first, she sits down first – as long as I watch her, I keep in time with Father Zubritsky. I don't know how she can do it, being not mentally normal and all.

After a while, though, I get a car-sick feeling from the up-down motion and the smoke. Auntie Rose's perfume isn't helping either. I lean hard on Sophie to make the church stop spinning. This is the worst I've ever felt at a wedding. I put my mouth on her ear to say, "Soph, I'm gonna throw up." Sophie doesn't look so well herself. She grabs my hand and holds it, hard.

For an hour and a half, Father Zubritsky talks and wails and out-and-out yells – all in Ukrainian. At the very end of the service, he finally switches to English. English with a heavy accent, but English nonetheless. The problem is that his English words have nothing to do with the wedding ceremony. He talks in English about young people. Young people who don't go to church. Father Zubritsky makes church a two-syllable word – *char*-itch – and he says it over and over again.

"You young people," he booms, "you've forgotten the CHAR-itch! You don't come to *char*-itch. For shame! You go to your discos in your fancy cars and you forget where you come from. *Hospode!* Too much English. You young people don't know your mother tongue. For shame!"

By the end of the ceremony, the bride looks like she's about to cry, and her parents storm out of the church after the wedding party with frowns on their faces. Auntie Helen and Uncle Dan don't look too pleased either, but they try their best to smile at the crowd as they walk toward their car.

The whole thing makes me sick – not just sick, but angry, too. Sophie's just as mad. And, on the drive from Szypenitz to Edmonton, Mom and Dad talk non-stop about the things that Father Zubritsky said.

"No wonder we don't go to church," says Mom. "What's wrong with him? Senile old goat, making a fool of himself like that. Making all of us look like a bunch of dumb Ukrainians in front of those English people."

We all cross our fingers that the priest won't show up at the wedding reception to make more speeches – and he doesn't.

Which is a good thing. Father Zubritsky would be outraged.

The Hotel Macdonald is a classy place, there's no doubt about it. It reminds me of the legislature with its ornate ceilings and marble floors. We're all directed by bellboys to one huge banquet room with plush carpet, a dozen enormous chandeliers, and a candlelit patio. The guests' tables are round, with bright white tablecloths and huge arrangements of white roses for centrepieces. The head table is long and rectangular, decorated with big white bows and bunches of white flowers and leaves, all strung together with vines – which are real because, after dinner, I have a look at them up close. Besides the vines, everything else is white. The tablecloths, the napkins, the flowers, the bows, the cake. The limo, the tuxes, the candles, the centerpieces on the tables, the tables. And the bride's and bridesmaids' dresses, of course – all bright white. You'd never guess that they all spent the afternoon in the gloomy little church at Szypenitz.

Now I'm not sure what to think. The Hotel Macdonald is beautiful. It's like something right out of the movies. The bride looks happy here, and relaxed. She looks like a movie star bride. But it's all wrong for a Ukrainian wedding. It's not the right place for a reception.

The seating has all been arranged beforehand, something we've never seen before. Sophie and I sit together – in our assigned spots, at the very back of the hall, behind two pillars and the bar, with the rest of my mother's family – sipping our orange pops, and sulking. The whole place makes us nervous. Are we allowed to leave our seats once we sit down? We hardly speak, and when we do, it's in whispers. We're afraid that if we move, we'll touch something white and dirty it.

I think that the uncles and the aunts don't like the idea of assigned spots either. They're all sitting quietly – barely talking, let alone laughing. Sophie says it's the white washed atmosphere. It's all too clinical.

"At a wedding," says Sophie, "the bride's gown should be the only all-white thing."

I disagree. The food, too, should be white, or nearly white. *Pyrohy, nalysnyky, holubtsi, pyrizhky.* I point to the food in front of us – green Brussels sprouts, orange carrots, red potatoes – and raise my eyebrows. Who wants to eat *this* at a wedding?

For dessert, we're served something brownish and semi-sweet and coagulated that looks like a poached egg in syrup. I almost gag. At a real wedding, after a real supper, we get up to stretch our legs. Then we help ourselves to real dessert – squares. Twenty different kinds, at least. Auntie Mary's matrimonial squares, with dates and oatmeal; Auntie Linda's seven-layer squares with coconut and butterscotch chips; Auntie Rose's rhubarb delights, Minnesota bars, and rocky road fudge; Mom's cookie sheet brownies and poppyseed *Pampushky.*

At a real wedding, we all sit at long, rectangular tables, wrapped in paper. We sit wherever we please. There are bells, streamers, and balloons, and two big cardboard hearts joined together, with the name of the bride and the name of the groom written in sparkles. Across the head table, we lay a piece of embroidered cloth and, on it, a jar of salt and the *korovai,* with tiny dough birdies squatting in golden braids of bread. Before the meal, we have a Ukrainian blessing and an English blessing. At a real wedding, Uncle Dave and Uncle Charlie and Uncle Andy take turns going to the bar during the meal, each bringing back to the table a tray of drinks in plastic glasses. From time to time while we eat, we clank our forks against our plates to make the newlyweds kiss. We sing *"Mnohaia Lita"* for the couple at least two times. And, at a real wedding, as the speeches begin, the men pull hankies from their pockets, so that the women will have something with which to wipe their eyes.

At Dean and Diana's wedding, we're too far from the podium to see who is speaking and the pillars seem to block what is being said. Diana's family and friends are all seated at the front of the banquet hall and each time someone at the microphone says something funny, we hear them laughing, but it's like we're all left out of the joke. We miss the Toast to the Bride completely, and the Toast to the Groom.

When a little streak of mauve takes her place behind the mike, though, we all know exactly what's going on. A little girl is about to sing.

A girl from the bride's family.

Not me.

I would like to make the secret party-on signal in the little girl's face, to stop her – or slow her down at the very least – from butchering "You Light Up My Life." As she starts singing, someone turns up the volume on the PA system, so we can all hear every word of the song. She sings it twice as fast as she should. Of course, I would sing it double-time too if my voice were that weak.

Because she can't sustain a note, she holds the microphone right against her lips, which makes her *p*s and *b*s explode. Amateur. When she hits her first semi-gutsy note, the mike squeals. Surprise. Any semi-experienced, semi-talented singer would pull the mike away on the loud notes. It seems to me she's had voice lessons because she's concentrating too much on rounding her lips and dropping her jaw and rolling her *r*s. I don't think about my mouth when I sing, or my lips, or my tongue. Instead, I tell myself that my voice is an arrow and that I've got to send it powerfully and precisely. Her voice is a half-dead jackfish, hooked in the gills, drowning in air.

I should be up there in front of the crowd, not her. I should be singing. I should be singing in Ukrainian. I'm better than her, and I always sing. I want people to look at *me*. I whisper in Sophie's ear a hundred times before Mom gives me a poke and a *"Shhh."*

It doesn't matter, though, if I whisper. It doesn't matter if I scream at the top of my lungs. Nobody in the hall can see us because we're behind the pillars, and nobody can hear us over the sound of the little mauve girl's voice.

After "You Light Up My Life," Auntie Helen and Uncle Dan take a turn at the mike, but someone turns down the PA again so we can't make out anything they say. They start at 9:36 and talk until 10:17. Wes times them. They talk and talk. All we can hear are boom-booms, lower when Uncle Dan takes the mike and a little higher when Auntie Helen speaks. After ten minutes or so, Sophie and I make our way to the front and stand by the wall, promising to report what we hear to the family. Wes tags along.

Auntie Helen thanks certain people for coming – Uncle Dan's business colleagues, mostly, who work with him in the industry. The oil industry, she means. Uncle Dan cuts in and makes some jokes about the industry, and some of the people in the front – industry people, I suppose – slap each other's backs and chuckle. Auntie Helen thanks the world-class florist and the world-class chef and the world-class photographer that they hired for the wedding. In front of the pillars, the ladies wear long gowns and big, gold hoops on their ears. The men don't wear regular suits like my uncles and my dad. They wear tuxes, like the groomsmen, with real cufflinks. Standing against the wall and staring, Sophie, Wes, and I look like little brown Indian kids, brown from the time we spend outside on the farm. Looking in, from the outside.

Uncle Dan takes over again, describing the difficulties the bride encountered in selecting her bridal gown. Our jaws drop when we hear that she couldn't find anything she liked in Seattle, Vancouver, Toronto, or Montreal. We've never been to any of these places. Uncle Dan says that Auntie Helen had to bring Diana to a designer in London. London, *England*.

"And, wouldn't you know it," says Auntie Helen, taking over from Uncle Dan, "the silk the designer needed was nowhere to be found in the Western World!"

The crowd rumbles at the joke.

"So it was off to the Orient."

The *Orient*.

Sophie and I simultaneously turn our heads to look at the bride, whose gown is long and white and has sleeves. From looking at the gown, it's hard to tell the difference between it and every other wedding gown we've seen. Unable to stop ourselves, Sophie and I cover our mouths and giggle into our hands. All the heads at the tables closest to us turn and stare. Auntie Helen's head turns our way as well. She gives us a horrified look, a look of embarrassment, disgust, reprimand. We are out of place, out of our assigned spots, on the wrong side of the pillars. Sophie and I blush and start to move back to our table. We've forgotten to party on. We've altogether abandoned the secret party-on signal.

At a real wedding, the band starts with a few old-time waltzes, seven-steps, and foxtrots. After their first break, they play the schottische and the heel-toe, and the bird dance, if it's requested. Polkas and butterflies just before midnight, when the fiddler and the *tsymbaly* player are warmed up; the *kolomyika* just after midnight, before they're too warmed up with liquor. The uncles take turns on the dance floor with the girl-cousins, half-carrying us as they twirl us around. Once in a while they take their wives for a slow two-step. If the band can manage "In the Mood," Mom and Dad jive. But mostly the women sit and talk after the meal and the dishes have been done.

This isn't a real wedding. Because this isn't a real band. There is no accordion, no *tsymbaly*. Nine musicians on stage, and not one of them plays the fiddle. Two play trumpets, one plays the trombone; there is a piano player, an upright bassist, three singers, a drummer. I was hoping for the Melodizers from Mundare in their matching black slacks and light blue velour shirts. This band doesn't have a name, even, and they wear tuxedos. They play elevator and shopping mall music.

When the industry people start stepping onto the dance floor, the uncles gather in bunches, leaning on the pillars, talking quietly and shaking their heads. The aunts cross their arms and their legs, press their lips together. They glance at their watches a lot. For us, there is no dancing.

At exactly midnight, the band stops and there is some commotion on stage.

"The throwing of the bouquet," Sophie whispers to me, smiling.

It's time for the bride to throw her flowers, and for the groom to throw her garter. We make our way toward the middle of the dance floor. We're single girls, after all, so we're eligible to catch the bouquet. The little mauve girl, too, I notice, is walking towards the dance floor. I'm going to stand beside her so that I can push her out of the way when the time comes – push her hard, so that she falls on her little mauve bum and shows the crowd her mauve panties. It will be her best performance of the day.

Only, she doesn't stop at the dance floor, she heads straight for the stage, mauve heels clickety-clacking on the hardwood. I don't think I can bear it. I don't think I can stand another of her songs. But here it comes, her grand finale, a special song for the special couple.

It sounds like the other song she sang tonight: weak, flimsy, bloodless, uninspired. Like the singer herself. *I am your lady and you are my man.* Give me a break. She looks like she's all of nine years old, ten at the most. She's got nerve. *Whenever you reach for me I'll do all that I can.* I wish that she would reach out to me on the dance floor. I'd smile up at her, and hold her bony little hand in mine. Then I'd squeeze. I'd grip her wrist with one hand and her marbly knuckles in the other; I'd pull her down, nose-first, onto the floor, and the mike would be mine. Nobody would take notice of her bawling her bulgy eyes out, her nose leaking blood and snot all over her mauve party dress, because they'd all be transfixed by my singing. I'd sing *"Chaban."*

Halfway through the girl's song, Kalyna appears at my side. I shift my weight from one foot to the other and look for Sophie, who is on the other side of the dance floor, getting us two more glasses of pop.

When the little mauve girl's song is finished and people are clapping and the band is preparing to start up again, Kalyna turns to me and smiles. She leans over close to my face, so close that I can feel her mouth warm on my neck, and she cups her hands around my ear, as if she has a secret to tell me.

"Mauve is my least favourite color," she whispers, and then she takes my hand in hers and twirls me around. "They're crazy, all of them, crazy crazy. You should be singing, Colleen. Sing a Ukrainian song. Sing now! Sing for me, Kalyna!"

But Kalyna's wrong. There's no room for my voice here, and no place for a Ukrainian song. The rules have all changed.

You'd have to be crazy not to see it.

TWO

At the end of the wedding summer, right before grade nine starts, Simone calls. As usual. Simone always calls this time of year. It's a tradition in our house, a sign that school is starting again. We only take piano lessons during the school year, from September until June. And every August, Simone makes a new schedule. She calls all of her students to ask which days we would prefer for our piano lessons. First she calls her most senior students, then her intermediate students, and finally her beginners. There is a sort of hierarchy to the days of the week. Senior students generally choose to have their lessons on Fridays. Friday lessons are high status. And beginners have their lessons on Mondays.

For the last two years, Sophie has been Simone's senior-most student. She's had Friday lessons. Wes has his lessons on Tuesdays. I go on Thursdays. This year, though, I'm moving into the top spot. I've been catching up to Sophie – doing two piano exams each year instead of one – and now we're in the same grade. Even though Sophie is two years older than me, we'll both be taking our grade nine piano exam this year. I've waited a long time for this day to come, and I've worked hard for it. For the first time, Fridays are mine for the taking.

Simone asks to speak to my mother first, so I'm forced to hover around the phone in the kitchen and wait. Sophie is in her bedroom, pretending she doesn't care that we're going to have

65

lessons on the same day. I know it bothers her, though. I know she secretly hates the fact that I'm younger than her and better than her. Lately, when she's practising the piano, and I come into the living room, she quits playing. Even if she just started practising, she stops as soon as I walk into the room. Sometimes she gets angry and bangs the keys before she gets up. Sometimes she gets a sad look on her face, like she'd like to keep playing but something is holding her back.

While Mom and Simone talk, I pace around the kitchen. There are butterflies in my stomach and my palms are sweaty. The thought of talking to Simone makes me nervous. I worry that when it's my turn to talk, I'll stutter and stammer. I like Simone so much that I'm afraid of her. She isn't that much older than Sophie and me. Simone just graduated from high school two years ago. But she's a pro. Some day, she's going to be concert pianist. When I'm older, I want to be just like her. I want to smell like cinnamon, I want to wear silver rings on my pinkie fingers. I want to play like Simone, with my back straight, my head tilted slightly to the right, my wrists up. I'm growing my hair out to look just like hers. Long, straight, no bangs.

Before I have a chance to talk to Simone, Mom hangs up the phone.

"Simone," she says, "is not teaching piano lessons anymore."

I'm too shocked to speak.

"She called to tell us that she's moving to Montreal. She's getting married there. Isn't that good news?"

Good news? I can't believe my mother would say such a thing.

"It's terrible news," I say. Why is this happening to me? It's my year for Friday lessons. "Simone can't be moving."

Not this year. Not yet. Not now.

My mother doesn't seem to notice the gravity of the situation. I was going to learn my first Rachmaninoff this year. I was going to play it at the Kiwanis Music Festival. Simone was going to take me. We were going to make a weekend of it, and stay in a hotel, and go shopping together at Gordon Price Music. How could Simone *abandon* me like this?

"Simone *can't* leave me," I say, my voice shaking.

But it isn't just that Simone is leaving me. She's leaving me to get *married*. Since our trip to Dauphin last summer, I've formed a new opinion of men. They're good-for-nothings, and they can't be trusted. Except for Dad and Wes, men are all liars and cheats. Why would Simone marry one?

"She doesn't even have a boyfriend," I explain to Mom. *"How could she be getting married?"*

"Well." Mom pauses. "She has to get married."

"Why? Why does she *have* to get married? Nobody *has* to do anything. This is a free country. Nobody has to –"

And then I get it. It's written all over Mom's face, the reason Simone has to get married. The reason she won't be teaching piano lessons anymore.

"Oh," I say. *"Oh."*

Mom tries to be cheerful. She rattles on as though nothing has happened, as though nothing at all has changed.

"Simone wants you to take her beginner students. All eight of them, including Wes. What a compliment to you! What a wonderful opportunity! Good experience and extra spending money. Simone says that you'll make fifty dollars a week. Fifty dollars a week! That's two hundred dollars a month."

On and on Mom talks. She talks about advertising for more piano students in the *St. Paul Journal*. She starts an imaginary schedule for the beginners. Four lessons every day after school, twenty students per week; Saturday morning piano recitals in our living room with coffee and doughnuts for the parents. The whole time, she doesn't even ask if I *like* beginners, if I *want* to teach piano lessons. And she doesn't consider for a second what Sophie is going to think of all this. Sophie is hurt enough that I caught up to her with my playing. How will she feel when she hears that Simone has chosen me to replace her?

"I guess that's it for me, then," I say to my mother, tears spilling down my cheeks. "No more piano lessons for *me*. I was going to have Friday lessons this year. I was going to play my first Rachmaninoff."

Mom tries to put her arm around me, but I shake it away.

"And what about Sophie? Sophie needs a teacher too. And all the other senior students. Did Simone ever stop to think about us? I hate her! I wish she'd never been my teacher!"

"You can play all the Rachmanoff you want," says Mom, mis-pronouncing the name. "We'll find a new teacher for you. In fact, Simone has suggested someone. Someone well-respected and very qualified. She wouldn't leave you without a teacher. We just have to make the arrangements."

"Is it Laurette Côté?" I ask, quietly.

Laurette Côté is one of Simone's former students. She plays the violin and the piano. One of her eyes wanders a little but she's nice, and an exceptional pianist. Though I don't quite understand how she focuses on the keyboard.

Mom shakes her head as she explains that Laurette has all the students she can handle.

"Oh Mom," I say, "don't tell me it's *Jablonski*. Please, not him."

Pavel Jablonski is my parents' age. Actually, he's *Dr.* Jablonski. He has a Ph.D. in Music. He's the organist at the Catholic church in town and the Director of the Polish Catholic Community Choir and the President of the Polish Catholic Cultural Association.

Mom shakes her head again. She says that Jablonski is on sab-batical this year in Poland.

"Good," I say, smiling a little. "I don't think I could stand his Polish nationalism. And, I mean, I'm sure he's a good teacher but he'd probably try to convert me to Catholicism."

"So who is it?" I ask, starting to cheer up a little. "A teacher in Edmonton? Will we have to drive all that way?"

Mom clears her throat. "No, that wouldn't be practical."

"Well *who* then? Who's going to be my new teacher?"

Mom clears her throat again.

"Maria Chapdelaine," she says.

Sophie appears in the kitchen as I'm explaining to Mom that I'd rather quit piano completely than take lessons from Maria Chapdelaine.

She's a nun. And nuns are old and old-fashioned and mean. Everybody knows it. You can catch a glimpse of the nuns in St. Paul walking around the convent on main street in their habits. They never smile, they're certainly not friendly, and they only speak French. I'm supposed to take piano lessons in French?

"What kind of woman would marry Jesus?" I ask. "A very creepy one."

Nuns hit their students' knuckles with rosaries. It's a well-known fact. They pray constantly, and when they're not praying, they're reading the Bible. They don't talk like normal people. They don't eat normal food. They don't like children, let alone teenagers. They have no sense of humour, they hardly laugh.

I wouldn't take piano lessons from a nun if she were the last piano teacher on Earth.

For some reason, Sophie disagrees with me. Apparently she's not at all sad that Simone is quitting, and she's perfectly happy to take lessons from Sister Maria.

"A lot of nuns these days are modern," she says. "Some of them are young, and they're allowed to wear regular clothes. It could be interesting."

Sophie says that she'll give Sister Maria a chance.

Of course she will. Because this is her big chance to get ahead of me. No wonder she's so cheerful about Simone quitting. If I stop taking piano lessons, and she continues, then she won't have to compete with me anymore.

So I change my mind – on the spot.

"All right," I say, glaring at Sophie. "Count me in, too."

"Well," Mom says, looking down at her hands, then up at the

ceiling. "It's a bit more complicated than that."

Mom looks straight at Sophie as she explains that Sister Maria has room for one student. One student only.

"So," says Mom, still looking at Sophie, "unless one of you decides that you don't want to continue with your lessons, then you're both going to have to audition for Sister Maria, and she'll make the choice."

Sophie and Mom stare at each other for a long time before Mom looks away. Something about the expression on Sophie's face gives me a lump in my throat. It's not that she looks sad exactly. It's more like – she looks old. She doesn't look like Sophie anymore, she looks like a grown-up woman.

"I'm graduating from high school in a couple of years," she says. "It probably makes more sense if Colleen takes lessons with Sister Maria. She'll be around longer."

"Are you sure?"

As Mom asks the question, Sophie nods, getting up from the kitchen table, as though, if she stayed a moment longer, she might change her mind.

Part of me wishes that Sophie had put up a fight, or that Sophie would have been the one Mom chose for Sister Maria. Deep down, I want to keep taking piano lessons, but it's hard to imagine playing for anyone except Simone. I don't even know how lessons will work with someone else. I've always had Simone. I know the routine with her. We start with scales, chords, arpeggios; then we run through my pieces; and we end with ear training and sight-reading. Is it the same with every teacher?

As Mom drives me to my first piano lesson, I sulk. I stare out the window as we head west down main street, as we pass the turn-off to Simone's place and approach St. Paul Elementary. Two more blocks, and we'll be at the convent next to the cathedral. I look down at the books on my lap, books Simone bought for me, books with Simone's notes in them.

"I don't want to go."

"I know," says Mom.

"I miss Simone."

"I know."

"I'll probably hate Sister Maria."

"If you don't like it you can always quit."

The more Mom agrees with me, the worse I feel. She's being too sympathetic, too *nice*. I want to fight with my mother. I want her to tell me I'm being childish so that I can tell her she doesn't understand anything. It would make me feel better. Instead, she parks the car at the side of the convent and says that she's proud of me.

"I'm really impressed with you, Colleen. You're being very mature about this."

I scowl at her. She smiles back at me.

Sister Maria meets me at the side doors, beside the little plaque on the convent wall that says *Les Soeurs de l'Assumption*. No smile, no hello.

I look back once more at Mom, waving to her as she pulls away.

"You're Colleen," she says. "I'm Maria." She rolls the *r* in Maria.

Now I'm alone with her, and there's no turning back.

Sister Maria is very tall and bone-thin. She's so thin that when I look at her face it's as though I'm looking at a skull. On her head, there's just a small patch of white hair – hardly any, in fact. I've never seen a woman with so little hair. And Sophie is right, some nuns don't wear habits. Sister Maria is dressed in normal clothes. But her sweater is black and stretched out of shape. Her pants are too big, they hang and sag as though they're about to drop off. Don't they feed them here?

The first thing Sister Maria does when we get to her music

room is motion for me to take a seat on the piano bench. Then, while I wait, she rummages around in her cupboard. Is she getting out her Bible? Do we pray before we play? I wonder if I should tell her, right off the bat, that I'm not Catholic and I don't intend to become one.

"You've been at school all day," she says. "No one can play music with an empty belly."

Sister Maria lifts up a bag of chocolate chip cookies. She pulls a chair next to the piano bench.

"You want to eat, you eat. I don't like my pupils to go hungry." She definitely has an accent. "Hungry" sounds like "hongry."

I'd rather not eat any of Sister Maria's cookies. She needs them much more than I do. But she doesn't help herself to any cookies. Instead, she keeps offering them to me, thrusting the cookie bag in my face. Really, she's acting an awful lot like an old *baba* – insisting that I eat, practically forcing food down my throat. She's French, though. Chapdelaine is definitely a French name. She has to be French. This is a convent for French Catholic nuns.

I give in, finally, and take a cookie.

"What do you want to play?" she asks.

Should I start with scales? I wonder. I should probably start with scales.

I start to play the A-major scale, two hands, four octaves, ascending and descending, with a cadence at the end to polish it off. But Sister Maria doesn't look too impressed.

"That's not really music. What *music* do you want to play?"

So she wants me to play a piece. I start to open my grade eight Royal Conservatory book to the Chopin waltz I played for my last piano exam. Actually, I can play it off by heart, the music is just for reassurance. It's my best piece. Simone says I was born to play Chopin. I can really show off with it. But halfway through the waltz, Sister Maria grabs the book and tosses it onto the floor.

"All right," she says, making a sour face. "That's enough.

Grade eight is finished. Understand? Grade eight is for babies. Let's move on."

I open my brand new grade nine book, then, hands trembling. Will I have to sight-read pieces that I've never seen before? Grade nine pieces?

Before I have a chance to play anything, Sister Maria pulls the grade nine book off the piano, dropping it onto the grade eight book.

"I don't like any of these books," she says, pointing at the floor.

"But I'm supposed to play from the books. For the exam at the end of the year. I have to follow the syllabus."

"Forget the books. Forget the syllabus. What music do *you* want to play?"

What do I want to play?

I don't understand her, I don't know what she means. I've never actually chosen my own pieces. Simone made all the decisions. I liked it that way. And Simone never threw my books around, never made faces. This is it, I think. Sister Maria is going to pull out her rosary right now and let me have it across the knuckles. God, this is worse than I'd imagined.

Sister Maria looks a little exasperated.

"I want you to play music that you love, understand? You tell me what you love and we'll learn it together, yes? You choose. I don't baby my students. I don't choose for you, the book doesn't choose for you. *You* choose. *Capice?*"

She's Italian! That's it! I knew the accent wasn't French. I try to think of some Italian music to impress her so that she'll stop picking on me. Something by Verdi? Did Verdi write piano music? Puccini. No, he's opera. Palestrina?

Sister Maria snaps her fingers. "Come on, come on. Say a composer. Give me a name. One name, your favourite. Someone you always wanted to play. Quick, quick. Let's go!"

"Rachmaninoff!"

I say Rachmaninoff in desperation because I can't think of a single Italian composer of piano music. It's not a lie, either. I really do want to learn Rachmaninoff. As soon as I say it, though, I want to take it back. I don't know how she'll react. There is a Rachmaninoff piece in the grade nine book. Is it too easy? Is Rachmaninoff for babies?

She is silent for several seconds, while Rachmaninoff hangs in the air between us, suspended, waiting for her judgment. Then she leans back in her chair and smiles. She actually smiles.

She can't be Russian. There's no such thing as a Russian nun. Is there?

"You like Russian music?" she asks.

"Sure. I like Russian music. I like it a lot. Shostakovich, Tchaikovsky. Bartók. I've always liked Russian music. Well. Of course, Bartók is Hungarian, not Russian."

I'm rambling now, but there's no turning back. If I'm lucky, she'll believe me, and stop her interrogation.

"I like Slavic music in general," I say. "Like Stravinsky, Dvořák. The Chopin Mazurkas. All of that. I suppose it would be really neat to play music by a Ukrainian composer, if there was such a thing. A Ukrainian composer, I mean. Because I'm Ukrainian myself. I mean, I was born here and everything, but, you know."

Sister Maria stares at me.

Now why did I go and say that? What's wrong with me? Ukrainian composers have never once crossed my mind. Never once. And I don't actually know any Russian music, except for the Rachmaninoff piece that Simone chose for me. I'm so scared of Sister Maria that I'm making things up – lying – blurting out anything that comes to mind. I'm so intimidated that I don't even know what I'm saying.

"Tell me," she says. "Tell me about being Ukrainian."

I'm not sure what to say. No one has ever asked me what it's like, or what it means, to be Ukrainian. I don't know how to explain it. I don't know where to begin.

"For starters, I've never actually been to the Ukraine."

"Ukraine," says Sister Maria.

"Right," I say. "I wasn't born in the Ukraine."

"Just Ukraine. You don't say 'the Canada.' Why would you say 'the Ukraine'"?

She's got a point.

"All right," I continue. "I was born here, and so were my parents. Their parents – I call them –"

"Baba and *Gido* –"

"Right," I say. *"Baba* and *Gido.* They were born in the – in Ukraine, but they came to Canada when they were very young, just babies, so they don't remember anything about the Old Country. They were farmers. Actually, my *baba* and *gido* on my dad's side are dead. I just have one *baba* and one *gido* left, and they're too old to –"

"You speak Ukrainian to them?" she asks, cutting in again.

"Not really. Actually, no, I don't speak Ukrainian to them. I don't talk to them at all, unless my mom or dad is around to translate. *Baba* and *Gido* don't speak English very well, and I only speak English."

"Yet your parents, they speak Ukrainian."

"They do, yes. My mother is the Ukrainian teacher at my school. She teaches me Ukrainian, and my brother and sister. She's teaching my dad to read and write it at home, too, because he never learned when he was young."

"So you do speak Ukrainian. All of you."

I shake my head again. "No. Just my mom and dad. It's like a secret code for them when they don't want us kids to know what they're talking about."

Sister Maria raises her eyebrows.

"We're Ukrainian in other ways," I say.

I want to explain to her that it doesn't matter if we don't speak the language.

"Church?" she asks. "You go to church?"

I shake my head. I tell Sister Maria that my parents used to go. "My aunts and uncle go all the time. But we only go once in a while. Like for a wedding or a funeral. My dad doesn't want us to get brainwashed."

Sister Maria sits back in her chair, crossing her arms over her chest. I should have left out the last bit, about brainwashing. She is a nun, after all.

Maybe it's time for me to ask a few questions of my own. Like why Sister Maria is so interested in my background. I'm starting to think that she's Ukrainian herself. Though it doesn't make much sense. A Ukrainian Catholic nun in a French Catholic convent?

The problem is that when I try to ask her questions about herself, Sister Maria doesn't give very clear answers. I ask her if she's French, and she says that she speaks French. What kind of answer is that? Then I ask her if she's Russian, and she says that she speaks Russian.

"So are you one or the other?" I ask. "Or both? Or something else?"

But Sister Maria doesn't answer. In fact, she pretends that she hasn't even heard the question. She gets up from her chair, pushing me off the piano bench so that I almost fall to the floor. For such a skinny person, she's surprisingly strong.

"Hold out your hands," she says.

Here we go. I'm getting it now. The rosary. On the palms of my hands instead of the knuckles. I've said something wrong. I've said everything wrong. Well, this will be the first and last time she beats me, that's for sure. If she lays one finger on me, I won't come back. I probably won't come back anyway.

But Sister Maria doesn't pull out her rosary. Instead, she opens the piano bench and from it she gathers a stack of paper into her arms.

"So you think there's no such thing as a Ukrainian composer?"

One by one, she plops sheet music into my hands, reciting

composers' names as she goes. Dmytro Bortniansky, Kyrylo Stetsenko, Stanyslav Liudkevych.

"You know these names?" she asks.

I shake my head.

Lev Revutsky, Borys Liatoshynsky. More music drops into my hands. Mykola Lysenko. Maksym Berezovsky. Artemii Vedel. Vasyl Barvinsky.

There is silence between us for a moment and then, while I'm still standing with the stack of sheets in my hands, Sister Maria plays for me, by heart, no music in front of her. She plays a song in a minor key, slow and melancholy, her arms outstretched like wings over the piano. From time to time, she leans over the piano, her fingers kneading the keys, her forehead almost touching her hands, as though she means to kiss the keys; then she arches her back and tilts her face upward, eyes closed. As she plays, her room starts to change. The plaster on the walls is cracked and chipping, I know. There is a dented metal filing cabinet in the corner. A yellowed poster of Beethoven hangs crooked by one nail over the piano. On another wall, a funny-looking, faded drawing of three musicians. Everything is drab and worn. Sister Maria's sleeves are worn, too, not black so much as grey. But when she plays, everything looks different. As though a window has been opened, bathing her in light, like an angel.

She finishes too soon, I think. I don't want her to stop. I want to hear more. I want to learn it myself – the piece she just played, and all the music that I hold in my arms.

"Can I learn that song?" I ask. "Can I buy the sheet music in Edmonton?"

"You can't buy the music anywhere. Nowhere at all. It's not for sale."

"How did you get it, then? Where did all this music come from?"

Flipping through the stack of sheet music, I see that it's all handwritten.

"Your mother is waiting for you, I think," says Sister Maria, her eyes on the clock above the filing cabinet. "Shall we meet again next week?"

It's dark outside by the time my lesson ends. Mom is outside the convent at six o'clock sharp, listening to the radio in the car. I come out of Sister Maria's room with gifts from her, a handful of cookies and several brown sheets of music – her piano adaptations of several pieces of music by Ukrainian composers. Before I get into the car, I shove the cookies into my jean jacket pocket. Then I slip the brown sheets under the cover of my grade nine music book. I don't want Mom asking any questions about my lesson. I decide that what goes on inside the convent is private, it's between Sister Maria and me.

"So," says Mom. "Should we call it quits with Mother Superior?" She laughs at her own joke. "Or is she a *nice* nun, like Julie Andrews in *The Sound of Music?*"

I hardly hear Mom's questions. I'm staring through the car window and into Sister Maria's window – trying to catch a glimpse of her as we drive away. I wonder how Sister Maria found her way here, to St. Paul, Alberta. I wonder who she is, and why she lives here. I think that maybe I'll bake cookies for her before my next lesson, and bring her a Tupperware container full of them. Fresh cookies, soft, still warm.

Mom reaches over to squeeze my hand and, as she pulls away from the convent, she sings – "The hills are alive with the sound of music." But as we drive home, the melody that Sister Maria played is the melody that I hear, over and over again.

THREE

After I get home from my piano lesson each week, I like to close myself into my bedroom. Just for an hour or two before supper. The others – Mom, Dad, Sophie, and Wes – think that I'm doing my homework. But I'm not.

Sometimes I'm playing cassettes that Sister Maria has lent to me, recordings of piano concertos played by big orchestras and famous concert pianists. Or I'm flipping through the music magazines that Sister Maria subscribes to, old issues that she has already read, and then passed along to me. I'm learning about all kinds of music, not just the songs for my piano exams, but other songs, and the history behind them. At the end of every lesson, Sister Maria always pulls out something for me to borrow. Video recordings of operas, music history textbooks. Every once in a while, she gives me something to keep – a dog-eared copy of *The Well-Tempered Clavier,* sheet music for *"Malaguena,"* an old metronome that she's long since replaced.

More often than not, though, after my lessons, I lie on my bed and I think about Sister Maria. I think that she must be lonely. She's not like the other nuns. Lots of them are so old they can hardly walk. For the most part, the convent is deathly quiet. Except, of course, when Sister Maria is giving lessons. She's too lively for the convent, too loud. She doesn't fit in.

The truth is, I don't really know much about Sister Maria. I think that she's Ukrainian, or has some connection to Ukraine, but

I don't know for sure. She's never given me the whole story. I think that when she isn't teaching, she's transcribing the works of Ukrainian composers so that they won't be forgotten. But I don't know where she finds the music in the first place.

I imagine that someone in Europe sends material to her because her desk is covered with envelopes from foreign countries. I imagine that she receives scratchy recordings, old scraps of manuscript paper. The occasional booklet of printed music, and maybe diaries or journals with the odd bit of musical notation. I imagine that she sorts through everything that is sent to her, making sense of it the best she can. And when she thinks that she's pieced together an entire song, then she transcribes it. At least that's how I imagine it. Sister Maria has never explained it to me.

I'm learning to play from some of her transcriptions, which seems to make her happy, but I can never really predict how she'll act at my lessons. What kind of a mood she'll be in.

After my first lesson, I spent hours at home trying to work out the song that she'd played for me, the sad song in the minor key. She didn't lend me the music, but I'm good at playing things by ear. I had the melody in my head – most of it anyway – so I made up my own version of it to play for her at my next lesson. Only she didn't like it. Not one bit. She said that I'd gotten it all wrong. I made it sound simple and cheap, like a folk song. And then she pulled out her sheet music to show me the real thing.

Sometimes, before I learn a new song by a Ukrainian composer, she tells me about the composer's life, and that's when she looks the saddest. Artemii Vedel, spent most of his life in prison for political reasons. Vasyl Barvinsky, sentenced to ten years in a Soviet concentration camp. Maksym Berezovsky, committed suicide in the eighteenth century. So many of their deaths were violent and ugly. She talks about composers who were gunned down, murdered, assassinated – composers who starved to death, or froze to death. They all suffered and died because they were Ukrainian, because they wanted to stay Ukrainian when other countries invaded Ukraine. I never know what to say after Sister Maria tells me their stories. I wonder if Sister Maria was like them. If she suffered, too, because of what she believed in.

I've given up trying to predict when Sister Maria will talk about her own work. Every once in a while, out of the blue, she'll mention it, and talk and talk, bringing out sheet music and playing excerpts. Once she held me over, cutting into the next student's lesson while she explained her latest piece. But when I ask straight out about her progress, she doesn't answer.

I have so many questions. I want to ask about the person who sends her the material. For all I know, it might be more than one person. Are they other nuns? Priests, maybe, or monks. Family members, old friends? Anything is possible. I want to ask how she knows these people, and how they come across this material, and why they send the music to her and not to somebody else. I want to know what she plans to do with her transcriptions once they're all finished. I want to know exactly why she does them in the first place.

More than anything, I want to talk to somebody else about Sister Maria — like Sophie. Sophie would be fascinated, like me. I know she would. I wish that I could tell Sophie everything I know about Sister Maria's music room, her work with the Ukrainian music. Everything about her seems so romantic, so mysterious. My guess is that she's seventy or seventy-five. Which means that she was born before the First World War, and lived through both World Wars — maybe in Russia, maybe in France, probably in both.

Sophie would help me fill in the details, come up with possible explanations for how Sister Maria wound up in Canada, because Sophie is studying the USSR in her grade eleven Social Studies class. Together, we could make timelines, and sketch out maps of Europe, and trace out Sister Maria's life story — potential versions of it, at least. We could bounce ideas off one another, like a couple of detectives. If Sister Maria is Ukrainian, then maybe she came to Canada, via France let's say, to flee from the Communists.

Or else she was running from the Nazis. Or Stalin? Stalin is a possibility, too. Of course, I could do the investigation on my own. It just wouldn't be as much fun.

But I don't dare talk to Sophie about Sister Maria because Sophie hasn't forgotten that I'm the lucky one who got to continue with piano lessons, and she won't let me forget it either.

"How's our Little Prodigy?" she says, after my lessons. "How's the Musical Genius?"

How's the Gifted One, the Golden Child, Our Very Own Virtuoso?

I can't talk to Sophie about the mystery of Sister Maria. She'd laugh in my face. "You're the Girl Wonder," she'd say. "Figure it out for yourself."

So I keep Sister Maria a secret, hoping that one day she'll tell me her story.

Maybe I spend too much time daydreaming about Sister Maria, making up tragic versions of her past. Maybe I'm too preoccupied about her composers and how they were persecuted just for being Ukrainian. But when I hear the rumours that the school board is canceling Ukrainian classes in our school, I can't help thinking that Sister Maria will understand my plight because it's the same thing, history repeating itself. Persecution all over again.

I hear the news from my best friends Kirsten Paulichuk and Tanya Yuzko, who hear it from Carla Senko, who says that my mom is being fired because she's a bad teacher. Actually, Carla says that I'm to blame, too. She says the principal found out that Mom has been favouring me – showing me exams at home, giving me marks that I don't deserve. So he's cutting the whole Ukrainian program, just like that.

Nothing could be further from the truth, of course. They're canceling Ukrainian because the enrolment is so far down.

Because of students like Carla Senko who switched from Ukrainian to French. Mom explains this to me one night over supper during the Christmas holidays. The numbers in her Ukrainian classes have been dropping for the past two years and now there simply aren't enough students to justify paying a Ukrainian teacher. But Mom isn't going to be fired. That's a lie, too. They're reassigning her to grade three.

After Christmas, according to Mom, when we go back to school, everything will be different. The last remaining Ukrainian students are going to be integrated into French classes. There are only four of us left in grade nine Ukrainian anyway, and not many more in each of the lower grades. To help us along, Miss Maximchuk, the French teacher, will give us extra French tutorials after school. Until we're all caught up. And Mom will have a new classroom in the elementary wing of the school.

My mother, I can tell, is relieved. She finally gets to teach normal kids in a normal classroom. No more homemade readers and workbooks, no more bingo games and flashcards.

I, on the other hand, am devastated.

Miss Maximchuk is the problem. While the rest of the family talks at the supper table, about how wonderful it is that Mom will be able to teach grade three, and about how useful it is to learn French in this day and age, I pick at my food and think about Miss Maximchuk and fume. Everything was fine until she showed up and took over the French program from Mr. Poirier. Mr. Poirier was old and strict. But once Miss Maximchuk came along – with her pink miniskirts and her snug, see-through blouses – French class turned into a big party. French crossword puzzles, French fold-out board games, French hangman. She gets her students to move their desks into a circle and read glossy magazines from Quebec. In the wintertime, they make *cabane à sucre*. They learn how to jig.

Jigging. That's the main attraction. Miss Maximchuk has

enormous breasts, and when she demonstrates the jigging, her breasts bounce and jiggle under her blouse. Most of the guys switched out of Ukrainian because of her boobs. Everyone knows that. They couldn't care less about French. My mom isn't full-breasted at all. How could she compete?

I can't believe that no one else in my family sees the injustice. Our language is being taken from us, and nobody seems to care. Nobody wants to fight it. Mom and Dad talk about French like it's a good thing, like it's the only language that counts because anyone who speaks French can get a good government job. They say that, if I want to keep learning Ukrainian, we can speak it at home. But that will never happen. We've tried it before – Ukrainian-only meals to practice our Ukrainian. None of us kids said a word.

Over the Christmas holidays, I try to convince Sophie and Wes that we need to protest. I want to get them on my side. I tell them that it's an outrage – having to join students who have been taking French for years. We'll look stupid. How will we ever catch up? But Wes doesn't care much. He's in grade seven, which means that he's only been in Ukrainian for three and a half years. It won't be as hard for him to catch up in French class. And Sophie isn't affected at all. She's in grade eleven, and she's finished all of her second-language requirements. In fact, she says that she wishes she'd learned French all these years instead of Ukrainian. She says that Wes and me are luckier than she was.

"It's not the end of the world," says Sophie. "It won't be so bad. And don't forget, you've had Ukrainian for almost six years. You should be thankful. Think about all of the kids in St. Paul who aren't French or Ukrainian and who never even had one year, not one single year, not one single class, in their languages. Now that isn't fair, is it? Yet we don't hear a peep from all of the Norwegian kids, the Germans, the Polish kids, the Italians."

For the first time in my life, I raise my voice to Sophie.

"Easy for you to talk, all high and mighty, in grade eleven. *You* were never oppressed, *your* language was never taken from you."

I storm into the bedroom, slam the door.

"And there *are* no Italians in this town!"

Secretly, I want Sister Maria to come to my rescue. I'm not sure how she would help me exactly, but it would make a big difference if I knew that she were on my side. No one else seems to understand.

Before we go back to school, after the Christmas holidays, I call the other three students in my Ukrainian class who are being persecuted, Tanya Yuzko, Kirsten Paulichuk, and Henry Popowich. I figure if we band together, we can make our voices heard and keep Ukrainian after all.

"We're victims," I say. "Our rights are being taken away. We have to speak out."

But the other three victims don't seem to mind. Henry Popowich speaks Ukrainian at home, so it doesn't matter to him if Ukrainian classes are cancelled. He'll keep on speaking Ukrainian at home. Tanya's mother is French, and she already knows lots of French words, so she's perfectly happy to take French. And Kirsten has been completely brainwashed. There's no other explanation. She can't possibly believe the things that she says. That we need French to get a good job; that French is easier anyway; that there are no Ukrainian classes in high school and we'll all have to switch sooner or later. I tell Kirsten not to include *me* in her *we*. I tell all three of them, Henry, Tanya, and Kirsten, that they're traitors: traitors, double-crossers, and turncoats. They're selling us out, selling us right down the river.

Kirsten says, "What's a turncoat?"

My piano lessons are cancelled for the Christmas holidays, but I'm desperate to talk to Sister Maria about the cancellation of Ukrainian. So I visit her on New Year's Day. When Mom and Dad ask me why I need a ride to town, I tell them that I need to pick up some music from the convent. Actually, I'm going to ask Sister Maria for advice.

"What would you do," I say, "if something terrible were happening, something *unjust*? And you were sure that you couldn't stand by and let it happen? But you were sort of *powerless,* and you couldn't do anything all by yourself?"

I'm hoping that Sister Maria will ask for details. Then I will tell her about the Ukrainian program.

She shrugs her shoulders. "Depends," she says, as she plugs in the kettle to make us tea.

I glance at her stack of transcriptions, all of her yellowed and dog-eared scraps of manuscript paper. The brown envelopes with foreign stamps and funny, foreign handwriting.

"What if," I continue, "your language were being taken from you? Your language and your whole culture?"

It's not exactly true that my whole culture is being taken away from me. It's really just that I won't be able to take Ukrainian anymore. I need to get across to her the gravity of the situation, though.

Sister Maria frowns. "This is about – ?" She doesn't finish her question.

I tell her the whole story, from beginning to end. Everything. Not just about the low enrolment in my mom's classes, and the competition between Ukrainian and French, and the school board's decision to cut the Ukrainian program. I go way back to Dauphin, and tell her how the Ukrainian kids keep their dancing a secret at school; how we're embarrassed to talk about all the Ukrainian things we do. I tell her about Dean and Diana's wedding, and how there was nothing Ukrainian about their reception. My story gets a bit confused in parts – when I try to explain why I quit Ukrainian dancing after the festival, and why I stopped singing Ukrainian songs, and why I hated listening to Father Zubritsky's lecture about being Ukrainian at the wedding ceremony. But eventually I come back to my main point.

"And now, my parents are forcing me to join Miss Maximchuk's French class, even though I don't want to do it."

For a moment, Sister Maria says nothing. She takes a sip of her tea, and plays with the rosary around her neck.

"Isn't it the same as the composers in Ukraine?" I ask her. "Isn't it?"

Sister Maria drop her rosary. "No," she says, quietly. "It's not the same."

"Why not?"

"It's not the same," she repeats.

"Just because no one is trying to kill me or put me in a gulag or —"

"Stay quiet," says Sister Maria, "about things you know nothing about. Think before you speak."

I can feel my face turning red.

Sister Maria leans over the table to touch my hand.

"It's not the same because you don't know what you want."

"I want to keep taking Ukrainian."

"But you don't want to listen to this Father Zubritsky when he tells you to speak your language."

My face is as red as a tomato, I'm sure.

"And you don't want to sing these songs your mother taught you, or do this secret dancing you just told me about."

I can't respond. I don't know what to say.

"No one is stopping you from being who you are, Colleen," says Sister Maria. "Except you."

I think about my conversation with Sister Maria for a day or two, and I decide that she doesn't really understand my situation. I mean, she's right about a few things. I probably shouldn't have quit dancing. When Mom wanted to teach me *"Chaban,"* maybe I should have let her. Much as I hate to admit it, Father Zubritsky was partly right when he talked about Ukrainians who don't speak

Ukrainian. But I know injustice when I see it. It's not my fault that the school board is cancelling Ukrainian. And it's definitely not fair.

After school starts again, while the school administration phases out the Ukrainian program, I start a letter-writing campaign. I do it in the school library, which is where the ex-Ukrainian students are supposed to sit together, working through the beginner French textbooks for a few weeks before they officially join the French classes. It's humiliating, if you ask me, being forced to do grade four exercises. I refuse to participate. It makes me sick to my stomach watching Tanya, Kirsten, and Henry throw themselves into this new language, as though they can't wait to forget everything they learned in Ukrainian.

I write one letter to the principal, one to the school board, and one to the *St. Paul Journal,* protesting our forced migration into the French classroom. My parents think I'm being melodramatic. Sophie and Wes think it's a big joke.

The *St. Paul Journal* doesn't print my letter to the editor, but I do hear back from the principal and the school board. The news isn't good. Two copies of the same letter arrive in separate envelopes with a different signature at the bottom of each copy.

> *We regret to inform you that your request to have Ukainian rein-stated has been denied. Please consider entering Miss Maximchuk's French program. Alternatively, we are pleased to offer you any one of the following options, designed specifically for our Young Ladies in the junior high school:*

> *1. Introductory Typing*
> *2. Introductory Food Preparation*
> *3. Introductory Beauty Culture*

It's hard to imagine what would be worse: sitting, ignorant and confused and mute, in a classroom with students who have taken French for five and a half years, who are practically fluent, or sitting through a course for Young Ladies.

Mrs. Heatherington plays records during her typing classes, old country and western 45s of Merle Haggard, Johnny Cash, Mel Tellis, Conway Twitty, and her students type their exercises in time with the music. She doesn't care what they type – most of the girls, I've heard, write notes to exchange with one another after class – so long as their fingers never stop and they keep to the beat. Food Prep is like home eeconomics without the sewing. I'm not sure what they learn in Beauty Culture. How to cut hair, I suppose, and give perms, and maybe how to wax facial hair.

I refuse to give up. If the principal and the school board won't take me seriously, maybe the government will. I write several more letters: to my MLA, the Minister of Education, and the Premier. Not one of them responds. Not even to tell me that they disagree with my point of view. I'm sure that when the *Edmonton Journal* publishes my letter to their editor the whole ugly truth of it will come out – *Blatant Discrimination in St. Paul School, Politicians Turn Blind Eye to Social Wrong.* Official invitations will follow, invitations to Ukrainian bilingual schools in Edmonton or Calgary or both. But the *Edmonton Journal* doesn't publish my letter either.

In the end, my letter-writing campaign fails. It fails miserably. The conspiracy is bigger than I originally imagined. As far as I'm concerned, the entire universe is against me. Colleen Lutzak versus the Whole World. My parents are in on it. They say that my campaign is nonsense, and they're forcing me to sit in Miss Maximchuk's classroom four hours a week. My brother and my friends are in on it, trying to convince me that French is fun. And Miss Maximchuk is definitely in on it, more than anyone else. She's Ukrainian. Why is she teaching French in the first place?

As for Sister Maria – I can't be sure. Maybe she's on my side after all.

Out of the blue, at the end of one of my lessons, in the middle of February, she asks me how my French is coming along.

I tell her that it's coming along fine. That's all I say, nothing more.

While I'm putting on my coat in the foyer of the convent, she says, "You're a very smart girl, Colleen."

I stop zipping my coat, and turn to face her.

"You're smart about music, of course," she says, waving her hand. "I don't need to tell you. I've never had a more gifted pupil. You have enormous talent, and you match it with hard work."

I resume zipping.

"But you're getting smart about life, too, no? You're learning that sometimes we have to do unpleasant things. Sometimes we have no choice. So we do these things. We do them on the *outside,* yes? So that everyone around us believes we have given up."

Sister Maria puts her arm around me, and squeezes.

"On the *inside,* though, we never forget – who we are, what we believe in. No, we never forget these things. It isn't easy. Of course it isn't easy. Sometimes we feel very lonely. But we survive, you see. We do what we must to *survive.*"

As Sister Maria talks, I get goosebumps. I'm glad that she understands. I'm relieved. I get the feeling, though, that she isn't only talking about my problems at school.

Just what else is she talking about?

Learning French, in fact, isn't that hard. Not nearly as hard as Ukrainian. And once I accept my fate, I'm determined to be the best. To out-French the Frenchest students in my class. From the time I get home from school until the time I go to bed, I work through my French textbooks and *cahiers,* conjugating verbs, memorizing vocabulary and numbers.

French is easy because there's no new alphabet to learn, and a lot of English words are the same in French – especially long words. When I write compositions in French, I use a lot of big English words that end in "ance" and "tude." After two months, I can hardly believe that Miss Maximchuk hasn't caught on. I've used *insouciance, délivrance,* and *solitude* in every French composition I've written. Fifteen compositions, fifteen *insouciances, délivrances,* and *solitudes,* for a grand total of forty-five red circles. Miss Maximchuk circles each of my big words in red pen and writes, *Ton vocabulaire est bon!* in the margin.

By the middle of April, I'm right where I want to be: at the top of the class. I've worked hard, and it's paid off.

What's harder, though — harder than learning French — is fighting the feeling that I've been carrying with me since I started Miss Maximchuk's class. The feeling that I'm floating and bobbing in a pool of water and that pieces of me are floating and bobbing away. When I lie in bed at night, I make mental lists of the new French words I've learned and I try to match each French word with its Ukrainian equivalent, to keep my Ukrainian memory fresh and strong. I even put my Ukrainian-English dictionary beside my bed.

At first, the exercise is easy. *Je* – *Я. Pomme* – *Яблуко.* Numbers, the days of the week. *Grenouille* – *Жаба.* But we go through chapters quickly in French class — thirty new nouns per week, five new verbs — and I can't find words like insouciance, deliverance, and solitude in the Ukrainian-English dictionary. I'm losing words now, daily.

So when I select my topic for the French final project, it's a matter of survival, just like Sister Maria said. The ninth grade French projects — *Les Thèmes et Les Variations* — are infamous in our school; they are Miss Maximchuk's *raison d'être.* Each year, she chooses a *thème* — this year's is *Canada, Le Pays Multiculturel* — then she asks her senior French students to pair up and work on *variations* of the *thème.* The presentation of *Les Thèmes et Les Variations* in June is a gala event, like the school Christmas concert, with parents, teachers, and school board members in attendance.

Peter Eliuk and Greg Pederson are doing Mexican Canadians. There is talk that they'll make real *papier mâché piñatas.* Sarah H.

and Sarah M. decide on Italian Canadians, and they're bringing *tortellini* for the audience to sample. Torn between the Scots and the Irish in Canada, Laurie-Anne and Jessie compromise – they choose the British. Carla Senko and Michael Holowaychuk pick French Canadians. They're a couple now, boyfriend and girlfriend.

I plan to work alone, *sans* partner. I won't even ask Miss Maximchuk for assistance. My project will be mine all mine. I plan to make maps, models, diagrams, and charts. I might even bring in my guitar and sing, or wear my old Ukrainian costume and dance. The title of my project is *Je Me Souviens Aussi: Les Ukrainiens au Canada*. My *coup de grâce*.

I make three huge maps – one of Canada, one of Alberta, one of the rough triangular area between Vegreville, Smoky Lake, and St. Paul – which show the demographic distribution of Ukrainians settlers in Canada and Alberta. Plus Ukraine, of course. I also make a giant map of Ukraine which shows the cities and the villages from which most of the Ukrainian settlers originally came. My written report is twenty-two pages long; in it, I describe the path that my family followed to Alberta. From Bukovyna to Frankfurt by train, to Halifax by boat, to Winnipeg again by train, and, finally, to Szypenitz on foot. I include recipes and real embroidery patterns. Some discussion of Ukrainian folk music and religion. Photos of Ukrainian dance costumes.

As the presentation day approaches, I decide to sing *"Tsyhanochka"* with my guitar – my first performance since Dauphin. I'm also going to bring several *pysanky*. I will need a table for my *pysanky* and also for my 3-D miniature replica of a traditional Ukrainian village, with its miniature corrals around its miniature chickens and pigs, its thatch-roofed and white washed miniature house. Around me, I will hang the maps and a poster on which I have printed an excerpt of the Taras Shevchenko poem "The Testament." Translated from Ukrainian into English, of course, and then into French.

I translate almost everything into French, except the names of people, like Clifford Sifton, Ivan Pylypow, Wasyl Eleniak, and Taras Shevchenko, and the names of Ukrainian dishes that I can't bring myself to translate. *Les petites crêpes au fromage* doesn't work. *Nalysnyky* are *nalysnyky*. *Pysanky,* too, remain *pysanky*, not *les oeufs de Pâques* or *les oeufs colorés*. For each Ukrainian word, I write two transcriptions, one in the Roman alphabet and one in the Cyrillic. *Pysanky, Писанки.*

Three nights before *Les Thèmes et Les Variations*, the telephone rings, and my mother talks quietly into the receiver for a long time before she calls me to the phone. I'm in the bathroom, putting the finishing touches on the three new *pysanky* I've made for my presentation. They've already been varnished. Now, one at a time, I hold the eggs over the sink and poke two small holes in each one. When I blow into one hole, my breath pushes the egg yolk and egg white through the other hole, until the insides of the three eggs are one long clot slipping down the drain.

Mom yells, "Collee-een, pho-one. It's Miss Maximchuk."

Miss Maximchuk is on the phone?

"Carla Senko is in a bind," says Miss Maximchuk.

I can feel the blood drain from my face.

"Earlier this evening, Carla caught Michael Holowaychuk behind the Red Rooster with a girl from the Catholic school. You can imagine that Carla is very distressed. She's been at my house with me for the last hour. This was totally unexpected, completely unforeseen. Carla's heart is positively broken. She feels, well, humiliated, frankly, and vulnerable. Right now she needs our encouragement and our support."

"Help, too, don't forget help!"

I can hear Carla's voice in the background.

Across the room, I see my mother shaking her head.

"Yes, and our *help*," says Miss Maximchuk. "I think that Carla needs our help most of all. We girls need to stick together!"

While Miss Maximchuk chirps through the phone line, I see Carla Senko, nine years old, pulling a cinnamon bun apart with her hands. It's the biggest cinnamon bun I've ever seen – bigger than both her hands put together – and when she unrolls it, raisins drop out and onto her desk. I have six poppyseed *pampushky* in my lunch. I offer to trade all six for her cinnamon bun. I will trade anything for a taste of her cinnamon bun. She takes my *pampushky* and gives me half of the cinnamon bun. Later, toward the end of the day, as I'm tossing away some pencil shavings, I see my *pampushky* squashed at the bottom of the garbage pail.

I see Carla Senko when she is eleven years old, in her gym clothes. Both she and I have been selected as the team captains in Mrs. Zalinsky's gym class. It's the end of volleyball season and we're having a mock championship. Each team captain must come up with a team name. Carla takes the Panthers. The panther is our school mascot. Most of the people she chooses for her team are members of the Junior High Volleyball team, so they have matching Panther uniforms; their team cheer is the Panthers roar. All in all, I don't think it's very original. I call my team the Volleyball Vultures. I like the alliteration. Plus it's fresh and innovative. "Vultures" says what we're about as a team: winning. More than winning, devouring. More than devouring even, our name declares that our opponents are dead and defeated before we even start. We're simply cleaning up the scraps.

I hear Carla teasing me, and her teammates laughing at me to impress her. Some of the Panthers caw like crows, others gobble like turkeys. None makes the sound of a real vulture, whatever that sound may be, but it doesn't matter. All my teammates mutiny halfway through the mock championship. All except Joe Jr., one of the kids in our class from the reserve, who walks off the court to speak with Mrs. Zalinsky.

After a few minutes, I hear Joe Jr. saying, "What're you teaching in this class anyways. Help her out already."

I think he means me; help *me* out.

Joe Jr. gets himself kicked out of class for being disrespectful and Carla tells everyone that he's my boyfriend. That I've gone

Indian, and that we're going to have half-breed babies. She says we should rename our team the Redskins.

I see Carla Senko at six, at seven, at eight years of age – I see her at twelve and thirteen. I see her telling boys that I stuff my bra with Kleenex, and that I sleep in the same bed as my brother. I see her saying mean and cruel things, horrible things that aren't true. I see Carla, in the second row of the school auditorium, laughing while I play the guitar for the first time in the annual talent show. I see her glare when I accept the award for highest average in grade six, grade seven, grade eight. I see her lips peel back and her jaw snap – spitting and hissing my new names, Four-Eyes, Book Worm, Goody-Goody.

But I can't see Carla in a bind, distressed or broken-hearted. If I could, I think that I would watch and smile.

"Michael will present the French Canadians by himself," says Miss Maximchuk, "and Carla will present the Ukrainians with you. This way, Carla can still be actively involved in the presentation of *Les Thèmes et Les Variations*. Of course, she won't be graded on the work you've put into your project. It's just that – well. She can't bear to stand beside Michael, you see. It would be too much for her, you understand. It's just for the presentation, just for the evening, so that she doesn't feel left out. I'm sure you can appreciate where she's coming from. You don't have a partner anyway."

Carla will present the Ukrainians with me.

Carla will present the Ukrainians with me.

I can't believe that this is happening. I try to argue with Miss Maximchuk but she won't take no for an answer.

Carla will present the Ukrainians with me.

One hour to showtime, the night of *Les Thèmes et Les Variations,* I'm dressed in my full *Poltavsky* costume, headpiece and boots included. Sophie has French-braided my hair and slicked back the bangs from my forehead with gel, as she would if this were a dance performance. I've rouged my cheeks, brushed blue on my eyelids, painted my lips dark red. Backstage in the school auditorium, I double-check that my maps and posters are firmly tacked to the display boards.

Under the guidance of Miss Maximchuk, who has made a full-time job of consoling the lovelorn Carla, as though Carla is her friend and not her student, Carla and I have rehearsed our parts. We've decided to take turns delivering the presentation, and we've both decided to wear Ukrainian costumes from Ukrainian dancing. My velvet vest is burgundy, hers is green.

But at the last minute, Carla tells Miss Maximchuk and me that she doesn't want to wear the velvet vest. It makes her look fat. She takes off the vest and gives it to Miss Maximchuk, who folds it into a square and stuffs it into her purse.

Then Carla decides that she hates her blouse. She claims that the sleeves are too puffy.

I tell Carla that she's just a little nervous.

"You look great," I say.

Plus she's Ukrainian danced all her life. She knows perfectly well that the sleeves are supposed to be puffy.

"What do you know?" says Carla. "Michael is going to be in the audience. *You* can afford to look all bloated and fat, but I *can't.*"

I take a deep breath.

"And this headpiece is retarded," she says. "It's stupid. I'm not wearing it. It makes me look like I've got horns growing out of my head. Forget it."

Carla pulls off the headpiece. I've rarely seen anybody wear the *Poltovsky* costume without a headpiece. Carla looks half-nude to me.

Miss Maximchuk takes the headpiece from Carla and tosses it onto the floor. I pick it up, hissing under my breath that this headpiece cost almost two hundred dollars. Miss Maximchuk ignores me.

"Let's pin the sleeves down," she says, "so that they look more tapered."

"The sleeves of *Poltovsky* blouses," I say, "aren't supposed to be tapered, they're supposed to be billowy. The billowier the better. Right, Carla?"

From her purse, Miss Maximchuk pulls a pincushion and, turning her back to me, she starts pinning Carla's sleeves.

I want to rip the costume off Carla's body, and leave her stark naked backstage. Miss Maximchuk would try to intervene, of course, so I'd have to knock her out first. I suppose I could choke her with the ribbons of the headpiece Carla refuses to wear – just enough to make her faint. With Miss Maximchuk out of the way, I'd stuff a *pysanka* in Carla's mouth to stop her from crying out. I'd hear the sweet sound of Carla crunching the eggshell and gagging and spitting. I'd bring my knee down on her chest. With one arm, I'd pin her hands down; with the other, I'd untie the apron and the skirt, and I'd rip down the slip. I'd yank the beads from her neck, sending them rolling above her head. There would be pins still in her sleeves and she'd yelp because the pins would poke her as I pulled the blouse over her head. Poor stupid Carla. Lying naked for all the world to see. She'd sob but I wouldn't care. I'd slap her face. "Shut up, Carla!" I'd say. Then I'd slap her face again.

Carla walks onstage first, no velvet vest, no headpiece, sleeves pinned tightly around her arms. I can't follow her. I can't stand next to her onstage. I can't move. There is a lump in my throat and I'm afraid that if I open my mouth I'll cry.

Miss Maximchuk tells me to get going.

"Let's go, Colleen! You're on!"

I shake my head.

"I'm not going."

"You *have* to go," says Miss Maximchuk, pushing me hard toward the stage.

I won't budge.

"What's wrong with you? Your final grade depends on this presentation, Colleen. There are more than a hundred people out there waiting for you."

Carla runs offstage.

"Do something!" she says to Miss Maximchuk.

"You do something, Carla. Get back out there and do the presentation alone, by yourself. Colleen has stage fright."

When Miss Maximchuk says that I have stage fright, something snaps inside me. I've never had stage fright in my life, and I won't have anyone accusing me of chickening out. I was born for the stage. I'm a natural performer.

So I grab Carla by the arm and drag her back out into the spotlight. And then I grit my teeth while we deliver the presentation like we planned. The performance goes off without a hitch. It's perfect. Absolutely flawless.

Afterward, as the audience claps, and as Carla bows, grinning smugly as though she's actually earned their applause, I think about Sister Maria. I think about the things she told me about not giving up. "We survive," she said. "We do what we must to survive."

Standing next to Carla on the stage, I just can't help feeling that something inside me has died.

Because I let it.

FOUR

I've always known that grade ten means going to a different school and merging with the students from Racette. I've been looking forward to it for a long time – passing Dad in the hallways, seeing Sophie at recess and lunchtimes. New teachers, new friends. A whole new routine. At Regional, there's no such thing as homeroom. Students go straight from their lockers to their classes. And we're allowed to choose our own lockers for the first time – either in the Social Studies Suite, the English Suite, or the Business Suite. I choose the English Suite. Sophie tells me it's the perfect place for me. The Social Studies Suite is for people who party more than they study; for hockey players, mostly, and their girlfriends. The English Suite is where the brainy students hang out. Everyone else winds up in the Business Suite.

My friends, though, Kirsten and Tanya, choose lockers in the Social Studies Suite. That's when everything starts to change between us. Suddenly they have boyfriends – mostly guys from the Catholic school – and they're borrowing their parents' vehicles on the weekends, and driving out to bush parties. They use fake ID to get into the bars in St. Paul, to buy booze at the liquor store, and to get into beerfests at the Rec. Centre. I'm too scared of getting caught, so I don't use a fake ID. I'm not even sure how to get one.

I try not to let it bother me, the way that Kirsten and Tanya have started acting. I tell myself that, even if they want to go to parties on the weekends and drink, they're still the same people inside. They're still my best friends. We've been close all our lives, since we were little kids. We're like sisters.

Maybe, if I could, I would be more like them. A lot of the time, though, when I'm not at school or at piano lessons, I'm supposed to be at home, helping Mom and Dad watch my cousin Kalyna. Kalyna's dad, Uncle Andy, isn't doing too well. He's got cancer, and it's impossible for Auntie Mary to take care of him and Kalyna at the same time. It's just too much for her. So Kalyna is living with us until Uncle Andy gets better. During the day, Kalyna goes to a special kind of daycare for mentally handicapped people, but during the evenings, she stays at home with our family. I seem to get stuck with her the most because Wes is too young to be left alone with her, and Sophie has to study for her departmental exams. Plus Kalyna likes me best. She rarely leaves my side.

So maybe it's my fault that Kirsten and Tanya start spending less time with me, and more time with Carla Senko. Carla is more fun than I am. Guys like her because she's wild. I'm not wild at all. It's hard to be wild when I have to keep up with my schoolwork, and do well on my piano exams, and babysit Kalyna full-time. No matter what I do, Kalyna is with me. If I'm doing my homework, she's next to me, flipping through my textbooks, pretending to do homework of her own. She hums along as I play the piano, never taking her eyes off my hands as they move across the keys. I can't talk long to my friends on the phone because Kalyna doesn't like it. She starts huffing and puffing, fidgeting with the phone cord. I've had to warn Kirsten and Tanya that we could get cut off at any time. Kalyna will just pull the receiver out of my hands and set it down – as if to say, enough of that, enough talking to them. Talk to *me*.

After awhile, Kirsten and Tanya stop calling.

I don't blame Kalyna. And I don't blame Mom and Dad for making me take care of her. Somebody has to be with Kalyna at all times. It's not anyone's fault that I'm her favourite. Sometimes she drives me so crazy I want to lock her out of my bedroom or yell at her to leave me alone. But mostly I feel sorry for her. I hear Mom and Dad talking in hushed voices about how Uncle Andy is doing. I don't think he's going to get better. Though they've never actually said it, we all know that Kalyna is staying with us until he dies.

I'm tired a lot because it's easiest to do my homework and my music theory assignments late at night, after Kalyna has gone to bed. Mom and Dad don't seem to see how tired I am – or if they do, they don't say anything. At my piano lessons, Sister Maria notices me yawning, comments on the dark circles under my eyes. I tell her about Kalyna, so she understands why my pieces aren't always as polished as they should be.

Every so often, instead of having a regular lesson, Sister Maria makes us a cup of tea and we visit, like two friends. When I have no one else to eat lunch with at school, I bring my lunch over to the convent and eat with her. We talk together about all sorts of things. Not just music, but big events in the news, local events in St. Paul, things I'm learning about in high school. I start looking forward to the feel of her arm around my shoulders, her gentle squeeze, before I head back to home or school. Sometimes it's hard to leave. Sometimes I don't want to leave at all.

While Kalyna lives with our family, I spend more time with her than with anyone else – except maybe Sister Maria. They're like my new best friends, though it isn't always easy to be with either of them.

After a year of piano lessons with Sister Maria, I give up on finding out about her past. Whenever I try to ask her about where she was born, or who her parents were, or how she learned to play the piano, she changes the subject. She seems to enjoy talking about my future more than anything because she's always asking me about what I'd like to do with my life, what I want to be some-day. Her eyes light up when we get on the topic of my musical career. I tell her that maybe I'll go to university and study piano there. Maybe I'll become a concert pianist. She likes this option best, I know. Not that she says so exactly, but when I talk about becoming a music teacher, she makes a sour face. And when I tell her that I wouldn't mind being a singer in a band, she says straight out that I would be wasting my talent. "You're far above that," she says. "*Far* above it."

I don't think that I'm above singing in a band. It would be neat, playing keyboards or rhythm guitar, and singing lead vocals. I could sing in a country and western group, like the bands that play at dances in St. Paul, and do a few rock and roll numbers, a few jazzed-up Ukrainian songs. Kalyna would be my biggest fan, there's no doubt about that. Her favourite thing in the world is to sit next to me on the piano bench while I play and sing songs from the radio. She knows all the words – not just to popular songs in English, but to a hundred different Ukrainian folk songs – and she comes up with perfect harmony lines to anything I sing. She's like the autistic kids you hear about on the news who have some sort of weird, inborn talent for music.

According to Mom and Dad, though, Kalyna isn't autistic. They say that no one knows exactly what's wrong with her, but she isn't autistic. She used to be completely normal. A half-dozen times, when Kalyna is with Sophie or Wes, I ask my parents what happened to her, why she changed, when she stopped being her old self. I can't believe that she was once a regular person. I can't imagine what she would have been like – what kind of personality she would have had. Was she married? Did she have children? For some reason, Mom and Dad won't talk about it. If I catch Mom alone, she says, "Go and ask your father." When I find Dad, he says, "Your mother knows more about it." Neither of them will explain anything to me.

All I know for sure is that Kalyna loves music. When she's angry or upset by something that's going on around her – me talking on the phone, or Wes changing the channel on the TV without warning – I know that I can calm her down by singing something. Anything. When I sing, she forgets everything else and focuses entirely on my voice. It's kind of creepy sometimes, the way she settles down. As though someone has put her in a strait-jacket, or given her a sedative.

I know, too, that whatever happened to Kalyna – whatever made her into this crazy person who loves my singing but who can't remember my name half the time – there are parts of her old life that she hasn't forgotten. Or parts of her brain that still work properly. She remembers Ukrainian things especially. The Ukrainian part of her brain is completely normal. Why else would she know all the words to so many folk songs? And how to act in church, at Dean and Diana's wedding? And what to do in the kitchen to help my mother make Ukrainian meals?

For the first few months that Kalyna spends with us, I talk a lot to Sister Maria about Kalyna. About how strange it is that Kalyna knows so much about being Ukrainian. I tell her that I'm learning a lot from Kalyna about cooking Ukrainian dishes – she knows more recipes than my mother – and embroidery and making *pysanky*. She's like a Ukrainian encyclopedia. I can't get over it.

After awhile, though, Sister Maria loses interest in my Kalyna stories. I guess I'm like a broken record. I can see that Sister Maria isn't impressed when I show her Kalyna's latest cross-stitched pillow, or when I bring her Kalyna's latest egg. She just doesn't care.

And then one day, after one of my piano lessons, when I'm singing a folk song for Sister Maria a cappella – a song that Kalyna taught me called *"O Ukraina"* – she loses her temper.

"Stop this!" she says, out of the blue, practically yelling as she pulls the lyrics out of my hands. "Stop it!"

I cower like a dog, wondering if she's going to strike me. Tears well up in my eyes.

"I thought you might like it," I whisper. "I thought you might –"

"You thought, you thought. You don't think! Yes? That's the problem. You don't think at all."

I try to tell her that it's a nice song, that I like the melody. That

I've worked hard writing out all the verses in Ukrainian.

"Then you're as simple-minded as your aunt."

"My cousin," I say, correcting her. "She's my *cousin*, not my aunt. And she has a name."

Sister Maria has never spoken to me this way. Why is she picking on Kalyna?

Sister Maria crumples up the lyric sheet and throws it in my face.

"You're better than this. If no one else can see it, if your mother and your father can't see it —"

"Quit picking on my family," I say, fighting back tears. "They haven't done anything wrong."

Sister Maria turns her back to me, walks away from the piano.

"And I haven't done anything wrong either." I speak up, trying to keep my voice from trembling.

"But you haven't done anything right," says Sister Maria. "Not for weeks now. Your playing isn't getting any better because your mind is somewhere else. It's miles away in some fairy-tale land that doesn't exist."

"What do you mean?"

"You think it's fun to be Ukrainian? You think it's so easy?"

"I never said —"

"You put on a costume, paint an egg. It means nothing to you."

Sister Maria spits her words at me. I don't understand why she's so angry. I thought she liked Ukrainian things. The music that she transcribes is by Ukrainian composers.

"It *does* mean something to me," I say. "It means everything to —"

"Make-believe nonsense. Throwing away your talent on foolishness. Singing about *Ykraina*. What do you know about Ukraine?"

Before I can answer her question, Sister Maria tells me that my lesson is over. That it's time for me to go home. She doesn't stop there, though. As I gather up my music books, she says that I need to take a break from seeing her.

I stop packing my knapsack.

Sister Maria says that I'm not to come back until I'm ready to get serious about my music. She's not going to continue teaching me if I keep wasting my time on Kalyna's songs. I'm supposed to make a choice.

I feel my chest tighten as I try to argue with her. I tell her that she's not being fair. What's wrong with Kalyna's songs? I like to sing them. They make me feel proud to be Ukrainian.

Again, Sister Maria tells me to leave. She says that I don't know anything.

She's wrong. I'm sobbing now, tears are streaming down my cheeks. But I won't go until I make her see that she's wrong.

"At least I'm not ashamed of who I am."

Sister Maria turns her head sharply to face me.

"You pretend to be French," I say, standing my ground. "But you're Ukrainian, too. I know you are. Otherwise you wouldn't be writing down all of that Ukrainian music. Only you won't admit it. You won't talk about your life. It's all a big secret because you're ashamed."

Sister Maria shakes her head, tries to interrupt me. I keep talking, though, shouting my words at Sister Maria, and trembling from head to foot.

"What do *you* know about Ukraine? What do *you* know about what it means to be Ukrainian? You wear a costume, too. You're the one who plays make-believe."

Wiping the tears from my face, I pick up my knapsack, make my way out of her music room. I'm in the hallway of the convent, halfway to the convent doors, when Sister Maria grabs me by the arm.

"You want to know what it means to be Ukrainian?" she says. "I'll show you."

I cry for a week, maybe more, on and off. Mostly on. I skip three days of school because I can't pull myself together. I keep seeing Sister Maria in the convent foyer, pushing up her left sleeve.

I can't tell Mom and Dad why I'm crying. I'm not even sure myself. I know what the numbers on Sister Maria's arm mean; I just don't understand why she has them. The Nazis put Jews in concentration camps, and she's not Jewish, she's Catholic. So they must have put Catholics in the camps too. But why is she so angry at Ukrainians? She's Ukrainian herself. It doesn't add up. And why is she angry at me? I haven't done anything wrong. None of it makes any sense.

My parents can't find the words to console me. Mom sits with me for hours in my bedroom, rubbing my back, stroking my hair. Dad wants to give Sister Maria a piece of his mind. He thinks she's done something unspeakable to me. I beg him not to call her. I tell him that I had a bad lesson, that's all.

Wes is scared by the whole ordeal. He wants to know why I'm crying so much. Am I in pain? I hear Sophie whispering to him outside my bedroom door, telling him that everything is all right. She doesn't sound too convinced or too convincing, so I yell through the door that I'm fine. There's nothing to worry about. I just had a bad lesson.

Kalyna, though, is the most concerned about what's going on. If Mom or Dad is with me, she stands in the doorway of my bedroom, peering in as though she wants to come in but she isn't sure if she should. While I lie on my bed, she drifts in and out of the room, asking me if I want a glass of juice or a cookie. One afternoon, I cry myself to sleep, and when I wake up Kalyna is sitting at the edge of the bed, like a little girl, staring at me. She's brought me an apple.

"I washed it for you," she says, setting it down next to my head on the pillow.

As long as I stay home from school, there's no reason for Kalyna to go to her daycare, so we're alone together for three days. Most of the time, she's normal. She puts all her energy into making meals for me, and then cleaning up afterward. She must think that eating is going to make me feel better somehow because she makes so much food – too much food for a single day, really. Too many meals. Or maybe she just can't keep track of the time. In her world, it's lunchtime every couple of hours. But cooking keeps her busy, and keeps her out of my hair. We end up eating her lunches for supper. For Mom, it's a nice break.

I cry for Sister Maria. Because she went through something so terrible that I can't even imagine it. On my days home from school, I search through my social studies textbook to find out what happened to Sister Maria but the book only has three paragraphs on the Holocaust, and it doesn't say anything about Ukrainians – what happened to them during the war, what happened to them after.

I cry for me, too. I don't think that I'll be having lessons with Sister Maria anymore. After she showed me her arm, she didn't say a word. She didn't even look at me. Maybe I should have said something. Followed her back to her music room. But I couldn't move. Mom waited for ten minutes in the car outside the convent while I stood in the foyer, stunned.

I spend the third day at home moping around, plunking a bit on the piano. I'm all cried out. Now I'm just depressed, and sort of sick to my stomach. I read the encyclopedia entry on the Second World War a half-dozen times, and the entry on Nazis. The encyclopedia doesn't make things any clearer than my social studies textbook. It doesn't say anything about Ukrainian Catholic nuns being put in concentration camps. I feel like I'll never find out the whole story. I'll never put all the pieces together.

And I don't think that I'll try to find another piano teacher. I'll just quit altogether.

Kalyna comes up behind me as I sit on the piano bench, my elbows on the keys, my head in my hands.

"The best thing to do," she says, putting her hands on my shoulders, "is sing."

As I shake her hands away, I don't even look up. Everything is so simple for her, so easy. I wish she would leave me alone for once. Go away.

"When I went to the hospital, I used to put my hands over my ears like this, so I couldn't hear anything except the music."

Slowly, I lift my head. Kalyna has never talked about a hospital before. She's never talked about anything from her past.

"What hospital?" I ask.

"The nurses told me that I have a beautiful voice," says Kalyna. "I don't know. Do you like my voice?"

"Yes, I do. I like it very much."

I feel my heart racing. I never thought of asking her to tell me – tell me herself – what happened to her. I didn't think she could remember.

"What hospital?" I ask, again.

Kalyna frowns.

"What happened at the hospital?"

Kalyna scratches her head. She looks confused. She must have forgotten the rest. The hospital was a fleeting memory, and now it's gone.

"First you have to tell the children to go outside," she says, walking away from the piano. "Michael can take the girls to the park. They like the park."

"All right," I say, playing along. "Take them to the park."

I have no idea what she's talking about.

"Not you!" says Kalyna, raising her voice, shaking her head. "You can't go with them. You can't leave the house."

Why not? I wonder.

"Why can't you leave the house?" I'm too curious to stop myself.

Too stupid to see that Kalyna is working herself up into a frenzy.

"Because he'll follow you! He'll hurt the children!"

And then she loses control.

There isn't much warning. All of a sudden, she stops talking, and starts doing weird things with her hands – clenching and unclenching her fists, rubbing them up and down her thighs. Then she paces back and forth across the living room, wringing her hands. By the time I start singing, to grab her attention and calm her down, it's too late. She can't hear me. She's listening to some-one else. Someone else is in the room with us, someone I can't see, and he's hurting her. One minute she's standing next to the piano, begging him to stop, the next minute she's crouched in the cor-ner behind the rocking chair, sweating and shivering.

She tries to push him away, then she tries to protect her face with her hands. She pleads with him in a voice that makes my skin crawl. She howls, like a wounded animal. Over and over again, she says his name. "No, John, no. Please, no. John. Stop. John. John."

I panic. I don't know what to do. Auntie Mary never told us what to do if something like this happened. I try to sing a few dif-ferent songs – her favourite Ukrainian ones, "Snowbird" by Anne Murray, happy tunes from *The Sound of Music* – but it's useless. It's absurd. Kalyna, lying on the floor in pain, and me singing *"Do a deer, a female deer, re a drop of golden sun."* I start to cry because I don't know what else to do. When I try to go near her, she howls even louder. She thinks that I'm going to hurt her too.

I wonder if I should call Mom and Dad, and tell them to come home. It's an emergency. They can leave school for emergencies. Or maybe I should call the hospital, call for an ambulance.

Flipping through the phonebook in the kitchen, I can't stop my hands from shaking. Where is the number for the ambulance? Isn't it supposed to be on the back cover of the phone book? Somewhere easy to spot?

While I fumble with the buttons on the phone, Kalyna keeps trying to defend herself from John in the other room. I'm crying so hard that I'm not sure how I'll talk to the dispatcher. Tears drop onto the open page of the phone book before I can wipe them away.

And then –

She stops.

As suddenly as she started, she stops.

I hold my breath, my hand suspended over the keypad on the phone.

Do I wait? Or do I call, in case she relapses? My heart is beating so fast I think it's going to burst. I don't know what to do.

I hear whispering and humming in the living room, so Kalyna must be calming herself down by singing. She must be talking to herself, saying that everything is all right again. Everything is fine.

I'm afraid to step into the living room, in case she thinks that I'm John, coming at her again. But I need to know if she's really going back to her normal self. Or if I have to call someone for help.

When I finally get up the courage to peep around the corner, I have to look twice at what I see. I think, for a moment, that maybe *I'm* losing my mind – seeing things that aren't really there.

Sister Maria is sitting on the floor of the living room. Kalyna is lying on the floor with her knees curled up to her chest, her head resting on Sister Maria's lap.

When I open my mouth to ask what she is doing here, Sister Maria presses her index finger to her lips as if to say, *"Shhhhh."* She points to the window in the living room. I glance outside, and see a car parked in the yard. The little green Honda that the nuns use to get groceries once a week.

"I tried to find you at your school," Sister Maria whispers. "Your father told me that you were at home. He suggested that I visit you here."

Sister Maria looks down at Kalyna, stroking her hair.

"I wanted to have a talk with you," she says.

I open my mouth to tell her that I'm sorry. That I know what the numbers on her arm mean. That I have so many questions. She's talking to Kalyna, though, in Ukrainian. I can't understand everything she says, but some of it makes sense to me.

She says, *"Tykho, malanko, tykho. Mama tut. Mama tut."* Quiet, little one, quiet. Mother is here. Mother is here.

By the time Mom and Dad get home from school with Sophie and Wes, Kalyna is asleep in my room, and Sister Maria and I are finishing our second cups of tea. We've decided that she's not going home until we both talk to my parents. They need to know what happened to Kalyna this afternoon. And they need to know what happened at my piano lesson, a week ago. Everyone sits at the kitchen table, Sophie and Wes included, and the conversation goes on well into the evening. When Mom gets up to make supper, Sophie motions for her to sit down again. While we continue talking, Sophie warms up some of Kalyna's leftover lunches.

As I tell Mom and Dad about Kalyna, they do a lot of sighing. They keep looking at each other, and shaking their heads. At first, they try to pretend that they don't understand exactly what happened to Kalyna, what she was remembering. But I can't believe them, and I won't. Kalyna has a husband, a man named John, and she has children, a boy named Michael and at least two girls. Why won't they tell the truth? He beat her, and he put her in the hospital. She went crazy because of it.

Dad says that it's not so simple. He says Kalyna was never really right in her head. John was a good man. A hard worker.

Mom says that it's just that simple. John beat her, and put her down, and convinced her kids that she was a lousy wife and mother, and eventually she cracked up. She just couldn't take it anymore.

That's why they don't talk about it . Because they can't agree on how to tell the story. When John put Kalyna in the mental hospital outside of Edmonton, and moved with the kids to Toronto, half the family called him a bastard. The other half called him a saviour. No one has seen him or the kids in twenty years, maybe more. No one really wants to. It's easier that way. Easier to forget that the whole thing ever happened.

"Nobody ever tried to help her?" Sophie asks. "Auntie Mary or Uncle Andy? Nobody knew what was going on?"

"They knew," says Mom. "Of course they knew. We all knew.

I was very close to her. We're almost the same age, you know. We were married the same year. I knew it was bad. She used to come to me when Michael was a baby."

"She left him a few times," Dad says. "Mary and Andy wanted to take her and the kids, help them find a place of their own in the city."

"But she always went back," I say. "Right?"

Mom shrugs. "John used to make promises."

"Maybe she'll go back to normal again," says Wes. "If she tries hard enough to forget what happened. Can't the doctors give her pills or something?"

Sister Maria smiles at Wes. Dad shakes his head. Mom says that there is no medicine to fix Kalyna. Sometimes people who are sick just don't get better.

Sophie asks me if I sang to Kalyna. When she was remembering John, did I sing to her to calm her down? I explain that I tried, but my singing didn't work.

"I was going to call the ambulance, when Sister Maria showed up. She did something to help Kalyna."

"You sang?" Mom asks, turning to Sister Maria.

Sister Maria smiles. "I spoke to her in Ukrainian."

Mom and Dad look surprised. They think that Sister Maria is French, like the other nuns in the convent.

"In Ukrainian?" says Dad.

Sister Maria nods.

"You're not French?" Mom asks.

Sister Maria shakes her head.

Then she goes back in time, back in space, to her childhood in Ukraine, and finally I hear her story. Not all of it but enough to see that Sister Maria was a daughter once, and a wife, and a mother. I can't take my eyes off her as she speaks. I can hardly believe what I'm hearing. Before she became a nun, she was a normal person. She had a family, like everyone else, and a house of her own. Before the war, she was a different person altogether.

My parents want to know how Sister Maria found her way from Ukraine to Canada – from Ukraine to a French Catholic convent in St. Paul. It seems impossible. Do the other nuns know that she's not French?

Sister Maria sighs. They know, yes. After the war, she lived for a while in Paris, then moved to Montreal. She changed her name when she entered the convent in Quebec.

I still can't get over the fact that Sister Maria used to be married. That she had a husband, and children.

"But why not a Ukrainian convent?" says Dad. "If you don't mind me asking."

"Is there such a thing?" Sophie asks.

"Yes," says Sister Maria, laughing. "There is such a thing."

"So why join a French one?" says Sophie.

Sister Maria becomes serious again.

"I didn't want to live among Ukrainians after the war."

I can see that Mom and Dad look uncomfortable now. Mom looks down at her plate. Dad gets up to make a pot of tea. We're Ukrainians. What's wrong with us?

"But all your work," I say. "The music you write down. It's all by Ukrainian composers."

Sister Maria says that it's complicated.

My parents look confused. Sophie and Wes look at me for an explanation.

"Sister Maria," I explain, "is writing down songs by composers from Ukraine. There's no one else to write them down because they were killed before they could publish them. They were killed for being Ukrainian. Lots of their music was destroyed, too."

"Right?" I say, turning to Sister Maria to see if I've gotten the story straight.

"That's right. More or less. I want to keep the memory of them alive, through their music."

I smile at my family, proud that I've kept her secret. Pleased that I can tell them about it now.

"So why don't you want to be around Ukrainians?" says Wes.

Sister Maria clears her throat before she starts to speak. Then she begins to explain how her parents met, studying music in Kiev. How she met her own husband at a concert in Paris where her mother was singing. She says that her parents were against the marriage because he was Polish and a Jew, and his parents were against it because she was Ukrainian and a Catholic, but they married anyway, and settled in Warsaw.

As Sister Maria talks, I feel as though she's handing me pieces of a puzzle to put together in my head. Little by little, her story starts to make sense.

She was a concert pianist; her husband was a conductor. Before the war, they had two children, two little girls. Then, in 1942, when the girls were still small, they were rounded up by ss soldiers – they and hundreds of other Polish people – and taken away.

"Taken where exactly?" says Wes, his eyes wide. Dad touches his arm, and shakes his head. As if to say that Wes shouldn't ask.

"To a camp called Auschwitz," says Sister Maria, quietly.

"Oh," says Wes. "Oh."

And everyone in her family – Sister Maria's husband, and her daughters – died there. All of them except Sister Maria.

I watch Sister Maria's face as she talks, but she doesn't cry. Her voice doesn't even shake.

"All this time," she says, "Colleen was asking me, 'Where do you come from, Maria?' and 'Why do you write the music of the dead composers, Maria? Why do you care so much?' I never answered Colleen's questions. I told her stories about these composers, but I never told her my own. I wanted to forget this story, yes? Best to forget. Easiest to forget. Like your family and Kalyna."

I nod.

"But if I don't speak of it," she says, "how will people know?"

Sister Maria pauses before she continues.

"You see, the soldiers who came for us were Ukrainians."

Ukrainian soldiers. Now I'm starting to understand.

"No," says Wes, shaking his head. "They were Germans. They were Nazis. Everybody knows that."

Sophie puts her forefinger to her lips to shush him.

"Not only Germans," says Sister Maria.

"But why would they do that?" Wes asks. "Didn't they know that you were Ukrainian? You should have told them. Then they would have let you go."

"It didn't matter. I was married to a Jew, you see. I was living in the Ghetto with other Jews. It didn't matter to them."

I see my dad is troubled by this part of the story, too. He frowns while Sister Maria talks about the Ukrainians who joined the ss. I don't think he likes hearing about bad Ukrainians. He wants to believe that we're all good people. I don't blame him. Those soldiers must have been brainwashed.

"Everyone suffered in the war," says Sister Maria, rubbing the rosary around her neck. "The Ukrainian people have always suffered. So I try to forgive those soldiers. It's hard to forgive, but I try. People do what they must to survive, yes? Maybe I would have done the same. Who am I to condemn them?"

We're all quiet after Sister Maria finishes talking. She looks so old, and so sad. I want to be put my arm around her, or hold her hand. As Mom gets up to clear the table, my dad thanks Sister Maria for coming to talk with us. He says that her story is remarkable. Someone should write it down.

I'm still a bit confused, and I think it's going to take me some time to figure out what Sister Maria has told us. I think Sister Maria is confused too. She's not ashamed of who she is. When she writes down the music of the Ukrainian composers, she is remembering the good things that Ukrainians have done. But she can't forget all the terrible things that happened to Ukrainians in the past. And she can't forget what Ukrainians did to their own people, and to Jews, in the war. What the soldiers did to her and her family. She doesn't want me to forget either, or my family. I think that's why she told us her story. We're supposed to remember, too. The good things, and the bad.

Before Sister Maria leaves, Kalyna wakes up from her nap. She walks into the kitchen, rubbing her eyes. When she spots Sister Maria, she introduces herself. Then she says, "Who are you? What's your name?"

Kalyna doesn't remember a thing about the afternoon. It's all disappeared.

Standing by Sister Maria at the door with Mom and Dad and Sophie and Wes, I catch Sophie staring at me with a strange look on her face — as though she's looking at me for the first time. And Wes stares at Sister Maria like she's a statue, like he's not sure if she's real.

Sister Maria ruffles his hair with her fingers.

"Your sister," she says. "She's going to be a great pianist some day, yes? A concert pianist. She's my best pupil. She has a gift."

Sophie rolls her eyes, but she smiles at the same time.

I don't know about being a concert pianist. Right now, I just want to have my piano teacher back.

"So I can keep taking piano lessons?" I ask. "With you?"

Sister Maria laughs.

"Of course," she says. "We'll start again tomorrow. Yes? Tomorrow, we start again."

FIVE

"New Mexico, Italy, Wales. Victoria, British Columbia."
Mr. Kaushal pauses to adjust his bifocals. He's reading to our grade eleven social studies class from a United World Colleges brochure. Mr. Kaushal is always reading to us from brochures. Last week it was the World Vision "Thirty-Hour Famine" and a UNICEF literacy program for Nicaraguan child amputees. The week before he was pitching the Foster Parents' Plan, and the week before that, the Christian Children's Fund. Mr. Kaushal isn't Christian himself. He used to be Hindu, now he's Buddhist. He's very open-minded. He believes in the united human consciousness, plus he doesn't eat meat. He supports animal rights. There are Green Peace posters all around his classroom.

Mr. Kaushal continues. "Italy, Wales —"

"You said that already."

The remark comes from the back of the classroom, from Ted Ross, the class troublemaker. Ted likes to fluster Mr. Kaushal, likes to catch him making mistakes in front of the class. Every so often, Ted poses hypothetical questions to Mr. Kaushal. "If your wife were being attacked by a rabid dog, would you kill the dog or let it maim her? If you were starving to death and the last piece of food on Earth was a hamburger, would you eat the hamburger or die of hunger?" To Ted's questions, Mr. Kaushal gives serious answers, as though he doesn't even know that he's being laughed at. "I'd try to soothe the dog. I'd eat the bun but not the burger." He's too nice to tell Ted to stay quiet, or get out.

Mr. Kaushal apologizes for repeating himself. "Sorry, sorry," he says.

Ted imitates Mr. Kaushal's accent under his breath – *sorry, sorry*. Ted's buddies and a few girls snicker.

Mr. Kaushal ignores them. "These colleges," he says, "unite young people from around the world. For one year, they live together – young people of every race, religion, and political background. They learn to live in harmony with each other. Then they return to their home countries to teach others about what they've learned."

Ted rolls his eyes.

"There is also a college in Singapore, and one in Swaziland. Swaziland is by South Africa."

Ted rolls his eyes again.

South Africa is a recurrent topic in Mr. Kaushal's class – partly because Gandhi came from there, partly because Mr. Kaushal wants us to know about the apartheid system and how wrong it is. He devoted a whole month of classes to the history of South Africa, starting with the election of the first white government in 1948, and their subsequent constitutionalization of racism. He talked about the Sharpeville Massacre in 1960, during which sixty-nine black protestors were killed by the white regime. We learned about the establishment of the African National Congress and the Pan Africanist Congress. About Nelson Mandela's trial and imprisonment on Robben Island. The rise of Black Consciousness, the story of Stephen Biko. All of the senseless killings of innocent people on June 16, 1976, the day of the Soweto Uprising.

A peaceful look washes over Mr. Kaushal's face after he mentions the college in Swaziland. "Gandhi came from South Africa," he says.

The bell rings, Mr. Kaushal jumps.

After social studies with Mr. Kaushal, I have ten minutes to get across the school to the Music Room for the last class of the day, band with Mr. Schultz. If it weren't for Mr. Kaushal's after-class routine, I could do it easily. The school isn't that big. The challenge is to slip past Mr. Kaushal without him noticing me. Otherwise, I'm in for a lengthy chat about his latest brochure. If I'm a second late for band, Mr. Schultz will close the door in my face and I'll be forced to get a late slip from the office. Mr. Schultz is nothing like Mr. Kaushal. He runs his classes like boot camp. I already have two late slips against me; one more, and I'll be kicked right out for good.

"Colleen?"

Mr. Kaushal calls my name as I head out the door. I pretend that I haven't heard him.

"Colleen!"

He scurries down the hallway to catch up with me, then taps me on the shoulder. As I turn to Mr. Kaushal, I see my friends marching off to band class. None of them has late slips. Why doesn't he tap one of them on the shoulder?

"I want you to take this home with you tonight." Mr. Kaushal passes me the United World Colleges brochure.

I glance down at my watch. Seven minutes and counting.

"Talk about it with your parents. See what they think."

I stuff the brochure into my knapsack, next to the Foster Parents' Plan pamphlet I got from him a few weeks ago.

"Thanks, Mr. Kaushal. I'll do that. I'll definitely do that."

"I'll be more than glad to help you along with the application process." He smiles.

I know what's coming. *Please don't start with stories about your daughter.*

"My own daughter was interviewed – how many years ago now? Let me think."

While Mr. Kaushal thinks, I look at my watch again. Five minutes. Four and a half. Mr. Kaushal's daughter speaks four languages and has a Master's degree in International Development and works for the World Health Organization in Cameroon. She is his favourite subject.

"Nine years ago." His voice gets soft. "Nine years, so long ago. You know, my daughter didn't make the interview. Though she was close. I'm sure that she was close. *You* could do better, Colleen. I know you could – with your grades, and your music, and your interest in international issues. I'll help you write your essays for the application. And I'll write a glowing reference letter for you. Positively glowing."

I hardly hear Mr. Kaushal's last words. I thank him again, then I start to run.

I don't like having to rush out of Mr. Kaushal's class every day to get to band. He's a bit of an oddball in our school, and I know that the other students make fun of him sometimes, but he's my favourite teacher. He's one of my dad's best friends, too, along with J.Y., the phys. ed. teacher, and Mr. Joly, who teaches drama. I like Mr. Kaushal because he has all kinds of ideas about the world – like how, if a butterfly flaps its wings in South America, the weather changes in North America. Or how, if you work it out, every person on earth is connected to every other person. Six degrees of separation, he calls it. Mr. Kaushal has lived all over the world. He's lived in India, and Sri Lanka, and he went to university for a while in London before he came to Canada. He says that we're not really as different as we all think.

At first, at the beginning of the school year, I wasn't in Mr. Kaushal's social studies class. I got put in Mr. Maletski's class instead. But I had some trouble getting along with Mr. Maletski. Actually, I had a lot of trouble. The principal had to get involved; my parents were called in – none of which is normal for me. I always get along with my teachers. Something about Mr. Maletski, though, rubbed me the wrong way. He'd start every class with a joke – he called it the "Joke of the Day" – and it was usually something insulting toward women, especially blondes. He told a few Ukrainian jokes, too, even though he's Ukrainian himself. I don't think anyone in class found them funny. Half of us were girls. More than half of us were Ukrainians.

But it wasn't just the jokes. It was everything. The way he stood up on a podium in front of the class, looking down on us like we were ignorant little children. The way he chuckled when someone asked a question, or got a fact wrong, or gave a wrong date. Mr. Maletski is crazy about facts and dates. "Facts and dates," he said. "They're the backbone of history." I got in trouble over facts and dates. I thought he was missing a few important facts and dates in our unit on Canadian history. He made Canadian history start with the arrival of the French and English. I reminded him that for thousands of years before the Europeans came on the scene, Native people lived here. Aren't they part of our history? Mr. Maletski said that their history isn't written down, so we can't study it.

It was all downhill from there.

I couldn't help wondering how Native students would feel if they were to hear Mr. Maletski talk about the settlement of the West like it was the best thing that ever happened. Like the West was just a big empty space, waiting to be filled up with pioneers. He hardly mentioned the Riel Rebellion, and when he did, he made Riel and Dumont out to be bad guys. Imagine if a bunch of Jewish students had to sit in a class, and hear about how great the Nazis were. I never said that in class, but I thought about it a lot.

In the weeks following our unit on the pioneers, I thought a lot about something else, too. There were – and still are – no Native students in Mr. Maletski's social studies class. And not just in his class either. When I went to Glen Avon, lots of kids in the school were Native. At Regional, there are just a handful of them left. Doesn't anybody notice how many Native students have dropped out? Doesn't anybody care? I tried to bring up the issue once in Mr. Maletski's class. He told me to stick to the textbook.

We had moved on to the chapter on multiculturalism in Canada, and how great it is.

Mr. Maletski didn't like my comments. He didn't like the questions that I asked in class. He said that he's the one who asks the questions, I give the answers. I thought that he was doing both.

Maybe I took it a step too far. On our social studies midterm, instead of answering Mr. Maletski's questions, I wrote an essay on the way that history is just a story — one version of a story, told from one point of view — and how the story always has holes in it. Mr. Maletski failed me. Then he called in the principal to talk to me. I refused to rewrite the test. The principal talked to my parents. In the end, we worked out a compromise. We decided that it would be better for everyone involved if I switched into Mr. Kaushal's class because Mr. Kaushal, the principal said, is a little less traditional.

Mr. Kaushal's class is a dream compared to Mr. Maletski's. Every day we have a debate about a different current event — the crisis in the Middle East, the Troubles in Northern Ireland. Native land claims. Quebec separatism. We're supposed to relate what we read in our textbook to what is going on around us. He invites us to make connections between different parts of the world and different groups of people — like the blacks in South Africa, and the Native people in Canada. Sometimes Mr. Kaushal brings in guest speakers who have lived in other countries; sometimes he plays excerpts from the news so that we can analyze the way that stories are reported. Social studies class never seems long enough. It always ends too soon.

So when Sister Maria isn't up for a visit from me at lunchtime, or when she's busy with her work, I eat lunch with Mr. Kaushal in the cafeteria. I like spending time with him because he doesn't treat me like a kid. He talks to me like I'm an adult. My friends think I'm weird for hanging out with him but I don't care. Grade eleven, for them, is just one big party. I know for a fact that Tanya's grades have dropped because her mother told Mom, and Mom told me. Kirsten isn't even talking about going to university any-more. She wants to do a hairdressing course so that she can work in her mother's salon. Carla Senko might not even finish high school. She's run away from home twice, and she's always skipping school to go drinking with the grade twelve hockey players.

Not that Mr. Kaushal could ever replace Sister Maria. But she's getting older, and she needs to rest a lot more than she used to. Mom says that I can't always expect her to have time for me. Since Uncle Andy passed away, and Kalyna moved back home with Auntie Mary in Vegreville, I have all sorts of free time. Sophie is at university. She has her own apartment now in Edmonton. Wes is playing hockey four times a week. Mr. Kaushal lends me books to read about religion and politics. He lets me listen to his cassette tapes of music from around the world – classical Indian music, reg-gae, traditional African songs. I learn from him about female folk singers from the 1960s and 1970s – Joan Baez, Janis Ian, Joni Mitchell. For my birthday, he gives me an old Buffy St. Marie record. After I listen to it, I start writing songs of my own about injustice and oppression. Starving children in Africa. Persecuted monks in Tibet.

Of course, I have to remind myself from time to time that not all my teachers are like Mr. Kaushal, and I can't get away from all of them. I'm not too crazy about my English teacher, for example, Mrs. Webster. But the only other English teacher in my high school is Dad. Even though he'd like to teach me, and I'd love to be in his class, the principal won't allow it. So I'm stuck with Mrs. Webster until I graduate.

She isn't very old. In fact, she's one of the youngest teachers on staff. As far as I know, she's only been teaching for five or six years. Mrs. Webster just isn't very young at heart. When Dad teaches *Hamlet* to his classes, he brings in a ceramic skull and gets Mr. Joly to visit his class so that they can act out the Yorick scene. He keeps a surprise in his pocket – a little wooden dagger that he whittled at the lake one summer – for Hamlet's "to be or not to be" speech. All the students in his classes get to act out scenes too. Mrs. Webster plays an ancient record of the play being read by a group of English actors from the 1950s. While the record plays, she sits at her desk marking essays. It's hard to stay awake. But then if you fall asleep, she'd never notice.

English picked up a bit after Halloween, when we finished *Hamlet* and started *Who Has Seen the Wind?* Mrs. Webster wasn't too impressed, though, when I kept commenting on how the town in the novel has no little girls and no Indians. What kind of prairie town is that? Mrs. Webster said that W.O. Mitchell is one of the finest writers in this country and we should think twice before we criticize one of our own.

Band class should be the best time of day for me. I should be Mr. Schultz's favourite. But Mr. Schultz has never liked me. In fact, long before I stepped into his classroom, I knew that there would be trouble. For as long as I can remember, my dad has been locking horns with Mr. Schultz over the way that he runs the music program at Regional. Mr. Schultz doesn't like me because he doesn't like my dad. The problem is that – with the exception of the percussionists, who are allowed to use the school drum kit – band students are required to buy their own instruments. If they can't afford to buy their instruments, they can't take music. Period. Dad says that there's more than enough money in the music account for Mr. Schultz to provide instruments for every single band student. Students could even rent instruments from the school for a nominal fee. Or Mr. Schultz could set up a rental program with National Music in Edmonton, and he could use the music account funds to subsidize students who can't afford rental fees. Mr. Schultz refuses. Every so often, at monthly staff meetings, he and my dad get into arguments about it. Dad says that Mr. Schultz is needlessly prohibiting a broad segment of the student population from taking music. He says that Mr. Schultz is making music a class for well-off students only. He's making it a class for the elite. Mr. Schultz says that he's keeping the riff-raff out of his classes. He doesn't want students in his class who think that music is a free ride. Anyone who is really serious about music will find the money to buy an instrument.

I think Mr. Schultz is a hypocrite. His class is a joke. I'm the most serious student in class, by far. I'm also the best. I could easily teach the theory part of the class each week because the theory we learn in grade eleven band is the theory I learned from my old piano teacher Simone when I was in grade six at school. I should be section leader of the trumpets. I should be the guest conductor when Mr. Schultz is away and the substitute teacher doesn't know how to lead the class. But I definitely shouldn't be penalized for coming to class two or three minutes late. What could I possibly be missing?

After Mr. Kaushal gives me the brochure for the United World Colleges, I race across the school to Mr. Schultz's room, cutting through the courtyard that separates the Social Studies Wing and the Music Wing, brushing past Dad and J.Y. as they talk together outside the gymnasium. I would stop and say hello except that Mr. Schultz is dying to catch me coming late again. I won't give him the satisfaction.

He's about to close the door to the Music Room when I come flying around the corner of the Music Wing.

"Wait!" I yell. *"I'm coming!"*

If Mr. Schultz doesn't see me, I'm sure that he hears me. But he's closing the door nonetheless – slamming the door, in fact. At the last second before the door shuts completely, I lunge forward, slipping my music folder between the door and the door frame. Mr. Schultz, shaking his head in disgust, is forced to let me in.

In my most cheerful voice, I say, "Thanks, Mr. Schultz."

"Last time, Miss Lutzak. Last time."

Mr. Schultz's voice is drowned out by the sound of the clarinetists and the flautists tuning their instruments, the drummer alternately tightening and whacking his snare. There are almost sixty students in our band class – fourteen clarinets, thirteen flutes, eight alto saxes, five tenor saxes. Some of our trombonists double as tuba players, depending on the piece we're playing. We have three percussionists, one bass guitarist. In the trumpet section, there are four of us split into firsts, seconds, and thirds. Two second trumpets, one first trumpet, one third. I play third.

As I take my place among the trumpets, Oliver Morgan waves to me from across the section. While I yank my music out of my folder – the words "3rd Trumpet" printed at the top of each sheet – Oliver starts on his inane warm-ups. He puckers and unpuckers his lips, massages his cheeks. Rolls his head clockwise, counter-clockwise, up, down. Then he swings his arms at the shoulder, as if to stretch them. All of this is done, I know, for my benefit. Oliver is in love with me. He's all but told me so with looks and smiles. The warm-ups are supposed to impress me, dazzle me. Make me swoon.

It's not that I *dis*like Oliver, really. He's smart in school, and he's not bad looking – blond, blue eyes, nice build. In fact, Oliver could be prime boyfriend-material if he weren't so eager to please Mr. Schultz. At the end of every band class, Oliver stays behind to straighten the chairs in the Music Room, to tidy the instruments in the storage room. At the beginning of every band class, he chats to Mr. Schultz about famous brass players, famous brass songs, famous brass recordings. In every piece for the last two years, Mr. Schultz has given the first trumpet part to Oliver, who can't play to save his life. It's a sort of running joke in band class, a joke that everyone is in on. Everyone except Oliver and Mr. Schultz.

Today, we're working on our Christmas repertoire for the Christmas Concert. We've been working on our Christmas repertoire since the beginning of September. As always, we start with "Christmas in Tijuana." Featuring Oliver's sixteen-bar trumpet solo. It's bad enough I had to sit through him squawking it out last Christmas, now I've got to endure it all over again. Mr. Schultz resurrects songs to save time and, of course, to put on a good show for the town. Only two or three of our Christmas pieces are new to us; the others are songs we learned for last year's Christmas concert. "Rudolph the Red-Necked Reindeer" and "The Rock 'n' Roll Noel" – those are new. But the "I Saw Mommy Kissing Santa Claus/O Holy Night Medley" – that's old. "Handel's Hallelujah Chorus for Band" – old. "A Classical Christmas," "The Christ-Child Samba," "A Christmas Tribute to Elvis" – old, old, old.

Midway through the "Tijuana" trumpet solo, Oliver quits his bleating. He's lost his place. Again. That's my cue. I've got the whole solo memorized and I play it in my head along with him so that when he falls apart I'm there to pick up the pieces. Mr. Schultz shuts down the band but I keep playing, all by myself.

"*Quiet!*" Mr. Schultz shrieks.

Oliver apologizes profusely.

I roll my eyes.

Thirty-six bars into our second run at "Tijuana" – just after the flute trills and before the trombone swell – Mr. Schultz stops us again. I know what's coming. I brace myself.

"Third trumpets!"

Why does he say third trumpet*s* when we all know that there's only one of us? "*What* are you doing?" he bellows.

When Mr. Schultz gets annoyed or angry, his German accent comes out. It sounds more like, "*Vot* are you doing." I give Mr. Schultz my most blank, most innocent look. I bat my eyelashes. Oliver smiles at me sympathetically, oblivious to *vot* I'm doing. Oliver has no ear for music so he has no idea that I'm playing my thoroughly *un*interesting, entirely *un*inspired third-trumpet line three times louder than I should. Once in a while, I play loudly like this to remind Mr. Schultz that I'm the best trumpet player in the band and that I've been unjustly relegated to the bottom of the trumpet section. He says that my attitude is the problem. But it's hard to change my attitude when I'm stuck playing third trumpet. Two years in the high school band and I haven't even been promoted to *second* trumpet.

"Softer!" says Mr. Schultz.

All right. You want *zovter*, I'll play *zovter*. We start the piece over. This time, I play my trumpet so quietly that it can't be heard over the other trumpets. I have marvellous control over my instrument. I can do anything with it. Mr. Schultz stops us again. He points his Nazi baton in my direction.

"Miss Lutzak, play louder!"

"Oh," I say, trying my best to look confused. "I'm so *sorry*, Mr. Schultz, I thought you wanted me to play softer. My mistake."

"You will play at the proper volume or you will not play at all!"

I generally know how far to push him. I behave myself for the duration of "Tijuana."

After "Tijuana," we muddle our way through "Elvis." Then "The Rock 'n' Roll Noel." We've been playing "The Rock 'n' Roll Noel" for three months now and we have yet to get past bar twelve. It's the alto saxes. They can't actually read music. Most of them have chosen to play saxophone because it's cool. And Mr. Schultz doesn't much care if any them — if any of us, really — can read music, he just wants us to sound good at concerts. Like clockwork, he silences the band after bar twelve. Time for the saxes' daily section work. Mr. Schultz walks them through their line, note by note, over and over again. A few more classes and they'll have their part more or less memorized. Enough to fake it at the concert, at least.

We're not permitted to make a sound while Mr. Schultz does section work, though I'm tempted to play the sax parts on my trumpet. I've heard them play their lines so often that *I've* got them memorized. But Michelle Glynn got bawled out in grade ten when she started practicing her xylophone as Mr. Schultz worked with the tubas. Since then we've all kept quiet. To the left of me, Kerri-Lynn Stratford opens her chemistry textbook. The clarinets pass notes back and forth between them. Oliver does more lip exercises, glancing in my direction to see if I'm watching. I pull out the brochure that Mr. Kaushal gave me.

Kerri-Lynn drops a note in my lap, onto the brochure. She's written in the margins of her periodic table. *Oliver + Colleen,* it says. Kerri-Lynn watches while I read. I roll my eyes, she smiles. In the margins of the United World Colleges brochure, I write, *Mr. Schultz + Oliver is more like it!!!*

As Kerri-Lynn and I giggle, I feel a hand on my shoulder. My heart stops.

There is silence, suddenly, in the Music Room – absolute silence. The saxes have stopped playing, the rest of the students in the room have stopped shuffling papers. Mr. Schultz leans over my shoulder, reaching for the brochure in front of me; I slide my hand over my lap to cover it. Mr. Schultz tugs, I press down hard with my hand.

"Release it!"

"It's private."

"Lift your hand!"

As Mr. Schultz scans the brochure, I turn my head slightly to the left, making eye contact with Oliver – half-expecting Oliver to speak up and try to take the blame. But there is no time for anyone to save me. Mr. Schultz crumples the brochure in his hand.

"Miss Lutzak," he says, "you have disrupted my class for the last time. You will take your books, you will take your trumpet – you will take everything *and leave!*"

Mr. Schultz's words get louder and louder, like a crescendo; his face starts to turn purplish as he says, *"unt leave."* In front of me, the clarinets and flutes have all turned around in their seats to watch what's going on. To my left, the saxophones are all leaning forward in their chairs, cocking their heads to the right. It occurs to me that I have an audience.

"Do you mean leave *today's* class? You know, just leave *for the day,* or do you mean leave *forever?*"

I smile sweetly at Mr. Schultz. He picks up my music folder and throws it across the room, scattering third trumpet parts across the floor.

Oliver gets up from his chair to pick up the scattered music but Mr. Schultz orders him to sit down. While I pack up my trumpet, Mr. Schultz warns me that my parents will be receiving a call, and that there will be a meeting arranged by the principal of the school. I mutter under my breath as he talks, taking in only half of what he says.

"Do you hear me?" Mr. Schultz yells. "There will be a meeting with the principal! *Do you hear me?*"

Pausing at the front of the class, on my way out the door of the Music Room, I twirl around to face Mr. Schultz. But it's like I'm facing Mr. Maletski and Mrs. Webster, too. All of them, all at once. What have I got to lose?

"Yes," I say, my eyes blazing. "Yes, I *hear* you, loud and clear. You're talking about how much you're going to miss me in the trumpet section. How much you're going to miss sticking me with the worst parts; how much you're going to miss *boring* me with the easiest, crappiest, *least important* lines. Yes! I hear you!"

On my way out, I slam the door to the Music Room. My knees are trembling, and my lips, and my hands. I'm in real trouble now. I've never spoken like this to a teacher. Will I be suspended? Oh *God*. For all I know, the principal could expel me. I should probably go to Dad's classroom, and explain the whole incident from beginning to end, so that he doesn't hear about it second-hand in the Staff Room. He'll be sympathetic, I'm sure. He doesn't have any use for Mr. Schultz. But Dad still won't like the idea of meeting with the principal about it. And Mom will be horrified. I should call her to warn her, so that she's expecting the news when it comes.

Of course, there's nothing I can do now. No way to change what I've done, take back what I've said. I doubt that an apology would do any good. And – say I did apologize. Say Mr. Schultz let me back into class. I'd be right back in the third trumpet chair. Right back where I started.

I'll go to the convent. Sister Maria will make me feel better, I know it. We'll share a pot of tea and she'll give me cookies. The thought of sitting in her music room makes my hands stop shaking. A feeling of calm washes over me. Like everything will be okay.

With a deep breath, then, I knock on the Music Room door – once, twice; when Mr. Schultz swings open the door, I nearly rap his forehead with a third knock.

"That piece of paper you took from me. That brochure."

I square my shoulders and put my hands on my hips.

"I want it *back.*"

SIX

Sunday morning – six days to my UWC scholarship interview – and I'm on my bed with my guitar, sifting through my *Original Compositions*. I'm trying to find the perfect song for the scholarship committee.

It's Mr. Kaushal's idea, actually, that I bring my guitar to the interview. I've played a few of my songs for him at school, and he loves them. He's asked me to perform a few times for our social studies class, and for his other classes. For the annual Earth Day concert that he organizes each spring to promote environmental awareness. In the letter that he wrote to the scholarship committee, supporting my application, he spent three paragraphs describing how I use music to speak the universal language of love. Mr. Kaushal says that if I can find a way to sing for the committee, I'll be a shoo-in.

When I told Sister Maria about Mr. Kaushal's idea, she was a bit skeptical. Not that she doesn't like my guitar playing or my singing. She just thinks that I'm a better pianist, and that I'd have a better chance of getting the scholarship if I showcased my abilities as a piano player. Sister Maria might be right about my playing, but I can't exactly take a piano into the interview with me. Even if I could, I don't see why the scholarship committee would be impressed by my playing. I'm not trying to get into a music school. As far as I can tell, the United World Colleges are schools for hippies. I should wear a tie-dyed t-shirt, and Jesus sandals, and John Lennon sunglasses.

Everyone, though, has a different idea about how I should prepare for the interview – not just Mr. Kaushal and Sister Maria. Wes
tells me that I should work on coming across like I'm well-
rounded, like I'm not just interested in music. He thinks I should
talk about sports, maybe mention the Stanley Cup playoffs, or
World Cup soccer. Sophie thinks that my number one priority
should be my outfit. She comes home from university one weekend to take me shopping for new clothes. We go to a half-dozen
dress shops in St. Paul before we find the perfect pants and the perfect shirt – not too dressy, not too casual; not too flashy, not too
drab.

My parents were more excited about my application at the
beginning, before I got an interview. We looked through the
brochure together, and they were thrilled with the whole idea of
me going away for a year to live with kids my age from around the
world. The application itself wasn't too hard. I had to fill out a few
forms, then write a couple of essays about why I'd be a good UWC
candidate, and what my future goals are. Mom and Dad read
through drafts of my essays, and they thought they were excellent.
They thought the whole UWC movement was a wonderful thing.

On one of the forms, though, I had to rank the six colleges
from 1 to 6 – from the place I'd most like to go, to the place I'd
least like to go. That's where the trouble started. Mom and Dad
assumed that I wanted to go to the college in Victoria. Victoria is
in Canada. It's one province away from St. Paul. They could drive
there to visit me. I could fly home on long weekends. But I made
Swaziland my first choice, the college in southern Africa.

Actually, I made Swaziland my *only* choice.

I didn't even bother ranking the other colleges. If I'm going
anywhere, I want it to be as far away as possible; a place that's completely different from St. Paul. I want to put the whole world
between me and Mr. Schultz, me and Mr. Maletski, me and my
friends. I don't have anything in common with Tanya and Kirsten
anymore. I want to see a part of the world that's strange and exotic

and new, where I can be a new person, spread my wings. I've learned a lot about South Africa from Mr. Kaushal. I know all about apartheid and the suffering of the black people. This is my chance to make a difference – leave my mark in a positive, meaningful way. Victoria would never do. I might as well stay home. It's Swaziland or nothing. Swaziland or bust.

After they saw my ranking of the colleges, Mom and Dad weren't so keen anymore about the whole UWC idea. Mom, in particular. I don't think she's pleased at all that I've made it to the interview stage of the selection process. She doesn't offer me any advice.

I almost think she'd like to see me fail.

Sometimes, I'm not sure myself if I really want to succeed. I've never been away from home before. I've always lived in the same town. I'd miss my family, Sister Maria, Mr. Kaushal. I can't imagine living somewhere else – away from everyone – for a whole year.

But the chance to finish high school in another school, in another country – I just don't see how I can pass it up. I have to try my best.

And anyway there's no turning back now. I'm halfway there.

So I pore over the songs that I've been writing over the past few months. I go through all eight of them, trying to find the one that will help me win. While I'm sitting in my bedroom singing, I try to picture my new bedroom in Africa. I try to imagine what my new bed will feel like. I wonder who will be sitting next to me in that room someday, listening to me sing.

It's not easy picking the right song.

I've been working on a song for Sister Maria called "Ashes and Dust" but it's not finished yet. And, even if it were finished, it's too personal. Too private to sing for strangers.

There's "Song for Leonard Peltier" and "Daddy Went to Vietnam," both of which I love. They're my favourites. The melody of the Peltier song is haunting, and the chorus to the

Vietnam song is absolutely brilliant. It's inspired. I sing it at least a
half-dozen times before I accept that it's not the one.

> Can a flag tell me about the man I never knew?
> Can a flag hold my mother like her lover used to do?
> Can this flag that flies for every war we've ever won
> Tell me if my daddy was the winner in Vietnam?

The problem is that Vietnam has been overdone. So has
Peltier, for that matter. They're both sort of dated, too. I need a
more current topic to sing about at the interview.

"Miss a Meal for Mozambique" might do the trick, except
that it's not particularly subtle. A good song shouldn't whack you
over the head with its message. When I get to the last four lines of
the refrain, I'm almost embarrassed. It's not very subtle at all.

> Miss a meal for Mozambique
> And stop a baby's crying
> Miss a meal for Mozambique
> And stop humanity - humanity - from dying.

But then "Hear the Cries," about the persecution of Buddhist
monks by the Chinese in Tibet – it's too subtle. Will the committee know what it's about? I refer to the monks as butterflies getting caught in a net of hate. It could mean anything, really.

"Holding Hands," I think, is probably safest. Because it's vague,
and it's meant to be vague. It's just a song about general world
peace.

> Holding hands
> Reaching out for others in other lands
> Caring for your brothers
> And holding their hands!

Brothers. The women on the committee could be offended. I have to scrap "Holding Hands." In fact, it might be a good idea to write a whole new song for the interview.

Before I go back to the drawing board, I leave my bedroom to make a cup of herbal tea. The stuff tastes like boiled grass and it looks like pee but I drink it because Mr. Kaushal says that it's cleansing for the body and mind. I need some cleansing to get a fresh perspective on my songwriting.

When I walk into the kitchen, I'm surprised to see Yolande Yuzko sitting with Mom at the kitchen table. I didn't hear Yolande come in. They're drinking coffee, eating poppyseed cake – my favourite. They're talking, too, though they stop abruptly when I appear.

"Hi Yolande," I say, leaning over her shoulder to grab a piece of cake.

Yolande gives me a funny look. A sympathetic sort of puppy-dog look.

"It's all right. If I get a scholarship, I'm fully prepared to give up my mother's poppyseed cake. It's only one year. Sister Maria says that we'll all blink twice and I'll be home again."

Yolande knows all about the colleges, the interview, the scholarship. Mom has been phoning her every second night to talk about it. Neither Yolande nor Mom laughs at my joke.

"Colleen," says Mom, "sit down. Join us for a cup of coffee."

"So that you can brainwash me into staying home? For-*get* it. Uh-uh. Plus Mr. Kaushal says that coffee kills brain cells and I've got songwriting to do."

Yolande runs her finger up and down the side of her coffee cup.

"Just five minutes," Mom says. "Yolande's brought us some news. Something you need to hear."

Wes barges in through the kitchen door, slamming it shut behind him. He's all decked out in Real Tree camo, his face smudged with black and green paint. He drops his rifle onto the linoleum.

Mom frowns. "Is that thing loaded?"

Wes ignores her. "Hey!" he says to Yolande, grinning. "You still here?"

"*Tell* me that gun isn't loaded," says Mom, raising her voice.

"Number one," says Wes, "it's not a *gun,* it's a *rifle.* And number two, no, it isn't loaded. It's empty. I emptied it into a rabbit about ten minutes ago." Wes lets out his war cry, *"Yee-hoooooo."*

"Killer," I hiss under my breath.

"Oh C'lleen," he says as he pours himself a glass of milk. "Sorry to hear about your piano teacher. That's a real bummer, eh?" He gulps down the milk.

"What about my piano teacher?" I ask him. Then I turn to Mom. "Sister Maria isn't teaching me anymore?"

Mom looks at Yolande.

"What?"

Is she moving? Getting transferred to another convent? Can they *do* that?

"Didn't you tell her?" says Wes, stuffing two pieces of pop-pyseed cake into his mouth at once.

"Tell me WHAT?" I say, getting distraught. What is there to tell me?

"She died," says Wes, his mouth full. "Sorry," he shrugs. "I thought you knew." He picks up his rifle, then goes back outside.

"How do you know?" I spit the words at Yolande. "Who told you?"

"I was working last night."

Yolande is an X-ray technician; she picks up all kinds of gos-sip working at the hospital.

"They brought her in around eight o'clock," Yolande con-tinues, softly.

"Who? *Who* brought her in?"

"The other sisters. Two of them, Sister Josephine and Sister Marie-Claire. But it was too late. The doctor on call said that she had a massive heart attack. Even if they'd brought her in sooner, it wouldn't have made a difference. It was her time."

"That's not true," I say, my throat tightening. "That can't be true. I just had a lesson with her a few days ago. Tuesday. Not even a *week* ago. She was fine on Tuesday, she was perfectly fine. It couldn't be her – there must be a mistake – someone else – it couldn't be her. She was fine."

"Colleen," says Yolande, "I *saw* her. I saw her after she went, and she looked beautiful. Very peaceful. She looked like she was at peace."

The phone rings and I seize the opportunity to get out of the kitchen, get out of the house. At peace. That's what they say about everybody who dies. Sister Maria was *peaceful*? Full of *peace*? Yolande doesn't know that. Nobody knows that. Nobody has any idea how Sister Maria felt – if she was in pain, afraid, alone. *Angry.* I run across the yard toward the bushes behind the house and down the trail that leads from the machine shed to the clearing at the top of the hill.

Here it's peaceful.

Dad keeps his three old granaries in the clearing, plus an enormous stack of firewood cut from deadfall, an old rusted-out threshing machine that he can't seem to part with, a broken-down John Deere tractor, and eleven snowmobiles. The snow-mobiles aren't any good. I stretch out across them and look up at the sky, my eyes wide open. They're Merc snowmobiles – all of them – and the newest is twenty-three years old. Really, they're antiques. Merc doesn't even make snowmobiles anymore. Dad loves his Mercs because his dad had one. He says that they're big, solid, working machines; good for overnight ice-fishing trips, not like the new fiberglass racing Ski-Doos. In the machine shed, he keeps two of his Mercs in working condition – more or less. They're always breaking down, and he's always trying to fix them. If you ask me, Dad doesn't really want to keep the snowmobiles going. He wants to keep the memory of his dad alive; the mem-ory of the times they spent together on late fall hunting trips, and ice-fishing trips in the winter. These snowmobiles – the ones that are nestled between the pines and the poplars, the wild hazelnut and cranberry and raspberry bushes – these Mercs will never run again.

Can Sister Maria see me in this snowmobile cemetery, crying? I can't believe that she's gone. I can't believe it. Tears trickle from my eyes, down my temples and into my hair. I need her. I need her to talk to me, to tell me things. To take my hands off the keys when I'm playing poorly, and waltz around her music room when I'm playing well. To ruffle my hair when I make a joke. To squeeze my hand when I'm feeling down. We were supposed to learn *"Malaguena"* for two pianos, four hands. We were supposed to go to Vivaldi's *Four Seasons* at the Jubilee Auditorium in Edmonton. I was going to write her long letters from the college in Africa. I promised to tell her everything about it once I got there. When we talked about my scholarship interview, Sister Maria didn't say *if* – she never said *if*. She said *when*.

What's going to happen to her other piano students?

What's going to happen to her work?

Because I am sobbing, I don't hear them approaching – our dog, Ralph, first, and behind him, Dad.

"Beautiful day," says Dad, scratching Ralphie behind the ears. "No mosquitoes yet."

I nod, wiping the tears from my face. Afraid that if I open my mouth, I'll start sobbing again.

"I guess you've heard," he says.

I don't say anything.

"Father Levasseur just called the house." Ralph curls up at Dad's feet. "He asked to talk to you, Colleen. I know this is all happening pretty fast but he'd like you to sing for Sister Maria's funeral. He needs to know if you'll do it."

I shake my head, sniffling. "Someone else can do it." Not me.

"He asked for you, Colleen, not somebody else. *You.*"

Ralph gets up suddenly, and starts pacing at the base of a

spruce. There must be a squirrel on the upper branches of the tree.

"That's crazy," I say. "Lots of Sister Mari – lots of her students sing. Claire Boisvert, Angèle Thibault. I'm not Catholic, I've never been to a Catholic funeral. I've never even been to *Mass*. Why me?"

"The sisters asked for you," says Dad. "Specifically. They asked for you to sing *'Ave Maria.'* Mom told Father Levasseur that you know the song and he said that he'd arrange for one of Maria's other students to accompany you."

Ralph starts scratching around the tree.

"Mom talked to him?" I ask.

Dad nods.

"Then she already told him I'd do it, didn't she?"

Dad watches Ralph scratching in the dirt.

"Didn't she?"

Dad doesn't answer.

"Well, she can phone him right back and tell him I'm not doing it. I'm not."

I'm *sick of* being asked to sing – every wedding, every birthday, every concert. And now funerals. Why me? Why am I the one who always has to practise and get nervous and puke? I won't do it anymore. I'm *sick* of it.

"I know that it's hard for you," says Dad.

"No you don't. You don't know the first thing about it."

"You think I want to be MC at every wedding?" he asks, softly. "At every graduation and every twenty-fifth wedding anniversary? I don't. You think I want to give the eulogy at every prayer service, every toast to the bride, every keynote address? I don't want to do it. I never want to do it. I know what it's like."

"So why do you keep saying yes?"

Dad shrugs. "Because they ask, I suppose. Because I'm good at it. Because I wouldn't be any happier sitting in the crowd. You and I, we're performers. That's our calling. And when we're called to do it, we have no choice."

Ralph starts barking wildly now, howling and jumping at the

lower branches of the spruce. Dad calls for him to stop but he keeps woofing and yowling.

"I'd sing *'Ave Maria'?*"

"*'Ave Maria,'*" says Dad. "That's what the sisters want, and Father Levasseur. He said that Sister Maria would want it, too."

Dad grabs the dog by the collar. "Come on, Ralphie. Let's go back before you bark yourself to death."

I cringe at the mention of death, and the tears return. Dad notices that I'm crying.

"If I were giving the eulogy," he says, "I'd probably say something like 'for everything there is a season.'"

He puts his arms around me.

"Doesn't make it any easier, does it?" he asks.

Ralph appears at my side, sniffing at something in the grass.

"There's one more thing," says Dad. "Some of the nuns, they've been sorting through Sister Maria's things, packing up her belongings."

I've never liked the other nuns at the convent. The thought of them poking around Sister Maria's music room makes me sick. Scavengers. They have no right. She hasn't even been buried yet and already they're clearing out her room, taking away all that she left behind.

"Her affairs were all in order. She was a very orderly woman, you know. She made her wishes very clear."

Ralph rubs his nose against my leg.

"She's left you her music," says Dad. "All of it. I thought you might like to hear that. It's yours, if you want it. Father Levasseur said that we could pick it up from the convent whenever you're ready."

As Dad walks back to the house, I lie down again on the snowmobile, turning my face toward the bush. I try to focus on the trees, the sound of the phoebes singing. The feel of the plastic snowmobile seat against my cheek. But all I see is Sister Maria sitting at her desk, writing notes in my dictation book. I hear her music all around me, echoing in the woods. I feel my hand on her arm while she plays, holding on tight. And I don't want to let go.

For the funeral, Dad wears a black suit and a black and red polka-dotted tie; Mom wears a plain black dress, long, with white appliqué daisies around the neckline. I wear the new outfit that Sophie and I picked out for my scholarship interview. Mom thinks that the outfit is inappropriate. "Slacks to a funeral," she says. "It shows disrespect." But she's letting it go. I don't own a skirt or a dress.

In the car, on the way to town, Mom says, "Just this once. Next time you're wearing a *dress.*"

But there will be no next time. Sister Maria will be buried only once.

Dad has the air conditioning in the car turned up full blast. It's twenty-seven degrees outside today so it feels more like the middle of July than the beginning of May. There isn't a cloud in the sky. It doesn't seem right, all of this brightness, this sunshine. I think that it should be raining – pouring rain. The whole world should be crying for Sister Maria.

Mom makes idle conversation about her garden and her bedding plants.

"I want to get the cucumbers planted this afternoon, and maybe my petunias if there's time."

Nobody responds but she continues.

"I wonder if there'll be frost. Middle of May, we usually get frost. Maybe I should wait with the cucumbers."

Dad looks at me through the rear-view mirror.

"You okay back there?" he says.

I clench my fist around the Kleenexes scrunched up in the palm of my hand.

"Fine."

"Just don't look at the casket while you sing," Mom says, matter-of-factly. "Or the congregation. Don't look at them, either. They'll all be crying, you know."

I don't know who will be in the cathedral for the funeral. Sister Maria has almost no family – just one brother from Montreal and his son. I wonder if they'll make it to the funeral. All of the nuns will be there, of course, and the priests, however many of them there are in town, and the bishop. Sister Maria's piano students, their parents. The odd friend she may have had from outside the convent. I can't imagine that there will be more than thirty or forty people. The church, I think, will be nearly empty.

I'm shocked, then, as we approach the cathedral. Cars line the street in front of the church, across from the church, beside the convent and the rectory. There are Saskatchewan and British Columbia license plates on some of the cars. Sister Maria's ex-students, maybe. Dad pulls the car around to the parking lot at the back of the church; it's full, too.

"So many people!" says Mom. "Where did they all come from?"

We end up parking in a residential area, three blocks from main street. Two cars follow us, and both park behind our car. I feel nauseous and nervous. What if I cry in front of all these people? What if I can't stop? While we walk up the stairs of the cathedral, a hearse parks at the side of the church. I press my fistful of Kleenex against my eyes.

"Dad," I whisper, as we enter the church.

He doesn't hear me.

"Dad!"

He puts his arm around me, leaning down so that I can whisper in his ear. My voice cracks.

"I can't do this, Dad. I can't. I can't do it."

Organ music fills the cathedral, "The Twenty-third Psalm." Mom hugs me and gives me a quick peck on the cheek before she joins Yolande in a pew near the front of the church. Dad pulls me aside at the back of the church. He takes the red handkerchief out of his breast pocket and gently wipes my eyes with it.

"Of *course* you can do it. It's not going to be easy but you're going to do it, and do it beautifully."

"No, I'm not, Dad. I'm not!"

I'm starting to panic now.

"Go tell the priest. Please, Dad. *Please.* Tell him I've changed my mind."

Dad puts his hands on my shoulders. "What would Sister Maria tell you right now? If she were here, what would she say to you? Would she let you quit?"

I don't know. I shrug. I have no idea what she'd say.

"Come on, *think!*" says Dad. "Before a recital, before a festival. What would she say?"

I blow my nose into the red hanky. "Concentrate. She'd say *concentrate* and *focus.*"

"All right, then." Dad grabs my hand as he makes his way toward the organ. There are special pews behind the organ for the organist, choir singers, and soloists. "I'm going to sit right here next to you. I'm going to be with you the *whole* time. And I'm going to concentrate with you. We're going to concentrate *together.*"

But I can't concentrate on Father Levasseur's words, the prayers or the hymns. I stare out into the crowd, into the sea of faces I've never seen before. The women dab their eyes with tissue, the men sit up straight and stoic. When they stand, I stand; when they kneel, I kneel. At the front of the church, up near the priest, lies Sister Maria. Her casket is open – half of it, anyway; flowers cover the rest of the casket. Bright pink and white orchids, pink roses, and deep green tendrils of ivy. There are bouquets of carnations and daisies on either side of the casket, too, and, beside the organ, an enormous basket of stargazer lilies. I'm close enough to the lilies that I can taste them. Not close enough to see Sister Maria's face. Not close enough to touch her.

From time to time while Father Levasseur talks, I watch the organist, Monique Delongchamps. I watch her for signs of nerves – shaky hands, missed chords, tempo problems – to see if she's as scared as I am. She doesn't make any mistakes. It's amazing. Not a single mistake. I look closely at her legs working the pedals of the organ. Her knees don't tremble. I look at her hands between songs; she doesn't wipe them on her lap, so they must not be sweating. She has flawless control – a true performer, a real professional. Sister Maria would be proud of Monique, playing her way through the service without so much as a wrong note. Years ago, Sister Maria was her teacher. I have to say that now, too. In the past tense. Sister Maria was my teacher, I was her student.

While I watch Monique, I try to go through *"Ave Maria"* in my head. The first time through, I mess up the words. *"Dominus tecum, gratia plena"* instead of *"gratia plena, dominus tecum."* On my second try, I think *"Santa Maria,"* then remember that it's *"Sancta Maria,"* then forget what comes after *"Sancta Maria."* It's the word *"Maria."* I can't get past it. And the smell of the lilies on the casket – such a thick, sweet smell, like incense – it makes me want to throw up. Sister Maria wouldn't have liked them; she would have liked smaller flowers, odourless flowers. Wildflowers, maybe. They hardly smell. Or bright red poppies.

It seems clear to me, after my third failed attempt to recite *"Ave Maria"* in my head, that I need the words written out in front of me. Usually I don't sing with words in front of me. In fact, I don't think that I've ever sung with words in front of me. There's something unpolished, Mom says, about a singer who can't even memorize her words. Now, as I sit waiting to sing, I don't care if I look at words. I don't care if I look unpolished. A wave of panic ripples through me. Having the words in front of me is the only thing that will get me through this, I'm sure of it. If only I'd thought of it sooner. If only I'd brought a copy of *"Ave Maria"* with me.

"Monique. Pssst. Monique!" I give Monique a poke. "Do you have an extra copy of '*Ave Maria*' with you?"

Monique shakes her head.

"Is it okay if I look off your copy then? I need the words and I forgot mine at home."

"My copy doesn't *have* words," says Monique.

She shows me the music she uses for *"Ave Maria."* It's the original Bach Prelude, photocopied from *The Well-Tempered Clavier.* And she's right – no words.

"Here," she says, handing me a pencil and a funeral program. "Quick! Write the words out on the back of this."

For a moment, I'm relieved. I'll write the words out, I'll be fine. I'll have something in front of me to focus on instead of the casket and the flowers and the pews filled with sniffling women. Then I try to write. I try to write but – besides *"Ave"* and *"Maria"*– I can't remember a single word of the song. It's crazy. I've known *"Ave Maria"* for years. I've practised it at least a hundred times, I know it inside and out. Backwards and forwards.

"Dad!" I tug on the sleeve of Dad's suit jacket. "Dad! I can't remember the words. What am I going to do?"

"Shhh," says Dad. "Try to relax, take a deep breath. When you get up there to sing, the words will be there. Don't worry. It's just nerves."

He puts his arm around me, pulling me close to his side.

"You'll be fine."

But when it's time for me to sing – when I'm standing up, behind the microphone, beside the organ – I'm not fine. The lily smell makes me dizzy and I sway while Monique plays the introduction. She plays it just like we practised – two bars of arpeggios – and then she gives me the bass-note cue, just like we practised. I sway in silence, listening to my cue come and go. Monique plays the two-bar introduction again, this time looking at me while she plays, her eyebrows raised. After her third time through the introduction, I open my mouth, get the first words out – *"Aaaaa-veeee Mariiiiiii-aaaa"* – then nothing. I can't remember the rest. Not one word of the rest of the song. While I stand, twisting the Kleenex in my hands, Monique keeps playing.

Finally, after ten or twelve bars, I motion for her to stop.

The organ music stops.

"I'm sorry," I say into the microphone.

My voice fills the cathedral.

"I'm sorry. I can't remember the words."

Two hundred, three hundred faces turn to stare at me. There is whispering and the rustling of funeral programs. The nuns fidget in their pews. Father Levasseur, frowning, starts to get up from his chair at the very front of the church – to take over, I suppose. But I go on. I have to. I owe it to Sister Maria.

"I hope you understand." This is really hard. I clear my throat. "I think that Sister Maria would understand."

With the mention of Sister Maria's name, the church falls still and silent. Everyone stops whispering, the nuns quietly clasp their hands together across their laps. Though Father Levasseur looks positively mortified, he sits down again. He glares at me as he returns to his seat.

"I'm going to try this one more time," I say.

My voice trembles a little and my nose starts to drip. I stop to blow my nose into the red hanky, get a hold of myself. Pull myself together.

As I return to the microphone, an idea comes to me – why didn't I think of it before? – and, with the idea, a feeling of calm. Utter calm. As though the crowd and the casket and the flowers have receded far into the distance, as though Father Levasseur has melted into the stained glass windows. I can almost feel Sister Maria behind me, nodding her encouragement; I can almost hear her voice. As if this is just another piano lesson, just another hour with her.

I say nothing by way of an introduction. The song needs no introduction, really. It's sad and slow and solemn – the traditional Ukrainian funeral song, *"Vichnaia Pam'iat."* Maybe the idea comes from her, maybe it's what she wants – to have it sung for her. Though I've heard it a few times, I've never actually sung it myself.

This is my first time. Monique can't play along, of course, because she doesn't know how.

It doesn't sound right, one voice singing *"Vichnaia Pam'iat."* Everyone should be singing – men and women, little kids – everyone. One voice. I go on but it just doesn't sound right.

Dad must think the same thing – that it doesn't sound right with one voice – because before long I hear him join in. I hear his voice, an octave lower than mine, strong and deep. I glance over my shoulder. He is standing up with his hands clasped in front of him and his mouth open wide.

Then I see my mother rise and I see her lips moving, too. She sings softly at first, in perfect unison with Dad and me, then louder. We are the only three people in the cathedral who are standing and who are singing.

Together, we sing the words to the song – *"vichnaia pam'iat"* – the same words, over and over again. *"Vichnaia pam'iat."* And because I'm not singing alone, it's all right if I cry. When my voice falters and breaks, their voices fill the cathedral. *"Vichnaia pam'iat, Vichnaia pam'iat." In everlasting memory* of Sister Maria.

In everlasting memory
In everlasting memory
In everlasting memory

SEVEN

"**Y**ou must be Colleen!"
    At my scholarship interview, a girl meets me outside
    the doors of the office building in downtown Edmonton.
She is Barbie Christianson, a recent alumnus of the Lester B.
Pearson United World College of the Pacific near Victoria, British
Columbia.

Before telling me about herself, Barbie locks my hand into a
death grip, then pumps it with all her might. My fingers are tin-
gling by the time she's finished shaking my hand. She looks like a
Barbie doll – tall, thin, tanned. No makeup, blonde hair swept off
her forehead and pulled into a single braid down her back.
Barbie's never had a pimple in her life, I can tell. My face, on the
other hand, is a whole other story. It broke out the day of Sister
Maria's funeral. I've got a constellation of pimples across my chin
and the North Star on the tip of my nose.

"Coffee, decaf or regular. Tea, juice, water. Help yourself," says
Barbie, as she leads me into the office lounge.

There are doughnuts and muffins on a coffee table in the centre of the room; a fruit tray, too, plus a plate covered in tiny triangular sandwiches arranged in a circle with sprigs of parsley for gar-
nish and radishes carved into the shape of roses. The sight of food
makes me nauseous. Mom and Dad and I stopped at McDonald's
for lunch. I only ate half a Big Mac, but I hardly got it down before
I threw it up again. The taste of vomit still lingers in my throat.

Since Sister Maria's funeral, I haven't been sleeping well. I've hardly been sleeping at all, in fact, and I haven't had much of an appetite. For the past few days, at suppertime, I've been staying in my room. When Mom and Dad knock on my door, I tell them that I'm not hungry. Sophie and Wes take turns bringing me snacks – licorice allsorts, chocolate chip cookies. My favourite potato chips. I just don't feel like eating. I lie on my bed – on my back, on my stomach, on my side – trying to find a comfortable position. Trying to avoid looking at the boxes of Sister Maria's music stacked up against the wall in my room.

Dad picked up the boxes from the convent. All of Sister Maria's books and her sheet music, her record collection, her cassette and video tapes. Stacks of manuscript paper covered in her handwriting. He offered to store the boxes in the garage for the time being – until I feel ready to go through it all. But I couldn't bear the thought of Sister Maria's music lying in some dusty corner of the garage any more than I can bear to look at it in my room.

I want to believe that Sister Maria is with me, that she is watching over me while I sit in the waiting room, getting ready for my interview. I want to believe that she's cheering me on, giving me courage to get through this morning. On my own, I don't feel very brave.

At the far end of the lounge, a couple and their daughter are seated around a TV set and a VCR. Barbie tells me that they're watching the latest UWC promo video, shot at various locations around the world.

"That's Vanessa," says Barbie, pointing to the daughter. "She's a candidate, just like you!" Barbie smiles a flawless Barbie smile.

Vanessa waves to me from across the room.

"Super person," Barbie whispers. "And super parents. Just *super*. So supportive! Are your parents parking their car or something?"

I nod.

Mom and Dad dropped me off so that they could hit a few

malls with Sophie and Wes while I do my interview. We're meeting at the Eaton Centre in two hours.

Barbie joins Vanessa's parents as they finish watching the promo video. Vanessa bounces over to me.

"I'm, like, *so* glad," says Vanessa, "that someone else decided to wear pants! I was, like, *so* worried that I was, you know, underdressed or something!"

Vanessa is wearing cream-coloured silk slacks with gold threads woven into the fabric. Her blouse is gold-coloured silk with gold buttons. All of her accessories are gold. There are gold sandals on her feet, a gold bracelet on her wrist, a thick gold chain around her neck, and gold teardrop earrings on her ears. My pants wrinkled on the car-ride from St. Paul. I've got a small dark stain on the collar of my shirt where I dropped a piece of lettuce covered in Big Mac sauce. I want to tell Vanessa that she is, like, *so* full of it.

To get away from Vanessa, I wander toward the coffee urn. She follows.

"Oh my God. I, like, *so* admire you for drinking coffee now. I'm *so* nervous. Coffee would, like, *totally* put me over the edge."

I try to block out the sound of Vanessa's voice. Her mannerisms might rub off on me. I take my coffee to a chair in the corner – a good place, I think, to tune my guitar, run through the words of the song I'm going to sing. I've brought a lyric sheet with me so that there is no repeat of my performance at Sister Maria's funeral.

Vanessa is about to plop herself into a chair next to mine when her name is called. She gives a little yelp, her parents dash across the room to embrace her.

Vanessa says, "Oh my God!"

In unison, her parents say, "This is it!"

They hug, they kiss. They hug again.

I try to concentrate on opening my guitar case. But Vanessa runs over to me, giving my shoulder a poke.

"Wish me luck!"

"You, like, *totally* don't need luck. You're going to be, like, *so* awesome."

It's too late. She's already rubbed off on me.

I'm about to take my guitar out of its case when another girl enters the lounge – another candidate, another set of parents. The girl looks like she's ready to attend a wedding – hair pinned up in a French twist, long green dress, spiky green heels. Her parents are dressed no differently. The father wears a double-breasted suit, dark grey with a royal blue tie and a puff of royal blue in his breast pocket; the mother wears a matching royal blue suit, short and sleek, with dark grey gloves and a dark grey hat. Maybe it's a good thing that my parents didn't come with me. They drove to Edmonton today in shorts and T-shirts. My dad hates suits. My mother doesn't own a hat.

This girl's name is Caroline Thompson. Barbie leads her across the room to introduce us.

"Another musician!" says Barbie.

Caroline has a violin case in her hand.

"I'll leave you two alone," Barbie says, "so that you can talk music! And UWCS!"

Caroline looks down at my guitar sitting in its case. The body of the guitar is covered with stickers – CFCW RADIO, Kehiwin First Nations, Jesus is Lord. It used to belong to an Indian guy, a gospel singer from Bonnyville. Dad bought it for me years ago at an auction sale when I first started talking about playing the guitar. Mom said that we shouldn't spend too much money, in case I changed my mind. Dad paid forty dollars for the Jesus is Lord guitar. A few times, after they saw that I really was going to learn to play it, Mom and Dad offered to buy me a new one – a better one. But I love the sound of this guitar. I don't care how beaten up it looks.

Caroline's violin case is made of black leather. Several Air Canada luggage tags hang from the shoulder strap.

I snap my guitar case shut.

"So, you play the fiddle?" I ask.

I'm joking, of course. I can see that she plays the violin. I'm just making conversation.

"*Violin*," says Caroline, correcting me. "I'm section leader for the Alberta Youth Orchestra and the Western Canadian Youth Orchestra. I also conduct two youth chamber groups and play in one professional chamber ensemble."

I try very hard to be friendly. "Oh. Wow. That's – wow. Doesn't get much better than that, does it?"

"Actually, I've been invited to play with the International Youth Orchestra four times – once in Berlin, once in Moscow, once in Stockholm, once in Peking. This year, we're meeting in Mexico City."

Egomaniac, I think. Braggart.

"That must be exciting for you. Mexico City. What a change from Edmonton."

"*Actually*, I'm from Calgary. But Mexico is a second home to me as well. My family and I spend our summers on the Yucatan Peninsula. I speak English, Spanish, and French. I'm in French immersion."

Summers on the Yucatan Peninsula. I speak English, Spanish, and French.

How can I compete with her?

My stomach turns. I excuse myself politely from Caroline, then make my way to the bathroom as nonchalantly as possible. I have to throw up again.

Dry heaves. There's nothing left to vomit. I should leave now, Mom was right. I don't have a chance. I'm out of my league – way out. I press my face against the toilet bowl. *Berlin, Moscow, Stockholm, Peking.* I've hardly been out of Alberta, let alone overseas.

I'm still at the toilet bowl when Vanessa and her mother walk into the bathroom.

"Everything, Mom!" says Vanessa. "I could answer, like, *everything* they asked. They asked me a bunch of questions about

multiculturalism and what is Canada and stuff – that was easy.
Then there was this big question about crime and criminals and
what I think of extradition and countries that use capital punishment and, like, you know how we had that debate on the death
penalty in social studies last semester? Well I just recited, like,
everything our team came up with and I'm just totally sure it was
exactly what they wanted to hear, you know, about the *sanctity* of
human life and the *futility* of an-eye-for-an-eye and all that. It was
a total dream interview. A *total* dream."

As Vanessa and her mother slip into their respective bathroom
stalls, I slip out of the bathroom altogether. I'm going to grab my
guitar from the lounge and run. We've never talked about capital
punishment in our social studies class. Extradition? I have no clue
what the word means.

Barbie meets me in the corridor outside the bathroom.

"You're up next!" she says, handing my guitar to me. "You've
only got twenty minutes with them. Make every word count."

I feel dizzy.

"Don't worry, though!" Barbie puts her arm around me and
squeezes. "Just relax and be yourself! The committee will call on
you when they're ready."

Barbie joins Vanessa's Dad and Caroline's parents and Caroline
on the other side of the room. Caroline is in the centre of the
group talking about herself. She's describing her volunteer work
with AIDS victims and homeless teenagers and heroine addicts. Are
there heroine addicts in St. Paul? I've volunteered at bingos for the
Ukrainian dance club, to raise money for our trips to festivals.
That's it, the extent of my volunteer work. Bingo.

The interview room is long and rectangular; it's decorated in
pastel colours. A pastel blue carpet, pastel blue and pink chairs –
high-backed, plush chairs that swivel – and pastel pink vertical blinds
on the windows. Hanging on one wall is a pastel pink print of coral
and seashells and, on the other wall, a matching pastel blue print of
the ocean. The room is filled with a long rectangular table, and faces.

Six faces, six people, each with a pastel pink name tag. Tim Van Leuwen, the committee chairperson, extends his hand. He's balding. The top of his head, I notice, is pale pink. It matches the decor.

Tim takes me around the table, introducing me to the other committee members one by one.

J.J. Bowers, physiotherapist, University of Alberta Hospital. Pacific College Alumnus.

Craig Jefferson, Immigration Canada. Pacific College Alumnus.

Gena Fontaine, Alberta Teachers' Association. Pacific College Alumnus.

Heinrich Bauer, Bauer, Franke, and Associates. Atlantic College Alumnus.

Fiona Clarke, Director of Marketing, PETA. Atlantic College Alumnus.

Three women, three men. The committee is perfectly symmetrical. They even sit symmetrically – boy girl, boy girl, boy girl. Half have attended the Pacific UWC in British Columbia, the other half, the Atlantic College in Wales. There are no alumni of the Adriatic UWC in Italy or the College of the American West in New Mexico. No representative from the Southeast Asia UWC in Singapore. No one from the Southern Africa UWC in Swaziland. What a disappointment. I wanted to ask questions about the college in Africa.

There is no small talk. The committee goes straight into the questions.

"It's standard procedure," says Tim, "for us to begin by asking each candidate to explain his or her response to question 32.2(d) on the United World Colleges application form."

Question 32.2(d)?

Craig takes a turn at speaking. "In your case, Colleen, we're particularly interested in the way you chose to answer 32.2(d)."

Craig has short, spiky hair. He's tanned, broad-shouldered. Well-built. The opposite of Tim, with his shiny head and his scrawny neck and his white-blue complexion.

I try to visualize the application form – 32.2(d), 32.2(d). It's been two months since I filled out the application.

"I don't quite recall question 32.2(d). Could you refresh my memory, please?"

Tim and Craig exchange glances. This, I think, is a test. A test of my memory. And I'm failing.

Tim clears his throat. "The question asked that you rank the colleges from one to six according to your personal preferences: one being your first choice, six being your last. On your application" – he sighs as he sifts through a stack of papers – "you failed to rank the colleges altogether."

Tim pushes my application toward me; I pick it up, my hands shaking. My response to question 32.2(d) has been highlighted in bright yellow.

I remember now, of course. Instead of ranking the colleges, I simply marked my first choice. I circled the college in southern Africa. I drew tiny stars all around it. I placed an enormous number one beside the words Waterford Kamhlaba United World College of Southern Africa.

"We would be less than honest," says Craig, "if we didn't communicate to you the degree to which your application form – particularly, your response to question 32.2(d) – stands out as *unusual* among the other candidates' application forms."

"All of our other applicants completed the question *as asked*," says Tim.

"That is to say," says Craig, "they ranked the colleges from one to six."

"And almost entirely without exception," says Tim, "they relegated Waterford Kamhlaba to the bottom of their list."

Craig interrupts. "You should know, Colleen, that we don't – as a rule – send students on scholarship to Swaziland. I imagine that – given your obvious interest in Waterford Kamhlaba – it must be disappointing for you to hear this now. Perhaps your guidance counsellor or your teacher – whoever passed the application on to you – perhaps that person wasn't aware of our policy?"

"The region is too volatile," says Heinrich, the lawyer on the committee. He leans back in his chair, crosses his arms behind his head. "Political upheaval, civil unrest. Violence. With the potential dismantling of the apartheid regime by militant black factions and makeshift guerrilla groups, it's simply not in the best interest of our committee –"

"– or our candidates," Craig says, interrupting him –

"– to involve ourselves with the college in southern Africa. It's too dangerous."

Craig cuts in again. "Safety," he says. "The safety of our students is our number one priority."

For a moment, nobody speaks.

"You don't know that it's not safe," I say.

"Pardon?" says Tim.

"You don't know that it's not safe. You don't really know what's going on in South Africa. How could you? You haven't been there and you haven't sent any students there."

The more I talk, the more assertive I become. My hands stop trembling, my stomach settles. It's like being onstage, like a performance.

"All you know is what you read in the newspapers, and what you hear on TV. Do you believe everything the media tell you? I don't. The media are in business. Selling papers, high ratings – that's their business. They sensationalize everything. I don't trust them. I want to know what's really going on in the world. I want to see apartheid first-hand. If you're worried about the danger, give me a waiver. Something that says the committee won't be held responsible for any harm that might come to me. I'll sign it. I'll sign it right now."

"What we're asking," says Heinrich, ignoring my little speech, "is that you select another college."

"Keeping in mind," Tim adds, "that Waterford Kamhlaba is really out of the question."

For a split second, I think back to a conversation that I had with Mr. Kaushal, about the colleges. A week or so before Sister Maria died.

"I've read about the other colleges," I say, "and they all sound wonderful. Don't get me wrong. They sound beautiful. The campuses in New Mexico and Wales are both built around castles. The college in Victoria is surrounded by the ocean. But I've also read in your scholarship literature that when scholarship recipients have completed their year at a United World College, they're obliged to return to their communities to share what they've learned from the United World College experience."

I'm not sure if this is the right or the wrong thing to say. Probably it's the wrong thing. I keep talking, though. I can't stop now.

I tell the committee that Waterford Kamhlaba interests me because it was the first multi-racial school in southern Africa. It was designed to challenge the apartheid system, to show young people that it's possible for individuals of all races to live and learn and work together. And the apartheid system – the system that forces black people to live in homelands – was modelled on Canadian Indian reserves.

Mr. Kaushal told me this.

"My hometown is St. Paul. And St. Paul is surrounded by five reserves. Saddle Lake, Frog Lake, Kehiwin. Good Fish, Fishing Lake. We've got our own apartheid happening right here, right now. It seems to me that if South Africa learned about apartheid from us, who's to say that we can't learn from South Africa how to dismantle it?"

Now I'm sure that I've said the wrong thing. The committee members are all writing in their notepads. I've insulted them by saying that Canada is like South Africa.

"Thank you," says Tim, pursing his lips. "I think that's enough. We can move on to the next question. Gena?"

Gena's hair is curly and red, her face is pale and freckled. She says, "If a – if a *Swazi* student, let's say, were to ask you what it means to be Canadian, what would you say?"

I pause, wondering how I should answer. Mr. Kaushal and I didn't talk about what it means to be Canadian. But Sister Maria and I did. I showed her a song, once, that I sang in my elementary school choir, and we had a good laugh together about all the clichés that the songwriter had packed into it.

Finish this sentence, says Gena. "My country, Canada, is –"

> Canada is fresh maple syrup
> Canada is red-coated Mounties
> Canada is the boreal beaver
> And the bison and the loon

Without thinking, I recite lines from the choir song. I should stop myself before I go any further. I don't think that I've ever tasted real maple syrup. We buy Aunt Jemima's, it's cheaper. And the RCMP only wear red on special occasions. I'm sure the committee members know a cliché when they hear one.

> Canada is the Rocky Mountains
> Canada is the northern tundra
> Canada is Niagara Falls
> And the Great Lakes and the plains

Tim tries to interrupt me. I ignore him. I'm on a roll, making up my own lines to the song. It's like I'm reliving my conversation with Sister Maria, and the memory of her laughing makes me smile while I come up with a new verse.

> Canada is the Maritime miner
> Canada is the Calgary oilman
> Canada is the Saskatchewan farmer
> And the West Coast –

"Great," says Tim. "That's great. Let's move on. We've got to keep our eye on the clock. J.J.? You go ahead."

Damn it. I'm not finished. I wanted to say something about the Québécois language and Hibernia and the midnight sun in the Northwest Territories.

"As Tim mentioned," J.J. says, "I'm a physiotherapist at the University Hospital in Edmonton. My primary interest is in body consciousness: healthy eating, physical fitness, active lifestyles."

It doesn't look to me as though J.J. is interested in healthy eating. It doesn't look like she's interested in eating at all. The skin on her face is stretched tight across her cheekbones and eye sockets. She wears a sleeveless shirt so I can see her arms, thin and sinewy, blue-green veins bulging down the length of her forearms and across the backs of her hands. I think she's overdone it with the physical fitness and the active lifestyle. She looks anorexic.

"I'd like you to elaborate on your involvement in sports. Team sports and individual sports."

I could lie. I probably should. Make something up about running, aerobics. Volleyball, tennis, badminton. I could play the part, pretend that I'm a jock. J.J. would never know the difference, I'm not wearing a sleeveless shirt. But what if they send me to a jock college? I've heard that the college in Victoria specializes in water sports like sailing and swimming and ocean kayaking. They do rock climbing in Wales, cricket in Singapore. I'd never make it at one of those colleges.

"I have to be honest. I'm not really one for sports, organized or individual. In fact. No. That's an understatement. I hate sports. I always have."

J.J. gasps. The other committee members lift their pencils off their notepads. They've probably never seen a candidate make so many mistakes in one interview. I have to be myself, though. I can't pretend to be something I'm not.

"I've never tried out for the school volleyball team, basketball team, track team. Never played after-school sports, like softball or soccer. Wait – no – that's not true. My parents signed me up for T-Ball one year."

"You know the game, right?" I ask. "It's sort of a tiny tots' version of softball."

Gena nods. Craig nods.

"The coach never played me. He said that I wasn't aggressive enough." I pause. "For T-Ball."

"So, I suppose that set a precedent in my life. Ten years of phys. ed. classes and not once – ever – did I break a sweat. Never. I don't think it makes me a bad person, really. Sports just aren't for everyone, and that's all right, in my opinion. For me, it's the competition that I can't stand. I mean – imagine. We're playing floor hockey in phys. ed. and my best friend is the goaltender on the other team. Now, why would I want to go and score on her? She's my best friend. I'm not going to shoot at my best friend. Or, let's say, my best friend is on the other team, and she's playing left wing and she loves to score. Scoring means everything to her – and she's good at it, too. Why not pass her the puck and let her score? Scoring doesn't mean a thing to me."

J.J. looks at me as though I've lost my mind.

"You're telling me," she says, "that you have never engaged in any cardiovascular activity? You've never worked out? You've never – perspired?"

"Oh no. No. I've perspired lots of times – just not in phys. ed. In Ukrainian dancing I used to get completely drenched. I Ukrainian danced twice a week, all my life. It's a pretty good workout. But, technically speaking, Ukrainian dancing isn't a sport. You asked me about sports."

I try not to look smug.

J.J. turns to Fiona, shaking her head. "Your witness," she says.

Fiona says, "I want to pick up on something that you mentioned when you were talking about Canada. You talked about the beaver in relation to Canada. You know, many of our students – past and present – are actively involved in the protection of endangered animal species. A lot of us are strict vegetarians. I've personally made a career of animal rights, working with PETA, People for the Ethical Treatment of Animals."

I look around the room at the other committee members. Gena has set her pencil down; Heinrich and Craig have crossed their arms over their chests. Tim interrupts Fiona, asking if she could perhaps get to her question.

"Could you tell us about your interest *in* and your experiences *with* animal rights activism?" says Fiona.

"Animal rights activism," I repeat. "That's a tough one."

It is a tough one. Mr. Kaushal and I have had an ongoing argument about animal rights. Fiona is on his side. She wants to hear that I volunteer at the SPCA with abused pets, that I write letters protesting the sale of ivory. That I spray paint on rich women's fur coats. I don't think that I can do it – play into her hand, tell her what she wants to hear. I can't and I won't.

"I'll be straight with you," I say. "I grew up on a farm. I'm fairly pragmatic about killing animals."

"Pragmatic?" Fiona raises her eyebrows.

"I'm all for animal rights. I really am. I think senseless cruelty to animals is awful. But – take gophers, for example. They spell trouble for farmers. Gophers are big-time pests. They destroy crops; cows break legs because of gopher holes. They can't be allowed to live. Not in large numbers anyway."

"And farmers' fields are more important than animal habitats?"

"Let me put it this way. If I had to choose between human life and animal life, I'd choose humans. Think about lab animals. Mice, rats, rabbits. Scientists need to use them in their research, to make medical advances. If we need to sacrifice a few rats to save human lives, so be it."

I explain, then, that some animal rights activists seem to be selective about the animal lives that they fight for. "Mice and rabbits are cute, so they deserve to live. Cows are ugly, so they deserve to die. Where's the logic?"

"By my logic," says Fiona, "*all* animals have the right to live. I'm against the killing of all animals, so-called 'ugly' cows included. We could feed entire villages with the amount of grain that a single cow eats. How do you respond to that?"

I shift in my seat. I hadn't thought of that.

"Is there not," she says, "something inherently wrong – something inherently cruel – about the ways in which we privilege livestock industries over human life?"

"But killing itself isn't necessarily cruel."

Fiona stares me straight in the eye as I repeat a story that I once told Mr. Kaushal when I was arguing with him about cruelty to animals. It's a true story.

"Have you ever taken a walk in the bush in northern Alberta in the spring? *I* have. My dad took me on a walk in the bush near our farm once in the spring. And we found fourteen half-rotten deer carcasses, all around the same spot, their undersides all red and raw and bloody. Dad says that we're over-populated with deer. So when there's not enough food for them in the winter, in the bush, they head out to farmers' fields to get at the grain under the snow. Except that there's this hard, icy crust over the fields and it scrapes the fur off their bellies. They don't usually get to the point of starvation. They freeze to death first, bleed to death sometimes."

"So you would support – culling, I suppose," says Fiona, "as distinct from killing."

"Exactly. I come from a hunting family. My dad and my brother Wes hunt. We all grew up on deer meat. Deer meat and moose meat, sometimes elk meat. We've got freezers full of wild meat. There's a friend of my dad's at Saddle Lake – one of the reserves by St. Paul – and he takes the hides and the antlers. We use everything except the guts. Dad leaves the guts for the coyotes. I don't think it's cruel, I think it's natural."

I'm feeling smug now. Like I've won the argument after all.

"And your dad," says Fiona. "Does he keep the heads of the animals he kills for trophies? Or the antlers perhaps?"

I feel the blood drain from my face, and then rush up again to my cheeks. I look down at my hands, wishing I could crawl under the table.

"Not always," I say.

"But sometimes?"

I clear my throat. "Sometimes."

"So there is an element of sport to it, you might say."

"You might say."

"It's not simply a matter of putting food on the table."

I nod, miserably. Now I've really done it. I should have lied. I've done it now.

Tim says that we're going to run out of time if we don't get to Heinrich's question. Thank God. He asks Fiona if she has anything to add. She keeps her head down as she furiously makes notes on the paper in front of her.

"Nothing to add," says Fiona, glancing up at me, smiling.

"For the final portion of the interview," says Heinrich, handing me a piece of paper, "we want you to look at these three questions. Take a minute. Read through the questions carefully. Choose the question that you feel best prepared to answer."

I start to read the questions.

1. Should Canada extradite criminals to countries for which the death penalty is law?

There it is. The word. *Extradite.* From the context of the sentence, I can figure out what it means: export, deport – force to leave, basically. I don't think that the committee actually cares much about the extradition issue. They want to know my feelings about capital punishment. Which is a touchy subject. And I've had enough of touchy subjects. I think that I'd better stay away from question one.

"Whenever you're ready," says Heinrich.

2. Give a brief explanation of the Meech Lake Accord and the con-

troversy surrounding Meech Lake in contemporary Canadian political affairs.

Meech Lake. It's been in the papers. Mr. Kaushal and I haven't gotten around to talking about it, though. Meech Lake, I think, has something to do with Quebec – or is it Native people? Maybe both, I can't be sure. It's probably best to stay away from Meech Lake altogether.

"All set?" says Heinrich, drumming his fingers on the table.

I shake my head. I think he's enjoying this, watching me squirm.

3. Define genocide. Provide an example. What punishment, in your opinion, is appropriate for perpetrators of genocidal crimes?

This could be the one. Genocide is mass murder. Example: World War II, Hitler. The Jews. Simple. But what about the punishment? If I bring up "an eye for an eye," then I'm opening the discussion to capital punishment again – and I don't want to go there.

I try to think of a better example of genocide, one that won't lead to the death penalty issue. The Beothuck in Newfoundland. Perfect. Their genocide happened so long ago that there's no one left to punish anymore. Punishment is a non-issue. It's just a terrible tragedy, a horrific chapter in Canadian history. The End.

And if someone on the committee asks me for details about the Beothuck people? I know that they lived in Newfoundland. Or New Brunswick. Nova Scotia maybe? They were killed in the 1800s, I know that. Or maybe in the 1700s. Who killed them? I wonder. The French or the English?

"Anytime now!" says Heinrich.

"All right," I say. "I'll take the genocide question, number three."

Still unsure of how to proceed, I swivel back and forth – left to right – in my chair. My foot bumps up against the guitar case beside me. My guitar. I'd forgotten about it. I brought it along with me, I really should *do* something with it.

"Genocide is the wholesale annihilation of a group of people for religious or political reasons. The Jews in World War II, for instance – well, Hitler's campaign against them, I should say – that's genocide. Or the Beothuck people of – of eastern Canada, who were wiped out completely by the – um – European invaders. That's genocide."

I reach down to my guitar case, lift out my guitar.

"Actually," I continue, "all Native peoples in Canada and the United States were victims of genocide. They still *are* victims – when you think about it – of an ongoing genocide, really."

Then I start plucking broken minor chords. One long A-minor arpeggio, one long D-minor arpeggio – brief E⁷ and back to A-minor. The chord progression is melancholy, plaintive. Mournful.

"It's not that we're murdering First Nations people outright. No, of course not. We're more subtle than that. We're perpetrators of a sort of *cultural* genocide."

"Yes," says Tim. "It's like apartheid. You made that point earlier."

I'm repeating myself. Oh dear.

As I pluck the guitar strings, trying desperately to think of something else to say without looking panicked, it strikes me that the A-minor, D-minor, E⁷ progression is the chord structure of a hundred Ukrainian songs. I'm an expert on Ukrainian people.

"Then again," I say, "cultural genocide in Canada takes different forms; it comes in different degrees. My own family – my people, the Ukrainians – we've experienced our own persecution over the last century. Culturally, I mean."

I change from plucking to strumming – softly, still – the same chord progression.

"When my parents and my aunts and my uncles were young, in the thirties and forties, they weren't permitted to speak Ukrainian at school. The teacher expected them to speak English but most of them didn't know *how*. They spoke Ukrainian at home. The teacher strapped them at school when they spoke

Ukrainian; the other kids called them names. My parents and their generation, they grew up ashamed of who they were, and of who their parents were. Ashamed of their food, their religion – everything. Their whole way of life. So they raised us to be English, thinking we wouldn't have to be ashamed, then. They gave us English names. They hardly ever spoke to us in Ukrainian."

For a moment, I stop playing my guitar. I haven't thought through what I'm saying but I have to keep on.

"We've all taken Ukrainian dancing lessons. My sister, my brother, me. At Easter time, we make *pysanky*. Ukrainian was even offered as a second language at school, for a while. Sometimes, though, I think – so what? I can't talk to my grandparents. They only speak Ukrainian. I can't read Ukrainian books, or Ukrainian poetry, or Ukrainian newspapers, or Ukrainian magazines."

"If I had more time," I continue, "then maybe I would tell you about my friend. Her name is – her name was Sister Maria, and she was my piano teacher. I can't tell you about all of the things she taught me, even when we were just talking, or listening to music together, or having a cup of tea. But I can tell you about one thing. Sister Maria had a project that was always on her mind. She was trying to collect music that was written by a group of Ukrainian composers. Composers who were killed because of what they believed in – like Dmytro Bortniansky, and Lev Revutsky. Mykola Lysenko, Kyrylo Stetsenko, Vasyl Barvinsky."

"So that's one kind of genocide right there. Sister Maria told me how horrible it was. They were murdered, or they died in concentration camps, or they killed themselves. A lot of their music was destroyed. Only – you see, I think there's more to it than that. Because, like I said, I'm Ukrainian. But until Sister Maria told me about these composers, I didn't know that they existed. I'd never heard of them. They're part of my history, and my parents' history, and my grandparents' history. Why didn't any of us know their stories? It's as though the worst genocide of all isn't killing people, it's taking away their history."

I start strumming again and this time I sing along. I sing *Vichnaia Pam'iat* just like I sang it for Sister Maria. The same words, over and over again. The same melody, slow and sombre and dark. It's a repeat performance after all, though I'm singing alone this time. The committee members are silent while I sing. Craig nods in time with the music, Gena wipes her eyes.

When I've finished the song, when my guitar strings have stopped ringing, I look around the room at all the committee members.

"Do you know what the words mean?" I ask.

Tim shakes his head. J.J. drops her eyes. Heinrich says, "No."

"*Vichnaia pam'iat* means everlasting memory. Memory everlasting. It's a song for the dead, for a funeral. At least, that's what my mother tells me. I can sing dozens of Ukrainian songs because I memorize them phonetically. The funny thing is, though, if you were to ask me what the words mean, I couldn't tell you."

I put my guitar back into its case.

"And I don't know how we'd punish people for that kind of genocide. I don't know where we'd begin."

The interview ends with another round of hand-shaking – "thank you's" and "goodbye's" and "good luck's." As Tim escorts me to the door of the interview room, he says that the committee will make their decision within the next fourteen days. Successful candidates will be contacted by phone; others will receive letters in the mail.

I think I'll be getting a letter.

Waiting for the elevator to take me to the main floor of the office building, I hear Caroline warming up on her violin. She plays scales first, then arpeggios, then part of a piece – a concerto, probably – filled with sixteenth notes runs and trills.

The elevator doors open. A father and his son – another candidate – emerge, both in suits and ties and shiny shoes. I wish the son luck as I get into the elevator.

"Break a leg!" I say, before the doors close.

As the elevator takes me to the ground floor, I look up, wondering if Sister Maria can see me now. I think she can.

Maybe it doesn't matter so much that I screwed up the interview. At least I taught the people in the room something that they didn't know before.

And I learned something, too. Since Sister Maria died, I haven't talked about her to anyone. I haven't been able to say her name without breaking down. Until today, that is. It felt so good to tell the committee about her — even if I didn't have time to say much; even though I couldn't tell them her whole story.

I'm beginning to think that Sister Maria is still here. She's gone, but she hasn't left. She's just with me in a different way now. It's going to take some getting used to, and it's going to be hard. Remembering her makes my heart ache. Forgetting would be easier. I'll take it one step at a time.

I said her name today.

That's a start.

EIGHT

I get the letter near the end of grade eleven. *We regret to inform you.... Although your application was very.... Unfortunately we cannot offer....* I don't bother reading all of it. I don't need to. I knew what it said before I even opened the envelope.

When Mom and Dad ask to read it, I tell them that they can't. I've crumpled it up and thrown it away, along with all of the UWC brochures and information booklets that I collected over the past few months. As far as I'm concerned, the application and the interview never happened.

So I go into grade twelve like everybody else. It's just as well. I don't have to worry about making new friends. I can keep my old locker in the English Wing, next to Dad's classroom. In September, I settle back into my old timetable – English, social studies, math. Nothing ever changes much at Regional. Same place, same faces. Same routine. The only difference between this year and last year is that I'm not in Mr. Schultz's class anymore. Dad has arranged for me to practise the piano in the auditorium at Regional while everyone else is in Band. I'm trying to finish grade ten piano on my own. If I do, I'll get credit for it – as though I were in Mr. Schultz's class.

My piano lessons are on hold, though, until I go away to Edmonton next year. I've decided to apply for the Bachelor of Music program at the University of Alberta. I'll have a new teacher – a professor – for private lessons twice a week, plus classes in history, ear training, and theory. There's no point trying to find someone to replace Sister Maria as long as I'm living in St. Paul. I'll only be here for another year.

Once in awhile, when I'm alone in my bedroom, I catch myself staring at the spot on the floor, between my bed and the wall, where I used to keep Sister Maria's boxes. A few weeks ago, I moved her boxes into the bottom of my closet. For a couple of days, I left the doors open. Lately, though, I've been keeping them closed. It's hard enough trying to work on the pieces we were preparing for my grade ten piano exam – hard enough seeing her writing in the margins of my music. *Softer! Watch your tempo! Let the melody soar like a bird in flight!* I miss her so much. More than I thought possible. I'm determined to finish grade ten, but I'm not ready to look through her papers. Not yet.

As long as I'm in St. Paul, I'm supposed to make an effort to enjoy myself, make the most of my grade twelve year. I'm supposed to do more socializing outside of school with people my own age. That's what Mom and Dad tell me at the beginning of the school year. They think I'm too serious. I've got my nose in the books too much. I'm missing out on dances and parties and boyfriends – all of the normal teenager stuff. I need to go out more. I should be staying out late. Dad says that I can help myself to his liquor cabinet, as long as I'm responsible about it. I'm almost eighteen anyway, and all the kids drink at parties. Mom says that I don't need to worry about curfews. "Just call if you're going to be out late," she says, "to let us know that you're all right." I must be the only teenager on earth with parents who want me to stay out all night, and go to parties, and drink.

I get the feeling that Dad talks to Mr. Kaushal about me, and that Mom calls Mrs. Paulichuk and Yolande Yuzko. Because, suddenly, Mr. Kaushal doesn't have time to eat lunch with me in the cafeteria. All of a sudden he has marking to do – every single noon hour – or staff meetings. Then, out of the blue, Kirsten and Tanya invite me over to their table in the cafeteria. It can't be their idea.

I've never been part of their group in high school. They ask me to go shopping with them after school. They want me to go to beer-fests with them on the weekend, and to the bar. I'm not interested. I wouldn't know how to act. I think Kirsten and Tanya are relieved when I turn them down. I'd probably cramp their style.

"At least graduation," says Mom one day over supper. "At least get into the spirit of graduation. I want you to go to the banquet with your friends. Maybe you could help plan it. Join the Graduation Committee."

I snort.

Plans for graduation at Regional start early. The ceremonies and the banquet take place in June, but the Grad Committee is organized in September so that the students in grade twelve have time to do fundraising to pay for the caterer, the decorations, and a DJ for the dance. As far as I'm concerned, it's all a joke. Even though the Grad Committee spends all year planning the banquet – and even though girls spend hundreds of dollars on their graduation gowns – nobody actually stays for the dance. Grad coincides every year with Rodeo Weekend in St. Paul. After the meal and the speeches are over, all the grads race out of the school gym so that they can change out of their gowns and tuxedos, into jeans and cowboy boots. Then they head over to the Rodeo Beerfest at the Rec. Centre across town. Sometimes they don't even stay for the speeches.

Mom says, "If you don't go to graduation, I'll go to –"

"I know," I say, rolling my eyes. "I know. You'll go to your grave with a broken heart."

"You might change your mind," says Dad.

I snort again. Fat chance of that happening.

I didn't count on being obliged to go to graduation.

After the first semester's grades are tallied, in early February, the grade twelve student with the highest average is named Valedictorian of the graduating class. And he – or, in my case, she – has to give a speech at the banquet. I don't actually have a choice about going to Grad. I have to go. I'm the Valedictorian.

Mom is thrilled. Three months in advance, she makes me an appointment with her hairdresser for the morning of Grad. She books one of the other teachers at her school – Mrs. Stefansyk, who sells Mary Kay – to do my makeup. Between February and May, Mom takes me to Edmonton three times to look at grad gowns. We spend three whole weekends in the city, overnighting at Sophie's place, before we find the perfect dress. Three weekends of fighting in various malls, in a dozen different dress shops. I refuse to spend more than a hundred dollars on my dress; Mom thinks we should spend no less than five. I want something simple, possibly short, preferably black. Mom wants a gown with satin and lace – full-length, with a hoop or a crinoline – in any colour except black. Maybe mauve. Or powder pink. Or fuchsia.

We finally settle on a navy blue satin dress. Long, but not puffy. Originally six hundred dollars, on sale for half-price.

But when Mom starts talking about what type of corsage I should have, and how we should make sure that my escort's bow tie and cummerbund match my dress, I put my foot down. No more compromising. I'm going to Grad alone. I'm not going to ask some guy I hardly know to escort me to Grad just because everyone else goes in couples. It's silly. Mom says that I could ask somebody in my class, like Henry Popowich, or one of the Babiuk twins. She says that I could ask my cousin Wayne or my cousin Darrell. I say that I'd rather not go at all than go on a boy's arm. I'd rather die than take one of my cousins.

I'm more concerned about my speech than anything else. The valedictory address is the highlight of the whole banquet.

Deep down, I sort of like the idea of being the star of the show. The problem is that I'm used to singing in front of crowds, not talking. I wonder if I should memorize my speech, or write it out on recipe cards. How long should it be? I don't want to talk too long. I'll lose the attention of the crowd. But it can't be too short, either. It has to be profound, thought-provoking – funny at times – and, ultimately, heartwarming. I'm just not sure if I can pull it off.

Eventually, I go to Dad for advice. He's always giving speeches, plus he's been to lots of grads over the years.

"Basically," he says, "there's a formula to it. You talk about the twelve-year journey you and your friends have been taking, and how you were helped along the way by your parents, your teachers, and each other. Thank the parents. Thank the teachers. Thank the friends. Then say something about how the journey isn't really over. You're just at a crossroads now, and it's time to pick a fork in the road."

I try to think of another metaphor. Something other than a journey. Something more original. We've been building a house, and now it's time to move in – or move out? No good. What does the house really represent? We've been on a quest to find the holy grail of success and we've finally found it. Dumb. A high school diploma isn't anything like a holy grail. It's just a high school diploma. We've been swimming down the great river of life, and now it's time to hit the open water. Forget it. The crowd will think about rough waters, stormy seas. Drowning.

I decide to stick with the journey metaphor. It might not be original, but it works the best. And I'm going to quote from the Robert Frost poem, "The Road Not Taken." Dad says that it's a nice touch.

Graduation day, I have to admit, is exciting. I try to play it cool, like I'm not really interested in all the hype, but it's not easy. I feel like I'm about to get married. Our house is filled with relatives on Saturday morning, and everyone is all dressed up. I have to leave periodically to have my hair done, my nails, my makeup. Dad takes pictures of me in my gown. Sophie is like the maid of honour, fussing with the straps of my dress, helping me get into the car without creasing the satin. Mom has tears in her eyes as we enter the church.

In the afternoon, before the banquet, there is a ceremony in the cathedral for all the graduands and their guests. We don't actually have to do anything. We just sit in the pews while the priests and the minister bless everyone. It's not just a Catholic service. And it's not just in English, either. Father Levasseur does the French part of the ceremony, then a minister from the United Church talks in English for a while. A Ukrainian Orthodox priest is on hand, complete with his smoking ball of incense. Plus two Native elders from Saddle Lake, who chant in Cree while they burn sweetgrass.

Three Native students from Saddle Lake are graduating – Joe Jr., Clifford Jackson, and Monica Whitford. Mr. Kaushal and my dad made sure that elders would be included in the graduation ceremonies.

I try to focus on what's going on in the church, but my mind keeps wandering back to the last time I was in the cathedral, a year ago, for Sister Maria's funeral. It feels like yesterday. It feels like no time has passed at all. The smell of stargazer lilies comes back to me – so strongly that I can't believe there aren't bouquets of them next to my pew. It's as though her casket is open in front of me. As though her funeral is happening all over again.

From the church, we go straight to the gym for the banquet, one long row of cars snaking its way down main street toward the school. More like a funeral than a wedding.

In a way, too, it feels like we're on the movie set of a John Wayne western. Because it's Rodeo Weekend, and when it's Rodeo Weekend, the whole town gets into the rodeo spirit. There are cowboy murals on storefront windows, hay bales in front of the grocery stores and gas stations and all around the pad for the UFO. DJ's from CFCW blare country music from their van parked beside the office of the *St. Paul Journal*. People walking around town are dressed in blue jeans and plaid shirts, cowboy boots and ten-gallon hats. I half expect to see horses tied up in the parking lot of the high school.

But we're back into wedding world once we get to the gym. There are long rectangular tables covered in white paper, streamers and balloons, a stage for the DJ, and a dance floor for the dance. It's exactly like a wedding. It even smells like a wedding; like cabbage rolls, garlic sausage, and roast chicken. Everywhere I look, the grad committee members have hung banners that say "Grad '89."

After we eat, all of the grads leave the gym. We line up outside the gym doors while we wait for the principal to announce our names. Then, one at a time, as our names are called, we walk up through an aisle between the tables, over a little bridge, under an archway of fake flowers, and onto the stage. Frankly, I'm a little disappointed that we don't get to wear black gowns and mortarboards — mortarboards at the very least, so that the principal can move the tassel from one side to the other, symbolizing our transformation from graduands to graduates. He just shakes our hands, instead, and passes each of us our diploma.

The whole thing happens fairly quickly — there are only sixty of us — so, before long, it's time for my speech.

Which is, without a doubt, one of the finest valedictory addresses in Regional High School history. I practised it so many times that I hardly need to look at my notes. I enunciate all my words, and pause at all the right spots. I speak with feeling.

Dad squeezes my shoulders when I return to my seat. Mom gives me a big hug. All of my relatives are smiling and nodding. Before the dance starts, Mr. Kaushal comes over to our table to congratulate me on a job well done. Even Mr. Maletski shakes my hand. And Mrs. Webster says that she appreciated my reference to the Frost poem.

But I still feel like a fool.

When I ask Sophie if she could see the reactions of my classmates to my speech, I'm reminded of why I didn't want to go to Grad in the first place. Sophie says that only a handful of them actually heard it. By the time I got to the podium, most of the grads were already out the door, on their way home to change for the Rodeo Beerfest.

Of course. I should have known.

My aunts and uncles try to tell me that it's nothing.

"Their loss," says Uncle Harry.

"Don't even give it a second thought," says Auntie Natalka.

"*We* heard your speech," says Auntie Mary. "And that's all that counts."

They don't understand. I wanted my classmates to hear. I wanted to impress them. It's not enough that my family heard, and my teachers. I was supposed to walk off the stage, and all the other grads were supposed to cheer. I thought they'd give me a standing ovation.

Waiting in the women's washroom for Sophie to come out of the stall before we head home in her car, I look at my reflection in the mirror. I look like a clown, with my clown makeup and my curly clown hair.

I just need red lipstick and black eyeliner to complete the costume. Around my lips, I'd draw a big red frown. Under my eyes, I'd draw two little black tears.

I don't know why I let my family talk me into going to the Rodeo Beerfest with Sophie. I should know better. When we get home, and all the aunts and uncles are having a drink with Mom and Dad, Sophie pours me a stiff rum and coke. It's probably the rum and coke that does it. I drink it too fast, too eager to forget what happened at the banquet. And then my defences are down. I can't fight back properly.

"You're the Valedictorian," says Sophie, passing me my drink. "You should go out and celebrate."

I shake my head.

"We'll go together," she says. "It'll be fun! Just pretend the whole speech-thing never happened. Show your friends that you're bigger than them."

"Maybe I'm not."

"Come on. You never go out anywhere."

"So?"

"So let loose for once in your life. I'll drive."

"Maybe next time."

"There won't *be* a next time!"

After awhile, Mom and Dad join in. They say that they'll pay for my admission to the Beerfest, and for Sophie's. They'll give us spending money for drinks.

"It's on us," they say. *"We'll* drive you. Call us when you're ready to come home, and we'll pick you up."

I shake my head again and again. I'd rather stay home and visit with the family.

Then the aunts and uncles get involved.

"Go, go!" they say.

"You're young. You shouldn't be at home with the old people."

"Go! Do some dancing, Maybe you'll meet someone. Some nice boy. Who knows?"

I tell them that, even if I wanted to go to the Beerfest, I'm not quite old enough. I'm only seventeen, and you have to be eighteen to get in.

Dad waves his hand as if to say, "Never mind." He says that some of his buddies from the Old Timer Hockey Team are selling tickets at the door and selling liquor inside the Rec. Centre.

"You're my daughter. They're not going to say a word to you."

In the car on the way into St. Paul, I sulk. I tell Sophie that if the Beerfest is boring, we're going home. And it probably will be boring. So then I tell Dad that we'll probably be phoning him as soon as he gets home, and then he'll just have to turn around and come right back.

They both laugh, as though it's a big joke.

Dad is right. His friends are working at the door, and selling liquor tickets, and pouring drinks at the bar. Ron Stranadka and Bill Chornohus stamp our hands in the foyer of the Rec. Centre. We buy liquor tickets from Dan Zarowny and his brother Dave. Gerry Bidulock hands us our drinks.

The crowd is a mixture of familiar faces – lots of grads – and people Sophie and I have never seen before. We find a spot at an empty table near the dance floor between a bunch of Junior B Canadiens – hockey players who graduated with Sophie two years ago but who still live in St. Paul – and a group of bona fide cowboys in town for the rodeo. The hockey players are already drunk, they're loud and rowdy. Their table is covered with empty beer bottles; some of them are drinking straight rye. All of them are smoking Colts. The cowboy table is quiet. It's hard to see their faces under their cowboy hats but a few of them appear to be chewing snuff and spitting yellowish-brown saliva into plastic cups.

Before Sophie even sits down, one of the hockey players, Andy Kostiniuk, approaches her. I give her a pleading look so that she won't leave me by myself. She gets up to dance anyway.

"Just one song," she says.

Sophie and Andy dance for the duration of my first drink. I get a second drink – rum and coke again, best not to mix – and I sip it slowly, trying to make it last.

I finish my second drink. Sophie is dancing with another hockey player now, Bobby MacTavish. She waves at me from the dance floor.

On my way to the bar for my third drink, I think that I catch someone looking at me. An older man, maybe twenty or twenty-five. His is one of the faces I've never seen before. On my way back to our table, third drink in hand, I'm sure of it: I'm *sure* that he's looking at me. He's a rodeo contestant, obviously. A real cowboy. Maybe he's a bull rider. His face is tanned leathery brown; his boots look old and scuffed. He wears Wranglers, snug and well-worn – there are faded creases in the denim around his crotch.

Very manly. Black cowboy hat, and no wedding band.

I guess I'll say yes if he asks me to dance. He's nice looking. And the idea of dancing with a cowboy is kind of romantic. Probably when he asks me, we won't even exchange words. He'll just take me by the hand and lead me to the dance floor.

My cowboy takes a swig of his beer. Adjusts his hat. Starts walking slowly, nonchalantly, across the Rec. Centre floor. Toward me, unmistakably. His legs aren't nearly as bowed as the legs of the other cowboys. As my cowboy gets closer, I down my drink for courage. I haven't liked anyone since Corey, in Dauphin, and that was years ago.

Closer.

What if the band starts playing a slow song?

Closer.

My heart races. He might kiss me right there on the dance floor.

The cowboy tips his hat. At me.

And then I feel a tap on my shoulder. I hear a familiar voice saying, "Hi C'lleen. Wanna dance? You look kinda lonely sitting here all by yourself."

My cowboy veers left, heads toward the bar. Sure enough, the band starts to play a slow song, "Amarillo By Morning," and I'm stuck in the sweaty clutches of Wendel Kotowich. Wendel Kotowich, my old Ukrainian dancing partner. Wendel with chubby, chipmunk cheeks and a bowl haircut and clusters of pimples around his nostrils.

Wendel, as it turns out, has a hundred things to tell me and we end up dancing to four songs in a row. Did I know that he's moving to Olds to study meat-cutting at the college there? Did I know that Brad Trachuk and Jodie Sosnowski are going out? Did I hear about the whole mess with Carla Senko and her grandpa? I nod miserably, trying to spot my cowboy in the crowd – and losing him in a set of cowboy hats by the bar.

The rumour is that Carla Senko's grandfather has been sexually abusing her. She was living at the Crisis Centre for awhile because her parents kicked her out for pressing charges against him. But then Carla dropped the charges, and now she's moved back home again.

Wendel talks and talks.

Did I know that Wendel's older brother Glen is playing drums with the band onstage? Did I know that they're thinking about touring around? That they might be recording an album? On and on Wendel talks, hardly stopping to breathe. With all the talking he's doing, it's a wonder he doesn't miss a step or slip out of time. But Wendel is a good dancer, I'll give him that. He was born to dance.

"They go by the name of Jerry Garwasiuk and Sons," says Wendel, as we lean against a wall listening to the band. "Though the old man doesn't play anymore, just the Garwasiuk boys. No market for old-time Ukrainian music. No one wants to hear fiddles and *tsymbaly* anymore. It's all top-40 country and rock and roll."

"That's Donald Garwasiuk on lead guitar," he says, pointing to the lead singer of the band. "My brother Glen says he's a real perfectionist. Kind of a control freak. Hard to work with. George Garwasiuk plays rhythm, he's the youngest. Nice guy that George. Real people-person. Martin Garwasiuk's the bass player. And, of course, there's my brother Glen behind the drum kit. He's a good drummer, isn't he?"

Wendel looks really proud of his brother.

But I'm ready to ditch Wendel now. Enough is *enough*. I didn't come here to spend the night with Wendel Kotowich.

I tell him that I've got to get a drink.

He says that he'll get one for me.

I tell him that I need some air so I'm going to take a little walk.

He says that he'll walk with me.

I tell him that I need to go to the washroom.

He says, "Me too."

"*Jesus* Wendel," I say. "If I didn't know better, I'd think that you *like* me or something."

Wendel looks uncomfortable. He shifts his weight from one leg to the other. He might even be blushing.

"Wendel," I say, "are you blushing?"

Out of the blue, Wendel tries to kiss me, pulling me awkwardly toward him and tilting his head to the side – like in the movies. Now would be the time for my cowboy to appear out of nowhere, knock Wendel out in one blow, then kiss me himself.

No cowboy appears. Wendel's breath stinks of garlic. I whack him across the head with my open hand.

I look for Sophie at our table, by the bar, in the foyer of the Rec. Centre. She's nowhere to be found. Into the ladies' washroom I go, sure to find her reapplying lipstick or fixing her hair – or both. When I find her, I'm going to tell her that I'm heading home. Wendel Kotowich. Of all people. Wendel Kotowich. Likes *me*. It's definitely time to go.

I peek under the door of each stall in the ladies' washroom, looking for Sophie's leg. I call out her name. At first, there's no reply. But then a voice from within one of the stalls starts to mimic me.

"Soooo-phie. Soooo-phie."

Carla Senko emerges from the corner stall, hair tousled, mascara smudged under her eyes. She stands beside the washroom sinks with her hands on her hips.

"Colleen Loose-sack," she says, slurring her words. "Long time no see."

Carla is thin. Thinner than the last time I saw her, two months ago, before she dropped out of school. There are dark circles under her eyes, her cheeks are sunken. There's a long brown stain down the front of her shirt where she's spilled a drink.

"Carla."

I don't know what else to say. Since the incident with the French project, we've hardly spoken to each other. That was three years ago. Face to face with her here, in the bathroom, all I can think about are the rumours about her grandfather. She looks terrible.

"How are you?" I ask.

"Pissed," says Carla, trying to wipe off the mascara under her eyes. "I'm totally pissed."

While Carla talks, she sways – nearly falling over, once. I reach out to grab her arm, to keep her from hurting herself, but she shakes my hand away.

"Get away from me!"

As I leave the washroom, I can hear Carla talking to herself – about me, I think.

"Little princess." It sounds like *"lil priss-ess."*

Wendel is waiting for me outside the ladies' washroom but I charge past him, pretending not to hear him as he calls out my name. I need to find Sophie. Wendel runs after me.

"Colleen," he says, grabbing my arm. "Colleen! I'm sorry. Listen, I'm really sorry, I was way out of line. I'm sorry."

"It's okay, Wendel," I say, yanking my arm away from him. "Really, it's *okay*, it's fine. I've already forgotten about it."

I start walking swiftly toward the doors of the Rec. Centre. Maybe Sophie is outside. Maybe she's making out with one of the hockey players in the parking lot.

"Wait up," says Wendel. "Listen. I've talked to the guys. I've arranged for you to sing a song with them. Up on stage. You and the band. It's your big chance to sing for a big crowd."

I stop dead in my tracks.

"I don't *want* to get onstage! I don't even want to *be* here!"

Wendel looks devastated. "I thought you'd like it. I thought it would be like a dream come –"

"We're going to take a little break, but don't you go anywhere. When we come back we're going to have local celebrity, songstress Colleen Lutzak onstage!"

As Donald Garwasiuk, the band leader, speaks into the microphone, Wendel pulls me by the arm across the dance floor, toward the stage.

"Just *one* song," he says. "Come on. You've got to do it. They're *asking* for you."

"I don't think this is a very good idea," I say to Donald as we shake hands on the side of the stage.

"Wendel tells me you're a great singer."

"I've mostly been singing at weddings and funerals, Ukrainian songs. Nothing the crowd could dance to, nothing – you know – upbeat."

"Not a problem," says Martin, the bass player. "We can do a Ukrainian song or two, and we're about due for a slow song anyway. What have you got?"

My mind goes blank. I can't think of a single song I know – fast or slow. I glare at Wendel.

George suggests *"Kazala meni maty,"* but I don't know all the words. He says that *"Oi divchyno"* could make for a good waltz. I'm not crazy about it. He says that *"Balamut"* is an old standard, everyone knows *"Balamut."*

Donald shakes his head at George's last suggestion. "Too many chord changes in the chorus. We couldn't do it without a rehearsal."

"Don't you know any country?" Martin asks. "Tanya Tucker, Crystal Gayle. Anne Murray. The kind of stuff they play on CFCW?"

When I tell the band members that I know a few Johnny Cash tunes, the guys all laugh. I don't know what's so funny.

"And a couple of Merle Haggard songs," I say.

"Has to be a *girl*-song," says Donald. The other guys in the band nod in unison.

By now, I'm ready to give up. Wendel is grinning at me from across the dance floor, as though he has single-handedly made all my dreams come true. Sophie, for all I know, is having sex in some hockey player's car.

I thank the band for trying. I say, "Well, maybe another time –"

"How about the Judds?" says George Garwasiuk, interrupting me. "'Why Not Me' or – what's that other tune of theirs?"

"'Rockin' to the Rhythm of the Rain,'" says Martin. "That's a good tune. You know that one?"

As it happens, I've just sung a Judds song at Uncle Charlie's 65th birthday party in Two Hills. Not "Why Not Me" or "Rockin' to the Rhythm of the Rain," but a Judds song nonetheless. I give them the song title. They can play it. At last, a song that we all know.

We take a minute or two to go over the order of verses and refrains. Donald unplugs his guitar and we all cluster around him while he runs through the song. He's playing in E, I notice. I sing the song in A.

"I don't mean to be difficult, but actually I'd prefer to do the song in the key of A if it's not too much trouble."

"The Judds do it in E," says Donald.

"Well, the Judds have higher voices than I do. *Way* higher voices. To sing their stuff I sort of *have* to key down. It's just three chords anyway. Four, I guess, if you throw the minor into the refrain."

I take a second to transpose in my head.

"A, D, and E," I say. "Those are the chords. Simple three-chord song. And then a quick B-minor at the end of the refrain, if you want."

The guys all frown. Who would think that one minor chord would bring about such long faces?

"Of course, we *could* drop the minor chord altogether. That would simplify things. It's really up to you. Doesn't matter to me. You decide."

In fact, I know that the minor chord is crucial − take it out and the whole poignancy of the song goes with it. But I'm willing to compromise just to get this show on the road. It feels as though we've been negotiating for half an hour at least.

"We can do it in A," says Donald. "Problem *is,* if we do the song in A then we've got to scrap the riff that comes at the beginning and at the end and between all the verses. *This* riff," he says, playing it in E. "You can only play the riff in E. It doesn't work in A. Only a guitar player would know that."

"May I?"

I snatch Donald's guitar out of his hands and play the riff in A. Flawlessly.

"To play the riff in A, you just have to be creative. It gives your fingers a little workout, but it *can* be done."

I play it a second time.

"Then again," I say, "you could always play in E and set your capo on the fifth fret. Of course, if you use the capo, then you run the risk of playing a quarter tone sharp or flat."

I snap the capo onto the fretboard and play the riff in E.

"Can you hear that? *Ever*-so-slightly flat. Just enough to hurt the ears. Well. The capo's the easy way out, isn't it? The lazy-man's transposer. I try not to use a capo if I can help it."

I try to hand Donald's guitar back to him.

"Go ahead and play it yourself," he says, turning his back to me. "I'm going to get a drink."

Glen counts us into the song by hitting his drumsticks together. One, two, three –

He's counting us in too fast.

I can do one of two things: grin and bear it, and muddle my way through the song at top speed; or stop him now and get it right. Four bars in, I make my decision. I step away from the mike and wave my arms for the band to stop.

"Glen, could you play it a little slower?"

Glen starts hitting his drumsticks together again. Still too fast.

To hell with it, I think. Ignoring Glen, I count the song in properly. Martin and George – and Glen, too, thank God – follow my count.

In a matter of seconds, the dance floor fills with bodies, all of them moving counter-clockwise in time with the music, almost in unison. If we sped up the song now, they would all dance faster. If we slowed down to a crawl, they would crawl with us. Most of the couples careen past the stage without so much as a second glance at us; they seem to take their dancing very seriously. Some of the dancers, though, recognize me as they shuffle along. People from my grad class. Greg Pederson and Cheryl Popowich give me the thumbs-up; Sarah Matwychuk wriggles out of Luc Langevin's arms to momentarily applaud. As I sing the first line of the refrain – the line about lovers falling in love and staying in love – I see Kirsten Paulichuk and Myles Litwinski strolling onto the dance floor. I see Sophie waving to me from the Junior B table, grinning from ear to ear. I smile back, sing louder.

The song is all about the good old days. How people used to keep their promises, and families used to pray together, and daddies never went away.

I know the next words, they're easy. But at the end of the refrain, I step away from the mike. I can't continue. Carla Senko is in the crowd. Near the back of the Rec. Centre, she is leaning against a wall, staring at the stage – staring at me. I wasn't thinking. "Grandpa." Of all the songs I could have chosen, of all the songs I could have sung. The words are addressed to Grandpa, who is supposed to know all about right and wrong. No one deserves this, not even Carla Senko.

When it comes time for me to start the second verse, I don't know what to do. I could stop the song altogether. Make up a new set of words, on the spot? Impossible. I pause on the A chord for several bars as I think. The band follows my lead. They stay on A, waiting for me to sing.

After six bars of the A chord, George moves close to me on stage. He whispers in my ear that it's okay.

"Just sing the first verse again."

Now Carla is on the dance floor. And in the split second that it takes for me to recognize her dance partner, I start singing again. The first verse of "Grandpa," all over again. Carla is dancing with the cowboy in the black hat. *My* cowboy. Not just dancing with him, *flaunting* him – pulling him up toward the stage, so that I can't miss what's going on. I send my voice like an arrow, clearly enunciating the word "grandpa" over and over again. So that Carla can't miss what I'm saying.

Carla drops her hand from the small of the cowboy's back to the back pocket of his Wrangler's. She must have seen me look at him, earlier. She must know that I like him. Hovering in front of the stage, Carla nestles up close to the cowboy. As I come to the end of the final refrain, she starts kissing his neck.

After we've finished the song and I've left the stage, the band starts up again, without me. Wendel is at the bar, getting a drink for me, I'm sure. Sophie is still with the hockey players.

As I make my way through the crowd toward Sophie, Carla steps in front of me, forcing me stop and talk to her. In one hand, she holds a cigarette. The cowboy in the black hat is beside her, holding her other hand.

"Did you sing that song just for me?"

She says the words sweetly but her stare is cold and hard. The cowboy's hand brushes her breasts as he wraps his arms around her waist.

Carla Senko doesn't wait for an answer. She leads the cowboy away, flicking her cigarette in my direction as they move toward the foyer. Now that I've seen the cowboy's face – seen it up close – I change my mind about him. There are deep creases around his eyes, patches of grey hair under his hat. He's older than twenty. Much older. He must be fifty, at least. Carla is eighteen. What is she doing with him?

For second, I watch Carla's cigarette smoulder on the dance floor before I crush it with the heel of my boot. Then the room starts spinning. I feel sick. Like I'm going to throw up any second. And I don't think it's just the drinks.

Wendel appears at my side with two drinks in his hands, asking if I'd like to dance. I shake my head.

"I'm sorry, Wendel. I can't stay."

I need to find my sister.

I need to end this night.

I need to go home.

PART III

Edmonton/
St. Paul

ONE

I can't sleep in Edmonton. At least not at night. As soon as I start to doze, something outside my window wakes me up again — the sounds of sirens, horns honking. City buses roaring down the street. I see every hour on the new clock radio next to my new bed. I try wrapping my pillow around my ears, pulling the covers over my head. I just can't block out the noise.

Daytime is even noisier. There's more traffic, plus our upstairs neighbours listen to music and stomp around in their apartment in their shoes. Sophie says that our building is quiet compared to other buildings she's lived in. But I hear everything that goes on above us, and on either side of us. Water running, toilets flushing. Telephones ringing. I usually lie down around two or three in the afternoon, and sleep until suppertime. Not because our building suddenly gets quiet. I'm just so tired from not sleeping at night that I can't keep my eyes open anymore.

Sophie says that I'll adjust to the noise in no time. I'm not so sure. I don't think I'll ever get used to it.

Mom and Dad move Sophie and me into our apartment near the beginning of August, which gives us a few weeks to get settled before classes start. Dad wants Sophie to show me around campus, to make sure that I know where all of my classes are. He asks her to help me register for my courses and give me a hand buying my textbooks. Mom says that we should go grocery shopping once a week, so that there's always food in the fridge. She suggests that we take turns making supper every night. That we draw up a schedule for housecleaning and laundry.

I can't wait for school to start. I know that I'm going to love university. Just like Sophie. Sophie has been living in Edmonton for two years. For two years, I've heard her talk about the coffee shops that she goes to with people she meets in her classes. They sit around in pubs late into the night, philosophizing over bottles of wine. They go to bars to listen to bands, and to cafés for poetry readings. I can't wait to do all the same things. I've been waiting a long time to leave St. Paul. Since grad, I've just been killing time at home until I could start all over again. New city, new friends, new piano teacher. I'm going to be a whole new person.

Mom and Dad buy me a new double bed, new sheets, and a new bedspread with clusters of tiny blue flowers against a bright yellow background. I buy big, colourful posters to put up in my new bedroom – prints of artwork by Picasso, Monet, Van Gogh. Mom helps me put up my posters while Dad and Wes assemble my bedframe. I hold up the pictures, Mom tells me whether they're straight or not. Then we tack them up together.

Dad and Wes move most of the furniture into our apartment – our beds and desks, our dressers. The couch, the kitchen table. Mom, Sophie, and I do the cleaning, put away the pots and pans and dishes in the kitchen cupboards. We organize the linen closet. Hang towels in the bathroom. Moving in takes a whole weekend, and there's lots to do. But it doesn't feel like work. We order pizza and Chinese food. Dad buys beer. It's like one long slumber party. Mom and Dad sleep on my new double bed, Sophie and me on her bed. Wes rolls out a sleeping bag on the living- room floor. We stay up late, talking and laughing. In the mornings, Wes and I run out to buy coffee for everyone, and blueberry muffins.

Eventually, of course, Mom and Dad and Wes have to go back to St. Paul. At the end of the weekend, Sophie and I say goodbye at the door of our apartment. As Sophie closes the door, though, I decide that I should walk them downstairs. I don't have anything else to do. So, in the entrance to our building, I say goodbye again, waving while Mom and Dad and Wes cross the parking lot. Then I run out to their car, to say goodbye one more time. I'm not sure why I feel like crying. I want to live in Edmonton. I can phone home as often as I like, and I can go home anytime. I could go home every weekend if I wanted to. It's not like I'm living halfway across the world. St. Paul is only two hours away.

But the apartment feels so empty after Mom and Dad and Wes leave. It feels bigger, too. I wander around from room to room, looking at my new walls, my new floors. Somehow, everything seems older and darker once they're gone. The linoleum in the bathroom is lifting at the seams. Some of the paint on the cup-boards is peeling away. On my bedroom carpet, I find cigarette burns that I never saw before. And the noise. When Mom and Dad and Wes go home, I start noticing how noisy our apartment is. I try playing my guitar to drown out the traffic. I try singing. Someone in the apartment next door pounds on the wall.

Sophie isn't too keen on my singing, either. She says that once classes start, I'll have to find a practice room at the university. When she's studying, she needs total silence in the apartment. My playing and singing will annoy her.

It doesn't take very long for me to figure out that everything I do annoys Sophie – not just my music. She doesn't like me to leave anything out on the bathroom counter. I'm supposed to keep everything in the medicine cabinet or in the cupboard under the sink. Only, there's no room for my stuff in the cabinet or the cupboard because Sophie's got so much of her own stuff stored there. I have to put all of my bathroom things on the top of my dresser.

I'm also not allowed to light scented candles in my bedroom because Sophie says that the smell makes her sick. I can't leave any books or magazines lying around the living room because Sophie doesn't like the mess. When I come in from outside, I have to put my shoes in the closet by the door – on the left side, not the right side. The left side is for my shoes, the right side is for her shoes. Same with coats. After I put up a few of my posters in the dining room and the living room – a print of Picasso's "Three Musicians," and two whale prints done by a Haida artist – Sophie makes me take them down. She says that they clash with her furniture. Almost all of the furniture in our apartment belongs to Sophie, and it's all black and white. Black couch, black coffee table, black end tables. White kitchen table, white drapes, white dishes.

The problem is that Sophie has been living by herself for the past two years, and she's not used to having a roommate. She's used to doing things her own way. Shopping for herself, cooking for herself, doing laundry by herself. After Mom and Dad leave, she tells me that she's not planning to baby me while we live together. When she first moved to Edmonton, she didn't have anybody to help her. Nobody held her hand. I have to be independent, take care of myself. Figure things out on my own.

During my first few weeks away from home, I phone Mom and Dad every night. My plan, each time I dial their number, is to tell them about Sophie. About how she's not helping me at all with registration, or showing me how to open a bank account, or coming with me to get my library card. But I'd feel like a tattle-tale if I told them. They'd give Sophie a talking-to, and Sophie would just get angry. So I keep my mouth shut. Finding my way around isn't that hard anyway. I have to get used to being independent. It's part of the new me.

Plus my parents are so cheerful on the phone. They're so excited that Sophie and I are living together, and that we'll soon be walking to campus together each day, studying together every night. I don't want to disappoint them by telling them that Sophie isn't planning to do anything with me. She spends a lot of her time out with her friends. When she's in the apartment, she stays in her room.

Mom and Dad pay for everything while Sophie and I go to university, so that we don't have to worry about anything except our studies. We're supposed to enjoy our university years without losing sleep over money. On top of paying our tuition, they give us a monthly allowance to cover the rest of our expenses. They do it because, when they went to university, they didn't have anyone to help them. Their parents couldn't afford to give them money. Mom worked part-time at a meat-packing plant. Dad had to quit university for a couple of years, and go work at the chemical plant in Duvernay.

I hate hearing their stories. How Mom used to ride the bus home late at night with pigs' feet in her purse for soup. How, once a month, Dad used to count up his savings from the chemical plant, dreaming about going back to school. I feel spoiled when I think about how easy it is for me. So what if Sophie doesn't like living with me? All I have to do is show up for my classes. Do my homework. On weekends, if I want to go home, I can just hop in the car. Mom and Dad buy Sophie and me a second-hand Ford Tempo to use while we're at university.

After living with Sophie for a few weeks, though, and after taking the car home to St. Paul three weekends in a row, I realize that I've made a big mistake. Mom and Dad have made an even bigger one. They should never have bought us the car. And I should never have used it. I should probably never use it again.

Sophie refuses to come home with me when I drive to St. Paul. At first, I think that she wants time away from me – she wants to pretend on the weekends that she's living by herself again. But then, one weekend, when I go home in the car, she catches a ride to St. Paul with one of her friends. And another weekend, she takes the Greyhound from Edmonton instead of driving home with me. Saturday morning, she shows up at the bus depot in St. Paul.

She's trying to make a statement. Sophie never had a car before I moved to Edmonton.

I'd give the car back, if I could. I tell Mom and Dad that they should take it back. They say that Sophie is just being silly. She'll get over it. Just be patient. She'll come around.

They're right. After classes start – once everything starts going wrong for me – Sophie goes back to her old self, more or less. She stops brooding about the car in her bedroom. Stops sulking around the apartment when I'm around. She smiles a lot more, and laughs again.

Mostly at me.

Three weeks into September, I'm convinced that I've chosen all the wrong classes. Maybe the wrong program altogether.

For starters, my new piano teacher is a man. I've never had a man for a piano teacher. He's a man, and he's hairy. He's got thick, black hair everywhere – on his arms, on his fingers. On the back of his neck. Curly black chest hair pokes out of his shirt, around the collar, and tufts of coarse black hair grow out of his ears. I catch myself staring at him during our lessons. I've never seen such a hairy man. There's almost no space between his eyebrows. He's got permanent black shadows on his cheeks where he shaves.

His name is Lazlo Kalman. I'm supposed to call him Dr. Kalman, though. And he doesn't call me Colleen. It's "Ms. Lutzak."

Twice a week, on Tuesday and Thursday mornings, we meet in his music room on the fourth floor of the Fine Arts Building. Almost all of my classes are in the Fine Arts Building, which is easy to get to. It's only a five-minute walk from our apartment. My lessons with Dr. Kalman are supposed to last an hour and a half, but sometimes we finish early. Which is fine with me. An hour with Dr. Kalman feels like an eternity. I can't wait for our lessons to end. On Monday and Wednesday nights, I try to think of excuses for leaving early. I have a meeting with another professor. A doctor's appointment. A headache. I secretly hope that Dr. Kalman will come down with something serious so that my lessons with him will be cancelled. I'd like a different teacher.

As far as I'm concerned, Dr. Kalman's office is more like a hospital room – or an operating room – than a music room. The walls are painted white, the bookshelves are white, the blinds on the windows are white. Sophie would love it. Except for the two black pianos at either end of the room, the whole room is white.

When I'm in his music room, I never know where to put my knapsack. I wish he'd tell me. Everything has a place. My bag seems to mess things up. On his desk, he keeps two sharpened pencils, an eraser, and a clean notepad of staff paper – nothing else. No loose papers. His bookshelves are lined with music books and sheet music, all arranged in alphabetical order. I think he's got something against fresh air and natural sunlight because he keeps the windows closed and the blinds down. Not that his office is dark. There are rows of fluorescent lights on the ceiling, and fluorescent lights on each of the pianos. The light on top of the piano makes me feel like I'm playing the piano in a dentist's chair.

Of course, I don't play very much.

At the start of my first lesson, three weeks ago, Dr. Kalman asked me to play something for him, but he didn't even listen to the whole piece before he stopped me. He said that everything is wrong with my playing – the way that I sit, the way that I touch the keys. Before I learn anything new, I have to unlearn everything I know. I've got tension in my whole body, apparently. Tension in my neck, tension in my shoulders, tension in my wrists. I strike the keys when I should stroke them. I try too hard to make the music come out of the piano, when it should flow out of my body. For the past three weeks, I've hardly touched the piano in his room. He doesn't touch it, either.

He touches me a lot, though. In a creepy way. Sometimes he massages my shoulders, and the tops of my arms. He rubs my wrists and my fingers to loosen them up. Once in awhile he puts his hands on the small of my back, and keeps them there to correct my posture. I don't know how to tell him that it makes me uncomfortable. Sister Maria used to touch me, but that was different. She only touched my hands. And I liked the feel of her fingers. They were softer. Gentler.

I don't understand Dr. Kalman. Sitting in his office — just sitting in that sterile room — makes me nervous. I get a tight feeling in my chest, like I can't breathe. My palms sweat like crazy, and my heart races. He tells me to loosen up, and he's always talking about how my body has to be fluid like water — how the keys should be an extension of my fingers — but he runs his lessons like a drill sergeant. He's a lot like Mr. Schultz, when I think about it. Worse even. There's no small talk at the beginning of my lessons. No chit-chat about how my day has been, how my other classes are going. Not even a "Hello" or a "How are you?" I get the feeling that I'm interrupting him when I show up for my lessons. Like he's got something more important to do, and I'm taking him away from it. I don't see how I'm supposed to relax.

I try not to compare Dr. Kalman to Sister Maria. I try not to think about her when I'm having my lessons with him. But it's hard not to. I know that Sister Maria's music room wasn't the neatest or the nicest. The paint was chipping on the walls, and the whole place smelled a bit funny — like mothballs and lemons. There were always papers scattered across her desk, across the tops of her pianos. She always had time for me, though. I never felt unwelcome in her music room. I definitely wasn't tense. I used to live for my lesson with her. I'd count the days between my last lesson and my next lesson. And I spent hours with her in between, just visiting at the table in her room. Or listening to her play for me.

I miss playing, period. After three weeks of lessons with Dr. Kalman, I start to wonder if I'll ever play again. He gives me exercises to practise instead of new pieces. All kinds of ridiculous exercises, like closing my eyes, and massaging the keys of the piano. Or rolling my shoulders forward and backward. The forward rolling isn't so bad, but the backward rolling makes my breasts stick out. I feel like he's always staring at me, studying my body.

I'm supposed to count myself lucky for getting placed with Dr. Kalman. All of the other first-year piano students tell me that he's the best. Even the woodwind and brass students have heard of him. He's a famous concert pianist, and he only teaches the top students in the piano program. Everyone talks about how famous he is, how great he is. How they wish that they could have just one lesson with him. I think they'd change their minds if they spent an hour with Dr. Kalman in his office. An hour is all it would take. An hour of rolling their shoulders around, never playing a single note. Getting touched with his hairy hands.

When I tell Sophie about my lessons with Dr. Kalman – about how much I hate the exercises he makes me do, and the way he looks at me – she says that I'm imagining things. She doesn't believe that I haven't played any music yet. She thinks that I'm exaggerating. When I tell her that I want to quit, or switch teachers, she tells me to toughen up. I'm just not used to criticism.

"For the first time in your life," she says, "you're not perfect. Welcome to the club."

But it's not just my piano lessons with Dr. Kalman. My theory class with Dr. Kitchener is just as bad. He spends two whole weeks going over material I learned two years ago. In sight-singing with Dr. Evans, we're assigned baby songs. Sister Maria would laugh if she could see me reading the four-bar, three-note melodies that we have to perform for each other. It's hard for me not to laugh when I hear the other students struggling. Haven't they ever done sight-singing before? Dr. O'Connor's course in keyboard skills is supposed to teach us to improvise chordal accompaniments to melody lines, and to make up melody lines to chord structures in our textbooks. The other first-year music students tear their hair out over it, especially the students whose first instrument isn't the piano. I've been improvising on the piano since I was twelve.

I try hard to make friends with the other music students. Especially the pianists and singers. I figure we have a lot in common, and I want to have friends like Sophie – a whole group of friends who go out together after class and in the evenings. I invite a couple of girls out for coffee after class one day – a piano major, and a voice major. They seem nice enough. Fairly talented. The voice major says that she doesn't drink coffee because caffeine is bad for the vocal chords, and the piano major says that coffee makes her hands shake. I suggest hot chocolate. They say it's got caffeine too. Tea? They don't drink tea. Herbal tea? No thanks. Orange juice? Maybe next time.

I can take a hint. They just don't want to hang out with me.

A few days later, I overhear them talking with some other music students – about someone in our keyboard skills class who is a real show-off. Someone they wish would drop dead. At first, I assume they're talking about Scott, a violinist in our class with perfect pitch. Then I notice that Scott is in the group, doing some of the talking. I hear Scott say my name. They're talking about me.

Sophie says that it serves me right. I should try a little harder to fit in.

"You don't always have to be the best. Try screwing up once in a while, Super Girl. Try being human for a change."

I don't care what the other music students think. It's not my fault that I'm good at what I do. *They* should try a little harder. Spend more time practising. I'd even be willing to help them, if they'd just give me a chance.

It doesn't matter. I don't like them anyway. As far as I'm concerned, they're the snobs, not me. When Dr. Evans asks us to bring in pieces of music for each other to sight-sing, and when I bring in a Ukrainian folk song, they all turn their noses up to it – even Dr. Evans. Like it's not real music because it's not written by a famous composer. In Dr. Kitchener's theory class, when I raise my hand to talk about common chord structures of country music, I hear whispering and snickering at the back of the room. Dr. Kitchener says that country and western music isn't interesting to real musicians because it's not challenging enough. I make a point of improvising honky-tonk songs when it's my turn to perform in our keyboard skills class. Music is music. And honky-tonk piano is plenty challenging. Real musicians would know that.

The bottom line is that my music classes feel like a big waste of time. I'm bored. I don't have any homework because I'm not learning anything new. If I'm lucky, maybe by Christmas Dr. Kalman will let me play beginner songs with one hand. Maybe by this time next year, in my other classes, we'll get past beginner theory, and beginner sight-singing, and beginner keyboard skills. I just don't see why I have to wait around, twiddling my thumbs, while everyone else catches up.

Of course, then there is my other class, Ukrainian 100 with Dr. Pohorecky. Which is harder, but not any better. In fact, I think it might be the worst. The tables are turned in Ukrainian, and I don't like it one bit.

I don't actually need a second language to get my degree in music. I just thought it would be a good idea to take Ukrainian as an elective – instead of something like psychology or anthropology – to reacquaint myself with my mother tongue after all these years. I found the course in the university calendar, in the Department of Slavic and East European Studies. "Introductory Ukrainian." For people who have never taken any Ukrainian before. In a way, I felt guilty enrolling in a class for beginners because I've taken Ukrainian before. I thought that I'd intimidate the other students. But it seemed like a chance to get some easy credits. I wouldn't have to work very hard to get a really good grade.

Apparently everybody in my class had the same idea. Except everyone else in my Ukrainian class is completely bilingual. And, as it turns out, I hardly remember anything that I learned in Mom's Ukrainian classes.

So I'm the class dumdum. The class idiot. The dunce. All I'm missing is the pointy hat. I've never felt so stupid in my whole life. I don't even remember how to read the Ukrainian alphabet properly. I keep getting English and Cyrillic letters confused. Aside from a handful of nouns that I recall from Mom's classes, and one or two verbs, I'm totally lost. French words pop into my head when I'm searching for Ukrainian words.

At home, when I'm working on my Ukrainian, Sophie beams.

"Still struggling?" she says, smiling. "Still flunking your quizzes?"

I'm not used to being at the bottom of the class, and I'm determined not to stay there long. I conquered French in grade nine, I can conquer Ukrainian.

I spend all my free time working on my Ukrainian – doing extra exercises in the workbook, memorizing vocabulary, conjugating verbs. I phone Mom and Dad at night to ask them questions, to try out my pronunciations on them. I just can't catch up. I'm always a step behind the class because the professor moves so quickly through the material. I can feel my face turn red every time she calls on me to answer a question. Half the time I don't know what she's saying and, when I do understand her, I don't know how to respond. After awhile, I realize that phoning Mom and Dad doesn't help. Dr. Pohorecky is from Ukraine. She pronounces Ukrainian words differently from Mom and Dad. She says that my accent is all wrong.

Sophie thinks it's hilarious that I'm suffering in Ukrainian. She says, *"Boh ne be bu kom."* God doesn't hit with a stick. It's payback for being a smartass in my music classes.

"How does it feel?" she asks. "Now that the shoe is on the other foot?"

I don't think it's the least bit funny. The other students in my Ukrainian class aren't just bilingual. They all come from the same Ukrainian immersion school in Edmonton; they all seem to go to the same Ukrainian church; and I think that nearly all of them belong to the Ukrainian Club at the university. How can I compete? They're the most Ukrainian people I've ever met. At least half of them are *Shumka* dancers. They've been on tour in Ukraine two or three times. One guy in class is the president of the National Ukrainian Canadian Students' Union. He travels across Canada during the summers, meeting with other Ukrainian

Canadian university students. Almost everyone in my Ukrainian class is in the Ukrainian Studies program, so they take all kinds of courses in Ukrainian literature, folklore, and history. A few of them have summer jobs at the Ukrainian Cultural Heritage Village by Elk Island. Four months out of the year they become role players, living like Ukrainian pioneers and talking to tourists who stroll through the museum.

Sitting in Ukrainian class, listening to the other Ukrainian students talk together day after day about how important it is to keep Ukrainian culture alive, I picture them dressed in superhero costumes — embroidered shirts, tight satin pants, velvet capes. In my head, I call them the Super Ukes. Whizzing around the world to save Ukrainian culture wherever it's being threatened.

During the third week of classes, though, when it's time for us to give our first class presentations in Ukrainian class, I come up with a plan to show the Super Ukes that I don't need saving. I might not speak Ukrainian, and I might not belong to any of their dance groups and church clubs, but I'm just as Ukrainian as they are.

Our assignment is to stand up in front of the class and speak for five minutes about ourselves. We're supposed to talk about our families, where we grew up. How old we are. That sort of thing. Of course, the Super Ukes hardly need to prepare. They can make complex sentences and use big Ukrainian words without even trying. Next to them, I'll sound like a five-year-old. "My name is Colleen. I have a mother. I have a father. I have a sister. I have a brother." I refuse to do it. I decide to do something more creative instead. When it's my turn to speak, I'm going to bring out my guitar. I'm going to sing *"Tsyhanochka."* Before I start, I'll say a few words about myself. Maybe something about how I've been singing Ukrainian songs all my life. But the main part of the presentation will be the song itself. My classmates are going to be stunned. Dr. Pohorecky is going to be impressed. For the first time since classes began, I'll finally get a decent mark in Ukrainian.

I almost wish that the students in my music classes could be on hand to see me perform. And my music professors, too. Dr. Kalman could hear me play a song for the first time from beginning to end. I'd show them all what real music sounds like. How a real musician performs.

On the morning of presentation day, Sophie hovers around my bedroom while I pack up my guitar. She makes a half-dozen sarcastic comments before I tell her to shut up. She doesn't listen.

"I have an idea," she says. "Why don't you wear your Ukrainian costume? That would be a nice touch. And you could do a dance after you've finished singing. Or you could dance *while* you're singing. Even better."

"Mind your own business," I say.

"Maybe you'll get the gold medal this time. Think your prof is giving out medals?"

"Get lost."

That was low. Bringing up Dauphin. Really low.

"Too bad Carla Senko isn't here to help you," she says. "Remember the last time you gave a presentat —"

"Get out!" I say, raising my voice. "Leave me alone!"

I don't need to be reminded of my grade nine French presentation.

Sophie mutters under her breath as she leaves my bedroom.

"Just trying to help. Just trying to be supportive."

I'm not the first to give my presentation in Ukrainian class, or the last. Dr. Pohorecky calls us up alphabetically, and I'm smack in the middle of the class list, right after Peter Kordan and before Tatiana Melnyk. I hardly listen to the other students' presentations. Even if I could understand them — which I can't, because their Ukrainian is too advanced — I'm too busy thinking about my song, and wondering what I should sing if Dr. Pohorecky asks for an encore, and daydreaming about my classmates' reactions. For the first time since the course began, the Super Ukes are going to be speechless.

While I strap on my guitar, I introduce my song. In Ukrainian.
"Ya zaspivaiu sohodni odnu pisniu – 'Tsyhanochka.'"

Three or four students snicker in the back of the class. Dr.
Pohorecky raises her eyebrows. The *Shumka* dancers – all twelve
of them – cross their arms in unison.

The performance doesn't go well. I've never performed for an
audience like this. I suspected that the other students would be
jealous, so it's not like I expected them to jump out of their seats,
clapping and singing along. But I anticipated a few smiles, at least;
a couple of heads bobbing in time with the music. What's wrong
with them? *"Tsyhanochka"* is a lively song. It's all about passion and
longing. I *sing* it with passion and longing. Nobody seems to
notice. I feel as though I'm performing for thirty-three statues,
their faces as blank as stones. Even Dr. Pohorecky looks bored.
Halfway through my song, she stops watching me, and starts writing on the notepad in front of her. For all I know, she could be
doodling.

They applaud, politely. No one says a word to me, though, as
I return to my seat. Not a single word. Dr. Pohorecky keeps her
eyes on her notepad. The strangest feeling washes over me as I listen to the next presentation, and the presentation after that. I feel
like my cousin Kalyna – like I can suddenly see the world through
her eyes. The other students in class tolerate me, but they don't
really want to know me. I'm too different. I don't belong, and they
know it. They don't even try to pretend. Polite applause. That's
how we treat Kalyna.

At the end of class, after Dr. Pohorecky has given everyone
feedback on their presentations, the other students drift out of the
classroom in groups, comparing marks as they go – in Ukrainian,
of course. They make jokes in Ukrainian. I'm the outsider, and the
inside joke. I know they're laughing at me.

If Sophie actually was supportive, maybe I could tell her how
badly the presentation went. I'd have someone to confide in. A
shoulder to cry on. But I don't dare tell her the truth. I won't give

her the satisfaction. In the evening, when she gets home from her classes, I'm all smiles. I announce that I got the highest mark in the class – ten out of ten. The prof loved me. The other students gave me a standing ovation.

Sophie raises her eyebrows, as though she doesn't quite believe me.

"I'll show you the prof's comments," I say, reaching into my knapsack, hoping that she won't call my bluff.

"Don't bother. It's enough to hear you gloat."

Dr. Pohorecky's comments are crumpled in a ball at the bottom of my knapsack. She didn't give me a grade on my presentation, just a couple of sentences explaining that I'll have to redo it. Singing a song doesn't count for anything. It doesn't show what language skills I've picked up over the past few weeks, especially since I mispronounced most of the words to the song. I'm supposed to go back to class tomorrow and talk for five minutes, like everyone else. Then she'll give me a grade.

Only I'm not going back to Ukrainian class tomorrow, or the day after that. I'm never going back. I'm never setting foot in that classroom so long as I live. I can't show my face in front of the other students. I'm not one of them. Nothing will change that.

I start skipping Ukrainian.

And then, after a few days of skipping Ukrainian, I start skipping the odd music class too.

It's not only that my music classes are boring. It's that, lately, I can't stop thinking about Sister Maria. I can't push her out of my mind. In my music classes, we're going through the same material that she taught me, step by step. When my professors talk, I hear her voice in my head. When they play recordings of music that she played for me, I see her at her piano, her arms outstretched over the keys. Sitting in class is like watching a movie of my piano lessons with Sister Maria. I try to daydream about something else – anything else. I shake my head to make her go away. But she always comes back, like a ghost, following me around wherever I go. Dr.

Kalman's lessons are the hardest. I wonder if Sister Maria can see me in his office – if she can see him touching me, breathing down my neck. If she can see me unlearning everything I learned from her.

By the end of September, I quit going to classes altogether, and I formally withdraw from the university – just in time to have my tuition refunded. My hands shake as I sign the forms in the registrar's office, and then throw my student card into the garbage can outside the students' union building. I don't feel relieved, I feel sick to my stomach. I have to tell Sophie. I can't keep pretending to go to classes every morning. I have to tell Mom and Dad. I can't keep taking their money. They'll be so hurt. So disappointed.

October 3rd is the deadline that I give myself. October 3rd I come clean, and tell everyone the truth. That gives me a few days to prepare. I need to show Mom and Dad that I have a plan. What's my plan? I'll get a job on campus. Or I'll move back to St. Paul, and get a job there.

Those are my options.

October 3rd is the day.

Then, on October 2nd, the phone rings, and, out of the blue, everything changes.

TWO

M om and Dad call first, to tell me that a fellow from the United World Colleges called them, looking for me. They can't imagine why. Mom's guess is that he's looking for a donation. Dad says that I should tell him where to go.

Then Tim Van Luewen calls to explain why he's been trying to get in touch with me.

According to Tim, one of the scholarship recipients has decided to give up her place at the UWC in Victoria. Because I'm on their list of alternate candidates, her scholarship is now mine for the taking.

I'm an alternate?

I tell Tim that I don't understand.

He says that I should have received a letter. The letter explained that, while I wasn't at the top of their list, I was near the top. Near enough to be named an alternate. The selection committee always chooses alternates, in case one of the scholarship recipients turns down a placement.

I should have read my rejection letter more carefully before I threw it away.

"So I'm going to Victoria?" I ask.

"Not Victoria, Swaziland. If you decide to accept the scholarship."

I have to sit down.

"The school year in Victoria has already started," Tim explains, "so it doesn't make sense to send a student there. Or to any of the colleges in the northern hemisphere. They all start their classes in August. The college in Swaziland is different. It's in the southern hemisphere. Which means that classes at Waterford start in January."

"But I thought you didn't send students to Africa. I thought Africa was out of the question."

Tim says that they're willing to make an exception. These are exceptional circumstances. They've never had a student give up a scholarship. And they've never had a candidate express interest in going to Africa.

"You're one lucky lady," he says.

Of course, I am in no way *obliged* to accept. I shouldn't feel pressured to go to Swaziland.

"It's a big decision. Take your time. Think about it, talk to your parents."

I tell Tim that I don't need to think about it. I don't need to talk to my parents.

A miracle has happened. I've been saved. It's divine intervention. I don't have to feel bad now when I tell Mom and Dad about withdrawing from university. They won't be disappointed in me after all. They'll be thrilled.

I do need some time, though, for the news to sink in. So much has happened since my scholarship interview. It feels like a lifetime ago. I haven't thought about my UWC application in months. Africa, Africa. I keep saying the word to myself. I'm going to Africa. It doesn't seem real. *Africa*. It doesn't seem possible. A-fri-ca.

I wait a few minutes before I call Mom and Dad.

But I can't tell them over the phone. The news is too big, too important. I pack a bag, quickly, and grab the car keys. Sophie is out with friends. I leave her a note. *Gone to St. Paul – going to Africa – call home when you get in!*

It's the shortest trip home that I've ever made. I crank up the radio and sing along at the top of my lungs. Every so often, I have to remind myself to ease up on the accelerator. I feel like I could fly.

Mom and Dad are waiting for me at the front door. Sophie has called them. She's told them about the note that I left her. They've put two and two together. Dad is grinning from ear to ear. Mom is white as a sheet. Wes joins us as we make our way to the kitchen.

"When?" says Dad.

"In January."

"You haven't accepted, have you?" says Mom. "We need to talk about this first. As a family. What about university? You can't just quit. We have to think this through."

"I'm taking it," I say. "I'm taking the scholarship. I've already told them."

"Have you thought about your sister?" says Mom. "You're her roommate now. You've signed a lease. Have you thought about that?"

Wes says that Sophie could find another roommate. She has lots of friends at university.

"She doesn't like living with me anyway," I say. "Living together hasn't been so great for either of us."

"What are you *talking* about?" says Mom. "That's nonsense. You girls have a beautiful apartment, a car, money. You have a perfect arrangement. We've given you everything, and you're going to throw it away to go to some godforsaken country on the other side of the world? What's wrong with you?"

Dad tells Mom that it's a once-in-a-lifetime opportunity. He says that we should consider it at least. The university isn't going anywhere. I can always go back.

"You think she's going to *come* back?" says Mom, her eyes blazing.

I'm not sure if this is the right time to mention that I've already dropped out of university, but I have to tell them sooner or later.

Dad takes the news well. He says that it doesn't matter now. What's done is done. We need to look ahead, focus on the future.

Mom gets up from the table after I've confessed. She says that she can't look at me; that, if my goal is to send her to an early grave, then I'm succeeding. She can hardly finish her sentence before she starts to cry.

Dad gets up to follow her, but then he changes his mind. He walks back to the table, shaking his head and grinning. Before I know it, he's lifted me off my chair, and he's hugging me, and swinging me around the kitchen.

"That's my little girl!" he says. "That's my girl!"

Wes is the most excited, though, by far. Shortly after I give him the news, he goes to his room. When he comes back to the kitchen a few minutes later, he's got a stack of books, magazines, and loose-leaf papers in his hands. Over the next few days, by consulting his hunting almanacs and wildlife encyclopedias and rifle magazines, Wes plans a complete safari. He makes a rough sketch of basic necessities – transportation (Land Rover), food (malaria pills?), camping gear (include mosquito netting). He compiles a list of big game animals indigenous to southern Africa – zebra, giraffe, lion, warthog, impala – all organized under the headings *Big Cats, Antelope,* and *Other.* Beside each animal, Wes notes the calibre of rifle he thinks would do the job.

When Sophie comes home for the weekend, she hugs me, congratulates me.

She says, "I'm so happy for you!" And she tells me not to worry about the apartment. She'll find a new place after Christmas, a one-bedroom. No big deal.

I'm not sure if Sophie really means it. I'm not sure if she really is happy for me. When Mom comes up with reasons for me not to go, and when I argue with her, Sophie leaves the room. She could stand up for me, but she doesn't.

Mom says that the night before I received the phone call from the UWC selection committee, she dreamt I was getting married.

"You were standing at the altar of the Greek Orthodox Church at Szypenitz," she says, "dressed in my wedding gown, of all things. The traditional Greek Orthodox wedding crown was on your head, pressing down on *my* veil. I don't know who you were marrying. I couldn't see the groom. Father Zubritsky was there, though. He was marrying you. In Ukrainian."

The dream is how Mom knew that something terrible was going to happen. She says that, in dreams, weddings mean death. That's what my scholarship is to Mom. Death. Mine or hers, she's not sure. Maybe both.

For the next few months, our house becomes a battle zone. Mom won't help me move out of the apartment in Edmonton. Dad and Wes come to pick me up and take my furniture back to St. Paul, but Mom stays at home.

She says that I'll miss the change of seasons here. I say that it's only one year and, besides, seasons change everywhere. Swaziland must have its own winter. Mom says that I won't be safe in Africa. I'll get mugged, or raped, or murdered. I say that I could just as easily get mugged, raped, and murdered right here in St. Paul. Mom says that medical care is substandard in a Third World country like Swaziland. What if my appendix bursts? I'll be three days away from a good, Canadian hospital. I say that the college will take care of me. There must be doctors on campus and Johannesburg is a hop, skip, and a jump away. Johannesburg is a major, modern city.

We fight non-stop – about the quality of the food in Swaziland, the water, the standard of living. Mom worries about diseases like bilharzia, yellow fever, malaria. She clips articles from the *Edmonton Journal, Maclean's, Time* magazine – anything that has to do with violence and bloodshed in South Africa.

My aunts don't help. Mom talks to them on the phone every week, and they all tell her the same thing: she and Dad shouldn't allow me to go. Auntie Mary, Kalyna's mother, is the worst. She's closest to my mother, and the most vocal about how dangerous it is for me to go to Africa by myself. Once, she even talks to me on the phone, trying to talk me out of it. Why am I so determined to hurt my mother? she wonders. Why do I want to break her heart? Auntie Mary says that I'm selfish and ungrateful. After all my parents have done for me, this is how I thank them. It's shameful.

I want to tell Auntie Mary that she's wrong, and that it's none of her business. But I can't. She's my oldest aunt. I can't talk back to her.

I phone the South African Embassy in Ottawa instead, requesting general information on the country. They send me a big manila envelope in the mail filled with pamphlets and brochures advertising sandy white beaches and flashy casinos and luxurious spas in Durban and Cape Town and Sun City.

I spend a lot of time in my room then, scanning the articles Mom has found and going through the Embassy package. It doesn't seem possible to me that South Africa is as bad as the newspapers say, or as good as the brochures suggest. So I take out a few books from the town library. Books, I think, will paint a more accurate picture. The St. Paul Municipal Library has three titles in its South Africa section: a novel, *Cry the Beloved Country,* by Alan Paton; a collection of Nadine Gordimer short stories; a dog-eared paperback on the history of apartheid. I borrow them all.

The books are all about apartheid – passbook laws, homelands, police brutality – even though they're written by white people. Nothing about surfing paradises and holiday spots. The more I read, the more worried I become. Maybe Mom is right. Maybe it is awful. Maybe it isn't safe.

By Christmas, though, I've got my passport, my transit visa for South Africa, and my Student Residency Permit for Swaziland. My itinerary has been confirmed by the scholarship committee, the headmaster at Waterford has guaranteed a place for me. All of my textbooks are waiting for me there. On January 19, I'll board the plane in Edmonton. Edmonton-Toronto, Toronto-Montreal. Montreal-Paris. Paris-Johannesburg. Johannesburg-Manzini. My route is the cheapest and most direct one that the committee could arrange at the last minute; the price tag is almost five thousand dollars. They've arranged and paid for everything – flights, tuition, room and board. They even give me spending money. I can't change my mind. Not now.

Whatever else I need, Dad buys. He buys mosquito netting for my bed, a special mosquito screen for the window of my dorm room, and a twenty-four month supply of malaria pills. Hiking boots, running shoes, leather sandals. A special leather pouch that fits snugly inside the front of my pants for my passport. And five hundred Canadian dollars in American Express traveller's cheques.

He's really excited about my trip. I think he wishes that he were going himself. The college sends me information about Swaziland, in general, and the college, more specifically – so that I can prepare. Dad pores over the fat photocopied booklet, making notes on Swaziland's climate, geography, average temperature, rainfall, humidity. Swazi history, the history of Waterford. Swazi culture. The relationship between students at the college and the Swazi people. He becomes a walking encyclopedia on the subject of Swaziland. Over the Christmas holidays, it's all he talks about.

"Now, isn't that interesting," he says at breakfast one morning, while he underlines a paragraph in the booklet.

My mom presses her lips together, takes a deep breath. I can see that she's getting fed up with Dad's mini-lectures.

Yesterday he told us all about the variety of ecological zones in Swaziland – rainforest in the northwest, dry savanna in the east; high veld and low veld; mountains and plains. Remarkable for a country that's not much bigger than Vancouver Island. The day before, he gave us a summary of colonialism in Swaziland, from the arrival of the British in the nineteenth century and the consolidation of their power in Swaziland after the Boer War, to independence, in 1968. English is still an official language, along with SiSwati. But the country – a kingdom, technically – is now ruled by King Mswati III. Mswati's father, King Sobhuza II, had over one hundred wives and close to seven hundred children. My mother winced when Dad talked about the old Swazi king. Sophie called Sobhuza a pig. My dad scolded her. He said that wives and children are signs of wealth in Swazi custom. The tradition, he explained, is for the king to take on at least one new wife each year at the Umhlanga, or the Reed Dance. It's an annual, eight-day ceremony during which hundreds of Swazi girls gather to perform for the king. He chooses his bride from the crowd.

"Isn't that *interesting.*" Dad repeats himself at the breakfast table, hoping that someone will take the bait.

Wes glances at Mom, cautiously. Then he says, "Isn't what interesting, Dad?"

"Well, it says here –" Dad points to the paragraph he's been underlining – "that the college takes students from the ages of eleven through eighteen. So it's not just for United World College scholarship students. Anyone can go, as long as they pass the entrance exam and pay their tuition."

"So I could go, too?" Wes's eyes light up.

"Absolutely not." My mother gets up from the table, starts clearing away dishes. "It's not enough that I'm losing one child?"

As Mom leaves the kitchen, I look at Dad. Dad taps his pencil against the table. I think *he's* getting fed up with Mom's negative attitude. For a moment, he says nothing. Then he resumes lecturing.

The college started out with sixteen students, all from South Africa or Swaziland, and six faculty members, mostly British ex-patriates. Now, more than four hundred students go to Waterford, and the staff has ballooned to forty-five. A quarter of the students are from Swaziland. More than half are from other African countries. But there are students from almost every continent. Over seventy countries are represented. And the teachers come from around the world, too – India, Belgium, Ireland, Japan.

Dad sighs. "Just imagine, teaching on a staff like that. Imagine the conversation in the staff room."

As usual, Dad and Wes get into a discussion about hunting in Africa. When Wes is around, and Dad starts talking about Swaziland, the conversation always turns to hunting – whether or not, hypothetically, they'd be able to bring their trophies back to Canada and, if so, how they'd go about doing it. I slip away from the kitchen table, and head toward Mom and Dad's bedroom. Sophie follows.

At the door of the bedroom, Sophie tells me that I should let Mom be alone for a while. If I go in, I'll just make things worse.

As if that's possible.

Mom hasn't been herself at all since I got news of my scholarship. She's trying hard to act tough and brave. I can see, though, that it's a struggle for her. There are dark circles under her eyes. She picks at her meals, never finishing the food on her plate.

When I knock on her bedroom door, she doesn't answer. When I let myself in, I find her sitting on the edge of her bed, wiping her eyes with a Kleenex. Wrapping paper and boxes are spread out around her – and a small pile of gifts. The gifts are for me, but she doesn't try to hide them. T-shirts that say "Canada" on them, and a small Zip-loc bag filled with "Canada" pins. A pair of moccasin slippers lined with rabbit fur. A cassette called *Canada: A Land and Its Songs*. Plus deodorant, shampoo, conditioner, tampons; toothbrushes, toothpaste, dental floss; and a mountain of Mars bars. My favourite.

"I'm not sure what you'll be able to buy there," she says, blowing her nose. "And I don't want you to go without."

I feel my chest tighten. Mom thought of everything.

I sit next to her on the bed, put my arm around her waist. Mom lets her head rest on my shoulder. "I'm scared," she says, tears rolling down her face. "I'm so scared."

"Me too." I wipe the tears from her cheeks, and from my own.

"I don't want you to go," she says.

But I don't know what to say, how to make her feel better.

Because I have to go. And I want to go.

Because I'm going.

THREE

She falls apart on Christmas Day.

Every year, on Christmas Eve – the regular Christmas Eve, not the Ukrainian one – Mom makes the traditional Ukrainian meal, twelve meatless and milkless dishes. Then, on Christmas Day, we go to *Baba* and *Gido's* house in Vegreville for a big turkey dinner. We don't bother doing the routine all over again on Ukrainian Christmas Eve and on Ukrainian Christmas Day. We're usually back in school by then, and Mom doesn't have time.

Christmas Eve is normal enough. Mom might be less cheerful than usual, but she tries not to show it. She makes all twelve dishes. She makes Sophie and me help. She sings carols with us around the piano. She allows each of us to open one present – our new pyjamas – before we go to bed.

On Christmas Day, though, after we open the rest of our presents, Mom goes into her room and won't come out. She says that she's not feeling well. She tells Dad that she's not feeling up to the trip to Vegreville. She'd rather stay home this year. She wants to spend Christmas Day alone with us – just us, not everyone else.

We're alarmed. We go to Vegreville every Christmas. Christmas Day at *Baba* and *Gido's* is a tradition. We've never *not* gone there on Christmas Day. Vegreville is central for everyone – the aunts and uncles in Two Hills, the cousins in Edmonton, us in St. Paul. Nobody misses Christmas Day in Veg. They can't. *Baba* is too old to cook for everyone. The meal depends on all of the aunts being there. Auntie Mary always roasts a ham, Auntie Linda brings the mashed beans and garlic. Auntie Rose brings *nachynka*. Auntie Marika and Auntie Natalka get together ahead of time to prepare the *nylysnyky* and *holubtsi*. Auntie Helen brings mustard pickles, beets and mushrooms, and pickled herring. Auntie Jean makes mushrooms in cream and *pyrizhky* in cream. For dessert, everyone pitches in. Each aunt brings her own assortment of squares.

It's possible that one or two of the aunts could skip out on Christmas Day and the meal wouldn't be ruined. Especially Auntie Pearl. Auntie Pearl could stay home and no one would notice. Her jellied salads are a flop every year. And Auntie Rose, too – she puts cinnamon in her *nachynka*, which makes me gag. *Nachynka* should be thick and creamy and a little on the salty side. There's no place for cinnamon in *nachynka*.

Mom, however, could never miss Christmas Day at *Baba* and *Gido*'s. Never. She brings the turkey and the stuffing. Usually she puts it in the oven right after we open our presents so that it's a glossy golden-brown by early afternoon, when we're ready to go. After she takes it out of the oven, she wraps the roaster in two or three dish towels to keep in the heat, then Dad carries it out to the car.

Today, after Sophie, Wes, and I have finished opening our presents – and after Mom and Dad have had a long conversation in their bedroom, all in Ukrainian – we see something that we've never seen before. We stand and stare.

Dad brings out the Butterball – the thirty-pound Butterball – from the fridge.

Not Mom, Dad.

He calls Sophie and me over to the turkey. Wes tags along.

"Girls," he says, placing his hands on his hips, "what do we do?"

Sophie takes over, like a surgeon in an operating room. I play the nurse, handing her salt, pepper, garlic powder, poultry spice.

Dad and Wes stand around with their hands in their pockets, nodding now and again. Seasoning and then roasting the turkey is easy for Sophie and me, we've done it lots of times. But neither of us has ever made the stuffing – not without Mom around to supervise. The recipe is in her head. She's never written it down. Even though we know what goes in the stuffing, we don't know the proper quantities.

Dad says that we can skip the stuffing this year.

Wes looks positively horrified. Stuffing is his favourite part of the Christmas Day meal. He says that, at the very least, we have to try.

"Be my guest," says Sophie, stepping away from the turkey.

We skip the stuffing.

In the end, Mom agrees to come with us to *Baba* and *Gido's*. Against her will, it seems. Dad has to coax her out of the bedroom and into the car. All the way to Vegreville, she stares out the passenger side of the car, as though she's searching for something way off in the distance. The rest of us chatter about the temperature and the state of the roads and the forecast. We want to go on one last ice-fishing trip before Sophie goes back to school in Edmonton and I leave for Africa. Mom doesn't say a word, doesn't join in. It's like she's not even with us.

Until we make the turn at the giant *pysanka*.

As we pass the egg on the outskirts of Vegreville, Mom starts sniffling, and talking in Ukrainian to Dad – too fast for me to catch a single word, let alone the gist of what she's saying. It sounds like she's pleading with him. I glance at Sophie to see if she understands but she gives me a helpless look, shrugging. Dad doesn't say much. Wes passes Mom a Kleenex from the back seat.

After we pull up in front of *Baba* and *Gido's* house, I want to ask Dad what Mom said in the car, only he's too busy plugging in the car and unloading the turkey. I want to ask Mom what she said in the car. I'm sure that it had to do with me. Me and Swaziland. Before I have a chance to open my mouth, though, Auntie Mary,

Mom's oldest sister, rushes out the door of the house, whisking Mom out of the car. She puts her arms around Mom, and then leads her into the house as though she's an invalid. Once or twice Auntie Mary glances back at the rest of us, glaring. Mom's the youngest in the family, the baby. Auntie Mary is very protective of her. Obviously she hasn't changed her mind about my trip to Africa.

As Wes and Sophie and I make our way up the front walk, Wes ruffles my hair. Sophie says not to worry, to relax.

"It was nothing," says Sophie. "Mom's just not feeling well. You can't blame her. She's been under a lot of stress."

I'm not convinced. When Mom and Dad talk Ukrainian, it's *some*thing. They talk Ukrainian to hide things from us. Secretive, confidential things. Serious things.

Baba and *Gido*'s house is filled with people, activity. Noise. Sonya and Robert's boys have set up their new electric racetrack in the middle of the living room; Paul and Kelly's boys are playing with plastic Star Wars spaceships. Dean and Diana's daughter is playing Barbies with Orysia and Danny's girl. The aunts and the older girl cousins are banging around in *Baba*'s kitchen – all except Kalyna, who's playing Barbies with the little girls in the living room. The aunts take turns warming their dishes in the oven. The older girl cousins take out the dishes and the cutlery, others set out their pickles and buns and *kolbasa* and squares. Downstairs, the men are visiting. *Baba* and *Gido* have a long table in the basement. The uncles sit around the table playing cards, drinking. All the way upstairs I can smell Uncle Ed's cigarettes mingling with the smell of garlic and dillweed and fresh farm cream.

One by one, Sophie, Wes and I greet *Baba* and *Gido* who sit next to each other in the living room, *Baba* on a corner of the green vinyl couch, *Gido* in the matching green vinyl armchair. Sophie is a whiz at talking to *Baba* and *Gido*. She's not the least bit scared of them. First she kisses them each on both cheeks, then she says, *"Dobryden Baba, Dobryden Gido."* Wes shakes *Gido*'s hand, then he sits next to *Baba*, holding her hand, letting her touch his face.

I do my best to imitate Sophie and Wes. I smile, I kiss them — *Baba* and *Gido* both — gently, my lips barely brushing their cheeks. I say hello in Ukrainian.

Then I walk away as quickly as I can. I escape to the kitchen or the basement, where I try to block out the sight of them. *Baba's* face is all veins — grey-brown liver spots and veins — and *Gido* looks like a skull. A bony, fleshless skull. I'm afraid to touch them, afraid that my kisses will leave bruises on their faces. Afraid that they'll have a heart attack or a stroke right in front of me.

Baba and *Gido* are too old to be normal grandparents. Normal *Baba*s and *Gido*s are much younger, and robust, and jolly. Normal *Baba*s bake cookies and cakes and fresh *borshch*. They keep cupboards full of chocolate bars and red licorice; they say, "Eat, eat, you're too skinny." Normal *Gido*s tease their grandchildren, tell dirty jokes. They like to sing.

Our *Baba* can't cook anymore, and she needs a walker to get around. Meals on Wheels brings food to their house every few days. Though he can't read it, *Gido* keeps a Bible beside him, tucked in beside the cushion of the armchair. He walks with a cane, and he hasn't driven a car in years. I've never seen him smile. He's ninety-one, she's eighty-seven. Neither of them speaks more than a word or two of English.

In the kitchen, the aunts are chattering non-stop in English — all at once, it seems, one interrupting the other, voices raised. They talk in English when they want to keep something from *Baba* and *Gido* — the nursing home plan, usually. Sophie and I know all about the nursing home plan, the aunts have been discussing it on and off for the last three years. Auntie Mary, Auntie Helen and Auntie Natalka are in favour; Mom, Auntie Linda and Auntie Rose are against. They argue openly in front of us. Sometimes it even gets ugly. Yelling, name-calling. Crying.

Today, though, when Sophie and I walk into *Baba's* kitchen, the aunts' voices drop to a whisper. Then they stop talking altogether. The silence is eerie. The aunts are never silent. If they need to hide something from us, they just switch from English to Ukrainian. They never actually stop talking.

After Sophie, Wes and I fill our plates in the kitchen, we head down the stairs to the basement. Everyone eats in groups around the long table in the basement – uncles, younger cousins, older cousins, aunts. We sit with the cousins who are closest to us in age. None of us is actually allowed to eat. Not until *Gido* says Grace. And *Gido* doesn't come downstairs to say Grace until the aunts have served everyone. While the aunts finish dishing out the food, we sit, talking, picking at our food. Waiting.

The cousins don't ask a single question about my trip. Nothing about when I leave or how I feel about going. It's like they've made a pact not to mention it. Kenny talks about his new snowmobile, Dalia tells us about her school ski trip to Banff. Darrell goes on and on about his Christmas hockey camp in Calgary with the Calgary Flames. I think maybe they're jealous about my scholarship so I don't bring up the subject of Africa. Instead, I ask them what they got for Christmas, how they'll be spending New Year's Eve.

Gido's Grace seems longer than usual. His Grace is always long, and always in Ukrainian. I never know exactly what he's blessing. The food, I suppose. His children, grandchildren. Great-grandchildren. As *Gido* says, "Amen," tears come to his eyes. He always cries during Grace. *Baba* hands him a hanky, he presses the cloth to his cheeks.

I've already got a mouthful of *nalysnyky* when my cousin Kalyna speaks up. I keep eating – we all keep eating – as though nothing out of the ordinary is occurring. When Kalyna is in a big group of people, she gets overexcited – starts singing, making up little poems. Carrying on about things that don't make sense to the rest of us. We've all learned to live with her outbursts; they're predictable, now – normal, in a way.

As Kalyna babbles, Sophie and I critique the Christmas dinner. We give Auntie Linda's mashed beans the thumbs-up. Just enough garlic, not too many sautéed onions, all-around good texture. Sophie makes a face at Auntie Natalka's *holubtsi*. The cabbage leaves are a greenish-white colour, which means that Auntie Natalka has used fresh cabbage instead of sour leaves. The edges of each cabbage roll are brown and crusty. Clearly, Auntie Natalka overcooked them all.

I'm about to express my annual disgust with Auntie Rose's cinnamon-laced *nachynka* when I hear Kalyna say my name. She talks in Ukrainian, adding my name in English – *Colleen* – loud enough for everyone to hear.

Before I can turn to Sophie for a translation, *Gido* says something back to Kalyna in Ukrainian. Something stern. A reprimand, I think. Kalyna repeats herself – repeats my name – only louder this time. *Gido* raises his voice at Kalyna, *Baba* asks Mom a question; Mom turns deathly white. She doesn't answer *Baba*; instead, she starts to cry, covering her face with her hands.

By now, everyone has stopped eating. I lean hard into Sophie's ear, asking her if she knows what's going on. Sophie's Ukrainian is better than mine, even though I took it for a few weeks at university.

Gido yells something in Ukrainian – yells at Mom, I think. Auntie Mary puts her arm around Mom, comforting her. Auntie Rose tries to calm *Gido* but he keeps yelling. In English, Auntie Linda tells my dad to *do* something. Dad says something to *Gido* in Ukrainian. *Baba* cries quietly, saying, *"Bozhe, Bozhe"* – God, God – as she rubs her eyes with the edge of her apron.

"Oh no," Sophie whispers.

"What?" I say.

Sophie covers her mouth with her hand.

"WHAT?" I give Sophie a poke in the arm.

Sophie talks quickly. "I'm not sure, but I think" – she turns away from me, listening to Dad and *Gido* argue – "I think *Baba* and *Gido* didn't know that you're going to Africa. I think Mom and her sisters have been keeping it a secret. I think Kalyna just blurted it out."

"That's crazy. Everybody knows I'm —"

"Shush!" says Sophie. "I can't hear what's going on."

Gido gets up from the table, still yelling, pointing his cane at Dad. Dad crosses his arms over his chest. He looks furious. They both look furious. Auntie Jean starts saying something in Ukrainian, Dad tells her to stay the hell out of it, in English. Uncle David, Auntie Jean's husband, gives Dad a hard push, sending Dad across the room. Uncle Harry pushes Uncle David back, calling him a goddamned son of a bitch. While the uncles fight, Kalyna crouches in the corner of the room behind the table, singing to herself, her hands over her ears.

Then *Gido* grabs Wes — Wes of all people — by the collar, shaking him and yelling at him. He's stronger than he looks.

Poor Wes. He can't fight back. It's *Gido*, after all. While *Gido* shakes him by the shirt, Wes pleads with Sophie and me, pleads with his eyes. He looks terrified and panicked and confused. Sophie and I sit frozen in our chairs. We try to make eye contact with Dad but he's busy holding back Uncle Harry's arms, keeping Uncle Harry from punching Uncle David. The uncles have been drinking, so they're rowdier than they'd normally be if they were sober. Mom is no good to us. She's surrounded by the aunts, and most of them are crying now. *Gido* drags Wes toward Dad. Wes looks like he's about to cry.

There are no goodbyes. Minutes after Dad sees *Gido* with his hands on Wes, we're out of the house.

We leave our plates of food almost completely untouched. Dad buys us burgers and fries on the way home, at the A&W in Vegreville. He says that Mom will be all right with her sisters. She'll probably spend the night with Auntie Mary, then call tomorrow, when she's ready to come home. As we pass through Two Hills, Dad asks if we'd each like a banana split for dessert, from G.O.'s Drive-In, just off the highway. But we've hardly touched our burgers. And G.O.'s isn't open on Christmas Day.

"It's for the best," says Dad, filling the silence on the car ride home. "Kalyna did us all a favour by telling *Baba* and *Gido*. Your mother just couldn't bring herself to do it. She was afraid of their reaction. Doesn't help that her sisters encouraged her to keep it a secret. I don't know. Maybe they were right."

Dad sighs.

"We've got to remember that Mom's parents are old," he says. "They're old and they're old-fashioned and they don't know any better."

It sounds as though he's trying to convince himself.

"Their way is to fear everything. Anything new, anything different. That's why those aunts of yours are the way they are. Not one of them knows how to swim, how to skate, how to ride a bike. Those girls were raised on fear."

"Mom can swim," says Wes.

"Only because I forced her to learn," says Dad. "She was petrified of water. Lakes, pools, you name it. She was scared that she'd drown if she went near water. She didn't know how to drive until after we were married, and I taught her. Imagine that. Those girls were raised on the farm and their dad never taught them how to drive a car."

Dad slows down as we approach the Duvernay Bridge. He asks if anyone needs the bathroom at Brosseau, then he picks up speed for the final stretch home.

"I offered to talk to *Gido*," he says, "a few times. Every time we visited there, I wanted to tell them. They had to be told, Mom knew that. I think your aunts would have told your *Baba*. I'm surprised they didn't tell her, the way they gossip. But your mother wanted to tell *Baba* and *Gido* herself, when she was good and ready."

"Why did he pick on Wes?" I ask, interrupting Dad. "*Gido*, I mean. Why did he yell at Wes like that, and shake him up?"

Wes looks out the window, blinking away tears.

"Well," says Dad. "After I told *Gido* that the arrangements had all been made, that your trip had been paid for, he suggested that we send Wes to Africa."

"Wes?" says Sophie. "You're kidding."

Dad shakes his head. "Don't forget, *Gido* hasn't seen much of the world."

"He immigrated from Ukraine," I say, "doesn't that count for anything?"

"He was eighteen months old. Too young to remember. Never spent a day of his life in school. Really, except for the odd trip to Edmonton, *Gido* never left the farm. So you can't expect him to understand. He figures you girls should be getting married right about now. And if anyone is going anywhere, it should be Wes. Because Wes is a boy."

I roll my eyes. Dad continues.

"*Gido* wasn't yelling at you, Wes. He was yelling at your mother and me, for sending Colleen instead of you. *Gido* told us that we're as cracked as Kalyna. Crazy. He called us crazy."

Dad slows down to fifty as we enter St. Paul.

"But you know," he says, turning north down the gravel road that leads to our farm, "sometimes I think Kalyna isn't crazy at all. Sometimes, I think that she's saner than all the rest of us put together."

I'm not sure that Dad is right. Kalyna should have stayed quiet. Then the fight wouldn't have happened. Mom would be driving home with us. Kalyna made a mess out of everything.

"Kalyna was the only one who had the guts to speak up. And she did it in an eloquent way, too. One hell of an eloquent way. She asked *Gido* to bless you, Colleen. She asked him to say a special prayer for you, for your journey. And when the stubborn old goat wouldn't do it – when he wouldn't pray for you – well, Kalyna did it herself. Right in *Gido*'s face."

Dad chuckles as we pull into the yard. The Christmas lights blink red and green along the eavestroughs of the house. Ralph greets us, barking, at the garage doors.

"So, Colleen," says Dad. "For what it's worth, you have Kalyna's blessing. Wherever you go, whatever you do, you have her blessing."

The automatic garage door kicks in and Dad eases the car into the garage. As the garage door closes behind us, I watch the snow-bank shrink, the full moon disappear. With a flick of the light switch, Dad turns off the Christmas lights outside, and the yard is black.

PART IV

Swaziland

ONE

My plan is to make a quick, clean getaway.

"Just drop me off when we get to the airport," I say. "You don't even have to walk in with me. We'll just wave and say, 'See you later.' Pretend that I'm going away for the weekend."

But Mom and Dad insist on staying with me as long as they can. Wes gets to miss school, and Sophie skips her morning classes at the university. We huddle in a group beside the Air Canada counter, Mom and Sophie and me. Wes lifts my hockey bags onto the weigh scale. Dad talks to the woman behind the counter.

I don't want anyone in the airport to know that this is my first flight, my first solo trip anywhere. I want to look relaxed and slightly bored. Like I know exactly what to do with my luggage, where to go with my boarding pass. I want the world to think that I've done this a hundred times before.

Hockey bags were Dad's idea, not mine. Two big hockey bags, cheap but durable. Experienced travellers don't use hockey bags for luggage. Experienced travellers carry tidy little Pierre Cardin suitcases and posh Pierre Cardin garment bags, and they definitely don't fill their baggage to the maximum weight allowance. My hockey bags weigh seventy kilograms each. Dad checked at home on the stainless steel scale he uses during hunting season, to weigh moose meat.

"Window seat or aisle?" says the woman in the Air Canada uniform.

"Window seat or aisle?" Dad repeats.

I pause, wondering what sort of seat an experienced traveller prefers. Before I have a chance to speak, a voice answers for me from across the departure lounge. A familiar voice. Loud.

"Window seat. Take a window seat!"

I turn around, glaring. Kalyna continues.

"From the sky, all the farmers' fields are like a patchwork quilt."

A few months after Uncle Andy passed away, Auntie Mary and Kalyna went on a trip to Hawaii. To take their minds off all the sadness.

Trailing behind Kalyna is her mom, Auntie Mary, and behind her, Auntie Rose and Uncle Bill, Auntie Pearl and Uncle Charlie, Auntie Linda and Uncle Ed, Auntie Jean and Uncle David, Auntie Natalka and Uncle Harry, and Auntie Marika and Uncle Dave. Seven aunts and six uncles – nearly all of my mother's sisters and their husbands. Plus Kalyna. Fourteen relatives altogether.

The uncles stand quietly in a circle, sipping coffee from Styrofoam cups, but the aunts all talk at once. Auntie Natalka asks Mom how she's holding up. Auntie Mary answers that she's a wreck.

"Look at her," says Auntie Mary. "Just look at her. The poor thing hasn't slept in days."

"I'd be a wreck, too," says Auntie Jean, nodding.

"If my Sonya were going to the other side of the world," says Auntie Linda, "I'd be in the mental hospital."

"It's not too late to change your mind, Colleen," says Auntie Pearl.

"Never too late," says Auntie Marika.

"But my Sonya would never go."

"My girls wouldn't go either. Never."

"You can come home with us right now."

"Right now."

"Honestly, I'd be in the *mental* hospital."

"ENOUGH!"

My mom yells so hard that strangers standing around us turn and stare. The aunts fall silent immediately.

"I'm *not* going to the mental hospital. I'm not going any-where. My daughter *is.*"

The aunts are too shocked to speak.

"My daughter is going to Africa and I'm so proud of her my heart is bursting. Colleen is doing something none of you – none of *us* – could ever dream of doing. Now give her some *peace,* for heaven's sake, before she goes. Give *me* some peace. Please."

My aunts look like a group of schoolgirls who have just been scolded by the teacher. They don't know what to do with them-selves. Their eyes all drop to the floor. Dad puts his arm around Mom. She keeps her chin up, her shoulders straight.

I reach out to hold my mother's hand, and I squeeze. I'm proud of her too.

Uncle Ed steps forward.

"We'll say our goodbyes now," he says, giving Mom a sympa-thetic look. "Let you have some time alone with Colleen."

Experienced travellers don't break down in public. I'm sure of it. They definitely don't cry in the airport. But one by one, as each of my aunts kisses me goodbye – as I press my face against each uncle's winter jacket, taking in the smell of cigarettes and after-shave – I start to feel my throat tighten. Then, watching them walk away toward the airport coffee shop, the tears come. Hot, wet tears spilling down my cheeks.

Wes tries to make a joke as he hugs me, but his voice cracks, so he buries his face in my shoulder.

Sophie wipes her eyes again. "We'll write all the time, right? And we'll talk on the phone all the time, right? And in no time at all –"

She stops talking as she puts her arms around me.

Then Mom and Dad hug me, together, and I hug them back, hard. The three of us stand together for a long time.

"We love you so much," they say. "We're going to miss you."

"I love you, too." I can hardly get the words out.

Then I force myself to walk toward the boarding gate – right, left, right. I do my best to straighten my shoulders, like Mom, and lift my chin. I try not to feel sorry for myself. But my nose is running. The strap of my knapsack keeps cutting into my shoulder. And each time I look back, Mom and Dad are further away, Sophie and Wes look smaller and smaller. In the distance, they're holding on to each other. I'm on my own.

I've never been through airport security before, so I don't know what to do. I glance back once more at Mom and Dad, take a deep breath. While I stand in line waiting for my turn to go through the metal detector, I watch the people around me, to see what they do. Ahead of me are two businessmen in three-piece, pinstriped suits and dark grey trench coats. They empty their pockets into a plastic basket while their briefcases roll down a moving belt through an X-ray machine. In front of the businessmen, a young woman stands with her arms outstretched. A security guard rubs a metal detector up and down her legs, across her torso, sideways along the length of her arms.

None of the other travellers is crying. I wipe the tears from my cheeks.

When my turn comes, I try to act like everyone else, like going through airport security is routine, so that no one will stare at me. I wish that I'd cleaned out my jacket before passing through the boarding gate. I've got used Kleenex, movie ticket stubs, matches, a tampon – a tampon, of all things – and two Tylenol caplets in my pockets. Do they let drugs through security? For a split second, I consider swallowing the pills. But there isn't time. The security guard is asking for my airline ticket and my boarding pass.

After my knapsack has passed through the X-ray machine – after the security guard has looked through my guitar case, rubbed his metal detector against my arms and legs – I'm home free. Nobody looks twice at my Tylenol. Nobody looks twice at *me*. I follow the other passengers down a long corridor toward my boarding gate. I'm on my way.

But halfway down the length of the corridor, I hear my name – a voice behind me, from the direction of the security check, calling my name. Several people around me stop walking to look around. I feel my face burning. Could I have forgotten something? I check for my ticket, my boarding pass. Knapsack, guitar. Nothing is missing. Have I broken a rule?

"Miss Lutzak? Miss Colleen Lutzak?"

One of the security guards taps me on the shoulder. I spin around to face him. And there, beside the security guard, in her bright red parka – out of breath, but grinning from ear to ear – is my cousin Kalyna. She's already said goodbye to me. Why is she here?

The security guard says that Kalyna tried to slip through security, that she put up quite a fight when they wouldn't let her through.

"I've got an older brother," says the guard, shrugging his shoulders. "My brother's sort of like your cousin, here. I didn't think it would hurt to bring her to you. She says that she forgot to give you something."

From the pocket of her parka, Kalyna brings out a long necklace of big pink and purple plastic flowers. A lei. She must have saved it from her trip to Hawaii.

With a solemn, ceremonious air, she drapes the lei around my neck.

"*Bon Voyage!*" she says. "*Aloha!*"

Five or six travellers turn to watch Kalyna as they make their way down the corridor. Some smile. I don't want them to stare so I give Kalyna a quick hug – a quick thank you and an even quicker goodbye. Once she has passed back through the security check with the security guard, I stuff the lei into my knapsack.

During the flight from Edmonton to Toronto, I'm seated next to an older lady. Gladys is her name. At first, I think that Gladys is the nicest lady I've ever met. She gives me Kleenex so that I can blow my nose and a whole pack of Trident to help my ears as we take off. Then, Gladys starts talking.

Gladys is visiting her daughter, Cheryl-Lynne, who is married to Gerald, a stockbroker from Windsor, originally. I see photos of the children from Cheryl-Lynne's first marriage to Adam, photos of the children from Cheryl-Lynne's second marriage to Bernie. Gerald is Cheryl-Lynne's third husband. They haven't started a family yet.

Now and again as Gladys talks, I glance out the window of the airplane. I rifle around in my knapsack, bringing out a book, my Walkman – anything to give Gladys a sign that I'm not interested in Cheryl-Lynne. Gladys doesn't take my hints. When the stewardess brings us our lunch, Gladys hardly touches her meal. She's too busy telling me about Cheryl-Lynne's job at Toronto's Sick Kids, Cheryl-Lynne's home in Etobicoke, Cheryl-Lynne's last holiday in Florida. By the time we've landed at Pearson International Airport, I know everything about Cheryl-Lynne.

And I've learned my lesson. From Toronto to Montreal, I don't even smile at the man sitting next to me, a bald, middle-aged man in a fancy suit. He orders a drink while he reads his *Globe and Mail*. I sip on a Diet Coke, flipping through the airline magazine. I'm learning how things work on airplanes. I know when to expect the liquor cart, the peanuts; when to listen for the captain's voice over the loudspeaker. I make sure that between the bald man and me, there is no exchange of names and no small talk. No conversation whatsoever.

On the flight from Montreal to Paris, I decide to take a nap. I want to be refreshed when we land in Europe. Except for family trips to the States, I've never been out of Canada before. I've never left North America. This is my first time overseas.

But the airport in Paris is a big disappointment. There's nothing European, nothing exotic, nothing remotely interesting about it. It's just like the airport in Edmonton, and Pearson, and Mirabel.

The same duty-free shops, the same magazine kiosks. I expected more. Marble floors, maybe, and gold fixtures. Indoor cafés with small, round, candlelit tables and checkerboard tablecloths and wandering accordion players. I thought the people, at least, would look different. Avant garde outfits, haut couture hairstyles.

After I exchange some of my Canadian dollars for French francs, I buy a coffee and a pastry. The coffee tastes like ordinary, everyday Maxwell House. The pastry is chewy and bland.

To kill time, I pick up a handful of postcards. For Mom and Dad, a picture of the Eiffel Tower; for Sophie, the Palace of Versailles. And for Wes, *L'Arc de Triomphe*. Neither *Baba* nor *Gido* can read English, or Ukrainian, for that matter. But I pick up a Notre Dame Cathedral postcard for them anyway, to show them that I'm alive and well. Maybe they can look at the picture, bring it out when people come to visit.

Once I start to write on the backs of the postcards, I realize that there isn't enough room to say anything meaningful. I want to tell Mom and Dad about everything that I've seen, everything that I've learned about airport security, and customs, and passport control. About changing planes, and changing money. The flavour and texture of airplane food, the way that airplane earphones work when you plug them into your armrest. I want to tell them about Kalyna's farewell gift to me.

The idea comes to me as I'm shopping for paper. I could buy a package of flimsy, see-through airmail paper to write letters home or – for the same price – I could buy a book. A bound, hardcover book filled with regular, lined sheets, all blank.

It's genius. Pure *genius*. To write a book about my travels starting with my departure from Edmonton, covering all of my adventures in Swaziland, and ending when I return to Canada, a year from now. After I've filled the book with stories of my trip, I'll present the finished product to my family. Of course, I'll still have to write letters every so often, and send the odd postcard. But nothing will compare to the book.

Paris to Johannesburg is, by far, the longest leg of my trip. Fourteen hours from takeoff to touchdown, including an hour-and-a-half stopover in Kinshasa to take on fuel and passengers. When the captain comes over the PA system, he explains that our flight will be long because all airplanes destined for apartheid South Africa are banned from a considerable portion of African airspace. Now that I have a book to write, the long flight doesn't bother me. Fourteen hours will pass quickly.

My first objective is to come up with a good title. Something clever and quirky. I make a list of possibilities on the airline barf bag. *Leaving on a Jet Plane* comes to mind. Not a bad title, except that it makes no reference to Africa. *A Passage to Africa* could work. *Into Africa,* even better. Or, *Hello the Beloved Country.*

As I'm covering the barf bag with possible titles, I get the feeling that someone is watching me. To my right is the window of the plane and to my left is an empty seat. On the other side of the empty seat, though, sits a guy about my age. A black guy with a pillbox hat tie-dyed yellow and green. He has a fat face and chubby hands. Around his neck he wears a big, leather pendant in the shape of Africa. I think that he's staring at me. But when I glance over at him, his head is down. He seems engrossed in a paperback novel. I decide that I'm just imagining things.

So I return to my list of titles. *The Story of My Life: Colleen Lutzak.* That's a title for a book by an old person. *As For Me and My Travels.* Cute. A possibility.

My train of thought is interrupted by the feeling that Mr. Africa two seats over is staring at me. In fact, I'm sure of it now. I'm positive that he's watching me write. I look up quickly, trying to catch him in the act, only he's too fast for me. By the time I lift my head, he's back to his novel.

Nosy jerk. He's dying to know what I'm doing with the barf bag, what I'm writing on it. He could just *ask.* I'd probably tell him, even though it's none of his business. I have half a mind to tell him off. Tell him to keep his eyes to himself, let me have a little privacy.

What I need is a secret code. To hide my writing from Mr. Africa. Numbers, maybe, 1 to 26 for each letter of the alphabet. On the first page of my book, I start to make the number-letter key. Then I rip out the page. Stupid. It will take me forever to write anything down and I'll lose all my artistic inspiration in the process. Stupid, stupid.

I could switch letters. A=B, B=C, C=D all the way to Z=A. Again, I start on a key to the code. Again, I rip out the page. Just as time-consuming, just as stupid.

Mr. Africa watches me ripping the pages out of my book. This time, though, he doesn't hide it. I give him my dirtiest look. He's making me waste time, precious time that I could be spending on my book.

Finally, just as the stewardess appears with lunch, I come up with a brilliant way to write my book. I'll be able to read it, and my family will be able to read it, but to all other eyes it will look completely cryptic. Totally unintelligible. Why didn't I think of it sooner? Using the Ukrainian alphabet, I'll write English words. Phonetically, that is. My writing will *look* Ukrainian; read out loud, though, it will sound English. I almost laugh out loud, it's such a perfect idea.

As we eat our meals, Mr. Africa decides to strike up a conversation with me. He makes small talk about our food, and the service on the plane. I'm not interested in talking to him. When he asks me questions, I answer, "Yes," or "No." Nothing more.

"Going to Johannesburg?"

"Yup."

"And are you from Paris?"

"Nope."

"It's a long flight, isn't it?"

"Uh-huh."

He has a funny way of talking, a funny accent – sort of British, I'd say, with a touch of something else. Long vowels. It must be African. South African, I suppose, since he is going to

Johannesburg. And he has a lisp. "Going to *Johannethburg?*" "Are you from *Parith?*" "Long flight, *ithn't* it?"

That's when it dawns on me that I should be friendlier with Mr. Africa. What have I been thinking? Here is my first up-close encounter with a real-life victim of apartheid, an oppressed person – with a speech impediment, no less – and I'm not even acting civil. He probably lisps because his family has no money for speech therapy. Maybe his lisp is a result of ill-treatment by the white regime. Really, now that I've come up with a way to protect my privacy, he's no threat to me. And I wouldn't want him to mistake my behaviour for racism.

"I'm Colleen."

Mr. Africa's mouth is full. He nods as he finishes chewing his food, then reaches out to shake my hand.

"Siya," he says, smiling. *Thiya.*

Siya talks a lot, and he talks quickly. He explains that for the last six weeks, he's been travelling in Europe. When he pulls out his passport, I see that nearly all the pages are covered in stamps. Siya was in London first, visiting friends of his grandparents; then in Berlin with friends of his parents. He spent Christmas in Geneva, New Year's in Brussels. After Brussels, he travelled around by train through the Netherlands and France.

It occurs to me that if Siya can jet-set around Europe, his family has more than enough money for speech therapy. The more he talks, in fact, the clearer it becomes that he must be rich. Prior to his holiday, Siya was finishing his last term at Oxford. I hear about nightclubs and jazz festivals; about driving at top speed on the *autobahn;* about the gardens around the Palace of Versailles – the *Palath* of *Verthailles* – and the red-light district of Paris, and *Le Louvre.* Buckingham Palace, Hyde Park. Shakespeare's birthplace in Stratford-upon-Avon. The Berlin Wall, and Lake Geneva. Swiss girls in Switzerland. French girls in France.

When Siya excuses himself to go to the toilet, I watch him walk down the airplane aisle, trying to imagine what sort of girl

would find him attractive. He's fat. From the waist up, he looks
fairly trim but from the waist down, his body widens like a pear.
And he's short. Shorter than me, even. So he walks on the balls of
his feet, to make himself seem taller. If Siya tried to have a real,
two-way conversation with me, he might improve in my eyes. He
talks about himself too much.

"Have you seen the statue of David?" says Siya, settling back
into his seat.

I shake my head.

"You're joking."

I shake my head again.

"You mean you *really* haven't seen the statue of David?"

This, I think, does not make for a real, two-way conversation.

"You haven't *lived* until you've seen the statue of David. Have
you been to the Leaning Tower of Pisa?"

I shake my head.

"You mean you *really* haven't been to the Leaning Tower of
Pisa? I don't believe it! But you must have been up the Eiffel
Tower."

Our entire conversation follows suit. Did I know that the
drinking age in Germany is sixteen? That marijuana is legal in the
Netherlands? That Jim Morrison's grave is in Paris, France? That
London Bridge isn't in London at all but somewhere in the
Mojave Desert of Arizona, USA?

I should fight fire with fire. Ask him about places and things
he's sure to have never seen. Only, I can't think of anything good.
I've hardly been outside of Alberta. West Edmonton Mall? The
giant *pysanka* in Vegreville? I could try the Rocky Mountains but
Siya would just one-up me with the Swiss Alps, the Andes. The
goddamn Himalayas.

Really, my only line of defence is to start ignoring Siya. So,
after an hour of his bragging, I tune him out altogether. I stop
nodding, stop answering his questions, stop pretending to be interested in his stories. With my book open to the first blank page, I

start to write. Siya, though, doesn't catch on. Like Gladys before him on the flight from Edmonton to Toronto, he keeps talking.

Writing English words with a Ukrainian alphabet is harder than I thought, especially with Siya babbling at my side. I'm out of practice. Plus, for some English sounds – like "th" and "j" and "w" – there are no corresponding Ukrainian letters. I have to substitute "dat" for "that," "dyust" for "just," "vell" for "well."

The title of the book, I decide, will come later. For now, a chapter heading will have to do. I start with *Чептер Вон, Ситінь Вит Сія. Chapter One, Sitting With Siya.*

"What are you writing?" says Siya.

I take a deep, annoyed breath. "Nothing much."

"Is it a diary?"

I pretend that I haven't heard his question.

"It *is* a diary, isn't it? You were writing in it earlier, before we ate. I saw you." Siya leans over, thrusting his nosy head down, inches from the pages of my book. "What language is that? Russian?"

I pull the book away from his eyes. "It's *Ukrainian.*"

"Uker-ain-i-an. As in, the *Ukraine?*"

"Ukraine," I say, correcting him. "Not *the* Ukraine, just Ukraine."

"Ukraine," says Siya, like a parrot.

"Wait, now. Don't tell me, let me guess. You've been to Ukraine. Not once but, what, twice? You've seen it all, done it all. And, let's see, you speak Ukrainian, too. Yes? Am I right?"

"Not at all!" says Siya, ignoring my sarcasm. "I've never been to Eastern Europe. But I'd love to go. You are Uker-ain-i-an, then! And all this time I thought you were American. *Tell me* about Uker-aine, tell me all about it. Say something in your language!"

I stare at Siya, speechless. How could he miss the sarcasm in my voice?

"Actually, I've never been to Ukraine. My grandparents were Ukrainian immigrants but I'm –"

I pause for a moment. How do I explain to Siya that I'm Ukrainian, even though I've never been to Ukraine? I could say Ukrainian Canadian. But then I'd have to explain how it works, being two things at once.

"– I'm Canadian," I say. "Not American. Canadian. This is my first trip away from Canada, away from home."

"And you're going to South Africa," says Siya.

"Swaziland."

"*Swaziland?*"

I nod.

"You're really going to *Swaziland?* This is too much! We're going to the same place, you and I! This is *too* much!"

Yes, I think. Yes, this *is* too much. Siya has the rest of the world to boast about. Swaziland is my only claim to fame, and he's just taken it away from me.

"How long are you staying in Swaziland?" I ask.

I've already resigned myself to the fact that Siya will be with me in the Jan Smuts transit lounge, on board the plane from Johannesburg to Manzini. I'll need a new chapter title. *Ситінь Вит Сія; Ен Епик. Sitting With Siya: An Epic.*

"Now that I've finished my studies," says Siya, looking down at his hands, "I'm going back to live in my country."

"Well, you might live in Swaziland. But you don't *own* it. I mean, technically, it's not *your* country."

This, I think, may well be the pettiest, cattiest thing I've ever said to anyone. Ever. And yet, I say it.

"Well, technically," says Siya, "Swaziland isn't a country at all. It's a kingdom. Therefore, technically, I do own Swaziland. Or at least my family does."

Siya's face becomes stern. "I am Prince Siyabonga Mabandla Liteboho Dlamini."

"Right," I say under my breath, returning to my book. "And I'm Abracadabra Yabba Dabba Doo, Queen of the Prairies." I know all about the royal family in Swaziland, but Siya doesn't look anything like a prince.

"The last king," Siya continues, "the great King Sobhuza II, was my grandfather. His Majesty King Mswati III, the reigning monarch, is my uncle."

I read about King Sobhuza in the information booklet from the college. He was the last king. His name is all over the paper-work I received from Waterford because he's the person who came up with the "Kamhlaba" part of Waterford Kamhlaba United World College of Southern Africa.

"Yeah, well." I feel myself stammering. "If you're a prince, shouldn't you be flying in a private jet? Or, I mean, first class or something?"

Siya smiles.

"And shouldn't you have, I don't know, *bodyguards* or something?"

Siya chuckles. "Look, Sobhuza had over one hundred wives. All of his children are princes and princesses, and their children are princes and princesses too. There are scores of us Swazi royals. It would cripple the economy if we each travelled with an armed entourage. Besides, who would ever want to harm a Swazi prince?"

I don't answer.

In the Jan Smuts Airport, Siya helps me drag my hockey bags off the luggage carousel. His luggage is small, dark green, and designer. Together we stand in line at Customs. Just as I suspected, just as I dreaded, we are taking the same flight from Johannesburg, South Africa to Manzini, Swaziland. Waiting for our bags to be searched, Siya tells me about his country.

Did I know that Swaziland has the second largest man-made forest in the world? I should go see it. The Usutu Paper Mill, too, if I have the chance. For camping out, there is the Malolotja Game Reserve and Mkaye, which is better but more expensive. Did I know that Swaziland has ritzy casinos in the Ezulwini Valley? Live entertainment nightly; world-class dining. For souvenirs, the Swazi

Candle Factory, Ngwenya Glass. African Fantasy by Armstrong
Artworks, in Mbabane, and Endlotane Studios on Oshoek Road.

I couldn't possibly remember everything Siya tells me, not
without writing it all down, and I've long since given up on my
book. Once I'm settled in at the college, while my memory of the
trip is still fresh, I'll bring it out again.

When my turn comes up at the Customs counter, I'm ready
with my hockey bags open, passport and plane ticket to Swaziland
in hand. Two fresh-faced teenagers in army fatigues greet me. One
has platinum blond hair cropped so short that patches of his
blotchy-pink scalp show through; the other has darker, slightly
longer hair. Both are tall and broad-shouldered, both carry rifles.
And beside them, tethered to a chain, alert and menacing, sits a
large German shepherd.

The dark-haired soldier takes a quick glance at my passport.

"Canadian," he says. "Don't believe what you've heard about
us."

The dark-haired soldier gives me a wink as he waves me
through. He doesn't so much as touch my bags. Then Siya steps up
to the Customs counter, and both soldiers turn their attention to
him.

They ask Siya to open all of his bags; with the tips of their
rifles, they poke through Siya's clothes and toiletries. One of the
soldiers, the blond, lifts out a framed certificate. The writing on the
paper is Latin, I think, and there's a gold seal on the bottom right-
hand corner. It's Siya's degree, from Oxford.

With the framed degree in his hand, the blond soldier says
something to the dark-haired soldier – in Afrikaans, I think. I don't
understand what they're saying. My guess is that they're going to
make trouble for Siya. For a moment, I glance around the airport,
trying to spot someone official who can help us. But there's no
one to turn to. The soldiers are the officials.

"It's mine," I say to the soldiers, blurting out my words. "There
wasn't room in my own bags, so Siya here agreed to take it for me.

It's just my degree. From a university in Canada. Right, Siya?"

I look at Siya, the soldiers look at Siya. Siya nods.

"It's from the University of Alberta. In Edmonton. Alberta."

The two soldiers exchange words, again in Afrikaans.

"You know," I add, "the city with the famous mall."

The soldiers seem to ignore me. For several minutes, they continue to poke through Siya's bags. Then the blond finally tosses Siya's degree in the direction of Siya's suitcase, missing the bag altogether. I pick up the frame, its glass cracked now right down the centre. Siya snaps his suitcase shut before he moves along.

As I'm about to follow Siya, the blond soldier steps in front of me, blocking my way. He stands so close to me, and he's so tall, I have to lift my chin to meet his gaze.

"*Kaffir-lover,*" he says, spitting the words in my face.

I push past him, rushing to catch up with Siya. My legs tremble as I run.

According to Siya, the flight to Swaziland is a piece of cake. "Up and down," he says. "Forty-five minutes and we're there."

But his hands are shaking, I notice, as we buckle our seat belts in the *Royal Swazi* plane. Beads of sweat have formed on his forehead. My own pulse is still racing. *Kaffir-lover.* I've never heard such awful words.

"Those soldiers," I say. "They wouldn't have – you know. They wouldn't have really *done* anything to you, right? I mean, you're royalty. And you've flown through Jan Smuts lots of times. They wouldn't have – they're not really allowed to – they can't *do* anything. Right?"

Siya pulls a handkerchief from his pocket, wipes the sweat from his forehead.

"Tell me," he says, ignoring my questions. "How do you say 'thank you' in your language? In your Uker-ain-ian language? I'm curious."

"Come on. I told you, Ukrainian isn't my language. I want to know about the soldiers. They wouldn't have taken your degree away from you, right? What would that prove? You'd just get another copy sent from –"

"In my language – in SiSwati – we say *'Siyabonga.'* To you, I would say, *'Siyabonga, Sisi.'* Which means, *'Thank you, Sister.'*"

"Wait a second. That's your name. Isn't it? *Siyabonga.*"

Siya nods, sweat trickling down the side of his chubby face.

"Well," I say.

Slowly, Siya wipes the sweat with his hanky.

"I guess, in Ukrainian, your name would be – here, repeat after me. *Dee-yak –*"

"*Dee-yak –*"

"*Dee-yak – oo –*"

"*Dee-yak-oo –*"

"*Dee-yak-oo-yoo, Diakuiu.*"

"*Diakuiu. Diakuiu.*"

TWO

By the time we touch down in Swaziland, Siya knows half a dozen words and phrases in Ukrainian. Hello, *Dobryden*. How are you? *Iak sia maiesh?* Merry Christmas, Happy Easter. *Khrystos rodyvsia, Khrystos voskres.* Cookies, *korzhyky. Ia pechu korzhyky.* I bake cookies.

In return, Siya teaches me Swazi words, and how to act when I'm with Swazi people. Once we arrive in Swaziland, Siya is back to his old, know-it-all self again.

"Remember," he says, as we make our way across the tarmac, "Swazis will greet you all the time. Nearly everyone speaks English, at least in Mbabane and Manzini. But, nonetheless, wherever you go, they'll greet you in SiSwati. You must greet them back in SiSwati. It's the custom. They say, '*Sawebona.*' You say, '*Yebo.*'"

Siya drags out the vowels of the SiSwati words. *Saweboooona. Yeeeeebo.*

While Siya talks, I stare straight ahead, across the runway, over the airplane hangars, and up along the horizon into the hills stretched out before us. Dark, wet-green hills speckled with blue-grey rock and clusters of tall, leafy trees. I didn't expect this. There were no photographs in the information booklet from the college, and when Dad talked about the different ecological zones in Swaziland, I didn't really pay attention. I expected savanna. Dry, flat grassland, like in movies about Africa. Almost desert. The odd spindly shrub; a few baobabs with bone-thin, twisted trunks.

Siya is giving me a ride to the college. On the plane, right before we touched down, I told him that I was prepared to take a taxi – Dad said that there should be lots of taxis around the airport – but Siya wouldn't hear of it. He said that the taxi drivers will know I'm a foreigner. They'll know that it's my first trip to Swaziland, and they'll adjust their fare accordingly.

I see what he means – about everyone knowing that I'm a foreigner. It's thirty degrees Celsius outside, and at least thirty-*five* degrees inside. No one else in the airport is wearing corduroy slacks or a heavy wool sweater. No one else is carrying a winter coat, lugging hockey bags across the floor of the airport.

No one else is so white.

There are dozens of other Caucasian people milling around me. The flight from Johannesburg was packed full of South Africans, all destined – according to Siya – for the casinos of the Ezulwini Valley. But the Caucasian South Africans aren't white. Each is tanned to a particular shade of brown. Deep bronze-brown, dark olive-brown. Golden yellow-brown. My skin hasn't seen the sun for months; it looks more blue than brown.

At the airport in Swaziland, it's me who needs help now, not Siya. I need help carrying my hockey bags; help understanding what the Swazi officials say as they examine my residency permit and stamp my passport. Their accents are so thick, they might as well be speaking another language. Siya translates for me. He shows me how to shake hands properly with Swazi people, according to their custom. As I extend my hand, I'm supposed to clasp my left hand around my right wrist.

Siya has his own driver. The driver is waiting for him in the parking lot near the airport in a shiny new black Mercedes. Siya teaches me that it's called a car park here, not a parking lot. He sits in the front seat of the car, on the left side, because the steering wheel is on the right. I sit in the back. As we ease out of the *car park,* I pull out my camera. And, on the way to the college, I shift from side to side, camera poised so that I don't miss a shot. This is my first real glimpse of the Swazi countryside. I want photos of everything. Women walking with baskets on their heads, babies tied to their backs with blankets; groups of schoolgirls in uniform, chatting on the shoulder of the road. Men in traditional Swazi dress, and little boys herding goats along the ditches.

By the time we reach Mbabane, though, forty-five minutes later, I've taken a dozen photos of cows. Cows grazing in the fields beside the road, cows walking along the shoulder of the road. The cows are fascinating. They're so skinny that I can count protruding ribs, and they have abnormally long, twisted horns growing out of their heads. Three times, Siya's driver comes to a full stop to avoid hitting a cow. I think that maybe he should plough into the poor animals, to put them out of their misery. Around Mbabane, the cows finally peter out, and then the shopping malls start, complete with supermarkets and gas stations and hamburger joints.

As we approach Mbabane, Siya decides that a tour is in order. He says that I'll be spending a lot of time in Mbabane, and I need to know my way around – where to open a bank account, who to see about cashing travellers' cheques. I need to become familiar with the South African Trade Commission, so that I know where to apply for my next transit visa. He wants to show me the Ekhwezi Bar and Grill, a good place to hear live music, and Marco's Restaurante, the best place in town for pizza.

According to Siya, it's easy to find your way around Mbabane – though I'm not convinced. I think it's going to take time for me to get used to the place. He shows me Allister Miller Steet – the main street of Mbabane, home of the Ekhwezi and Marco's, and Barclay's Bank. He says that Indingilizi, the only art gallery in town, is nearby. Allister Miller is the centre of all the action; at the south end of it is the Mbabane Market, a great place to buy cheap local crafts – soapstone carvings, wooden masks, swatches of the brightly coloured fabric – and west of the town centre are the two shopping centres, The Mall and the Swazi Plaza, with supermarkets, drugstores, ice cream shops, and clothing stores. Siya says that I should check out the shops in The Mall for upscale, locally made souvenirs — handbags, jewellery, T-shirts, and ceramics.

Siya points to all of the places he talks about, but they pass by so quickly — and there's so much to see — I'm not sure that I'll remember anything from our tour. Oncoming traffic makes me squeeze my eyes shut constantly because I feel like we're on the wrong side of the road. Our driver seems reckless the way that he takes corners, ignoring pedestrians who are trying to cross the street. I see poor people everywhere, many of them old and crippled and begging. I know that Swaziland is a Third World country. Somehow, though, this isn't what I expected to see. They're dressed in rags. They have no shoes. Some are children who couldn't be older than seven or eight.

As we make our slow ascent to Waterford, along the narrow road that winds up and around the Waterford hill toward the college near the top, I spot a mud shack with a thatched roof, an open cooking fire, two children chasing each other around their mother. My camera is lifted and I'm ready to take the perfect photograph — a bit of Swazi shrubbery framing the scene, the African sun setting in the background — but I just can't snap the picture. The woman looks up as our Mercedes passes by; her children wrap their arms around her legs and stare at us. I feel ashamed, pointing my camera at them as though they were animals in a zoo. As though their poverty is something fascinating for my scrapbook.

Welcome, says the sign at the gates of the college.

WELCOME

Waterford Kamhlaba United World College of Southern Africa

WE ARE ALL OF THE EARTH, WHICH DOES NOT SEE DIFFERENCES
OF COLOUR, RELIGION, OR RACE.
WE ARE 'KAMHLABA' — ALL OF ONE WORLD.

King Sobhuza II

But the earth does see differences. It sees differences all the time. I'm seeing them too, for the first time.

There's nobody at the college gates to greet me, and nobody at the main office – except for a night watchman who says that everybody else is at dinner, and that I should make my way over to the cubies straight away. He's not particularly friendly. I tell him that I don't know what the cubies are, let alone where they are. I ask him to show me. But the watchman doesn't seem too thrilled about the idea. He pretends that he doesn't understand what I'm saying.

So I walk back to the car park. Back to Siya, who is waiting for me in the car for the word that everything is all right. Everything isn't all right. I'm starting to dread the moment that Siya drives away. What will I do without him?

Siya talks to the night watchman himself, and he promptly finds out exactly what and where the cubies are. Cubie is another word for room. It's short for cubicle. My cubie is in the senior girls' hostel, not far from the main office. The watchman says that Siya can't help carry my bags there, though. Unless he's a student or a teacher, Siya isn't allowed on campus. We have to say our goodbyes in the car park.

I feel my heart race. I don't want him to leave. I've gotten used to him. I like him. How will I carry my bags by myself? How will I know where to go? How will I understand what people are saying?

After Siya arranges for the night watchman to help me with me bags, he gives me his phone number in Mbabane. Pressing it into my hand, he says that I can call him anytime. "We should get together sometime," he says, "downtown." He says that he'll pick me up at school, anytime.

And then he shakes my hand – the Swazi way.

"*Hamba Kahle,*" says Siya. Goodbye, in SiSwati. And then, with a grin, *"Do pobachennia."* Goodbye, in Ukrainian.

I throw my arms around his neck and thank him for everything.

"Thank you, Siyabonga. Siyabonga, Siyabonga."

If I weren't on the verge of tears, I'd probably find it funny.

It isn't hard to find my cubie once I know where the senior girls' hostel is. Every cubie has a name on it. Inside my room, I find a copy of *Official Rules and Regulations,* a timetable, all of my textbooks, and a letter that tells me what to expect over the next few days. I'm welcome to spend this evening exploring the campus, figuring out my way around. First thing tomorrow, though, I have to be in the assembly hall for the headmaster's opening remarks. Then classes begin. They don't waste much time.

Or much space.

Each cubie is five feet by six-and-a-half feet, with a cement bed built right into the wall, and a mattress on top of it. Across from the bed, there's a desk; beside the desk, a cupboard, also built into the wall. The cubie door doubles as the cupboard door, so that when the cupboard is open, the cubie is closed, and vice versa.

Settling into my cubie isn't my first priority. Showering *is.* I've been wearing the same clothes since I left home. Shower first, unpack later. I can almost feel the water pelting my shoulders and back, rinsing away the last three days of traveling.

Are there rules against showering at this time of day?

Flipping through *Official Rules and Regulations,* I hear water running, voices echoing against tile. It must be all right.

But it isn't all right. It isn't all right at *all.* Two steps into the bathroom – soap, shampoo, conditioner, and razor wrapped inside my towel – I realize that I'm in trouble. There are no walls between the shower heads, and no curtains. Nothing to divide the shower area from the toilets and the sinks. Just one, big steamy room filled with wet, naked bodies. Three girls stand side by side under three jets of water, chatting as they lather their armpits and crotches. At the sink, two girls brush their teeth, bare-breasted, towels wrapped around their waists.

My heart races as I slip back into my cubie, shutting the door tightly behind me. I'm a private person. Showering is a private activity. What if I have my period? Other girls will see me. They'll stare at my nude, menstruating body. I won't do it. I won't shower in a group. If I have to, I'll get up in the middle of the night. I'll shower at four in the morning, if that's what it takes.

For now, a change of clothes will have to do.

Of course, nothing is left unwrinkled in my hockey bags. I packed my bags well over a week ago, so all of my clothes are creased. I pull out a pair of brown walking shorts, a white cotton T-shirt. The girls' hostel is split into two corridors, connected by the bathroom, and each corridor, I discover, has a communal iron and a communal ironing board. Shorts and T-shirt in hand, I head down my corridor to press my clothes.

Another girl has beaten me to it. A girl in a beige bra and a long, black skirt. A black girl ironing a blouse with black-and-white polka dots.

My first new friend.

I decide that while she irons, I'll introduce myself — find out her name, where she's from. Then I'll ask her if she wants to come with me to find out where we eat, and whether dinner is still being served. I'm starving.

Except that, by the time I reach the ironing board, the girl is walking away. She's walking away quickly, though I can see that she hasn't finished. Half of her blouse is still criss-crossed with sharp creases.

"Hang on!" I say. "Come back!"

The girl stops dead in her tracks. Slowly, she turns back toward the ironing board.

I point to the ironing board. "You can finish." I smile.

The girl doesn't smile back. Without a word, she lays her

blouse again across the ironing board.

"Are you from here?" I ask, trying to be cheerful. "From Swaziland, I mean?"

The girl shakes her head as she passes the iron across her blouse.

"From South Africa?"

She nods, her eyes focused on the blouse in front of her. She's shy, I think. I'll have to do the talking.

"I'm from Canada. My name is Colleen."

I wait for the girl to introduce herself. She keeps her head down, keeps ironing.

"What's your name?" I ask, after several moments have passed.

"Thandiwe."

"Thandiwe. What a nice name. Well, Thandiwe, I've been travelling for the last three days. My clothes are so wrinkled. Just *look* at these shorts. I don't know how I'll ever get them straightened out."

Thandiwe looks up from the ironing board. "Shall I press them for you?" she says, quietly, whispering almost.

Why would she press my shorts?

"If you want," she says, "I could show you how to press them yourself. It's not very hard once you get the hang of it."

"I've *got* the hang of it thank-you-very-much," I say, laughing. "Who do you think has been ironing my clothes all my life?"

The girl shrugs. I stop laughing.

"*Me!*" I say. "*I* have. *I've* been ironing my clothes all my life!"

Thandiwe doesn't seem convinced. She looks at me as though I'm lying. She must think that I have servants at home to do my ironing. I'm sure of it. But not all white people grow up with servants. We don't all have nannies and maids and housekeepers.

Making friends here is going to be tricky, I see. Trickier than I thought. I'm going to need time to come up with a strategy.

I apologize for disturbing Thandiwe. I tell her that I'll come back later. Slowly, I walk back to my room.

Staring at the walls of my cubie, I open a Mars bar. Thank God
for the Mars bars Mom bought me. I start to plan where I'll hang
my pictures, and where I'll set out the odds and ends that I
brought from home. Above my bed, posters of my favourite singer,
Joni Mitchell. Joni Mitchell in blue jeans and a tie-dyed shirt, sitting in a pile of straw next to her yellow acoustic guitar. Joni
Mitchell close up – pensive – her hair long, hanging limp and
straight. Joni Mitchell live, in concert. Eyes closed, mouth open.

On the back of my cubie door, with thumbtacks, I'll pin up
my print of Picasso's "Three Musicians." Beneath the Picasso, I'll
tape up the small paper Canada flag that I saved from last year's
Canada Day celebration in St. Paul. And around the burglar bars
in my window, I'll wind a red and green flowered scarf. The ker-
chief that I wore during my last year of Ukrainian dancing.

Unrolling my close-up of Joni Mitchell, I hear voices nearby.
Voices chattering and giggling; girls on their way back from dinner. When I open my door, I see three girls walk into the cubie
across the hall: three Indian girls in brightly coloured saris. I watch
them settle onto the bed together, and light a stick of incense.
Ribbons of smoke drift out of the half-open cubie door. It's not
like Father Zubritsky's incense, though. The Indian incense is rich
and spicy. I inhale deeply.

For a moment, I hesitate. I can't just barge in, and push myself
on them. I can't exactly force them to be my friends. I could ask
to borrow masking tape for my posters. A tea bag maybe. Some
sugar? Then I remember my Canada pins. The tiny plastic
Canadian flags that Mom gave me for Christmas. Gifts for the
girls, icebreakers. Conversation starters.

Pins in hand, I knock on the half-open door. *"Helloo-oo.
Saweboooona!"*

The giggling stops. One of the girls pokes out her head.
"Yes?"

"I'm your new neighbour!" I reach out to shake her hand.
"Colleen Lutzak, from Canada."

The Indian girl gives my hand a polite squeeze. Her name is Preeya. Inside her cubie, I meet Vijia and Samina. After the three girls thank me for the Canada flag pins, the four of us sit together.

I ask questions – "Where are you from? How many years have you been at Waterford? How many years have you known each other?" – and they give one word answers.

"Botswana." "Seven." "Seven."

A few minutes later, I excuse myself, explaining to Preeya, Vijia and Samina that I've got bags to unpack, posters to put up. Back in my cubie, I hear one of the girls mimicking my voice with a thick drawl – *"I'm your new neighbour from Canada."* Another girl says, *"Shhhh."* The giggling resumes.

I try not to let the Indian girls bother me. I try to concentrate on decorating my room. But tears come to my eyes as I stare at my empty cubie, my blank walls. Up the corridor, girls gather outside their rooms, talking and laughing. Down the corridor, someone turns on a stereo. Outside my cubie door, two girls reunite for all the hostel to hear.

"I've missed you so much!"

"I've missed you, too!"

The two girls gossip about their travels over the Christmas holidays, they share news from home.

It doesn't take me long to figure out that most of the girls have been going to Waterford for years. They all know each other. They're old friends. For all I know, I'm the only new student in the senior class. I'll never make friends here.

With tears in my eyes, I plunge my hands into my hockey bags. I pull out all of my jeans, t-shirts, shorts. My one-piece bathing suit, my two-piece bathing suit. Socks, panties, bras. Flannel pyjamas. In one of my bags, there's an envelope of photos taken at home over the last year. I'll put the pictures up around my bed, above my desk. In the spaces between Jonis, between Picasso and the Canada flag.

I know that I packed them. Photos of Mom and Sophie in the

summer – Mom lifting her first batch of *pyrohy* from the outdoor clay oven that Dad had just built; Sophie at Mom's side, holding back our dog Ralph as he jumps at the loaves of bread. Photos of Sophie, Wes and me posing one Halloween in matching green costumes. We went as three peas in a pod. Dad and Wes ice fishing at Blacket Lake in red and black Merc snowmobile suits, the two of them holding up thermos mugs of rum and coke, saying "Cheers" to the camera.

Where are the photos?

Panicking now, I turn the hockey bags upside down, shaking their contents onto my bed. A box of Tampax drops out, scattering tampons across the floor. Plastic cassette cases crack against the cement; my hardcover copy of *One Hundred Years of Solitude* drops onto Joni Mitchell's torso, ripping a hole in her guitar. I don't care.

When I finally find the envelope, I ruin half the pictures inside. Tears drip onto the photos, onto Ralph's nose, onto Mom's bread. Onto Sophie's green hands.

My first night at the college is a rough one. I see every hour on the clock, hear every strange noise outside my window. I consider showering at three in the morning, but I don't want to wake up the hostel, and I'm scared to walk around in the dark.

At a quarter to six, just as I'm nodding off, a troop of girls starts traipsing up and down the corridor, to the shower room and back to their cubies.

When I find my way to the dining hall, two hours later, and then the assembly hall, my eyes are bloodshot and swollen from lack of sleep, and from crying.

The assembly hall is a long, rectangular auditorium filled with rows of benches that slope down to a stage at the front. Dark red velvet curtains frame the stage; there's a podium in the centre, and a piano in the wings. Everyone has an assigned area in the assembly hall – senior students at the back, junior students at the front, faculty on stage behind the podium. The headmaster, Mr. Harrington, starts the opening assembly with the Swaziland

National Anthem, followed by a reminder that Waterford was founded in 1963 as a challenge to the separate and unequal educational systems in apartheid South Africa. He quotes King Sobhuza – the same words that are on the sign at the college gates. *We are all of the earth which does not see differences of colour, religion, or race. We are 'Kamhlaba' – all of one world.*

I sit with my books on my lap up near the top of the hall, looking down at the other students. They all sit in clusters – white students separate from black students separate from Indian students. Boys sit with boys, girls with girls. Boarding students apart from day students.

While Mr. Harrington runs through the college rules, I take notes in the book that I bought in Paris. Attendance at breakfast is mandatory. It's served from 7:00 a.m. to 7:50. There is a compulsory morning assembly from 8:00 a.m. to 8:20. Classes from eight-thirty to twelve noon. Lunch until one, classes until three. Afternoon sport from three to five. Between five and six, more classes. Between six and seven, dinner. Study period from seven and nine. Check-in and lights out by ten-thirty.

Every other Saturday morning, we have classes. Four extra hours of classes every second weekend.

For a minimum of one term, all students are required to perform Community Service: four hours of mandatory volunteer work in Mbabane, eight kilometres from the college.

Walking, hiking, or jogging in the hills behind the school is prohibited, unless we have permission from the on-duty staff member. Swimming in the college pool is prohibited, unless we're supervised by the on-duty staff member. Day trips to Mbabane are prohibited, unless we have permission from the on-duty staff member.

No loud music is ever allowed in students' cubies. Boys and girls can mix in the common room only but never in each other's cubies.

No smoking, drinking, or drugs, on or off campus.

It takes me a few days to find my way around campus – to figure out where I'm allowed to go, and when. All of the school buildings are situated around a central, quadrangular courtyard – the senior and junior hostels, connected by the dining hall; the classroom block; the assembly hall; the library; the sick bay; and the main office. We're allowed in the dining hall at mealtimes, but not before or after. During class time, we have to be in the classroom block; between classes, we're supposed to socialize in the courtyard. Most of the buildings on campus look the same. They're made of whitewashed concrete and they have flat roofs. Teachers, though, live in round, thatched-roof rondavels built higher up in the hills, just past the playing field and the pool, a few minutes' walk from the main part of the campus. We're not supposed to go near their houses.

The school grounds are lush and green – there's grass everywhere, and flowers I've never seen before with big, bright blossoms. A huge avocado tree grows right outside the senior hostel – complete with real avocados. The assembly hall is surrounded by poinsettias. I've only seen poinsettias in pots, at Christmastime. I didn't know that they grew into trees. I can't wait to tell Mom.

I'm not the only new senior student at Waterford, taking in everything for the first time. Six new students in total have come to Waterford on United World College scholarships. Six including me. All girls. We meet each other during the first day of classes, while we're all stumbling around, trying to orient ourselves to our new surroundings. We all have History together. That's where I learn their names and their nationalities.

Maria is a doll. Literally. She's four foot nine, maybe four foot ten, with miniature doll hands and miniature doll feet. We spend five full minutes in our first history class trying to figure out where she's from. "Eets-TSEEL-ay," she says. "Eets-TSEEL-ay." Italy? "Eets-TSEEL-ay." Italy. "*EETS-TSEEL-AY.*"

She points to her country on the globe in the corner of the classroom.

Ah. Chile.

One of the scholarship girls, Nikola, speaks five languages. Spanish, unfortunately, isn't one of them. She's German. Tall, stick thin, no shape. Her hair is blue-black but dyed, obviously, because there is a quarter-inch of blonde growing out along her centre part. Her real eyebrows are almost completely plucked away and she draws fake brows over her eyes with black pencil. Nikola only wears low-cut, sleeveless shirts. Short, tight skirts. Her legs are covered with fine, blonde hair.

Then there is Katja, who is from Poland, apparently. Listening to her talk in class, I would have guessed she came from England. In her voice, there's no trace of a Polish accent – nothing remotely Eastern European – and her grammar is impeccable. Katja dominates the history class. She's good with dates, good at analyzing events. A brain, actually. Katja is a total *brain*. She never takes her eye off the teacher, Mr. Afseth. Never talks out of turn. Never smiles.

Shelagh is bright, too. Bright in class. Bright blue eyes, bright red hair. But foul-mouthed and hot-tempered. Two or three times during each class, Mr. Afseth has to remind Shelagh to clean up her language. I don't mind it myself. Shelagh is Irish and Catholic, from Belfast. Even when she's swearing, I like to listen to the lilt in her voice, the rhythm of her language.

We almost never hear Hannah's voice. She doesn't say much, and she's soft-spoken when she does speak. She sits beside me, alternately chewing her fingernails and the end of her pen. Her hair is black – *real* black, not dyed like Nikola's. Sometimes Hannah takes a strand of it in her fingers and twirls. When I glance over at her paper, I see that she takes notes from right to left, in Hebrew. She's from Israel.

After History, I try to strike up conversations with the other scholarship students. Three days in a row I try. Three days in a row, the girls brush past me, rushing to get to their next class. Almost all of them are taking the same subjects, so their schedules are identical. I'm the only scholarship student in my English literature class, and the only scholarship student in my French, environmental studies and economics classes. The exception is music. Katja, the girl from Poland, is in my music class. The two of us are the only scholarship students taking music. We're the only senior music students, period.

It's just my luck, getting stuck with Katja Malanowski three hours a day, five days a week. History isn't so bad, because the class is big. As long as Katja isn't talking, I can ignore her. Music is a different story, though. I can't block her out. There are only two of us, after all, and we're both piano students. I wish that she played a different instrument, or that she screwed up once in awhile. But she doesn't. Katja understands theory inside and out, she's got a good ear, her playing is impeccable – and she knows it. She struts into music class every day. When our teacher, Mrs. McBain – who is also the head of the Senior Hostel – asks us a simple question, Katja gives complicated, ten-minute-long answers. She's never stumped, and she never second-guesses herself. She makes Siya look humble.

If she were friendly, music class would be better. Everything would be more fun. During the evening study periods, Katja and I are the only students allowed outside the hostel because we need to go to the music room to practise. We could walk across the courtyard together, quiz each other on ear-training and melodic dictation. Bring cups of coffee with us, and do our harmonic analyses together at the stereo. I try to get to know her before our music classes start, and when I run into her in the practice rooms at night. I ask her questions about her training, her piano teacher in Poland. She just doesn't like me. And I don't know why. It's as though she can't wait to get away from me. I annoy her.

In the evenings, after study period ends, I don't always go back to the hostel. Sometimes I stay in the practice room to do extra work on my playing. I'm rusty. When I sit at the piano, I feel stiff and tense. I can hear Dr. Kalman telling me that I need to relax, but I can't. I'm worried that I've lost my touch, and I won't ever find it again. Scales don't come easily to me anymore. My fingers don't work properly. I can't remember pieces that I used to play, that I used to have memorized. Katja is ten times the pianist that I am, and she never has to stay late in the practice rooms.

On my way back to my cubie for check-in and lights out, music books pressed against my chest, I have to pass by Katja's door. I have to listen to the voices of the other scholarship students in her room, talking and laughing. After every study period, all the scholarship girls congregate in Katja's cubie. They come out to the common room for check-in, but then they go back to her room and stay there long after lights out. I can hear them as I walk to the bathroom to brush my teeth, as I walk back to my cubie to go to sleep. Sometimes I linger outside Katja's room, trying to work up the courage to knock. Katja likes the other girls. Why doesn't she like me? I wish that her door would open on its own, magically, and that the girls inside would clear a space for me on the bed.

I've looked into Katja's cubie before – once when she was in the shower, once when she was filling her cup with water from the corridor kettle. Her walls are plastered with maps of Eastern Europe, maps of Poland. There are black and white photos of Katja and a man – her boyfriend, maybe – in dark, heavy coats, holding hands as they stand next to a sign that says SOLIDARNOSC. Over her bed, she's hung a poster of Lech Walesa. For a bedspread she uses a giant Polish flag, its red and white bands lying vertically down the length of her bed. Red and white, just like the Canadian flag.

Shelagh is the one who catches me one night standing outside Katja's door, my toothbrush in hand.

"Don't be shy now," says Shelagh as she leads me into Katja's cubie. "We've been wanting you to join us for days but you're always off in the music room."

Maria gets up from the chair beside Katja's desk, motioning for me to take her seat. As Nikola hands me an empty ceramic cup, Shelagh reaches into Katja's cupboard for a bottle of Polish vodka tucked under a pile of clothes. Katja and Hannah are stretched out on the bed, both smoking. Shelagh lights a cigarette, and offers me one. I shake my head.

While all of this goes on, the girls keep talking. The conversation never stops. It's as though nothing has happened. Nothing at all. But I feel my spirits lifting like the smoke from Shelagh's cigarette.

I don't actually like vodka much – years ago, when Sophie and I were kids, we tried some of Dad's vodka. We drank three glasses each before we started throwing up. It makes for a funny story, I think. I'm about to tell it, in fact, when the girls start talking about politics, sharing stories from home, about events that have changed their lives.

Nikola goes first. Her chin trembles as she describes the demolition of the Berlin Wall, the first time she set eyes on her aunts and uncles and cousins from East Berlin.

Katja breaks in, telling us about the last few months in Poland – the rise of the Solidarity party, the introduction of democracy. The celebrations in the streets.

Katja's eyes are bloodshot. While she talks, she refills her cup with vodka.

"We never thought we'd see them," says Nikola. "Never in our lifetimes."

Maria places her tiny hand on Nikola's arm.

"You're lucky," says Maria, playing with the crucifix that hangs around her neck. "My uncle was a member of a local trade union. My father's brother. He disappeared a few weeks after Pinochet took over the country. We pray for him but –"

Shelagh nods. "I know. You pray and you pray. You wear your bloody *knees* out praying. And what comes of it? Twelve years ago, two cousins of mine were taken from their homes. IRA sympathizers, both of them. They could've been my brothers, or my father. A few years later and they could have been my husband. For twelve years, I've watched my aunts and uncles pray for my cousins. I've listened to them pray. For *twelve years*. I used to pray with them. Got down on my hands and knees beside them. What good has it done? Let me tell you something: I'm not doing it anymore. I'm not praying *anymore*. I've bloody well had it up to *here* with prayer."

Shelagh waves her hand over her head.

Hannah looks down at her hands. "You can't stop praying. You just can't. You can't give up what you believe in, who you are. You've got to fight for it."

"And you're willing to do it?" says Shelagh. "You're willing to fight?"

"I've got no choice. In Israel, military service is compulsory. For everyone, male and female. When I go back home to Tel Aviv, I'll spend two years in the army."

Katja downs the vodka in her cup, pours herself another shot. Her eyes settle on me.

There is silence in Katja's cubie. Awful silence. Everyone in the room has spoken. Everyone except me. I look down into my cup, swishing the vodka clockwise, counter-clockwise, clockwise. In my mind, I run through my family's history, searching for something horrible. Some kind of real oppression or injustice. Some tragedy.

If only we were – I don't know – French Canadian, maybe. Then I could bring up the FLQ Crisis. If my family were Native then I could talk about self-government, land claims, racism. Reserves. Or if we were Metis. The Metis don't even have reserves. For a moment, I consider talking about Sister Maria. But her story doesn't have anything to do with me. I wasn't there, I didn't suffer. I can't talk about Ukrainians in Canada, either, like I did at my scholarship interview. About how my parents had to stop speaking Ukrainian. It would sound silly. They didn't disappear, or die. They weren't killed. I have nothing to say. Nothing at all to contribute to the conversation.

Shelagh, I think, can sense my discomfort because she changes the subject. She starts talking about our classes and our teachers. The academic workload at the college. In order to graduate, each of us has to complete a big project, like a thesis. It's called the Extended Essay, or E². All of the teachers have been encouraging us to pick our topics early, to get started on our research as soon as possible.

Shelagh asks if anyone has thought about their E².

As the other girls answer Shelagh's question, my stomach turns. I don't know what I'm going to write about. I have no ideas.

Hannah is going to examine the events leading up to the Beijing Massacre in Tiananmen Square, June 4, 1989 – from a feminist perspective.

Maria lets out shriek of approval. For her E², Maria is going to analyze the role of Nicaraguan women in the Sandinistas.

At the moment, Katja is undecided. Her essay is going to have something to do with the fall of communism in Poland. Maybe an in-depth study of the Catholic church in relation to Solidarity. She's not sure. Mrs. McBain wants her to write a piece of music instead of an essay. Music students can submit original compositions as Extended Essays. She might go with the music option.

Shelagh is going to analyze IRA murals in Belfast. Nikola says they should work together. She wants to focus on the Berlin Wall – specifically, on the graffiti of the Berlin Wall. Graffiti as art, art as politics.

And we're right back where we started.

"Let's hear from our Canadian friend, shall we?" says Katja, lifting her cup in my direction. A Polish accent is creeping into her speech now, and she's slurring her words a little. "You can speak, I assume?" Katja pours more vodka into her cup.

Shelagh touches my leg, gently. "Yes, Colleen. Are you going to do something related to music?"

"Music? Yes, music. Definitely music. Probably Ukrainian music."

Without thinking, I blurt out the words – the first words that pop into my head – anything to fill the cubie with my voice.

"Really," says Katja, staring me straight in the eye. "Ukrainian music."

"You mean, *classical* music?" says Hannah. "By Ukrainian composers?"

"Sounds fascinating," says Nikola. "From what perspective?"

"How will you do research?" says Maria.

The questions make me dizzy. Or maybe it's the vodka. I squirm in my chair, trying to dream up a political angle. I think about Sister Maria's work. I have all of her transcriptions in a box in my bedroom at home. Maybe I should do something with it. Pick up where she left off. But it would be a lot of work. Sister Maria spent years collecting music and writing it down. I don't know exactly how she put the transcriptions together. Where would I begin?

"Ukrainian folk music," I say, gulping down the rest of the vodka in my cup – for courage, to buy time. Ukrainian folk music is easy. Plus I know all about it, so this is safe territory.

"I'm going to study Ukrainian folk music in Canada." The vodka burns in my throat. "Ukrainian Canadian folk music, I mean. You know. Over the last – well – from the turn of the century, I guess. To the present day."

Shelagh gives me a nod of encouragement, Maria and Hannah smile. Katja yawns. I continue improvising, gaining momentum as I go.

"I'll be looking at traditional songs, traditional instruments. Melodies and harmonic structures. Using songbooks. And recordings, to some extent. To understand how the old music has changed in the new world. In Canada, I mean. Under the influence – the *oppressive* influence – of dominant, Anglo-Canadian culture."

I sit back in my chair, relieved. Relaxed. Not bad for spur of the moment. Not bad at all.

Katja leans forward.

"And," she says, "you've chosen this topic because – ?"

"Because I'm Ukrainian."

"Oh." Katja crosses her arms over her chest. "I thought you were Canadian."

"Both. I'm both, actually. Ukrainian Canadian."

"Dual citizenship, two passports," says Hannah.

I shake my head. "No, I've just got one passport. But my grandparents immigrated to Canada from Ukraine. So –"

"So you're not Ukrainian, then," says Katja. "Your *grandparents* are Ukrainian. *You* are Canadian."

I feel my face turn bright red. My ears start to burn.

"I'm both. It's hard to explain."

"Try." Katja drinks from her cup, her eyes focused on me.

I clear my throat.

"Come on," says Katja. "Explain it to us. Explain it to *me*. Please. I'm wondering what it feels like to be Ukrainian."

"Well, it feels just like – well, I'm sure it doesn't feel any different than –"

"Any different than *what?*" says Katja, interrupting me. "Come on. How does it feel? You said you were Ukrainian. How does it *feel?*"

"What do you mean?"

"Your people are cowards. Cowards and traitors. They have no conscience. They murder innocent people without a second thought. Tell me. How does it feel to be one of them?"

"I don't know what you're talking about," I say.

But I do. She's talking about the war. She's talking about Sister Maria.

"I'm talking about Kiev, 1941. Do you read your own history? Maybe not. It happened a long time ago. When your people were still – how would you say it? – Ukrainian *Ukrainian*. Before they came to the – what was your phrase? – the new world. To sing songs."

Katja chuckles.

"What the hell are you on about, Katja?" says Shelagh. "Spit it out, for Christ's sake."

"Thirty thousand Jews systematically murdered by the Nazi regime in Kiev," says Katja, "that's what I'm on about, and countless Ukrainians who turned their backs on their own people to collaborate with the Nazis. They hunted Jews out of hiding in Ukraine. They did it all over Poland, too. Ukrainian soldiers hunted Ukrainian Jews and Polish Jews, and then they stood by to watch them die."

"It wasn't me," I say, my voice trembling. "I wasn't there. My grandparents weren't there. They never lived in Kiev. They were farmers. They moved to Canada before the war, years before. In 1899."

"Right," Katja says, nodding her head. *"Right.* Brave settlers taming the wild west. Stealing land from the –"

"Enough!" Shelagh glares at Katja. "What is *up* with you?"

"Just as many Polish people settled in Canada," I say. "Maybe more."

"No one I know." Katja shakes her head. "No one from my family. My grandparents didn't run from the Communists. They *stayed.* They committed themselves to the –"

"All *right,* Katja!" Shelagh breaks in. "Jesus *Christ,* could you shut your bloody trap already and let us talk about something else? Christ."

But I'm already halfway out the cubie door. Katja pours herself another drink as I go. The other girls – Hannah, Maria, Nikola – keep their eyes on the floor.

"Don't go, Colleen!" Shelagh follows me up the corridor.

As I fumble with the keys to my cubie door, my eyes blurred with tears, Shelagh places her hand on my shoulder. I shake it away.

"I'm sorry. Really, I am. Katja was way out of line. You didn't deserve that. No one deserves that. She just had too much to drink. Give her the night to sober up, and tomorrow morning she'll be apologizing. I'll make sure of it."

I close the door of my cubie quickly, and stand for a moment with my back to it before I slide down to the floor, and press my knees to my chest, my head down, crying.

A week passes. Two weeks.

Katja doesn't apologize. In history class, she won't even look at me. We don't say a word to each other in the music room. Shelagh sits with me at breakfast sometimes. She says that Katja is too proud to say she's sorry. Every so often, two or three of the other girls drop by to visit me. We talk about the weather, our history assignments. No one mentions the incident in Katja's cubie.

I can't forget it, though, can't put it out of my mind. I think about Katja all the time, and the things that she said to me. I think about my grandparents, about *Baba* and *Gido* sitting at their old kitchen table in their house in Vegreville, eating their Meals-on-Wheels suppers with shaky hands. I think about Sister Maria. Her music room. The boxes and boxes of unfinished manuscripts stacked in my old bedroom at home.

Finally, after study period one evening, I slip into the college library, diary in hand.

There aren't many books to choose from. Nearly all of the college history books are devoted to South African history. They're organized under tiny cardboard headings. *Archeology: Rock Paintings. Early History to 1500. Arrival of the Europeans. British Conquest. The Mfecane. The Difaqane. The Great Trek. The Anglo-Boer War. The Establishment of South Africa. Apartheid. The African National Congress. The Anti-Pass Campaign and the Sharpeville Massacre. Black Consciousness and the Soweto Massacre.*

Under the *World History* heading, I find two Polish books. One skinny paperback about the history of Polish aviation and a hardcover biography of Jozef Poniatowski, some eighteenth-century Polish hero. I come across three or four World War II history books, too, and I run my finger down each table of contents, each index, looking for the word *Poland* or the word *Ukraine*. I find

Auschwitz. Gdansk. Majdanek, Treblinka. Warsaw Uprising. Nothing about Polish people committing injustice. But nothing about Ukrainians committing injustice, either, in 1941, in Kiev. Nothing at all about Ukrainians.

This is stupid, I think, slipping the World War II books back into the shelf. It's juvenile. Playing into Katja's hand, stooping to her level. It's childish. What do I care about events that took place fifty years ago? Nothing. What does any of it have to do with me? Nothing.

That's when I find something – a book tucked into the bottom of the shelf marked *Agriculture and Forestry.* Somebody made an error with the book; some librarian miscategorized it. I wouldn't have noticed it at all, in fact, except that the book is enormous – four inches thick, at least – and there is a drawing of embroidery on its spine. With two hands, I lift it from the shelf, lug it across the library to a carrel. *Ukraine: A History.* The book is brand new. I must be the first person to open it.

No, not the first. Someone has written on the title page. *A donation from E. Shabalala to the students of Waterford Kamhlaba.*

Ukraine: A History is a reference book, which means that I'm not permitted to take it out of the library. Three nights in a row, then, during free time before check-in, I sit in the library, leafing through the pages of the book, scribbling notes on the pages of my diary. Some sentences – some entire paragraphs – I take down word for word; some I paraphrase. I record all of the corresponding page numbers, the author's name, the copyright information – everything. For Katja. So that she can double-check, if she chooses. So that she knows every word is true.

There is more information in *Ukraine: A History* than I ever dreamed I'd find. When I've finished, twelve pages of my diary are covered in my handwriting. I write down dates, facts, names. In my cubie, on loose-leaf paper, I recopy the best parts, neatly, organizing the information chronologically, underlining the words *Poland, Polish,* and *Poles.*

History of Ukraine, especially Western Ukraine: marked by centuries of domination by Tsarist Russia; by Austro-Hungarian Empire; by White Russians; by Bolsheviks; by Germany's Nazi Regime; by <u>Poland</u>.

1340-1366. <u>Polish</u> King Casimir the Great leads <u>Polish</u> forces in the occupation of Galicia and Volhyna.

1500's. Ukrainian nobles assimilated to <u>Polish</u> culture and religion. Ukrainian language and customs, as well as Orthodox religion, therefore increasingly associated with the lower classes of Ukraine.

1600's. Five major Cossack/peasant revolts against <u>Polish</u> aristocracy. All revolts brutally suppressed.

November, 1918 - July, 1919. <u>Polish</u>-Ukrainian War. <u>Polish</u> troops (experienced in WWI battle) easily defeat Ukrainian army of volunteers (teenaged boys, mostly, and peasants, without arms, without food, without shoes).

1920. <u>Poland</u> declares that it will protect the rights of Ukrainians and other minority groups living within its borders.

1924. Entente Powers, through League of Nations, declare <u>Poland's</u> right to Galicia in Western Ukraine. Ethnically "pure" <u>Polish</u> settlers given Ukrainian land. Ukrainian language periodicals abolished. Ukrainian cultural organizations banned. Ukrainian language schools shut down. Laws passed to ban use of Ukrainian language in government agencies

Autumn, 1930. <u>Poland's</u> "Pacification" or "Pasifikatsia" campaign against Ukrainians in Galicia. Ukrainian buildings and monuments demolished. Ukrainians arrested, beaten, tortured, denied medical care. Hundreds die, hundreds more suffer permanent, debilitating injuries.

1934. <u>Polish</u> government takes back promise made to League of Nations to protect rights of minority groups in <u>Poland</u>. <u>Polish</u> officials establish concentration camp at Bereza Kartazka for Ukrainian nationalists.

It's past midnight when I make my way to Katja's cubie, stack of papers in hand, heart beating fast. The corridor is dark and quiet, for the most part. Outside Katja's room, I can hear hushed voices and smell cigarette smoke. The scholarship girls, like clockwork, have gathered again. For a few minutes, I stand outside

Katja's door, unsure of how to proceed. I could leave the pages outside her door, or slip them under her door, or tack them to her door. I could barge in, making a dramatic, impromptu speech about Katja's ignorance and *her* people's cruelty.

In the end, I settle on knocking. A second later, the cubie door opens and Katja appears. Behind her, I see the other girls – some sitting, some lying – around the room, their eyes wide.

"Katja."

"Yes?"

"You didn't do your homework."

Katja looks puzzled. Katja the brain, the straight-A student. The head of the class. When has Katja ever been caught with her homework not done?

"Tell you what," I say, handing her the sheets of paper covered in my handwriting.

"You can copy *mine.*"

THREE

Monday. February 12. Мондей. Фебруері твелвт. 1990. The day starts like any other. Five-forty-three and water is running in the bathroom down the hall. A half-dozen girls – always the same half-dozen African girls – are singing their hearts out in the shower. Led by Thandiwe, the girl I met at the ironing board, they sing African songs. At the top of their lungs.

Every morning I hear them – the same songs, the same voices, the same harmonies – and every morning I tell myself that this is the day I'll join them. I've heard the songs so often now that I know all the words, even if I don't know their meanings. I know which parts I'd sing. A few times, I grab my towel and make for the shower room, determined to push my way into Thandiwe's little choir. I never get past the ironing board. Halfway to the bathroom, I lose my resolve. It's not the showering that bothers me. Not anymore. I'm getting used to being naked around the other girls – I've had to. It's that I'm afraid of the African girls – afraid they'll stop singing if I try to sing with them. So I hum along softly, instead, in my cubie, where no one can see me, and no one can hear.

Six-fifteen and I'm out of bed. The girls have finished singing. By six-thirty I'm dressed, but I have nothing to do until seven, when the dining hall opens for breakfast. So I fix myself a cup of instant coffee. From under a pile of books on my desk, I grab my diary, and the latest issue of *Maclean's* magazine. I bring my guitar, too, in case I'm struck with the inspiration to write a song. Then I make my way to the hill behind the hostel.

The senior hostel, the dining hall, and the junior hostel are one long building connected by a corridor. At the midpoint of the corridor, two sets of doors open onto opposite sides of the building. On one side, there is the quadrangular courtyard, where students gather between meals and classes; on the other side, a hill overlooking the maintenance area.

Students stay away from the maintenance area. They don't go near the laundry building, where we send our dirty clothes once a week to be cleaned and dried and pressed by Swazi women with babies tied to their backs. Nobody hangs around the gardeners' building, where the grass-cutters and hedge-trimmers keep their equipment, take their meals. There are never any students outside the dining-hall kitchen, where our food is brought and where our food is prepared and where our dishes are washed.

In the mornings, though, I like to sit here, above the maintenance area, away from the rest of the students. I like the sounds here. Water drumming against the sides of galvanized steel wash-tubs, forks and spoons clattering against plates and cups. Lawnmower engines sputtering, roaring, sputtering, dying.

I get *Maclean's* second-hand, from home, in care packages. It's almost embarrassing, how much mail I get. In the senior hostel, only three people have received letters. No one else has yet to receive a package. I've gotten two.

My packages aren't small, either. Each one contains fourteen letters – seven each from Mom and Dad, written daily – plus Hallmark greeting cards from Sophie, and postcards from Wes. There are photos and fresh film for my camera. More Mars bars, jars of peanut butter, soda crackers, bags of Oreo cookies. Copies of the *St. Paul Journal* to keep me up-to-date on the local news, and *Maclean's* magazines, for Canadian current events.

On the hill behind the hostel, I open the latest issue of *Maclean's*. Which isn't, in fact, the latest issue at all. Packages from home take some time to arrive in Swaziland. Today, February 12, I'm reading the February 2 issue.

The commotion begins as I am reading about recent developments in South Africa. The unbanning of several political parties. The African National Congress, the Pan African Congress. The South African Communist Party.

From behind me, from within the senior hostel, comes the shrieking of voices, male and female. There is hardly time to close the magazine before girls start spilling out of the hostel doors onto the hill – onto *my* hill – overlooking the maintenance area. Some of the girls are crying – wailing, really – and all of the senior boys are chanting as they fill the quad, lifting their knees to their chests and stamping their feet to the ground. From the kitchen there is cheering and singing. The kitchen workers rattle spoons inside pots. Gardeners and laundry women rush out of their respective buildings to find out what has happened.

I follow the crowd too, diary and magazine and guitar in hand, watching the other students, and listening. I'm afraid to stop someone. I'm afraid that I'll look stupid. Everybody seems to know what's going on. All of the students, the workers. I should know, too. February 12. Is it a national holiday? Siya never talked about national holidays. Maybe everyone just heard the news about the unbanning of the political parties. Maybe it's bigger news than I think.

Around the courtyard and in the assembly hall, a few senior South African boys are setting out stereos and microphones and loudspeakers. Within minutes, African music is blaring throughout the campus. I can feel the bass drum and the bass guitar thumping under my feet. Several groups of African girls are spreading long sheets of paper across the lawn in the quad, using wide brushes to paint banners of yellow, green, and black. ANC colours. From time to time, one of the South African guys presses a microphone to his

lips. Over the music, he calls out, *"Amandla!"* The girls stop painting, drop their brushes. They thrust their right fists into the air.
"Awetu!"

By the time the assembly starts, at eight o'clock sharp, I've figured it out. Actually, the African girls' banners spell it out.

NELSON MANDELA! FREE AT LAST!

I'm excited – as excited as everyone else at the college – to
bear witness to this historic event, to *history.* With my guitar at my
feet, my books in my lap, I watch the assembly hall come alive
with laughter and spontaneous singing. Students dance in the
aisles, up on the benches, in front of the stage. Mr. Harrington tries
for five full minutes to bring the student body to order, and when
he has finally succeeded in settling the crowd, he has only a few
seconds to declare that all classes are cancelled before the auditorium roars again with cheering and whistling and applause. The
energy – the elation – is contagious.

After Mr. Harrington's announcement, the students take over
the assembly. The microphone is open for anyone to use. Theo, a
senior South African student, starts by talking about the history of
apartheid in South Africa. The assembly hall falls silent as Theo
speaks. He talks about the first white government formed by the
National Party in 1948; the 1960 Anti-Pass Campaign, which
resulted in the Sharpeville Massacre – sixty-nine people killed by
the white regime – and the banning of black political parties like
the ANC and the PAC. He talks about the rise of Black
Consciousness, the banning of poets and novelists and musicians
and political leaders.

Theo's speech gives me the shivers. I'm familiar with the
names and the dates that he mentions – 1961, 1963, Rivonia, 1976,
Soweto Uprising, Biko, SiSulu, Thambo, 1985. Mr. Kaushal taught
us all about the history of South Africa in his social studies class.
But none if it seemed real before. Not really. It does now. This is

Theo's history – a real person's history. A real person who is my age.

When Theo has finished speaking, Nhlanhla, another senior student, steps up to the microphone to recite several poems he's written about growing up black in South Africa, in Soweto. His poems are more like stories – about sitting in an unheated class-room in winter with forty-five other students, twenty textbooks to share between them; about being forced to learn Afrikaans; about the older sister he never knew who was shot and killed during the Soweto Uprising in 1976.

I think about Sophie. What if I'd never known her? What if she were murdered like Nhlanhla's sister? I can't even imagine it.

Then there is Robert, a boy in Form One. He's brave, I think. The only junior student to address the assembly. He reads a short story whose main character is a little coloured boy named Bobby. Bobby receives an invitation to a friend's birthday party – a white friend's birthday party. Bobby buys a special gift for his friend. Dressed in his Sunday best, Bobby goes to the birthday party in the white area of town. Only, when the white friend's mother discovers that Robert is coloured, she won't let him into the house. Robert's hand – the hand that holds the paper – trembles as he reads, his voice quivers. It's a true story. I'm sure of it. Bobby, the boy in the story, is Robert.

This is what I came here for, I know – to see apartheid, first-hand. To see what it's really like. But the reality of it knocks the wind out of me.

The only girl to stand up to the microphone is Natasha, a Form Five student. She speaks slowly as she shares the details of her best friend's death eleven years ago. This isn't make-believe either. Natasha was there, walking home from school one day, hand in hand with her friend, when, for one reason or another, the friend stepped out onto the road. At precisely that moment, an ambulance happened to be passing and it struck her – struck Natasha's friend – leaving the little girl bleeding and unconscious.

The assembly hall is so quiet, I can hear the girl beside me breathing.

According to Natasha, the ambulance that struck her friend was a Whites Only ambulance. So the ambulance driver raced away from the scene of the accident to call a second ambulance. But by the time the other ambulance arrived, Natasha's friend had stopped breathing. Her heart had stopped beating.

I sniffle quietly for the next few minutes, hardly listening to the other stories and speeches. There are girls crying all around me, dabbing their eyes with tissues. By the time I've pulled myself together enough to focus again on the stage, Mr. Harrington is paying tribute to Nelson Mandela.

"Let us never forget," he says, "the suffering of this great man. Let us remember the *years* that he gave to us, the *years* that he gave to all the people of South Africa, white and black. Let us celebrate his role in the struggle for freedom in South Africa!"

The assembly hall breaks into applause.

"Let us celebrate his *leadership* in the struggle for freedom in South Africa!"

More applause, cheering. Whistles.

"Let us celebrate his *achievements* in the struggle for freedom in South Africa!"

Students pound the benches with their fists, stamp their feet. They stand up, clapping their hands high over their heads.

"Freedom for South Africa! Freedom for Mandela!"

Mr. Harrington raises his voice to a feverish pitch over the cheering of the crowd. His face is red now.

"Amandla!" he yells.

"Awetu!" the crowd explodes, hundreds of fists raised.

"Amandla!"

"Awetu!"

Then several senior girls rush to the front of the assembly hall, ANC banners in hand. They tack the banners onto the curtains at the back of the stage. Across the front of the stage, ten senior boys in gumboots line up in a row. A group of forty or fifty students from the lower and the upper forms crowd in behind them. Waist-high cowhide drums are pulled onto the stage from the wings. One of the Spanish teachers runs onstage with his guitar. Mrs. McBain rolls out the college piano.

Thandiwe starts the singing, and everyone onstage joins in. As I listen to her lead the other voices, I remember her talking to me beside the ironing board. I remember the sound of her voice – a half-whisper. She hardly parted her lips then. Now, her jaw is dropped, her throat is open. She fills the assembly hall with her singing. Hers is a woman's voice, deep and full with a rich, con-trolled vibrato. She stands with her legs spread wide, back arched. Chin lifted. There is power in her voice, in her posture, in her stance. Thandiwe's whole body is singing.

Watching Thandiwe sing, hearing her voice soar above the crowd, I don't want to join her: I want to *be* her. I want to sing with my eyes closed and my arms out – not thinking about the notes or the words but *feeling* them in my belly, and making every-one else feel them too, in their bones. I've never seen a singer like Thandiwe. I've never heard singing like this. I've never sung like her. I wonder if I can. If it's even in me to try.

It seems to me that the students onstage have rehearsed beforehand – that they've all rehearsed their parts. They must have. But there are two, maybe three hundred voices in total now – onstage and off – singing song after song in perfect four-part har-mony. They all couldn't have rehearsed together. How do they know what to sing, and when? They don't just sing, either. They dance too. Girls swinging their hips and their arms in unison, boys lifting their knees to their chests. As though their movements were choreographed. And after nearly every song, the fists. The refrain.

"*Amandla!*"

"*Awetu!*"

"*Amandla!*"

"*Awetu!*"

Over the course of the singing, more students and teachers flood down the steps of the assembly hall in groups of two or three until the stage is packed tight with bodies. Katja and Nikola, I notice, are among the first to go running to the front, their fists raised. Maria follows, holding hands with Hannah. Shelagh trails behind.

Before long, the assembly hall benches are almost completely empty. Everyone, it seems, is onstage. Some students stand with their arms around each other as they sing, some hold hands while they dance together. I start to feel ridiculous sitting in the audience. Sitting alone and silent, watching the crowd perform. Sitting with my guitar beside me – my mute guitar in its unopened case. I feel as though my face is glowing white.

It's different, of course, for other white students. For scholarship students like Maria and Nikola and Katja. They have a right to be onstage because they've been oppressed. They belong. I don't. I've never survived hardships or struggles or strife. I'd feel like a fraud if I joined them onstage. Katja would probably push me off.

So I stay seated. As the celebration continues onstage, I open my diary across my lap. Try to look busy with writing.

On the bench in front of me, another girl is also still seated. I hadn't noticed her before. Though I have no classes with her, I know that she's a senior student. She's sitting in the section of the assembly hall reserved for senior students. She's writing, too. Like me. Drawing, actually, in a small sketchbook bound with metal rings. With a charcoal pencil, she's making lines, then smudging them with the back of her fist. Her arms and hands are freckled, her hair is long and strawberry blonde. From time to time, her hair falls over her eyes, but she can't use her hands to sweep it back because they're covered in charcoal. Instead, she throws her head back and to the side, swinging her hair over her shoulder.

She's drawing a globe, I think. Her picture isn't quite finished.

I'm guessing that her sketch is political. The globe represents a

new world: new because Mandela is free and apartheid is collaps-
ing. It's not a very subtle symbol, really. And I'm not sure about the
girl's talent. The continents on the globe aren't recognizable at all.

The girl catches me staring and says something to me, but I
can't make out the words over the singing onstage.

"Are you spying on me?"

The girl swings her hair over her shoulder as she steps over the
bench and settles in beside me. Her voice is teasing, though, not
angry. She's Australian. Her accent is a dead giveaway.

"Just admiring your artwork."

"Artwork," she repeats, enunciating her r's. "You're American,
aren't you?"

I wince.

"Oops. Sorry. Canadian, then?"

I nod.

"I know how it feels. I'm from New Zealand. I've only ever
been to Australia twice. But when people hear me talk, they always
assume I'm an Aussie. It drives me nuts."

While the singing onstage continues, we introduce ourselves,
shake hands. With the music so loud, we have to raise our voices
when we talk, and lean in close.

Her name is Rosalind Richardson. I can call her Rosalind or
Rosa. Or Richardson, even. Anything but Rose. She won't answer
to Rose.

"Rose," she says, "is an old lady's name. The kind of old lady
who wears flowered housedresses and puts a blue rinse through
her hair every month –"

"And has a moustache –"

"– and whiskers growing out of a mole on her chin."

Rosa and I giggle.

Onstage, the drumming stops.

I look around me to see what's going on. Why has the music
stopped?

Maybe Rosa and I are in trouble. We've been caught talking

about trivial things on a historic day when we should be singing and dancing with everybody else.

But as Rosa and I turn our attention to the front of the assembly hall, Thandiwe starts another song. No drums this time. No guitar or piano. She sings the first line by herself, *"Nkosi sikelel'i Afrika,"* then the other voices join in.

"It's the African National Anthem," Rosa says. "Sacred song."

"Why aren't you up there?"

Rosa shrugs her shoulders. "I just don't feel like it's *my* celebration."

For a moment, we listen. The boys onstage sing, *"Woza moya."* The girls echo back, *"Woza moya,"* an octave higher.

"How about you?" says Rosa. "Why aren't you up there?"

"Same reason, I guess."

Nkosi sikelela
Thina lusapho lwayo

"What about your drawing, though?"

Rosa is staring at the stage, so I give her a poke to get her attention.

"What about your picture?" I ask. "Your *globe*. Isn't it sort of a celebration of a new world? A new world free from injustice?"

"What?" Rosa looks confused.

I try to repeat myself but the singing is too loud now.

Sechaba saheso
Sechaba sa Afrika

The songs ends. There are more *Amandla - Awetu* calls. And the assembly finally draws to a close. Mr. Harrington announces that there will be a half-hour break followed by more celebrations on the playing field.

"Your *globe*," I say to Rosa, pointing to her sketchbook as we stroll back to the hostel. "It's a celebration of a new world free from injustice. Right?"

"Oh, my *embryo!* Yes, I suppose it *does* look something like a globe, doesn't it? But – no. Sorry to disappoint you. It's an embryo, not a globe."

Which explains why the continents on her drawing don't look like continents.

"Nothing political about it," she says. "I don't do politics. It's just not my thing. I'm sort of infatuated with embryos and fetuses. What's the plural of fetus? *Feti?"* She laughs. "Come on. Let me show you something."

Rosa's cubie is on the opposite end of the girls' hostel, far from my cubie, in the other corridor. That's why we've never run into each other before.

It's wall-to-wall embryos.

She's drawn them in pencil crayon, in oil pastels. In ink. Over her desk, there are dozens of charcoal sketches of wombs, each filled with swirls of black and white fluid and one tiny, rounded body. In every drawing, the face is featureless, save for a half-formed eye, the beginnings of a nose. The hands are more detailed. Long, delicate fingers reaching out beyond the uterus walls. Above her bed there are plump watercolour embryos in pale blues and pinks and greens. They have enormous heads, smiling mouths, and shrunken bodies. Some are underwater, surrounded by coral and seaweed and fish of all sizes. Words rise out from the lips of one embryo that rests on a sand-yellow sea floor. *Hello fish! Hello fish!*

She has several darker pieces leaning up against the wall under her desk. Paintings done in oil, I think, because the canvas is textured with thick paint. The oil embryos are long and thin, their bodies sinewy, fleshless. Their faces are grey, and wrinkled with age, like the faces of old men and old women. Like corpses, even, wrapped in a dark green – almost black – shroud of womb.

I stare for a long time at Rosa's art, then at Rosa herself. Her freckled face is framed by soft, curly tufts of hair. She looks like the girl-next-door, like a cheerleader. Not like an artist. Where do these paintings come from?

And then, as though she's heard my question, Rosa tells me.

"It started about a year, year and a half ago. By accident. I was studying for my A-Levels. Biology, actually. I'm good at sciences. And art, too. Though art is supposed to be my hobby. My parents want me to be a doctor. They're both doctors, and my two aunts. I get a ton of grief from my parents for doing art. They think it's a colossal waste of time. But I found a way to put my art classes to use when I was studying for my A-Levels. I started drawing these amazing diagrams of zygotes. Have you studied biology?"

I nod.

"Okay, then you know that zygotes are fertilized eggs."

I nod again.

"Which eventually become embryos."

She stops, then, grinning. Waiting for me to respond.

"All animals start out as zygotes," she continues. "And all zygotes look the same. They're identical."

I feel as though I should say something, but I don't know what Rosa is getting at. So they're identical. So what?

"I-den-ti-cal," she says, repeating herself. "Can you grasp it? Can you see what it *means?*"

I can't. I give her a blank look.

"It means that for a brief, beautiful period in their initial developmental stages, every single animal from every single animal species looks identical to every other animal from every other animal species."

Rosa sits back in her chair, crossing her arms over her chest.

"That's political," I say. "You said that you don't do politics, but that's the most political idea I've ever heard. Equality. You're talking about the equality of all living things."

"Uh-uh," Rosa shakes her head. "It's science, not politics. Put two animal embryos in front of us, and we couldn't tell them apart. Pig, cat, horse, cow, sheep, mule. *Human*. They're all the same. *We* are all the same."

"Sounds political," I say.

Rosa ignores me.

"So when I draw an embryo, I'm not drawing one single thing. I'm drawing *everything*. Figuratively, I mean. I'm drawing the whole spectrum, the whole taxonomy, of living, breathing creatures. What artist can say that he – or she – has captured the entire living, breathing universe in one picture? What artist in the history of the *world?*"

"So you really don't see your art as political?"

"After my first embryo," says Rosa, pointing to a pencil sketch beside her window, "there was no going back for me. I knew that I'd found my lifelong passion. The art teachers aren't exactly thrilled about it. They want me to make still-life portraits of – I don't know – cabbages, I guess. Or avocados. Or pears. I refuse. Pears have been done to death. I'm never going to draw anything but embryos. It's my calling."

I still think that her art is political, but I don't think that I should mention it again. I'm starting to sound like a broken record.

"Enough about me!" says Rosa, clapping her hands. "Get me started on embryos and I can't stop. How about you? What are you into?"

I pause, unsure of what to say. I think Rosa is fascinating. She's not like anyone I've ever met before. I'd like to impress her. Should I talk about my piano playing? My music? It's not the same as her embryos. I wish that I had a weird, all-consuming, lifelong passion, too. Sister Maria's eyes sparkled like Rosa's, when she talked about her transcriptions of Ukrainian music. I want to sparkle too.

"Wait a second," says Rosa, before I have a chance to speak. "Hold that thought. I want to show you something else. One more thing and then I'm shutting my mouth for good. I promise."

Rummaging in her cupboard, Rosa pulls out a piece of

yellow fabric. She spreads it across her bed. In the centre of the cloth, there's an outline of two embryos, their heads and tails touching to form a complete circle.

"I'm experimenting with different art forms, and different media. This is my first batik. And my first set of twins."

Batik, Rosa explains, is an ancient Indonesian art form. A Javanese art form, actually, that dates back at least two thousand years.

"The word batik comes from the Javanese word *ambatik*, which means drawing and writing. Artists in Java discovered that when portions of fabric are covered in wax they repel dye. So it's possible to make pictures on pieces of cloth by drawing on the fabric with wax, and then dipping the fabric in different coloured dyes."

"Sure. Like *pysanky.*"

"Piss-on-*what?*"

"*Pysanky.* Ukrainian Easter eggs."

Then I talk.

I tell Rosa everything I know about *pysanky.* How Ukrainian women have been drawing on eggs each spring for two thousand years, maybe longer, with beeswax and *kistky.* To celebrate the renewal of the natural world. You start with a white egg, and you draw designs on it with a writing tool that transfers hot wax onto the shell. When the egg is dipped into yellow dye, the white parts of the egg that are covered in beeswax stay white. I explain that *pysanky*-making is based on the same principles as batik. The egg goes through several dyes — yellow, orange, sometimes green or blue, and red — before it's dipped in the final black dye. After the egg has been dyed black, you hold it next to a flame, to melt off the layers of beeswax. And the egg comes to life with colour.

Pysanky. I teach Rosa to pronounce the word properly. I tell her that it's *exactly* like batik. *Pysanky* comes from the word *pysaty,* to write.

When I've finished, Rosa grabs hold of both my hands.

"I want to learn," she says. *"Teach* me. Will you teach me? Promise you'll teach me."

I try to cut in, to explain that it's not as simple as teaching and learning. There are special materials involved, special tools. Where would we find beeswax and *kistky?* We'd need the proper dyes, and fresh farm eggs. Dye doesn't stick to eggs that have been washed with chemicals.

Rosa doesn't hear me, though.

"This is fate. You know that? It's *destiny.* You think it's an accident? A coincidence? That you just *happened* to come all this way to Africa, all the way from Canada, to *Swaziland* of all places?"

I shrug.

"No," she says. "Uh-uh. It doesn't work that way. This friendship – you and me, us – it's all been written in the *stars,* Colleen. Preordained by some higher being."

Rosa's face is flushed. She grabs my hands again, and squeezes.

"You have been *sent* to me," she says. "I'm going to make embryos *on eggs."*

Rosa and I spend the remainder of the day together. After lunch, when the Mandela celebrations start up again – dancing on the play fields, readings of banned poetry in the assembly hall – we take a long walk around campus. Then we sit together on my bed, sharing crackers and peanut butter from one of my care packages. Rosa asks about my family and my hometown, about life in Canada. I show her photos of Mom and Dad, Sophie and Wes. Photos of our dog Ralph. Our house. The farm.

Rosa is amazed by my photos. She doesn't think they're real. She wonders if we're really like this – arms around each other, cheeks pressed together – or if it's put on for the camera. I tell her that it's real. We're not just posing. Rosa flips through the pictures again to take another look. She says that it must have been hard for me to leave. Hard for everyone. I nod.

Her oldest brother, she says, is in London studying medicine, and her next-oldest brother works for some big computer company in Singapore. There are three of them in the family. Plus her mother and father, of course. But Rosa hasn't lived with her mom and dad – or with her brothers, for that matter – since she was very young. She was sent to boarding school in New Zealand when she was seven.

I don't understand why she would go to boarding school. Why her parents would send her away.

Rosa says that her parents started their medical careers in the tropics and never really left. They were in Surinam for seven years before Rosa was born, and in Tanzania for nine years after. For two years they worked in Cameroon, then another two years in Swaziland. Rosa's parents have been working in Zambia for the past three years. For the last five, Rosa has been boarding at Waterford.

She can't believe that my family has never moved. That we've always lived in the same house on the same farm by the same town. That every day – day after day – my brother and sister and I came home after school, and that we slept under the same roof as our parents. I can't believe that she didn't.

Walking into the dining hall for dinner with Rosa at my side, I catch myself smiling. For the first time in more than a month, I'm smiling. I look from side to side across the room, at the students and the teachers eating in groups. Yesterday, and the day before, and the day before that, I sat alone, making it seem as though I enjoyed being by myself. Now I have someone to sit with too. I don't have to pretend anymore.

Over supper, Rosa asks me to tell her more about my family. More stories from home, about all of my aunts and my uncles, my cousins. Grandparents. Do I see them all the time at home? Do they live close by? Rosa has two grandparents, two aunts and one cousin – in the whole world, they're all she's got. And in her whole life, she's seen her grandparents twice.

"What about the eggs," says Rosa. "The *pysanky*. Do all the women in your family make them? Do you make them together?"

Before I can answer, Rosa leans across the table so that we are nose-to-nose. So that I can hear her whispering.

"I have to tell you about this crazy thought of mine. It's about my twins. My batik twins. I think that they're prophetic. I think that they're *us*. I know it sounds crazy, but I think that I made a drawing of you before I ever even knew that you existed. Is that crazy? I mean, do you think that I've lost my mind completely?"

Rosa stops grinning, then, and she stares me straight in the eye.

Is that crazy?

I stare back, at her green, green eyes, islands in a sea of freckles.

Slowly and solemnly, I shake my head.

"No."

FOUR

At the beginning of May, two months before the end of the first term, Mrs. McBain corners me. After check-in, she pulls me aside, saying that we need to have a chat. I'm supposed to stop by her house for tea the next day, after class. I can tell by the tone of her voice that she's not happy. She half-whispers, half-hisses her words at me. I've heard her use the same tone with other students when they've been in trouble. But she's never spoken to me this way. I wonder what I've done wrong. The night before our meeting, I hardly sleep.

Nobody likes Mrs. McBain. She's the least popular teacher with the senior students. A lot of the other teachers are lenient when they're on duty. Especially the younger teachers. Mr. Afseth, our history teacher, doesn't mind if we hang out in each other's cubies during the homework period in the evening, as long as we're quiet about it. The art teacher, Miss De Silva, hardly ever patrols the corridors. And our English teacher, Mick Dawson, doesn't pay attention to any of the college rules. He lets us call him by his first name. We have our English classes in the common room, where we can pull our chairs into a circle, or outside the hostel, on the grass in the courtyard. If someone has been drinking in town on a Saturday night, Mick looks the other way. He says that we're adults. Why should he treat us like children?

Mrs. McBain isn't like the other teachers. Behind her back, a lot of the girls call her Mrs. McBitch, or just McBitch, because she seems to enjoy catching rule breakers, and she's notorious for the punishments she comes up with – anything from picking up garbage around campus, to being denied weekend exeats, to being suspended and even expelled. She's a stickler for rules, there's no doubt about that. Even when she's not on duty, she has her eyes on us. Every Thursday night before check-in, Mrs. McBain inspects our cubies to make sure that they're tidy. She can show up anytime, though, in anyone's room, for a random inspection – and she does. Plus we've all seen her in Mbabane on the weekends, strolling through the mall and popping into restaurants down-town, making sure that none of us is smoking or drinking. Once, she dragged two guys out of the Ekhwezi bar before they ordered. Before they even had a chance to do anything wrong.

I don't think Mrs. McBain is so bad, really. As long as we fol-low the rules, we have nothing to worry about. Rosa disagrees. She's had a few run-ins with Mrs. McBain over the past couple of years. Rosa doesn't trust her. I tell Rosa that Mrs. McBain is in charge of the whole senior hostel, which is a big responsibility. It's her job to keep us in line. Without her, there would be no order. The place would fall apart. Rosa thinks Mrs. McBain goes over-board, spying on us and invading our privacy. She says Mrs. McBain is like a prison warden. I say she's more like a mother.

Of course, in music class, I see a different side of Mrs. McBain. Five times a week, I see a side of Mrs. McBain that Rosa never sees. On Mondays and Wednesdays, Katja and I meet with her for classes in ear-training, sight-singing, and melodic dictation; on Tuesdays and Thursdays, the three of us do harmony, counter-point, and composition; Fridays we have individual piano lessons. Mrs. McBain must see Katja and me glaring at each other over our books, but it doesn't seem to bother her. When she steps into the music room, everything about her changes. Her face lights up as soon as she spots us sitting in our desks, and she doesn't stop smil-ing until the end of the class. We're the best part of her day, I can tell, because she always looks disappointed when the bell rings.

Every class starts with a few minutes of small talk about how we're feeling, how our other classes are going. Mrs. McBain likes to hear about our families, and our former piano teachers. What we like about Swaziland. Whether we miss home. She talks about her husband – who lives with her on campus but works as an architect in Mbabane – and her two daughters, both studying music at university in England. I think we must remind Mrs. McBain of her girls. I know she misses them.

It feels weird talking about myself in front of Katja, and hearing Katja tell stories about Poland in front of me – since we don't like each other, and we never talk to each other outside of music class. When it's my turn to talk about my old piano teachers, I don't mention anything about Sister Maria or her work on the Ukrainian composers. I don't want Katja to know about Sister Maria. I'm not sure that I want Mrs. McBain to know about her either. So I tell them about Simone instead, and Dr. Kalman, and I pretend that my lessons at the convent never happened. It's easier this way. I'm afraid that if I talk about Sister Maria, I'll start to cry, and I won't be able to stop.

The truth is, I think about Sister Maria all the time – more than I think about Mom and Dad, or Sophie and Wes. I'm homesick for her from the moment I wake up in the morning until the moment I go to sleep at night. It doesn't make any sense, I know. She's been gone a long time now. Plus I have Rosa. I spend all my free time with her. And I have Siya. I have no reason to feel lonely.

For the past couple of months, on weekends, the three of us have been meeting downtown for lunch. We meet at The Mall and then go for walks together, window shopping and eating ice cream. When I first phoned Siya, and made plans to meet him in Mbabane, at the market near the centre of the city, I wasn't sure if I should bring Rosa along. I thought they might not get along. They hit it off, though, from the moment they met. As though they'd known each other all their lives. For three hours straight, they talked about art galleries in Europe, and the art scene in southern Africa. Ever since then, we've made a point of getting together at least once a week, and we always have a good time. Siya isn't much of a know-it-all when Rosa is around. He's actually pretty normal.

Mrs. McBain reminds me of Sister Maria. That's the problem. The way she paces around the music room when she's teaching us something new. The way she bobs her head up and down in time with the music when we play well, and frowns when she doesn't like something she hears. All sorts of little things make me think of my lessons at the convent. Like how Mrs. McBain sits at the piano with her eyes closed for a moment before she starts to play, and how she taps the side of the piano bench with her pencil to keep us in time when we're sight-singing. She's nothing like Dr. Kalman. From the first time she heard me play, she's given me nothing but praise.

So I don't understand why Mrs. McBain is angry with me now. She's my favourite teacher. I'm not like the other girls. I don't call her McBitch. And I know that I'm her favourite student. During my piano lessons with her, when it's just Mrs. McBain and me, she tells me that I'm exceptional. My playing is outstanding, my ear is remarkable, and I have a special talent for composition. In all her years of teaching, she's never come across such a gifted musician. Katja, she says, is a very good pianist. Technically, Katja's playing is almost flawless. Maybe too flawless. There's no emotion in her performances. Katja reads lines of music like a scientist. I read between the lines, like an artist. Pieces sound new when I play them. I make them my own.

How can I be in trouble with Mrs. McBain?

I try to read between the lines, but I just don't get it.

While Mrs. McBain fixes our iced tea, I pace around her sitting room, touching the odd ornament, picking up candles and pottery vases, then setting them down again. I don't know what to do with myself. Rosa and I sat up half the night trying to guess why I've been summoned to Mrs. McBain's place. I tossed and turned until morning, replaying everything I've done over the past few weeks.

Her house isn't at all what I expected. From the outside, it looks like the other teachers' houses on campus. Thatched roof, whitewashed walls. A little garden out front next to a small drive-way. I've seen the inside of Mick's rondavel, and it's tiny. His floor is tiled like the floor of the classroom block, and he's hardly got any windows. Mrs. McBain's house is huge and bright. It might have started out small and round, but Mrs. McBain's husband has obviously done a lot of work on the place. He's added at least a half-dozen extra rooms, some of them round, with low ceilings; others long and thin, with vaulted ceilings. I've seen Mr. McBain around campus a few times – going for a swim in the college pool, joining Mrs. McBain in the dining hall for lunch. She introduced me to him once at an evening assembly. He seemed so ordinary. Short, balding. Friendly, but quiet. Ordinary clothes, ordinary glasses. I would never have guessed that he had it in him to trans-form their house like this. One wall in the sitting room is practi-cally all glass. There are plants in every corner of the kitchen, and big paintings of African animals in the sitting room. Blown-up photographs of the market in Mbabane, and sunsets over the hills behind the senior hostel. The McBains' furniture is covered in wild animal prints – zebra, cheetah, giraffe – and they've got Swazi spears and shields propped up against the fireplace. I thought their house would be more prim and proper. More British, somehow. Plainer. I never imagined it would feel so African.

I could understand if Mrs. McBain had asked Rosa to come to her house for a meeting. Rosa's been in trouble with Mrs. McBain before because she breaks the college rules all the time, and she doesn't seem to care if she gets caught. I'm always a little on edge when we go to town together. Rosa smokes cigarettes in restaurants downtown – openly, without keeping her hand under the table in case a teacher walks in – and she orders wine or beer with all her meals. She buys liquor in town, too – Southern Comfort and brandy – to drink in her cubie after lights out. It's easy to buy booze and cigarettes in Mbabane. No one ever asks for ID. Rosa knows where to go to buy *dagga,* too, and sometimes she goes for walks in the hills behind the hostel to smoke it. Which is really asking for trouble, since we're not allowed in the hills, and we're definitely not allowed to smoke pot. Once in a while, after lights out, Rosa smokes right in her cubie – cigarettes and *dagga* – even though Mrs. McBain could walk in at any time. I never join her. I'm too afraid of losing my scholarship. And I ask her not to do it, either, but she just laughs. She says that they wouldn't dare kick her out. They need her tuition fees.

Mrs. McBain takes ages to come back to the sitting room. By the time she reappears, carrying a tray with a glass pitcher of iced tea and two glasses, I've gone through her record collection beside the stereo, and I've read nearly all the titles in her bookshelf. She's obviously been in Swaziland for a long time because everything in her house is African. The pitcher and the glasses are etched with outlines of the African continent, like see-through maps.

She starts the conversation by asking about my school work. How am I doing in my other courses? She doesn't seem angry, just curious. Am I keeping up with the workload?

I don't know why Mrs. McBain bothers to ask about my other courses. We talk about them all the time at the beginning of our music classes. She knows that my grades are excellent, and that I get along well with the other teachers. I stay on top of my readings and my assignments.

As Mrs. McBain pours our iced tea, I explain to her that my classes are fine. No problems at all.

Next she asks me about my Extended Essay. Have I settled on a topic? Have I given any thought to her suggestions about it?

Again, I'm not sure why Mrs. McBain is asking about my E^2. She knows that I'm going ahead with Ukrainian Canadian folk

music. I've already done most of my research. Mom sent me a box
of material at the beginning of April. Cassette recordings of old
LP's, Ukrainian songbooks, history books about Ukrainians in
Canada. I've gone through it all. Now I'm ready to write the
actual essay. When I first mentioned my topic to Mrs. McBain, she
was a bit hesitant. She thought that I should do something more
creative, like Katja — compose a piece of music, and then submit
it instead of an essay. But I told her that I wanted to stick with
Ukrainian folk music. It's important to me. Rosa agrees. She
thinks it's a brilliant topic. We're going to make *pysanky* together,
with the supplies that Mom sent along with the material for my
essay. Then we're going to photograph the eggs for the title page
of my essay.

I tell Mrs. McBain that I'm still working on "The Evolution
of Ukrainian Folk Music in Canada." That I'm about to start writing. I tell her about the *pysanky* and the title page.

She frowns.

Then she asks how I'm enjoying my free time. Whether I'm
making friends, taking part in college life. Getting out to experience Swazi culture. Have I decided where I'm going to do my
Community Service next term?

This is weird. Of course I'm making friends. Mrs. McBain sees
that Rosa and I spend all our time together. She's signed all our
weekend exeats, so she has to know that we go to Mbabane every
Saturday and Sunday. Plus I've told her about Siya during my
piano lessons — how we met on the flight from Paris to
Johannesburg, how I introduced him to Rosa. How the three of
us have become friends. And we've already talked about
Community Service. Mrs. McBain knows that Rosa and I are
going to volunteer at the hospital in town, starting in June. Siya is
going to join us there on Tuesday mornings.

I tell Mrs. McBain that my social life is good. I'm happy. Still
planning to do Community Service at the hospital. Nothing has
changed.

"That," she says, crossing her arms over her chest, "is precisely what I feared."

I don't understand.

"Have I done something wrong? Because I seem to be in trouble, and I don't know why. Can you just tell me what I've done?"

Mrs. McBain uncrosses her arms, then crosses them again.

"I'm concerned about you, Colleen. I've asked you here today because I'm very concerned."

She looks down at her sweater, picks off a piece of lint from her sleeve. I wait for her to continue.

"I don't need to remind you that there is more to being a good Waterford student than fulfilling the college's academic requirements. You're part of a community here, part of a large family, so to speak. And when you're part of a family, you participate in family activities."

I nod.

"I didn't see you at Sunday dinner this week," she says.

Every Sunday, the kitchen staff puts on a special meal for students and staff, with turkey or roast beef. All of the tables in the dining hall are covered in tablecloths, with fresh flowers and real plates instead of metal trays. Rosa and I have been skipping Sunday dinner. Not just last Sunday, but a few Sundays before that too. We've been meeting Siya at Marco's Italian Restaurante downtown.

"I also noticed," she says, "that you haven't been joining the other students for afternoon sport."

She's right. I haven't. I don't like sports. Neither does Rosa. So we've been spending our afternoons in the music room. I practice the piano, or write songs, and Rosa sits in one of the desks beside the piano, drawing in her sketchbook.

"We don't have to do afternoon sport," I say, trying to defend myself. "It's optional. Isn't it?"

"Three weeks ago," says Mrs. McBain, ignoring me, "you and

Rosalind Richardson were the only senior students who did not run in the 24-hour Relay. Every other student in your class made an effort to secure pledges and raise money for the Quedusizi Primary School at the base of the hill. Where, may I ask, were you and Rosalind?"

My face starts to get hot. We were camping at Malolotja with Siya. Rosa said that lots of students skip out on the 24-hour Relay. It's just a big show to make the college look good.

"I've kept quiet about this for a long time." Mrs. McBain moves from the armchair to sit beside me on the couch. "I'm telling you this for your own good, not for any other reason. I don't believe that you are to blame for your behaviour. Not entirely. Rosalind Richardson is a very troubled young woman. She's not good for you, Colleen. She's not a good influence."

Rosa isn't perfect. I know that. But when I try to argue with Mrs. McBain, when I try to point out all of Rosa's good qualities, she doesn't listen. She says that Rosa has a history of acting out. Since Form 4, she's been in numerous power struggles with faculty members. Mrs. McBain suspects that Rosa is experimenting with alcohol and drugs. When she was in Form 5, she ran away from the college to stay with her boyfriend in town, a coloured boy working at one of the casinos in the Ezulwini Valley.

I don't know what to say. Rosa never mentioned running away.

"She has difficulty accepting authority," says Mrs. McBain. "The only reason she's still at Waterford is because her parents can't handle her themselves. They've made several large donations to the college. As much as I'd like to see her go, Mr. Harrington doesn't feel that it's in our best interest to expel her."

No wonder Rosa doesn't care about breaking the rules.

"Now, I can't speak about this Swazi boy you've befriended, but I find it troubling that you spend all your time with him and with Rosalind. You've made no attempt to get to know the other students here at Waterford. Even Katja. Katja is someone with whom you have a great deal in common, yet you have no social interactions with her whatsoever."

"That's not fair. I tried to be friends with Katja. Honest, I tried. She's just impossible. You know what she's like. She's not exactly friendly."

"And the other students in your class?"

She doesn't understand. They all have their own groups. The students who have gone to Waterford all their lives aren't interested in making new friends, and I don't fit in with the scholarship girls. I'm lucky to have Rosa and Siya. They're my group.

What am I supposed to do?

Mrs. McBain says that I'm supposed to think back to the reasons I came to Swaziland in the first place. She talks about the essays that I wrote when I was applying for a UWC scholarship – essays that she has on file, in case I want to reread them. What happened to the girl who wrote those essays? she wonders. What happened to the girl who wanted to extend the hand of friendship to young women and men from around the globe? Who talked about breaking down borders and building a new world, free from racism, poverty, and prejudice?

She's not gone. I want to tell Mrs. McBain that the girl who said all those things is still here. I'm still her. I just can't find a way to do the things that I set out to do. I think about Thandiwe at the ironing board, and the Indian girls who laughed at my accent. I think back to the day Mandela was released; how out of place I felt when the other students were celebrating. When I was writing my essays, at home in St. Paul, anything seemed possible – it was easy to talk about saving the world, or making a difference at least. Real life is different. I can't explain to Mrs. McBain how lonely it is, and how scary. How complicated. How hard.

Mrs. McBain says that I need to spend less time with Rosa. Less and less time with Rosa over the next few weeks, and more time with the other girls in my class. It's as simple as that.

I shake my head. I'm not giving up Rosa because Mrs. McBain has something against her. Rosa is my best friend.

But Mrs. McBain keeps talking, as though she can't see me shaking my head. She says that I can start making new friends by selecting a different Community Service project. By joining the daycare volunteers, or the group of students who run tutoring sessions at Quedusizi.

Impossible. I tell her straight out that I'm not changing my Community Service. Even if I wanted to – which I don't – I can't. Rosa and I signed up for the hospital a long time ago, and all the paperwork has been done. We've been issued special identification tags to get into the hospital. Siya had to make special arrangements to take time off his work at the Ministry of Transport. The three of us are volunteering together. It's all been planned.

"All right," says Mrs. McBain. "Then you cut back on your weekend trips to Mbabane. Instead of going to town every Saturday and Sunday with Rosalind, you stay on campus. Try mixing with the students who stay on campus for soccer tournaments and evenings of watching videos."

Now I'm starting to get angry. Mrs. McBain can't tell me what to do. She can't control who I'm friends with, and how I spend my free time. I haven't done anything wrong. The last thing in the world that I want to do on weekends is watch soccer matches and outdated movies.

"I'm sorry, but I won't do it. Rosa is my friend. I like her. You can't stop me from being her friend."

Mrs. McBain takes one last, long drink of her iced tea. "Unfortunately, I can."

"How?"

I look her straight in the eye.

"Starting today, you're banned from leaving campus. For the next eight weeks, I'm blacklisting you. No exeats, except for class-related, teacher-supervised trips to town."

I try to stay calm as I explain to Mrs. McBain that she can't blacklist me. I haven't broken any rules.

"But I'm afraid you have," she says. "It's almost mid-year, and you haven't made any progress on your Extended Essay. *That* is grounds for blacklisting."

What's she talking about? The research for my E² is complete. All that's left is for me to write the actual essay, which shouldn't take long. Researching is the hard part, writing is easy.

When I remind Mrs. McBain that I've made plenty of progress of my E², she gives me an icy look.

"You no longer have my approval for your current topic. You know that I was never keen on the topic in the first place, Colleen. It's not challenging enough. I want you to spend the next eight weeks coming up with something more interesting and more creative. Something more provocative. Perhaps you could approach Katja. Have a look at the piece of music she's working on. You could attempt something similar. And you could develop a friendship with her in the process."

This isn't happening to me. I can't believe that this is happening to me. What can Katja Malanowski teach me about composition? She's half the musician I am. Mrs. McBain has said it herself. I'm too angry to cry. I want to scream.

As I leave Mrs. McBain's house, I slam the door behind me. I wish that I'd told her about Sister Maria when I had the chance. I wish that I'd told Mrs. McBain how many times I defended her when Rosa called her Mrs. McBitch – because I thought she was just like Sister Maria. Just as kind, and thoughtful, and motherly.

I was wrong. She's nothing like Sister Maria.

I wish that I'd told Mrs. McBain how much I used to like her. Then I could tell her that I've changed my mind.

Eight weeks is a long time to be stuck at Waterford. By myself. It wouldn't be so bad if Rosa stayed with me, but she doesn't see why we both have to suffer. I don't tell her the truth about why I've been blacklisted. Maybe I should. I just don't want to hurt her feelings.

The first weekend of my blacklisting, Rosa says that we're in it together. My punishment is her punishment. We'll show Mrs. McBain that we're tough. That we don't need to go to town.

One weekend is enough for her, though. In fact, she doesn't even make it until the end of the weekend. On Sunday morning, she says that she'll go crazy if she spends another minute on campus. So she calls Siya, and he picks her up in the car park, and they wave to me as they drive away. Rosa says that she'll bring me back a pizza from Marco's. Siya promises me an ice cream from the mall. I don't bother to mention that Marco's doesn't do takeout. That the ice cream will melt long before they reach the top of the hill.

I try not to feel sorry for myself, and jealous of Rosa and Siya, and angry at Mrs. McBain. It's just eight weeks. Eight weekends. The time will fly by. I'll still see Rosa during the weekdays and in the evenings. Siya and I can talk on the phone. If Mrs. McBain thinks that her plan is going to work – that she can break up my friendships with them – then she's got another think coming. And I'm not changing my E² topic, either. During my first weekend on campus, I spend all of my time in the music room, transcribing Ukrainian folk songs, analyzing different recordings of them. Tracing the way that the melodies and lyrics have changed over the years. I'm going to write the best Extended Essay Mrs. McBain has ever read. By the time I've finished, she won't have a choice. She'll be so impressed that she'll have to approve it.

It's hard, though, eating by myself again in the dining hall. Lots of the senior students leave campus to go to town on Saturday or Sunday, and the ones who stay behind sit in their usual groups at their usual tables. The scholarship girls hang out on the edge of the playing field, braiding each other's hair, sunning themselves. Thandiwe and her friends gather in the quadrangle to do homework together. I don't belong with any of them. When I take breaks from writing my essay, I consider watching soccer for a few minutes. I just can't do it without Rosa. Since February, we've been inseparable. Without her, I feel naked.

The worst part is that Rosa doesn't seem to feel the same way. She doesn't think twice about calling Siya on Friday night to make plans for Saturday and Sunday. Sometimes she calls him in the middle of the week, too, for no reason. Just to talk. Now that I'm blacklisted, I only have weekdays with her, so I don't understand why she's wasting our precious time together on phone calls to Siya. What do they talk about? The thought occurs to me that Rosa and Siya might like each other. But it's not possible. Rosa has never said anything to me about liking Siya, about the two of them becoming boyfriend and girlfriend. Siya's not good-looking anyway. He's overweight. And he has that annoying lisp.

After the fourth weekend of my blacklisting, the halfway point, I've almost had enough. Rosa has been disappearing most evenings after homework period and before check-in. She doesn't tell me where she goes, but I can guess what she's doing. She's meeting Siya somewhere on campus, maybe in the art room. She's with him all the time.

When I ask her straight out if something is going on between them, she shrugs. I take it as a yes.

Wonderful. So Mrs. McBain's plan has worked. Rosa doesn't care about our friendship anymore. She doesn't need me. She's got Siya now.

I pull out my trump card, to see if there's any hope left for us.

I tell Rosa that I'm ready to start making *pysanky*. This weekend. I'm going to the art room to mix the dyes on Friday evening. Saturday morning, I'm getting eggs from the kitchen staff.

Rosa is excited.

"So you're in," I say.

"Can Siya come along? " she asks.

I shake my head. "He's not allowed. He can't be on campus. It's against the rules."

"You're already blacklisted," says Rosa. "What have you got to lose?"

You, I think. I've got you to lose.

But I've already lost Rosa, really. She won't make *pysanky* without Siya. It's both of them, or neither of them.

I choose them both.

It was a crazy, hopeful, desperate idea; a frantic, last-ditch effort to hang onto Rosa, and doomed from the start. She's lost to me now. Completely won over by Siya. And it's my fault. Why did I bring them together in the first place? If only I'd known.

The hostel is quiet and empty on Saturday afternoon, when I get back to my cubie with my *pysanka.* I only made one. Rosa and Siya are still in the art room, as far as I know. Or maybe they've left by now to grab a bite to eat in Mbabane. They hardly noticed me go. Siya was starting on his fourth egg; Rosa had just finished her third. They were giggling. Talking their stupid, lovey-dovey language. She calls him Sweetpea. He calls her Nymphet.

I should never have agreed to let Siya make *pysanky* with Rosa and me, but I was naive. I had no idea how in love they are. I thought that Siya would feel left out, not me. Rosa and I were supposed to study the *pysanky*-making books that Mom sent, mapping out our designs together. We were supposed to chat about the meanings of colours and symbols. Siya was supposed to hang around for a while, watching Rosa and me plan. I guessed that he might try to get involved. But I didn't think that he'd actually be interested. He was supposed to see the unbreakable bond between Rosa and me — strengthened by our *pysanky*-making — and then he was supposed leave us alone. I wanted him to disappear, wordlessly acknowledging that Rosa is my friend first, his girlfriend second.

So I laid out newspaper on one of the art room tables, and set out the dyes — yellow, orange, green, red, black. I made three workstations – trusting that Siya wouldn't stay long at his – each with a soft cloth to cradle the eggs, a *kistka,* a cake of beeswax, and a candle. I provided pencils and paper, too, so that we – so that Rosa and I – could practise our designs before drawing on our eggs. Beeswax is permanent. Once you draw with it on an egg, there's no turning back. There's no room for mistakes. Making *pysanky* is a slow, painstaking process. It takes planning and patience. I explained to Siya and Rosa that we probably wouldn't finish in one afternoon. Some of the eggs that I made at home took three or four days to complete.

I might as well have been talking to myself. They flew through their eggs as though it were a race; like little kids, competing to see who could finish first. I hadn't settled yet on a design for my egg and Siya was already dipping his in the yellow dye. Rosa was right behind. Later, while their first eggs were sitting side by side in the orange dye, each of them started on a *second* egg. They wasted no time. Oh no. No time thinking, no time planning. And all the while they jabbered together – to each other – non-stop, about politics, music, sports, the weather. They talked about anything and everything except *pysanky*. It's like I wasn't even there. I felt used. I felt insulted.

I felt invisible.

The real slap in the face, though, came later, after they'd lifted their eggs out of the black dye and started melting away the beeswax over a candle. I hadn't paid much attention to what they were actually drawing on their eggs, I was too absorbed in my own work. I made a Forty Triangles *pysanka,* one of the most difficult designs to execute. The pattern looks simple enough – it's just a series of lengthwise and widthwise bands that criss-cross around the egg, forming a mesh of forty triangles. The tricky part is spacing out the bands so that all of the triangles are identical in size. It's harder than it looks. If a single band is out of place – even by a hair – the whole egg is ruined. Symmetry is key. Absolute symmetry.

I chose the design and the colours carefully. Among traditional *pysanky* designs, Forty Triangles is the most Easter-like of all. The triangle represents the Holy Trinity: the Father, the Son, and the Holy Spirit. The number forty symbolizes the forty days of Lent, and the forty days that Jesus spent in the desert. I made all my lines yellow, which stands for youth, happiness, and wisdom. Then, after I dyed my egg orange, I filled every other triangle with beeswax. Orange stands for endurance. Red was my final colour. Red for hope and passion.

The finished product was bright and colourful: twenty orange triangles and twenty red, all outlined in a rich, warm yellow. It was perfect.

It still is. But when I look at it now, back in my cubie – my perfect, precious *pysanka* swaddled in paper towel and Kleenex – all I can think about are Siya's and Rosa's eggs. I won't even call them *pysanky*, because they're not. Neither Rosa nor Siya made any attempt at following traditional patterns. A bit of creativity I could accept – a little embryo or two in the corner, maybe; a few abstract African symbols added to the basic Ukrainian designs. Siya and Rosa didn't so much as glance at my *pysanky*-making books. He drew Swazi shields on one egg, a map of Africa on another, and African animals on two more. Stylized elephants, giraffes, impala, and – of all things – warthogs. I think my jaw dropped. She stuck to embryos, of course. Weird, chicken-like embryos with spindly legs and long, skinny necks.

I didn't say a word. I left them without saying a single word. I grabbed my *pysanka* and slammed the door of the art room behind me.

I try to do some homework in my cubie, try to work on my Extended Essay. I crawl into bed to take a nap, then crawl out again. I can't stop thinking about Siya and Rosa, rubbing noses across their candles, placing their eggs in the same jar of dye. Warthogs on a *pysanka*. It's ridiculous. And Rosa's eternal embryos. I'm sick to death of them. I wish she'd grow up and move on.

I decide to take a shower. I might as well. I can't concentrate on anything. Plus no one else is in the girls' hostel, so I'll have the bathroom to myself. I won't have to worry about socializing in the nude. I gather up my shampoo and conditioner, my soap, my razor. Waiting for the hot water to kick in – it always takes a few minutes – I brush my teeth.

At least if they were healthier-looking embryos. Chubbier ones.

When she steps into the shower beside me, my eyes are closed, and I've got my back to the sinks. She's so quiet that I don't hear her until she's turned on the taps. The sound of the second showerhead surprises me.

I jump. We say hello.

And then nothing. Just the sound of water beating against the tile.

I've never showered with Thandiwe before. She always showers in the early morning, with her friends. I try to shower alone, late at night, or in the afternoon, when there aren't too many other girls around.

Standing next to Thandiwe in the shower, I have the sudden urge to talk to her about our encounter at the ironing board, during my first day at the college. I want to say how sorry I am for walking away that day. I should have stayed. I should have made an effort to get to know her right from the start. Maybe we could have been friends.

My heart races. It's now or never. This is my chance. Why can't I speak? Why can't I just open my mouth and *say* something?

Thandiwe soaps up.

Speak, speak, *speak*.

She rinses away the bubbles.

Or sing.

I don't know what the words mean, and I don't know if she'll laugh if I pronounce them wrong, but I have to try. I decide to sing one of the songs that I've heard Thandiwe sing every morning in the shower.

Thula, thula mama, thula
thula mama, thula
thula mama

The song is sweet and slow; as I sing it, I keep my eyes straight ahead, focused on the wall of the shower. If I turn to Thandiwe, and she's frowning, I don't know what I'll do.

Samthatha sambeka ekhaya
wasuke wakhala
wathi mama thula

When I start in on the second round of *"thula, thula mama, thula,"* Thandiwe joins in.

I let her take the lead part.

I let her lead me through the rest of the song.

From time to time my voice falters and cracks. Her voice gives me the shivers. I can't believe that I'm finally singing with her. I'm so happy, I could cry. Thandiwe keeps going, solid and strong.

Thula, thula mama, thula
thula mama, thula
thula mama

Afterwards, when we're towelling off, side by side, I ask Thandiwe if she can translate the Zulu song for me. What does it mean? I wonder. What were we singing about?

She explains that it's a kind of freedom song, in the form of a lullaby. It's a song of comfort for mothers whose children have been imprisoned. *"Thula mama"* means "hush mother." Hush mother, don't cry. Hush.

I wish that I could give Thandiwe something in exchange for the gift she's given me. Something as simple and as beautiful as this Zulu lullaby.

Later in the evening, after dinner, I walk over to her cubie. I take along my *pysanka,* my Forty Triangles *pysanka* that has no white on it, and no black. She cradles the egg in her hands like it's a baby bird, thanking me with a nod, a smile.

But it's me who's thankful. Something changed today, in the shower. From the outside looking in, it might not seem like such a big thing. Thandiwe and I sang a song together; I gave her my *pysanka.* It might not seem so important. I feel different, though. What happened in the art room doesn't seem to matter anymore. I feel warm all over.

I almost feel – reborn.

FIVE

The smell.

Late Monday night, and it's here already. In my cubie, in the air. In my nostrils.

In my head, I know. But I can't get rid of it.

For three months now we've been volunteering at the hospital – Rosa, Carlo, a guy from Brazil, Siya, and me. Not the Raleigh Fitkin Hospital in Malkerns, where well-to-do Swazis go when they get sick; not the private clinic near Manzini, for diplomats and Waterford students and foreigners in general, those who can afford a private bed and a European doctor. We volunteer at the Government Hospital in Mbabane, on the Children's Ward – once a week, every Tuesday morning. Twelve Tuesdays in total, so far. I should be used to the place, the patients. The smell. I should be at home with all of it.

I should be used to seeing Rosa and Siya together, too, holding hands as they walk up the wheelchair ramp to the Children's Ward. Sneaking kisses when they think no one is watching them, and giggling at private jokes. From time to time, though, I still catch myself staring at them. As far as I'm concerned, they're the oddest couple. Rosa is tiny. She can't weigh more than a hundred pounds. Siya is short and fat. He's at least fifty pounds overweight. I try not to pay attention to the colour of their skin, but she seems so white next to him, and he seems so black. All of the nurses on the Children's Ward notice it, too. I know they do. They're all

Swazi women. When Rosa and Siya walk through the corridors of the hospital, the nurses' heads turn.

Rosa and Siya don't care.

I'm allowed to leave campus again, but I don't spend as much time downtown. During my blacklisting, Rosa and Siya found a new favourite restaurant in Mbabane. They have a regular table that seats two. On Saturdays, I usually head back up the hill in the afternoon, instead of staying in town until evening. Most Sundays, I don't leave campus at all. I don't want to be a fifth wheel.

Mrs. McBain seems satisfied. She smiles when she sees me eating Sunday dinners with some of the other scholarship students – usually Shelagh and Nikola – or with Thandiwe and her friends from Soweto. During my piano lessons, when Mrs. McBain asks about my E^2 composition, I tell her that it's coming along fine. Should be finished right on schedule.

In fact, I'm still working on Ukrainian folk songs. So far, my essay is forty pages long, and it's only half-finished. My *pysanka* pictures are ready to go, and I have two cassette tapes of folk music recordings to accompany the final draft. I can't wait to show Mrs. McBain. She's going to be stunned.

I just wish that I'd chosen another Community Service. Because Monday nights are starting to take their toll. I dread them. By the middle of August, I'm looking for any excuse not to go to the hospital. When I try to go to sick bay with make-believe migraines, the nurse on duty just sends me away with headache tablets. Homework doesn't work. Everyone has homework. At the beginning of the term, in June, I tried to use my wardrobe as an excuse. Women have to wear long skirts in all government buildings. I only had one – short – skirt. The nurses on the Children's Ward didn't approve the first few times that I wore it. Rosa bought a skirt for me, though, in town – a long, black skirt with white stripes.

Rosa and Siya aren't the problem. The skirt isn't the problem. It's the smell.

Late Monday night, and the smell is back again. I've noticed that it comes earlier and earlier every week. At first, the smell woke me up; now, it keeps me up.

Rosa, I know, doesn't notice the smell. She's been asleep for hours, dreaming about Siya, I suppose, her eyes darting from side to side beneath their freckled lids. Twice I've brought my sleeping bag and pillow to her room, thinking that maybe I would make a bed for myself on her floor. Thinking that I would drift off – peacefully – taking in traces of Rosa's oil paint, Rosa's *Nivea* cream. *Anais Anais,* Rosa's perfume. Twice, though, my plan has failed. The hospital smell follows me to her cubie.

In my cubie, I try incense – a gift from Rosa who uses sticks of it to mask the smell of *dagga* in her room – and squirts of my own perfume, *Sung.* On the bookshelf over my bed, I light a scented candle. Apple blossoms and cinnamon sticks.

And hospital smell.

A lot of senior girls are Pre-School Playleaders, tending to staff members' toddlers – two- and three- and four-year-olds who smell of baby powder, Johnson-and-Johnson baby shampoo. Or tutors. I could be a tutor on the Adult Literacy Team, or the Quedusizi Primary School Team. The tutors work with blackboards and chalk. They're surrounded by the rubbery smell of pink erasers on fresh, clean, white paper. I'm a decent swimmer, I could join the Hot Springs Group, and dip school-aged, water-winged kids in the Hot Springs, in the Ezulwini Valley, every Wednesday afternoon. I could be bathing in chlorine each week. Breathing in chlorine.

I chose the Government Hospital because of Rosa. She's been volunteering at the Children's Ward for years. She said that it was the most effortless Community Service project. The most effortless, and the most rewarding.

"Just show up," she said. "That's all you have to do. You'll really make a difference there."

Rosa didn't mention the smell.

She described to me the sort of Developing World hospital

that I've seen on *World Vision* commercials, on hour-long *Christian Children's Fund* programs and *Foster Parents' Plan* fundraising telethons. A place bustling with men and white women in khaki cotton slacks, white cotton shirts – cheerful doctors, nurses, and volunteers, all bottle-feeding malnourished infants, spoon-feeding children with spindly legs and distended stomachs. Bringing them all back to life. Doling out vaccinations and advice about breast milk. Rosa mentioned cement floors, cracking plaster on cement walls – a rundown building, all in all, but clean, more or less. She didn't say a word about the smell.

No. Not the smell. Not the smell, the *reek*.

The reek of shit. The reek of piss. The metallic, iron reek of afterbirth and menstrual blood. The toilets on the Children's Ward – a three-room sub-ward of the Maternity Wing – only sometimes flush, and diapers are hardly ever changed, and if there are showers or bathtubs, I've never seen them and I fear that they're rarely ever used. The sweet rotting reek of open, festering bedsores; of bedsheets rarely washed, caked in dried blood, sweat, pus. The rancid reek of oil from the fried fish – the whole fried fish, complete with heads and tails and fins – that the children never finish at lunch but save in swatches of greasy toilet paper to eat later. The reek of charred human flesh, too; of children rushed in with bone-deep burns from their mothers' open cooking flames. Children who have no skin left for grafting and who die on the floor, in the hallway, their bodies still feeling the fire.

Sometime before the sun rises, I fall asleep with the smell.

When I open my eyes, Rosa is standing over me. Oblivious to the hospital smell still strong in my cubie, she is smiling, telling me that I let my candle burn down in the night, and that a pool of hot wax has collected and cooled on my bookshelf.

"We'll have to clean it later," she says. "We don't want to be late for the hospital."

As I get out of bed, Rosa rummages in my closet for the skirt she bought me in Mbabane.

I think it isn't fair that we have to wear skirts. Carlo and Siya don't have to wear skirts. It isn't fair that Carlo can bring his soccer ball, either, and bounce it non-stop in the bus on the way to Mbabane and grin from ear to ear the whole time. Carlo is in love with the sport; he signed up for Community Service at the hospital so that he could play it every Tuesday morning. So that he could take the healthiest children from the ward and play football with them for four full hours. Siya usually goes with him. It isn't fair. Carlo and Siya leave Rosa and me with the sickest and the feeblest.

Of course, Rosa never grumbles about Carlo. She never complains about the bouncing of his football or the fact that both he and Siya can, and do, wear jogging shorts to the hospital each week. She's trying to play matchmaker, that's the problem. And she's not very subtle about it. Siya and Carlo have started to play soccer on the same team in Mbabane. Rosa wants me to join her in town to watch them play; then she'd like the four of us to go out together, on double dates. So she's always pointing out Carlo's best qualities to me.

"Look at the scar on his knee," she says. "Isn't it sexy?"

"Listen to his accent," she says. "Doesn't it just make you melt?"

Carlo injured his knee playing soccer, and he's had five surgeries on it. I think it's about the ugliest, lumpiest criss-crossed mess of scars I've ever seen. Looking at it makes me nauseous. Plus he's almost as chubby as Siya. How can he be serious about soccer when he's overweight? He probably injured his knee because he's too heavy. When he opens his mouth, he sounds like Cheech and Chong.

Forty of us ride the Community Service bus together on Tuesday mornings. Members of the Quedusizi Primary School Team, the Adult Literacy Team, and us, the hospital crew. On her lap, Rosa carries a cardboard box filled with art supplies – her own finger paints, wax crayons, oil pastels and pencil crayons, plus construction paper from the Community Service supply room at the college. Carlo's got the inevitable soccer ball. This week, for the first time, I've brought my guitar. Siya meets us at the hospital.

Rosa's got her Extended Essay all planned out, and the hospital kids are part of it. She's writing about art therapy, how drawing can be a way of healing. That's why she brings her art supplies to the hospital every week. She encourages the children to draw. They can draw anything, whatever they please. And then, in her cubie back at school, she analyzes the pictures, interprets them. This way, she can learn about the children's lives without asking them straight out. She can find out about their individual traumas. Rosa compares pictures, too. Comparisons are the main part of her essay. She tacks up pictures on the walls of her cubie – pictures drawn by the same child over a period of weeks, and months, if possible. Then she studies them for signs of progress. Her thesis is simple. The more the children draw, the more they heal. The pictures are supposed to get happier and happier. Figures with smiles on their faces, figures dancing. Figures sheathed in more, and brighter, colours.

The bus stops first at the base of the Waterford hill, where the Quedusizi Primary School is located. It's a rundown, one-roomed cement building next to a clay playing field that turns to mud in the rainy season. The tutors from Waterford take groups of students out to the playing field when it's dry. When it rains, they hold their classes inside.

Next, we stop at St. Marks School, a few blocks north of main street Mbabane, where the Adult Literacy Team meets their students – Swazi men and women who have never learned to read or write. St. Marks is bigger and newer than Quedusizi – though still nothing like Waterford. Waterford is a five-star hotel compared to other schools in Swaziland. There's no lawn around St. Marks, no flowers or shrubs. The paint is peeling on the outside of the building.

Our last stop is the Government Hospital, south of the

Mbabane city centre. It doesn't look so bad from the outside. There's a patch of grass in front of the main doors, and the outside walls have been freshly painted. But I know what's inside. I know what it's really like.

As the bus pulls up to the front doors of the hospital, Rosa can hardly wait to get out. She searches the parking lot for Siya's car. Siya greets her at the doors of the hospital with a big hug. I take a deep breath of fresh air — my last, I know, for the next four hours. Rosa, Siya, and Carlo walk quickly up the ramp that leads through the hospital — past the surgical theatres, past the geriatric wing — to Ward Eight. The Children's Ward. I lag behind, lingering at the doorway of the playroom — where the children also take all their meals, where some of them sleep at night. The smell here is worse than in any other part of the hospital; it makes me dizzy. I have to lean on a wall to steady myself.

Six or seven little boys run to Siya and Carlo — all under the age of seven and healthy, for the most part. Almost ready to go home. Some are in hospital with fractured wrists, broken arms; some are recovering from minor burns to their faces and chests. One boy grabs the football from Carlo's hands, the others race down the ramp to the doors of the hospital. I hear their giggles in the distance as they move toward the empty lot beside the hospital, as they move away from the playroom.

There are healthy girls here, too — at least three of them, between ten and twelve years of age. They are healthier even than the little boys who play football with Siya and Carlo. In fact, the healthy girls are only here because their siblings are ill. Their mothers send them to the hospital to watch over their sick infant sisters and brothers. The healthy girls never play football, never join in Rosa's arts and crafts. They hardly smile.

The other children, though — the children who are really ill, terminally ill, and abandoned, some of them, and alone, and never going home — they smile. When they see Rosa, they smile so hard that I think they might hurt themselves.

Rosa has trouble, sometimes, setting her box of art supplies onto the table in the playroom. The children hug her arms and legs, clinging to any part of Rosa they can grab hold of, and refusing to let go. I have to step in, taking the box from her, freeing her limbs. Rosa makes sure to greet all of the children. Kneeling down to them, one by one, she folds them into her arms, kisses their cheeks. Some are too frail to be embraced, so she strokes their faces, gently, and their hair. They like to touch her face, too – her hair, especially. She lets them.

Over the last five years, Rosa has formed a bond with several of the children on the ward – the permanent residents, the children who are stuck here until they turn eighteen. Or until they die.

Mbuso isn't supposed to have lived this long. His face looks to be about ten, maybe eleven years old, and his body seems even younger. But he's sixteen. He wears a hooped earring in his right ear, shaves his head like a Mohawk. Mbuso is paralyzed from the waist, possibly the chest, down, I'm not sure. He gets around by dragging himself with his arms and hands. There is no money for a wheelchair for Mbuso, or a catheter, or a colostomy bag. Around his waist, and down around his hips, he wraps raggy strips of bedsheets for a diaper. I think that he probably washes the rags himself.

Rosa knows a lot about spina bifida from her parents. It starts, she says, in the womb, shortly after fertilization. Two or three weeks into the development of Mbuso, something went wrong, and his tiny neural tube – which, in normal embryos, becomes the spinal cord and the brain – didn't close properly. Rosa says that underneath Mbuso's clothes, underneath his diaper sheet, there is an open lesion. A hole in his back, with damaged spinal cord protruding. The hospital has no money for an operation that would close it.

The nurses say that no operation will help Dumi. He'll almost certainly die soon. They talk about it all the time – in his presence they talk about it, as though he can't hear them, as though he can't understand. He's new to the ward, actually. Dumi's only been in the hospital for two weeks, lying on a cot in the corner of the playroom, his burnt body swathed in gauze. He is ten years old and fully conscious. When Rosa bends down to him, he whispers into her ear. The nurses feed him every two or three hours with a bottle, like a baby.

On occasion, the nurses let Gugu feed Dumi, to teach her about child care. Gugu is a big girl with Down's Syndrome. She's seventeen, tall, big-boned, and full of energy. She also helps the nurses sweep and tidy the playroom, put the babies down for naps. Gugu has spent her life in the Children's Ward. As far as I know, she was delivered in the Maternity Wing, and then left here by her mother. In a year's time, when Gugu turns eighteen, she'll have to go. They'll sterilize her first. Where? I wonder. Where will she go?

To a government asylum, maybe, in another part of Swaziland. Sipho, nearly fifteen, has to go too – and soon. Because the nurses at the Government Hospital aren't trained to deal with him. They don't know how to begin helping him. When Sipho was very small – a baby, they think – his mother went away, or died, more likely, leaving her husband to care for the boy. The husband, though – the father – didn't know anything about babies; when he left for work on the mines in South Africa, he left Sipho for weeks on end locked in a sort of backroom – a closet, really – in a shack in rural Swaziland with hardly enough food or water to survive. A relative found Sipho seven years ago.

This is the story, at least – the story I heard from Rosa, who heard it from Siya, who heard it from the nurses. There are plenty of holes in it, if you ask me. Maybe something got lost in the translation. I don't think that Sipho was just tied up and abandoned by his father. Something worse happened to him.

Sipho is like an animal. Sometimes he's violent. I've seen him kicking or slapping the other children, and frequently – very frequently – touching his genitals, playing with his stool. He can't walk. When the nurses untie the rags that bind him to the play-room table, he moves around on all fours, grunting, snarling. Supposedly, he can't talk either. But we've all heard Sipho utter swear words, clear as day. And not in SiSwati, either. In English. People in rural Swaziland don't speak English. Where did Sipho learn English swear words like *asshole* and *bloody hell* and *cock*?

Precious is terrified of Sipho – terrified of his grunting and snarling. Really, any loud noise drives her under a blanket in the corner of the playroom. So long as the ward is quiet, though, Precious is fine. Relaxed, and calm. Looking at her, in fact, she seems like a completely normal thirteen-year-old. As normal as any child her age. Except for her fear of loud noises, and the long, white line across her neck. According to the nurses, Precious was raised by a grandmother who yelled at the girl constantly. After the yelling came the beating. And then, to further discipline the child, the grandmother tied her to a wall. By the neck. With copper wire.

I'm a little suspicious of the nurses. They look chronically bored. When they do anything – wash a face, fold a towel, even walk – they do it slowly and reluctantly. The nurses at the hospital are badly paid, I'm sure. But sometimes I wonder if they've had a hand in scarring the children – if they untie Sipho only when we're present, watching them; if they really care to teach Gugu a few basic life skills, or if they enjoy seeing Gugu do their work; if they themselves haven't resorted to yelling on occasion. Sometimes I think that better pay wouldn't make any difference at all.

I've never seen a doctor in the Children's Ward.

There is, though, on the Children's Ward, a kind of social order among the children. A set of rules, unwritten, of course, but under-stood by everyone. I've seen it with my own eyes. The healthier children belong at the bottom of the pecking order; the sicker the child, the higher the status. Mbuso, the boy with spina bifida, is at the top; he's the enforcer, the ringleader of the ward who polices the healthy and protects the weak. No one is to tease Precious, no one is to intentionally frighten her with a raised voice. No one is ever to point to or laugh at Sipho, regardless of what he might say or do. No harm must come to Dumi – his cot is sacred. No balls can be thrown his way, no toys tossed in his direction. Gugu is to be treated like a woman, with respect.

I've also learned that Mbuso has a crush on Rosa. I've seen it with my own eyes – the way he stares at her as she lays out her art supplies on the table and on the floor in the playroom; the way he watches her as she helps the other children draw or paint, guiding their hands across the paper, and praising their work. He looks at her with such longing, such craving. As though he could at any moment break down and cry for her.

Mbuso loves Rosa, without a doubt. And he hates Ayanda. He would bash Ayanda's head against the cement floor, I think, if he could. If he had the strength.

Ayanda is a baby, three or four months old, and new to the ward. A month ago he was brought in by a taxi driver who found him in the Mbabane taxi rink. Ayanda – the nurses named him – is not likely to last in the hospital. The nurses know it, Mbuso knows it. I know it. He's an infant, and he's perfectly healthy, and it's only a matter of time before somebody adopts him.

Rosa won't hear of it. Today, for the fourth week in a row, she carries Ayanda in her arms for the full four hours of Community Service. She refuses to put him down. While she directs the other children's art work, she bounces Ayanda, rocks Ayanda, talks baby-talk to Ayanda. Holds the bottle to his lips, sings him lullabies.

I'm not like Rosa. I'm nothing like her. I'm not tough enough for the hospital. I don't know how to get through to the children, how to make them see that I'm their friend. I don't speak SiSwati, like Rosa. That's part of the problem. And none of the children speaks English. But it's more than that. Most students who have volunteered at the hospital over the years couldn't speak SiSwati – Rosa is an exception – and they never had problems. It's me. I'm scared of the children. They're so sick, and so fragile. I'm afraid that if I touch them, I'll hurt them. I'll make them cry. They'll break in my hands. Mbuso eyes me like a mother protecting her brood. He knows that I don't belong here. He can sense it. He watches me constantly, ready to catch me if I make one wrong move.

When I first started coming to the hospital, some of the children who have always lived on the ward – Mbuso, Precious, even Gugu – flocked to my side, asking for Steve. They all asked, "Where is Steve?" – in SiSwati, of course, with the nurses or Rosa translating so that I could understand.

"When is Steve coming? Today? Will Steve be here today? Will Steve come tomorrow?"

Steve, apparently, was a Waterford student on scholarship from the United States who used to volunteer on the Children's Ward. He came to the hospital before Rosa started her volunteer work here. Which would make it six or seven years ago. He must have made quite an impression, this Steve, because the children and all of the nurses remember him, after all this time. The children miss him the most. They're still waiting for his return, hoping that one Tuesday morning he'll stroll though the playroom doors. In my voice – in my accent, I suppose – they hear Steve.

But the children aren't stupid. After the first few weeks of asking for Steve, they figure out that I'm not going to bring him back. Sometimes I think that they blame me for it, too. As though I'm keeping Steve from them, by taking his place. As though if I were to stay away, there would be room for Steve again.

I wish that I were Steve. I wish that I were Rosa. I wish that I were anybody but me.

Today, though, I'm trying something different. Instead of sitting with the children, and trying to play with them – pulling out the second-hand toys that have been donated to the Children's Ward – I'm going to try playing my guitar, and singing. For the past few weeks, I've been talking to Thandiwe about my problems at the hospital, and she suggested that I bring my guitar with me to the hospital. She said that I should try singing some of the African songs I've learned from her and her friends.

It's not actually a new idea. When I first started volunteering at the hospital, my plan was to bring my guitar with me every week. Every Tuesday morning, I was going to brighten the Children's Ward with music. Music is the universal language, after all. Everyone speaks it.

Rosa talked me out of it. She didn't like the idea at all. Rosa thought that the children at the hospital would feel intimidated by my guitar; many of them have never seen or heard a guitar, and it would frighten them. Mbuso, she said, could grab for it, and break it. Gugu might run away. Sipho would almost certainly become agitated. No – no guitar. Rosa was adamant.

I'm starting to see why.

Rosa doesn't actually want me to connect with the children. She wants the children all to herself. Carlo and Siya can take some of the healthier boys outside – that's all right. But the sickest children are hers and hers alone. It's so obvious to me now. Why didn't I see it before?

After I pull out my guitar, a half-dozen children gather at my side. As soon as I start strumming, others join them. They might be a little shy, at first – but not for long. I sit on a chair in the corner of the playroom – the kind of chair meant for a child's body – and, shortly after I start singing, the whole ward comes to a stop, nurses included. Precious stands right next to me, her hands on my shoulders. Gugu kneels at my feet, brushing her fingers softly – gently – against the guitar strings. Sipho, who has been growling all morning in the corner, starts rocking back and forth, sucking on his fingers. I sing "Row Row Row Your Boat," "My Bonnie," "Twinkle Twinkle." I sing pop songs, and rock and roll songs. I even try some of the Ukrainian songs that I'm analyzing in my Extended Essay. Lively, uptempo songs like *"Oi chorna ia sy chorna"* and *"Chervona rozha."*

It doesn't seem to matter what I sing. The children aren't fussy. They clap their hands, their tiny bodies swaying in time with the music. Mbuso sits a few feet away from me for awhile, watching, cautiously. But within minutes, he's given me the nod of approval. After a few songs, I take a break. I put the guitar in his hands and show him how to strum with his right hand while I use my left hand to form the chords. Mbuso is thrilled. He's playing the guitar.

Mbuso is thrilled, the other children are thrilled, I'm thrilled.

And Rosa is furious. I can tell by her body language – by the way she stands apart from the rest of us, bouncing Ayanda on her hip, pretending that she's not interested in the little concert that's taking place. She paces from one end of the playroom to the other, frowning. She starts watching the clock. Usually I'm the one who watches it. At a quarter to twelve, she announces that it's time for us to pack up. Usually *I'm* the one who notes the time. I pretend that I haven't heard her. I'm not ready to leave. As I start to sing *"Thula Mama Thula"* to the children – a song that they take to immediately, because Zulu is so similar to SiSwati – Rosa marches over to my corner of the playroom, demanding that I put my guitar away. For the first time ever, the children want to be with me – they want to sing with me, they want to touch my guitar – and she can't stand it.

At ten minutes to twelve, Siya and Carlo return to the ward with their entourage of panting, perspiring little boys. One of the nurses takes Ayanda from Rosa. Normally, I would be relieved. I would be counting the minutes to my hot shower, and my fresh towel. Today, I want more time. I'm not ready to go.

At three minutes to twelve, the Sisters of Mercy start to arrive, and our time is up for the week.

When I first heard about the Sisters of Mercy, I thought they were a group of nuns. Like *Les Soeurs de l'Assumption* in St. Paul, Sister Maria's order. But they're not nuns. Their founding mother may well have been Catholic but all present members are British – *English* British, that is. Church of England, I assume, though they rarely talk about religion. They talk, instead, about their children, who board at private schools in England, and their husbands, who are – any day now – expecting re-appointments to

London. All of their husbands work, I assume, for the British High Commissioner. That or they run The Club in Mbabane. Because the Sisters of Mercy – Charlotte, Mae, Lenora, and Blanche – are always chatting about tea at the Consulate or tea at The Club. As far as I can tell, their primary objective is to make tea parties for the hospital children every Tuesday and Thursday afternoon. I half expect them to turn up one day in flouncy hats and short, white gloves.

They mean well, of course. Rosa is always reminding me that they mean well. They bring second-hand toys for the children, and second-hand books. Second-hand clothing, blankets, towels. More like third-hand, I think, or fourth-hand. More like scraps that their servants have thrown away.

Today, the Sisters of Mercy bring a new woman with them to the Children's Ward. She's so unlike the other Sisters of Mercy that Rosa, Siya, Carlo, and I stop in the doorway of the playroom to stare.

She's sinewy and lean, and taller than the regular Sisters of Mercy. Or at least she seems taller. Her hair has been teased and lifted and hairsprayed into a great copper ball on the top of her head. Her skin is copper, too. Her arms, ankles, neck – they're all tanned copper. She wears black, slip-on, backless sandals with four-inch spiked heels and a form-fitting backless, sleeveless halter top that ties around her neck. There's a leopard-spotted scarf around her neck, too, that perfectly matches her leopard-spotted jeans which are, I would say, three-sizes too small.

Jeans. In a government building.

Next to the copper woman, the regular ladies – Charlotte, Mae, Lenora, Blanche – look smaller and plainer and paler than ever in their cotton print blouses, their brown cotton skirts, their flat-soled, practical shoes.

One of the Sisters of Mercy, Blanche, clears her throat as she introduces the new woman.

"This is *Bernadette*. Bernadette is one of our *German* friends."

As she struts around the playroom, surveying the children, Bernadette ignores Rosa, Siya, Carlo, me. The nurses. Blanche, and the other Sisters of Mercy. All of us.

"Bernadette," Blanche continues, "is going to be taking little Ayanda."

"Bernard!" says Bernadette, lifting Ayanda from the arms of the nurse who is holding him.

Rosa's face turns blotchy, I feel her body stiffen next to mine.

"What do you mean *taking* Ayanda?" says Rosa, addressing the Sisters of Mercy, I think, but glaring straight at Bernadette.

"Taking him to *Germany,*" says Blanche. "As soon as he's healthy enough to travel. Bernadette is *adopting* him. Isn't that lovely? Good for little Ayand – er – Bernard. Good for him! Good for everyone! Think how all the children will benefit from Bernadette's generous contribution to the Children's Ward."

One of the other Sisters of Mercy shoots Blanche a dirty look and Blanche suddenly stops talking.

Carlo declares that we have to be going. The bus is waiting for us by the front doors.

"His name is Ayanda," says Rosa, raising her voice to the Sisters of Mercy, Bernadette, whoever will listen.

I touch Rosa's arm, whispering that we have to leave now. She shakes my hand away, then starts to move toward Bernadette. Siya and I exchange glances.

"Ayanda," Rosa says. "Not Bernard. *Ayanda.* And he doesn't *want* to go to Germany. He wants to stay in Swaziland. Swaziland is his *home.* He can't talk yet but if he could, he'd tell you himself. He'd tell you that he wants to stay *here* and –"

Bernadette turns her back to Rosa.

Mae says, "Oh dear."

Rosa tries to pull Ayanda from Bernadette's arms. Bernadette, who doesn't seem at all upset by Rosa, pulls Ayanda back, lifting the baby high over her head, out of Rosa's reach.

Charlotte says, "Oh *heavens.*"

Ayanda starts to cry. In the corner, Mbuso, I see, is smiling.

"See?" says Rosa, nearly crying herself. "Ayanda doesn't want you. He doesn't need *you*. You have no right to take him. You can't just buy children. You have no right! There are *laws*." Then the tone of Rosa's voice changes. "Come, sweetheart. Come, it's all right. I'll take you, now, my darling."

Beneath Bernadette, Rosa stands wiggling her fingers, her arms outstretched to take the baby. Bernadette – entirely unaffected by Rosa – walks to the other side of the playroom, bouncing Ayanda in her arms, talking to him in German. The only word I can understand is "Bernard." She says it again and again.

Crying, now, and yelling – yelling terrible things about Krauts and Nazis – Rosa follows Bernadette around the playroom. Bernadette keeps moving, spitting the odd German phrase over her shoulder at Rosa. There are more *"Oh dears"* and *"Oh heavens's"* from the Sisters of Mercy who wring their hands helplessly. The nurses busy themselves with folding diapers, putting toys away in the cupboard. All of the other children stand and stare.

Siya and I have to half-carry, half-drag Rosa out of the ward, comforting her as we go. Carlo walks behind us, carrying his soccer ball and Rosa's art supplies. Rosa fights us the whole way, hanging onto railings, trying to dig in her heels.

Through her sobs, Rosa says a half-dozen sad, crazy things – things like *"My baby, my little one. My sweetheart, I'll take you home. I'll take you."* But we have to go – Ayanda has to go – and she knows it.

As we approach the bus, Rosa changes tactics. She tries pleading with us. When the pleading doesn't work, she lists things that she has forgotten in the ward. "I forgot my pencil crayons, I forgot my pastels, I forgot my purse." But Carlo has her box of art supplies. Rosa doesn't own a purse.

She lashes out at Siya and me, then. "Let *go* of me, you *bitch!* You *son of a bitch,* let *go!*"

I forgive her for this before she's even said it. I remind her that the bus is full of people, that everyone can see her. What I want to tell her – what I will tell her later, and what she will come to accept because she has no choice but to accept it – is that Ayanda is lucky to have a future, now. A future filled with good food to eat and a regular home and nice clothes.

Siya helps me settle Rosa into her seat on the bus before he gets into his car. I promise to call him when we get back to the college.

Eventually, Rosa's crying peters out and she starts hiccuping. On the ride back to the school, she says nothing. Not a word. This has been a hard day for her. I understand. First, I sang for the children, and they sang with me. Then, Ayanda was taken away from her. When we arrive back at the college, she heads straight for sick bay, electing to spend the rest of the day there. I let her go.

After supper, as the sun sets, I go to the infirmary with Oreo cookies for Rosa. Rosa loves Oreos. She is sitting up on a bed with her back against the wall, her knees pressed up to her chest. I sit beside her on the cot. Her eyes are bloodshot, and her freckled lids are puffed up from crying. The place smells of ammonia and lemon soap.

"That horrible woman," she says, looking out the window, not touching the cookies.

Tears well up in her eyes.

"If it was anybody but her –"

I hand her a tissue. She presses it to her eyes.

"*I* could have adopted him."

I look away, toward the empty bed next to us.

"I *could* have," she says. "With Siya."

I nod, though I know – we both know – that she's wrong.

Then Rosa says that she's tired. She doesn't want to talk anymore but she doesn't want to be alone. So I stay with her, and like a very small child, she curls herself up with her head on my lap, wetting my jeans with her tears as I rock her to sleep.

SIX

At six o'clock in the morning, in the middle of November, my cubie is twenty-nine degrees Celsius. I know because one of Dad's Christmas gifts to me was a keychain compass with a miniature thermometer attached to it. These days, I sleep naked – no sleeping bag, no blanket. Not even a top sheet to cover me. When I wake up, the bedsheets beneath me are damp, my pillowcase is damp. My hair is damp. By midday, the temperature approaches forty degrees. To class, I wear thin shorts and thin T-shirts, and during study period, I strip down to my underwear. I don't care if one of the male teachers catches me like this. I've never been so hot.

Someday, I think, some November when I'm back in Canada, back in Alberta, I'll miss the warm weather. I'll tell stories about it. "Twenty-nine degrees above zero," I'll say, "during the coolest part of the day. Imagine! November and no snow, no sleet, no ice."

No rain, either. No relief from the heat. Spring in Swaziland officially started two months ago, which usually means showers. The rainy season should begin in a few weeks. Only we haven't had any rain yet and the college water reservoir is at its lowest level in fifteen years. The college pool has been drained; the gates to the swimming area have been closed and padlocked. Water trickles out of taps. Once a week, students are permitted a shower – one shower per student per week. Swazi officials are calling it a drought, college officials are rationing water.

We're supposed to feel fortunate that we can shower once a week, that we have water for sponge baths every other day of the week, that we have water to drink whenever we like. Several schools in Mbabane and Manzini have shut down – closed their doors indefinitely – because of the water shortage. Dozens of people from rural Swaziland are going to hospital, sick from the heat, sick from drinking bad water. But our sick bay is busy, too, with students stricken by heat exhaustion, dehydration – students with fair skin and fair hair, especially. Like Rosa. Since the heat wave started, she's been to the infirmary three times.

Each time Rosa goes to sick bay, I go with her. I stay with her as long as I can between classes, at lunchtime, before study period. She's not at all herself while she's in the infirmary, and it worries me. Her mind seems to wander when I'm talking to her. She's always asking me to repeat myself. And I'm not sure if she even hears me the second time. Mostly, she just sits in bed with her sketchpad, drawing pictures of embryos. The embryos bear an unmistakable resemblance to Siya. One is resting on a green field surrounded by perfectly round black and white spheres – soccer balls, clearly. Another is superimposed on a map of Africa with the words *Sawebona, Sisi* – Hello, Sister – floating up from its mouth.

The heat isn't the only thing bothering Rosa. Siya has been away from Swaziland for the past two weeks, and he's not coming back for another two months. Which means that Rosa won't see him for a long time. He's doing a course in London, for work, and then holidaying in Scotland and Ireland. By the time he gets back to Mbabane, Rosa will be living with her parents in Zambia. She's going to try to apply to art school in Johannesburg – if her parents agree – but nothing is for sure. I think she's worried that Siya is going to fall for someone else on his travels. They had a big fight before he left. I don't know exactly what they fought about, but Rosa has been depressed ever since.

I do my best to cheer her up, take her mind off Siya. Before he went away, Rosa and I started planning our own holiday, a two-week backpacking trip through South Africa. When I visit her in sick bay, I chat to her about our plans.

Neither of us has much money for the holiday, so we're going to hitchhike to Johannesburg and stay at a cheap youth hostel near Hillbrow, the artsy part of the city. Rosa's been there before. She says that Hillbrow has all kinds of cafés, restaurants, and art galleries, plus a big, open-air market where artists sell paintings, ceramics, jewelry. You name it. Thandiwe has invited us to spend a day or two with her in Soweto, too. She's going to show us around the township; show us where she grew up, and where she went to school before she came to Waterford. After Joburg, we're planning to hitchhike to Cape Town. We'll pass through Durban, East London, Port Elizabeth, and Mossel Baai. It should take us three days. Four at the most. Siya has some friends who go to the University of Cape Town. They have an extra room. We'll stay with them for two or three days before we head east again.

From Johannesburg, Rosa is flying to Zambia. I'm flying back to Canada.

Of course now, sitting beside Rosa in the sick bay, I'm beginning to wonder if the trip will happen. If the heat wave continues, she won't be able to go anywhere. Rosa seems to be getting worse. She doesn't show much interest in our holiday. While I talk, she gets up from her bed to throw up. Three times.

During Rosa's fourth afternoon in sick bay, I leave her with a glass of orange juice and a damp facecloth. I've got my music lesson with Mrs. McBain, but I promise to return to sick bay as soon as I've finished.

With the heat, my piano lessons have generally become shorter, and more informal. The music rooms are stifling hot – unbearably hot – so Mrs. McBain asks that we meet in her home. Of course, her house isn't much cooler, really, so we end up running through one or two short pieces before Mrs. McBain declares that it's iced tea time. Then, for the duration of the lesson, we chat about various things. My plans for after graduation, and whether I'm excited about going home. Sometimes Mr. McBain joins us. He talks about his work, the buildings he's designing for the king. I ask about the McBains' daughters, how their studies are going, if they're planning to come for Christmas.

Mrs. McBain is back to her old self. She's like Sister Maria again. I'm going to miss her when I leave. Since my blacklisting ended, we've never talked about Rosa or Siya. I think we've reached a compromise without actually saying so. I've spent less time with Rosa — so that she could be with Siya — and more time with other girls, like Thandiwe and her friends. I'm happy, Mrs. McBain is happy, Rosa is happy. Everyone is happy.

It doesn't seem real, though, that my year in Swaziland is almost over. Living at home again is going to feel strange. Seeing Mom and Dad, and Sophie and Wes, and all my aunts and uncles. I haven't told Mrs. McBain yet — or Mom and Dad, for that matter — but I'm thinking about applying to universities in South Africa. Wittswatersrand, maybe, or the University of Cape Town, if I like it there. I can't imagine living in Edmonton again, going to university there. I want to stay in Africa.

Today, Mrs. McBain skips my lesson entirely, leading me, instead, straight to the sitting room where the iced tea is ready to serve in her Africa pitcher. She says that she has something to ask me. A favour, of sorts.

In early December, at the local Rotary Club in downtown Mbabane, a concert is taking place. A concert featuring a number of Waterford music students. Mrs. McBain is organizing it, and she'd like me to perform. If I'm interested.

As she pours our iced tea, Mrs. McBain gives me all of the details. She explains that three years ago, the Mbabane Rotarians donated a generous sum of money to the college's Music Department. The money, in fact, made possible the construction of the new practice rooms, as well as the purchase of four new pianos, a complete stereo system, and a small library of classical recordings. Every year now, in return, Waterford sends a group of students to perform at the Rotary Club's annual Christmas luncheon. The gesture is meant, in part, to show our appreciation for the Rotarians' cash donation and also to demonstrate that their money has directly benefited students from around the world.

I tell Mrs. McBain that I'd love to perform. How much time do I have on stage? I could do a couple of Debussy pieces, and a Schuman waltz. Or my Rachmaninoff concerto, if she'd prefer a longer piece.

Mrs. McBain ignores my suggestions.

"Colleen," she says, "the annual Christmas luncheon is a complicated affair. We've got to be strategic with the Rotarians. You see, to be perfectly frank, these gentlemen would like to believe that their donation is bringing music to the – to the underprivileged, if you will."

I watch the ice cubes melting in my glass as I wait for Mrs. McBain to finish.

"Ideally, we would like to bring a large group of African music students to them. *Black* Africans representing countries from the poorest countries on the continent. And we are doing our best to recruit pupils from the lower forms who fit the bill, so to speak."

She pauses again as she pours more iced tea into our glasses.

"Of course, regardless of how many black Africans we find in the lower forms, we still need you there. We need you because you are one of our senior students, and we must put our best foot forward. So to speak."

"Katja won't be performing?" I ask. Innocently.

As Mrs. McBain shakes her head, I smile to myself. Naturally Katja isn't performing. She isn't half the performer that I am.

"Actually, Katja doesn't sing. And what I need is a vocal performance."

"You want me to *sing?*" I ask.

I didn't think that Mrs. McBain liked my singing. When I sing and play her my original songs – which isn't very often – she's never very excited.

"I want you to sing in Ukrainian. One or two of the songs that you were going to write about in your Extended Essay. You could accompany yourself on the guitar. That would be a nice touch."

As Mrs. McBain mentions my Extended Essay, I shift in my seat. I haven't told her the truth yet about my E². That I'm still writing about Ukrainian folk songs.

"You see," she says, "it won't do for you to perform a classical piano piece. There is nothing exceptional about a Canadian student playing a classical piano piece. A Ukrainian student, however, performing a Ukrainian folk song is altogether different. The Rotarians will be thrilled to see what we've done with a Ukrainian music student. I'd like you to represent the Ukraine at the luncheon."

I flinch when she says "the Ukraine."

"But I'm not –"

"I know you're not." Mrs. McBain frowns as she interrupts me. "That isn't the point. The point is that you can pass for one and not a single Rotarian soul will know the difference. Eastern Europe is widely recognized as a less-than-developed part of the world, Colleen, and it goes without saying that we haven't any other Eastern European music students, in the lower forms or in the senior class, who can showcase their culture like you can. Katja isn't able to sing or play Polish folk songs. It isn't in her."

Mrs. McBain taps the side of her glass with her fingernail.

"There is, of course," she says, "the small matter of national dress. Which we shall have to quickly iron out, so to speak. Genuine Ukrainian attire would be best, I realize. With the time constraints we're dealing with, though, it would be naive, really, to imagine that we could locate –"

"I'll call my mom. She'll send my full *Poltavsky* costume. First thing tomorrow morning."

This is perfect. After I've performed at the luncheon, Mrs.

McBain will have to approve my E². She'll owe it to me.

"Your parents *could* send the costume. And certainly, by all means, they should *try*. Do we rely, however, on the Swazi postal services to deliver in time for the luncheon? No. We prepare a backup."

What does she mean *backup?*

"In fact, the backup has already been prepared. I've taken it upon myself to organize a costume for you. Not genuine Ukrainian, mind you, but close enough. Katja Malanowski has been kind enough to lend us her national dress."

I nearly spit out my iced tea.

"Forget it," I say. "I won't wear it. Does Katja even know what it will be used for? Because she won't lend it to us if she knows why we need it. The cultural differences between Poles and Ukrainians are huge. She knows it, I know it. She knows that the Polish costume would never —"

"Katja knows that I need her help. Which is all that she *needs* know. Come now, Colleen, you're an intelligent young woman. Use that intelligence to set aside whatever cultural differences you may perceive. We're talking, after all, about a donation to the college of a half-million rand, every cent of which you *have* enjoyed, *are* enjoying, and will *continue* to enjoy as long as you remain a student at Waterford. If members of the Rotary Club are favourably impressed by us at the luncheon, they could potentially double — even triple — that amount in future donations to the Music Department."

Mrs. McBain sets down her glass.

"Under the circumstances," she says, "I think that the Polish costume will do just fine."

"You're assuming that I'll agree to wear it."

"I'm not *assuming*. Trusting is the word. I'm *trusting* that you will wear it."

After I leave Mrs. McBain's house, I march straight to the phone in the common room of the senior hostel. With the difference in time zones, my call is going to wake Mom and Dad, I know. When they hear the ringing of the phone at two o'clock in the morning they're going to think that something has happened, that someone is in trouble – Sophie, Wes, or me. There has been an emergency. A car accident, a rape, an aneurysm. A death.

Dad answers the phone, accepts the collect call. I say that I'm all right but that I need help.

He says, "Tell me what to do. You need money?"

In the background, I hear Mom getting out of bed, asking, "What's going on? Is it Colleen? Is she all right?"

The costume, they promise – relieved that all I need is a costume – will be on its way by eight o'clock the next day. Blouse, boots, headpiece. Slip, skirt, apron, socks. Beads, velvet vest. Everything.

Dad talks to me for a few minutes, then Mom. I get letters from them all the time, but I hardly ever hear their voices. And talking to my parents is different than writing to them. I don't want to hang up. There's so much I want to ask them, so much I want to say.

I ask about Sophie and Wes, about Ralphie, our dog. I wonder about the rest of the family – my aunts and uncles, my cousins, *Baba* and *Gido*. What's the weather like? How's school? Is there any news from home?

As Mom and Dad answer my questions, I close my eyes. It doesn't seem real that we're talking to each other from across the globe. Their voices are so familiar to me, and they feel so close. But I feel as though I'm talking with ghosts from another world. They don't belong here, in this world. Dad tells me that Sophie and Wes are fine. Wes scored two goals on Lloydminster last night; Sophie was home from Edmonton for the game. The roads were bad. It's been an especially cold winter. Mom says that she's getting an early start on her Christmas shopping; that Dad has been out ice fishing, twice now.

After we've said our goodbyes and I love you's, I stand for a long time staring at the phone. Nothing has changed. And every-thing has changed. It's as though I was talking to strangers I've known all my life. What will it be like when I go home again? Exactly the same. Completely different.

For now, I have to focus on the Rotary Club luncheon. I tell myself that if the costume doesn't arrive in time, I won't go. Simple as that. I'll feign sickness – the stomach flu, maybe, or sunstroke, even better.

The closer the date of the luncheon and the longer I wait, the more I hope for no rain. Without rain, sunstroke is good and believable.

Two days before the Rotary Club show, my Ukrainian cos-tume is still in transit, and I'm getting nervous. We've had three rehearsals for the performance and none of the lower form acts is much good. The Form Three choir has a sort of song-and-dance routine worked out for "Puttin' On the Ritz." Their singing isn't bad but their movements are clumsy, out-of-synch with each other. A Form One Nigerian soloist keeps forgetting the second verse to her rendition of a Mariah Carey ballad. There is a Somali flautist from Form Five whose act seems promising – she's playing a piece from *The Nutcracker Suite* – provided she doesn't faint from stage fright.

My songs, *"Tsyhanochka"* and *"Chervona rozha,"* are the strongest of the group by far. The other students put no energy into their performances, and they have no stage presence. Their songs don't engage the audience. When I sing, Mrs. McBain's head bobs in time with the music. She taps her foot, too, and claps her hands periodically during the refrains.

I suggest that the African students perform different material. I tell Mrs. McBain that they would do a far better job of African music. Aren't we supposed to be showcasing different cultures? They could wear their national costumes, too.

Mrs. McBain shakes her head. She says that the Rotarians want to see that the Africa music students have been civilized, so to speak, by the music program. The Rotarians want to hear Western music.

I remind her that I'm performing non-Western music.

Mrs. McBain glares. She says that I'm an exception. The African students look African. But if I don't sing in Ukrainian, how ever would the Rotarians know that I'm Ukrainian?

I have to go. I have no choice. I'm the show's only hope. I have to perform, with or without the Ukrainian costume. I think. I'm not convinced. A few days before the Rotary luncheon, I imagine that Katja is watching me as I dress in her costume. I see her throwing back her head, and cackling like the Wicked Witch of Poland. "You don't know who you are, do you?" she says, in my daydream. "You don't know what you want to be. Canadian? Ukrainian? No! It's best to be *Polish*, isn't it? *Isn't it* Colleen?"

What I need is Rosa's advice. There's only one day to go before the luncheon. Twenty-four hours. My Ukrainian costume is never going to arrive in time. Do I give in and wear the Polish costume? It's just clothing, really. Just fabric. Right? And I *have* benefited from the Rotary Club's money. And the concert is going to be a flop without me. And this could be my big chance to get Mrs. McBain to approve my Extended Essay.

While I talk, Rosa lies on her back in the sick bay bed. This is her sixth visit. She knows the whole story because I've been talking about it ever since Mrs. McBain asked me to perform at the luncheon.

I ask her if I should wear the Polish costume.

Rosa says, "No. Yes. Maybe. "

I tell her that I'll feel guilty if I disappoint Mrs. McBain.

"So wear the costume."

"But I'll feel like her puppet if I put the thing on. And it would be degrading, after all that's happened between Katja and me."

"OK. Don't wear it."

"Or maybe I should rise above Katja."

"Or rise above."

Then Rosa turns her face to the window of the sick bay. She's thinking about Siya again. I know it.

"So I should wear the costume?" I say.

Rosa turns back to face me. "Sorry, what costume are you talking about exactly?"

I walk away from sick bay angry. Rosa didn't hear a word I said. She couldn't set Siya aside for five minutes to help me, to think about me.

By the morning of the luncheon, the package from home still hasn't arrived. Packages arrive at the college once a day, in the evenings. My costume hasn't made it in time.

Mrs. McBain knocks on the door of my room. She's come to help me with Katja's costume. To make sure that I wear the outfit, is more like it. When she enters my cubie, I'm lying in bed with my blankets pulled up to my chin. I tell her that I'm coming down with something, a flu bug probably; that I've got the chills. I'm dizzy. All my joints are aching, my head hurts, my throat is sore. I tell her that I should probably go to sick bay for the rest of the day.

"Sick bay," says Mrs. McBain, "is occupied *again* by Ms. Rosalind Richardson."

In one, fluid motion, Mrs. McBain drops a garment bag on my bed and yanks the blankets off my bed.

I ask if I could do the performance in regular clothes. A nice skirt and a nice blouse maybe? High heels? Or I could wear half of the costume. The Polish blouse only, with a pair of black slacks.

Out of the question.

Mrs. McBain unzips the garment bag, handing me pieces of Katja's costume. Katja, thank God, is in class. Otherwise, she would see that I look ridiculous in her outfit, that none of it fits me very well. Katja's blouse and vest are too snug in the shoulders, I swim in the waistband of her skirt, and my feet are pinched in at the toes by her boots. Mrs. McBain pins the waistband tight before she pulls the blouse over my head and my shoulders. Then she helps wedge my feet into the boots; arranges the lace around my collar; adjusts the headpiece. When she's finished dressing me, Mrs. McBain says that the costume is flattering to my figure. I look absolutely lovely.

But as Mrs. McBain and I make our way through the girls' hostel, on the way to the car park, we pass by a full-length mirror, and I see for myself. I see the frilly, round clown's collar around my neck, and the bulky wreath of cheap, waxy plastic flowers on my head; the fabric of the skirt, pleated and plastered with enormous roses and giant leaves; the billowy sleeves of the blouse embroidered with garish red and yellow and blue flowers. I don't look the least bit lovely. Katja's costume isn't the least bit flattering to my figure. All in all, I look short and fat and Polish.

Mrs. McBain waits until I'm safely seated in the college bus before she informs me – informs all of the performers on the bus – that she won't be coming along to the Rotary luncheon.

"Urgent hostel business," she says, making her way down the stairs of the bus. "Mrs. Dlamini will be with you every step of the way. Remember: break a leg!"

I nearly do break a leg chasing after Mrs. McBain, tripping on the last stair of the bus as I race toward her across the car park. I tell her that I'm not going without her. I'm not going alone. Going alone wasn't part of the deal. What if someone recognizes that I'm not wearing a real Ukrainian costume? That I'm not a real Ukrainian?

In a half-whisper, half-hiss, Mrs. McBain orders me to get back on the bus. She says that we have to keep in mind the well-being of Waterford's music students. We have to sacrifice, and do what's best for the Waterford Music Department as a whole. For the last three years, the Rotary Club has seen Mrs. McBain direct the Waterford performance. This year, the Rotarians will be impressed to see that the show is being coordinated by a black African music teacher, a *Swazi* teacher.

"I'm not going," I say, setting down my guitar.

"Consider it a personal favour to me," says Mrs. McBain, the corner of her mouth twitching, her voice hardly audible. "I need not remind you, Colleen, that I am a powerful woman. Let me assure you that there are steps I can – and most certainly *will* – take if you don't get on that bus instantly. Do we understand one another?"

I understand that I'm condemned to go through with the charade. Go through with it or be sent home. Mrs. McBain's threat is unmistakable. On the drive to Mbabane, through the pre-luncheon cocktails, through the meal, her words echo in my ears. I talk to no one – not the other students, not Mrs. Dlamini, not the Rotarians. I'm supposed to be Ukrainian, after all. I can't exactly talk in English with a Canadian accent. The banquet room is filled with two hundred bodies, but I might as well be alone.

The lunch itself is a blur. A blur of multiple forks and knives, fine bone china plates, and crystal glasses of various shapes and sizes. I'm seated between two Form Five Zambian cellists who don't seem remotely underprivileged, who know exactly what to do with each course of the meal and each utensil. They raise their eyebrows when I use the same fork and knife for the salad and the main course, and when I use the same teaspoon to stir my coffee and to eat my dessert. To keep my spirits up, I daydream about my trip with Rosa. She'll come around. Final exams are probably worrying her. And the heat really is hard on her. Once we hit the road, she'll be herself again.

When the meal is over, several Rotarians make after-dinner speeches. Most of them are fat, and all of them seem drunk. The President sways a little at the podium, and the Treasurer tells a half-dozen vulgar jokes. One ancient Rotarian at the front of the room snores loudly throughout the speeches. His ascot is askew. It looks like he's spilled wine on his shirt.

The order of the Waterford program is organized according to age, youngest to oldest. I'm the last to perform. After the other students have stumbled through their numbers, Mrs. Dlamini gets up to introduce me, mispronouncing my name – *Colleen Loose-Sack* – and placing the wrong emphasis on *"Tsyhanochka."* It should be *TsyHANochka*. Mrs. Dlamini says *TsyhanOCHka*. She says *Ukrainian* properly, at least, and *Ukraine*. But if there is an encore, I'll have to introduce *"Chervona rozha"* myself.

I'm midway through the first refrain of *"Tsyhanochka"* when I first spot the Rotarian near the back of the banquet room. He's hard to miss, actually, as he's the only black person in the room – aside from the Waterford students, and Mrs. Dlamini, and the meal servers. He is the only black Rotarian at the luncheon, and he gets up from his chair while I sing to move closer to the stage. Most of the other Rotary Club members seem to be enjoying my performance. Some are smiling, others are nodding their approval. The black Rotarian is the only man in the crowd who looks puzzled, who appears to require a closer look.

By the last refrain of the song, I've got him figured out. It isn't hard. Once he settles on a spot against the wall at the front of the room, I can see his face, watch his eyes. His expression isn't one of amazement or awe – he doesn't look impressed by the power of my voice or the intricacy of my guitar accompaniment. Instead, the black Rotarian has a sort of smug look on his face, a look that has I-know-you're-an-impostor written all over it. Maybe his work brings him in contact with Polish people or he's married to a Polish woman. Or he's an expert in Slavic languages. Or he's visited Eastern Europe.

Regardless, he knows. And I know that he knows. And, the longer he stares at me, the more nervous I get. Is there, I wonder, a law against what I'm doing? He could be a lawyer or a Swazi judge. I could be deported for impersonation. For fraud. There will be no encore this afternoon, no *"Chervona rozha."*

After I've finished my song, I can't put away my guitar fast enough, can't get out of the banquet room soon enough. There's no time to enjoy the applause. While the rest of the Waterford students take their time disassembling their instruments, as they chat with members of the Rotary Club, I'm at the curb outside the building, waiting for the college bus to arrive. The temperature must be forty degrees. Several minutes on the street and my entire body is wet with perspiration.

He follows me, of course, the black Rotarian. When I feel his tap on my shoulder, I'm not surprised. I'm sick to my stomach, but I'm not surprised.

Then he starts speaking to me. In Ukrainian.

What am I supposed to do? Mrs. McBain wants me to pretend that I'm from Ukraine. A Ukrainian would understand this man, would respond – in Ukrainian. I can't. I can't say anything. If I start speaking English, he'll know that I'm not Ukrainian. If I say "I don't speak Ukrainian" – in Ukrainian – he'll know that I'm not Ukrainian. Either way, I'm in trouble.

We should have had a backup plan, in case something like this happened. Mrs. Dlamini should have been instructed to step in. She could have told the black Rotarian that I'm – I don't know – deathly shy, and then whisked me into the bus. But who could have guessed that there is, in Swaziland, a man who speaks Ukrainian? Who would have known?

The man is puzzled by my silence.

"You don't speak Ukrainian, do you?"

"No. Not exactly."

The bus pulls up beside us. One by one, the other Waterford students start boarding.

"Allow me to introduce myself," says the black Rotarian. "My name is Eduardo Shabalala."

He's the person who donated *Ukraine: A History* to the library at Waterford. I'm sure of it. I remember his handwriting in the book. *A donation from E. Shabalala to the students of Waterford Kamhlaba.*

I try to slip away. I tell Mr. Shabalala that I'm in a hurry. That the bus is leaving any minute. No sooner are the words out of my mouth than the bus driver steps out of the bus to smoke a cigarette. Mr. Shabalala takes it as his cue to tell me his life story.

He works for the Swazi government at the Ministry of Agriculture in Mbabane, but he's not from Swaziland, originally. He's part South African, part Mozambican. That explains his name, apparently. "Eduardo" is Portuguese – Mozambique was colonized by the Portuguese – and "Shabalala" is Zulu. I'm not actually interested. My goal is to get in the bus as soon as possible. End this conversation before it turns ugly.

The bus driver sits down on the curb, in the shade of a tree. Mrs. Dlamini joins him. They talk together in SiSwati, laugh at a shared joke. Neither seems in any rush to get back to school.

Mr. Shabalala explains that he was raised in Maputo. After he graduated from high school, he spent six years studying in Kiev. There, he learned Russian and Ukrainian. He speaks both. Not to mention Zulu, Portuguese, and, of course, English.

"I enjoyed your song," he says. "But I wondered about you. You didn't pronounce the words correctly."

Here we go again. It's Dauphin all over again, and my Ukrainian class at the university in Edmonton. My pronunciations aren't good enough. I sing with a Canadian accent. My Ukrainian is all wrong.

"And the costume that you're wearing." Mr. Shabalala leans in close to me, as though he's about to let me in on a secret. "I believe it's *Polish.*"

Yes it's Polish. I feel the blood rise to my cheeks. I *know* that it's Polish. Mr. Shabalala has no idea what I went through with Mrs. McBain. How I begged her not to make me wear Katja's costume.

As the bus driver meanders over to the bus, Mr. Shabalala asks how I came to learn the Ukrainian song, who taught it to me. Did I learn it, perhaps, from a book? Before I have a chance to answer, he comes at me with more questions. Where do I come from? What part of the United States? How long have I been in Swaziland? I feel like I'm being interrogated. He wonders if I've ever been to Ukraine – to Poland, perhaps? And then he tells me about his fondness for Ukrainians.

"Everywhere I went in Ukraine," he says, "the people loved me. They said, 'You're one of us! You learn to speak our language, you touch our hearts!' I feel very close to the Ukrainian people. I feel –"

"I'm Canadian, actually." I interrupt Mr. Shabalala, mid-sentence. "Ukrainian Canadian. My grandparents immigrated from Ukraine. I've never been there. My mother taught me the song."

End of conversation. The bus driver revs the engine a few times. As I pick up my guitar, I tell Mr. Shabalala that I really have to be going.

"A Canadian, singing Ukrainian songs in a Polish suit!"

Mr. Shabalala laughs while he follows me to the doors of the bus.

"My head is spinning!" he says, shaking his head.

Mine too, I think, from the heat, and the strain of talking to Mr. Shabalala. Mrs. McBain is going to hear about this. I'll never forgive her.

"You're a fine singer," he says, calling after me as I make my way up the stairs of the bus. "Not much of a Ukrainian, but a fine singer!"

The bus driver closes the doors on Mr. Shabalala, as he chuckles to himself, and waves to me from the curb.

Not much of a Ukrainian. What does he know? Who made him the expert on being Ukrainian? I'm tired of people telling me what I am. The adjudicators in Dauphin, Dr. Pohorecky in Ukrainian class, Katja – and now Mr. Shabalala. Total strangers, all of them, who have judged me without bothering to get to know me first. I might not speak Ukrainian, but I still feel Ukrainian. And I might feel Ukrainian, but that doesn't mean I'm guilty for every historical injustice perpetrated by other Ukrainians. So what if I've never been to Ukraine? The Ukrainian people accepted Mr. Shabalala. Why wouldn't they accept me? A person can be more than one thing at the same time. Mr. Shabalala said so himself. He's South African *and* Mozambican. I don't see why it's so hard for people to get. Ukrainian Canadian. Ukrainian and Canadian.

The bus snakes its away out of Mbabane, along Oshoek Road, then up the Waterford hill to the car park near the gates of the college. By the time we arrive, it's five o'clock, nearly dinner-time. The senior hostel is empty. Everyone is in their final class of the day.

I'm supposed to slip into my history class, but I'm going to skip it. I'm going to take off my clothes – *rip* them off, tearing seams if I have to – and then, with Katja's national dress in a plas-tic bag, all of the garments rolled into one wrinkled ball of sweaty cloth, I'm going to pay a visit to Mrs. McBain. Maybe I'll spit on the costume after I dump it out of the bag and onto the floor of her house. This is her fault. And she wasn't even there to help me.

Standing outside my cubie, fumbling with the lock to my door, I spot Katja out of the corner of my eye. She should be in the classroom block but instead she's walking up the corridor towards me. My first impulse is to run. Run *where,* though? To my left are Katja and the only entrance to the girls' hostel; to my right are several girls' cubies and a dead end. As she approaches, I start to walk away from her, in the direction of the dead end. I'll be trapped but I have to try something. I can't face her. Not now. Not while I'm wearing her clothes.

When Katja calls my name, I'm forced to stop, forced to wait for her to do with me what she likes. There will be no yelling, I'm sure. Yelling isn't Katja's style. She'll question me quietly but firmly – "What are you doing in my clothing?" – and then she'll give me a stiff reprimand, a scathing lecture on Ukrainian oppres-sion of Poles, or some sarcastic praise for the way I look in Polish national dress.

Here we go, I think, my back to Katja, my eyes closed.

"I had no choice!" I say, panicking as Katja reaches me. "Mrs. McBain gave me no choice. I didn't want to –"

"Forget that, now. Put it out of your mind. McBain told me everything, I knew beforehand. It doesn't matter."

"But I didn't want to —"

"Quiet!" says Katja, pulling me by the arm down the hostel corridor. "Listen to me while we walk. It *doesn't matter*. We have no time. She's gone. She's been gone for hours, since you left. Her cubie is empty. Nobody knows yet. They were all in class. I wouldn't have known myself except that I had to come back for a book I left in my cubie."

Katja leads me through the hostel corridor.

"Who's gone? Gone where?"

"Rosa," says Katja, as we pass through the hostel doors. "She's been sent home. After you left campus, while the rest of us were in class, Mrs. McBain escorted her to the car park. I saw it with my own eyes. Rosa had all of her belongings in her arms, she was crying. There was a taxi waiting for her."

My heart races as we follow the dirt path that leads to Mrs. McBain's front door. Mrs. McBain sent Rosa away. She must have arranged it all. That was her urgent hostel business. I feel dizzy.

"We'll talk to her together, and find out what's happened. Don't worry. I'm staying right here with you. Maybe we can reason with her. Maybe it's not too late."

As Katja knocks on Mrs. McBain's door I'm thinking about drugs. Rosa smoked a lot of *dagga*. The *General Information Brochure* is clear about the penalty for being caught with drugs. Or alcohol. Rosa had a half-empty, twenty-six-ounce bottle of Southern Comfort in her cubie. If Mrs. McBain wanted to, she could find plenty of reasons to expel Rosa, no questions asked. The Brochure is crystal clear about *no questions asked*.

Then, as Mrs. McBain opens her front door, I wonder about Katja. Why is Katja helping me?

"There has been an injustice," says Katja, pulling me by the arm into Mrs. McBain's foyer.

Mrs. McBain tries to invite us into her sitting room, where

we'll all be more comfortable. Katja refuses to budge.

"Rosalind Richardson is gone," Katja continues, "and we have the right to know why. All of us. Every one of us in the senior hostel has a right to know why. Colleen, especially. She is Rosa's closest friend here."

Tears come to my eyes when I hear the words *Rosalind* and *she's gone*. In the same sentence.

"You are out of line, young lady. What went on with Rosalind is between Rosalind Richardson, her parents, and the administrators of this college."

"Was it alcohol?" says Katja. "Was that it? Because all of the senior students drink. If you expel Rosa for drinking alcohol, you might as well expel the entire hostel, every last one of us."

"Don't you *dare* presume to tell me," says Mrs. McBain, pointing her finger at Katja, "that you or anyone else in the senior hostel has no idea why Rosalind Richardson was asked to leave."

"Drugs?" says Katja.

"Ask Rosa's closest friend." Mrs. McBain turns to face me. "Go ahead, Colleen. Katja claims to be in the dark, so to speak. Enlighten her. Explain to her why Rosa was suddenly asked to leave."

With Katja's eyes and Mrs. McBain's eyes on me, I feel my face turning red. I have nothing to say. I don't know why she was asked to leave. I'm in the dark, too.

"Suffice it to say," says Mrs. McBain, "that as a result of particular steps taken on *my* part – steps I was in no way obliged to take – Rosa *will* return to Waterford. I am permitting her to come back to write her final exams."

I feel myself smiling. Rosa hasn't been expelled at all. She'll be back. We'll still be able to go on our trip.

"So she *will* be back?" I ask. "For *sure?*"

"Under normal circumstances, Rosa would never again be permitted to set foot on campus. However – and I urge you to keep this to yourselves, girls – I have withheld the details of the matter from the headmaster, opting instead to contact Rosa's parents, both of whom are doctors, as you know. Having made them fully aware of the situation, I was able to extract from them the assurance that her condition, so to speak, would be taken care of as efficiently and as quietly as possible. She *will* be back, yes, provided all goes well."

At the mention of her condition, I start to lose my balance. Katja grabs hold of my hand.

"Consider it," says Mrs. McBain, "a personal favour to *you*, Colleen. In return for the performance you gave today at the Rotary Club luncheon. Another girl in Rosa's position would be treated – less generously. So to speak."

"And the father?" Katja asks, tightening her grip on my hand. "What happens to the father? Is he punished as well?"

Katja assumes that he's another Waterford student.

"Unfortunately," says Mrs. McBain, looking me straight in the eye, "we have no way of knowing who the father is. Rosa wouldn't come forward with a name. She is protecting him, it seems, from any embarrassment."

From Mrs. McBain's house to the senior hostel, Katja walks beside me, offering to sit with me awhile, saying that she has vodka and that Mrs. McBain would think twice, today, about punishing us for drinking. Katja says, too, that Rosa is a lucky girl, to have been granted such a break. We should celebrate the second chance Rosa's been given. But I decline Katja's company. Katja doesn't know Rosa like I do. *Taken care of. Efficiently. Quietly.* Rosa won't agree to it. What will she do?

Slipped under the door of my cubie is a memo from the college secretary, a note stating that there's a package for me in the General Office. My costume has finally arrived, a day too late. And there's a drawing under my door, too, small and untitled, with a signature at the bottom in Rosa's handwriting.

It's a sketch of a girl-embryo facing forward, her face blank. Her embryo abdomen is round and distended. The fingers of both hands touching to form a heart-shape over her midsection. She's encased in a rose-shaped womb; the umbilical cord, thick with barbs and thorns, winds twice around her neck. If I look closely at the centre of the picture, I can see a second embryo. A tiny, baby embryo in the belly of the first.

With the tips of my fingers, I run my hand along the surface of the paper, to touch Rosa. To feel her on the page.

But the charcoal smudges, and my tears drop onto the drawing, smearing Rosa's signature into the petals of the womb, and I have to put away the picture before I ruin it completely.

SEVEN

I have no place to go after Rosa is sent away. Everywhere I turn, I'm reminded of her. My cubie is the worst. We spent hours together in my room, and I have embryo pictures on all of my walls. The music room isn't much better. She used to sketch there beside me, while I practised the piano. The dining hall, the courtyard, the classroom block – they're all the same. There isn't an inch of campus that we didn't share. Even sick bay. Especially sick bay. On my first day without Rosa, I go to the school nurse with a headache. Only I can't stay. Being in the infirmary makes me feel worse.

Why didn't she tell me? Why didn't I see? I keep asking myself the same questions, over and over again. Classes are over now. I'm supposed to be putting the finishing touches on my E², and studying for final exams, but I can't concentrate. Does Siya know? Did Rosa tell him before he left? I wish that I could talk to him. That he'd left a phone number in London, or an address, at least. Mrs. McBain says that Rosa will return to write her exams. I hope so. I hope that she listens to her parents. I don't think that they'll really give her a choice. She's not ready to have a child. She's still a child herself.

Most of my essay is written. All that's left for me to write is the conclusion. One or two pages. Three, at the most. I want to wrap up the paper with a discussion of folk music and *pysanky*, to connect my title page to the rest of the essay. I've placed a photograph of my Forty Triangles egg on the title page – but unless I explain it, the picture won't make sense; the person who is reading my essay won't understand the significance of the Easter egg.

In fact, the whole concluding section of the paper is supposed to be like a story. It's the part of the essay where I explain my reasons for writing about Ukrainian folk music. I want to say something about my grandparents immigrating from Ukraine, and how they struggled to keep their culture alive, and what my parents have taught me about my heritage. Folk songs are an important part of it. But they're not everything. That's what I really want to say. Then I introduce my *pysanky*. Because they're a part of it, too.

I can't write it, though. Every time I try writing the conclusion, I get stuck. I have too much to say. It doesn't seem like enough, talking about folk songs and *pysanky*. There's more to it than that. I consider adding a paragraph or two about Ukrainian dancing, and the Ukrainian costumes that my mother made. A few sentences about embroidery, maybe, which is related to costumes. Still, I feel as though something is missing. Food? I could write ten pages on Ukrainian food if I wanted to, and another ten on what it's like to sit through an Orthodox church service. Then I'd need to explain that my family hardly ever goes to church, except for weddings and funerals, and why.

The problem is that, if I'm not careful, my conclusion will turn into a separate essay altogether. At some point, I'd like to mention Sister Maria and the Ukrainian music that she worked on. How she came to St. Paul after the war, why she left Europe. I can't discuss my Ukrainian heritage without talking about her because she's a part of it, too, even though she wasn't interested in folk songs. I'm just not sure how much I should say about her, how far back I should go. Someone could write a book about Sister Maria. Where do I begin?

Or maybe I should drop the story conclusion – drop the *pysanky* altogether – and just write a regular conclusion to my essay, focused on the music and nothing else.

But Rosa was crazy about the *pysanky*. I have to include the *pysanky* in my essay. They were her idea, after all. She thought that my essay wouldn't be complete without them, and she'll be crushed if I leave them out. I just wish that I'd told her more before she left, that we'd talked more about being Ukrainian. It would have helped me figure out my conclusion. We could have sorted out what I should and shouldn't say.

I wish that Rosa had talked to me about Siya, too, before she was sent away. I wish that she'd told me about her pregnancy. We could have come up with a solution, together; a way to hide it until the end of the school year. I could have talked to Mrs. McBain, tried to reason with her. Sitting at my desk, staring at my Extended Essay, I run through a dozen different scenarios. Siya and I could have approached one of the doctors at the hospital. We could have taken Rosa to the hospital in Malkerns, or the clinic near Manzini. I could have talked to her about her options, Siya would have lent her money. I wish that Rosa had talked to me months ago. Birth control pills are sold over the counter in Swaziland. You don't need a prescription. Rosa knew it. Why didn't she use them?

After a week has passed, and I still haven't settled on an ending to my essay, I set it aside. I set my books aside, too, since I haven't gotten much studying done either. Then I take a pad of paper and a pen to Rosa's old cubie, and I sit at her old desk to write her a letter. I tell her that I need her here. That I miss her, and that I'm sorry I wasn't a better friend.

But everything will be all right, I write. Just come home.
Come home soon.

A week before final exams begin, Mrs. McBain asks me over to her house again.

I'd like to believe that she's concerned about me. That she's worried about how my studying has been going since she sent

Rosa away. But I know that Mrs. McBain has another reason for seeing me. Our Extended Essays were due yesterday. All senior students were supposed to hand in their papers to their supervising teachers. Mine isn't finished.

With classes over, Mrs. McBain and I haven't seen much of each other. I try to avoid her as much as possible, and she hasn't exactly gone out of her way to check up on me. A few times, when she's been on duty, she's asked if my studying is going well. I've nodded, politely. Otherwise, we've hardly spoken.

As I make my way through Mrs. McBain's garden, I run through the little speech that I've prepared for her. A speech that's long overdue. I think back to the way that she blacklisted me for being friends with Rosa, and how she tried to tell me how to write my Extended Essay. The way she forced me to sing at the Rotary Club luncheon in Katja's costume, and then sent Rosa away behind my back. I haven't forgotten any of it, and I won't. While I've been at Waterford, Mrs. McBain has been nothing but heartless and mean, trying to control me. Always telling me what to do. I'm going to give her a piece of my mind once and for all. I have nothing to lose. My essay is almost finished. I'll show her everything that I've written, all seventy pages, and then I'll explain that I'm waiting for Rosa to return before I write my conclusion. It's Mrs. McBain's fault that the essay isn't complete. I just can't finish it while Rosa is away.

Once I've submitted my E^2, and written my final exams, I'll never have to deal with Mrs. McBain again. I can't wait. I'm sad about leaving Swaziland, but I'm looking forward to getting away from her. And backpacking in South Africa with Rosa. Any day now, Rosa should be back. I'm counting on her to go through with our plans. I'll convince her, if I have to. The trip will do her good. We'll have lots of time together to talk about what's happened, and I'll give her plenty of time alone to sketch. Drawing will help her heal. Like the children at the hospital.

When I arrive at Mrs. McBain's house, she and her husband

are in the kitchen, setting out a pitcher of iced tea, two glasses, a plate of chocolate cupcakes. Mr. McBain says a quick hello, then disappears. As Mrs. McBain pours me a glass of iced tea, she offers me a cupcake. I sit, but I don't touch the glass in front of me. I don't take a cupcake.

"This must be a difficult time for you, Colleen."

I say nothing, keeping my eyes on the floor.

"It's difficult for all of us," she says, shifting in her chair. "The end of the year. It's a terrible time. And I *am* sorry that we needed to send Rosalind away. I know that you two were very close."

When Mrs. McBain mentions Rosa, I look up from the floor, to glare at her across the kitchen table. Then I stare down at the floor again.

"I suppose you want to talk about my essay."

"Partly. Yes, partly. I haven't received it yet. But I understand that you're having some trouble finishing it. I understand that you've chosen not to write an original composition after all."

I raise my eyes. "Katja?"

Mrs. McBain nods.

Now I'm not sure how to proceed with my speech. Katja has already told her about my Extended Essay. I should never have confided in her.

"You should know, Colleen, that you are far and away the most talented student I've ever had the pleasure of teaching. I shall miss you."

I look up again, briefly. Long enough to see that there are tears welling up in Mrs. McBain's eyes.

"You have always done excellent work. First-rate work. And I'm sure that your Extended Essay is no exception. You can hand it to me when you've finished it. There's no rush. I know that Rosalind's situation has been hard on you. Perhaps I haven't been as supportive as I could have been."

I'm speechless. I wasn't expecting this.

"I'm sorry," says Mrs. McBain, touching my arm.

How can I tell her off now?

"Actually, I didn't really call you here to talk about your essay. I called you here to talk about Rosalind."

Mrs. McBain gets up from the table, then moves toward the kitchen counter, leaning against it as though she needs something to hold her up.

"There is no easy way to tell you this, and I wanted to avoid upsetting you before the exam period. But I know that you're anxious for news about her."

"You've heard from Rosa? How is she?"

"Colleen," she says, sitting down again, "I'm afraid that Rosalind won't be coming back."

"What do you mean? She's not going to write her exams?"

From the drawer in her desk beside the kitchen counter, Mrs. McBain pulls out a small, cream-coloured envelope. She presses it into my hand. "I think you should have this."

"What is it? A letter from Rosa?"

So far, I've sent three letters to Rosa in Zambia. She hasn't answered any of them.

"Read it," says Mrs. McBain, sighing. "Please."

I open the envelope, unfold the sheet of paper inside. It's a letter, handwritten on fancy, gold-embossed letterhead. The name on the letterhead is *Florence Richardson, M.D.* I scan the contents of the letter quickly once, then I scan it again. And then I read it a third time, slowly, carefully, from start to finish, pausing on every word. It doesn't take long. The letter is just a short note, really. To the point.

When I've finished, I refold the letter. I push it across the table.

"This must be a joke."

"No. It's not a joke."

The letter says that they found her shortly after she arrived home, and that she was laid to rest in a cemetery in Lusaka. In time, the Richardsons intend to establish a scholarship at Waterford in her memory, for art students.

I get up from the table, numb. Mrs. McBain tells me to take some time before I go. She follows me to the door, asking me to stay awhile and talk with her. I keep walking. She calls out for me to stop, to come back. But I walk straight out the door of her house, and through her garden, and across the playing field toward the hostel.

When I reach the hostel doors, though, I turn. I don't want to see the other girls, don't want to walk past Rosa's old cubie, don't want to go back to my room. Her embryos are still up on my walls.

So I head out along the path beside the senior hostel, past the college water reservoir that's still low with the dry weather, and deep into the hills behind the school, where Rosa liked to walk. From here, high above the college, the world looks different. The buildings are like doll's houses. Miniature paths, miniature trees, all neat and orderly, everything in its place.

I know, of course, that I can't sit here forever, rocking back and forth with my knees pressed to my chest. Eventually, I have to come down from the hill. Sooner or later, I have to go back to my cubie and face Rosa's drawings. Not just her drawings. The photos of her that I've taken over the past year, the stone carvings that we bought at the market downtown. All of the ticket stubs that I saved from movies we watched at the theatre in Mbabane, and the brochures from the universities in South Africa that we were thinking about applying to.

When I get back to the hostel, I'll have to contact Siya, too. Rosa's mother requested that we let him – the father – know. But he won't be back from Europe for another month, so I'll have to write him a letter, and send it to the ministry in Mbabane. Poor Siya. At least if I could tell him in person.

As the sun begins to set, I start to wipe my eyes, start making my way down the hill.

On the path that leads down to the hostel, beside the sign at the border of the campus – the sign that separates Waterford from the rest of the hill – I stop for a few minutes to catch my breath. I've never paid much attention to the sign. It was painted by a group of students in one of the lower forms. *You are now leaving Waterford Kamhlaba United World College of Southern Africa,* it says, in letters that are slightly crooked, slightly uphill on the plywood sheet.

At the bottom of the sign, in the lower right-hand corner, there's a painting of the college mascot, the phoenix, in black and white. Half-hawk, half-angel, it's engulfed in fire, stretching its enormous wings upward to escape the flames. I like the painting. I think it's good. It has imagination.

Though Rosa, I'm sure, would disagree.

Rosa would find all kinds of flaws in the students' drawing. Real talons don't curl like that. Put those wings on a real bird and he'd topple over in an instant, never take flight. She'd redraw the phoenix, turning the flames into a fiery womb, and transforming the phoenix into a baby bird with tight wings wrapped around its body to protect it from the fire. In fact, she'd redraw it and redraw it until there was no fire around the phoenix at all, just glowing red coals. Until it wasn't even a baby bird anymore. She'd redraw it until it became a tiny fetus – an embryo with wings in a warm little incubator, but an embryo nonetheless.

An embryo like all the rest.

The call comes after I return from my walk in the hills behind the senior hostel. Shelagh comes to my cubie to get me. She says that Katja sent her to find me. Katja picked up the phone when it rang. I should run to the common room. It's long distance, and important. The person on the other end of the line says that it's urgent.

For a split second, I think that it must be Rosa. Then I shake my head. It can't be her. She's gone.

"It's a man," says Shelagh. She overhead Katja saying "sir" on the phone.

Then it's Siya. I take a deep breath as I pick up the phone. I have to tell him about Rosa, and I'm not sure how.

After Katja passes the phone to me, she stays in the common room. Not right next to me, but close by. She and Shelagh whisper quietly as I press the receiver to my ear.

"Hello? Siya?"

It's not Siya.

It's my dad. Why is he calling me?

"Is everything okay?" I ask, my heart in my throat. Katja and Shelagh glance over at me.

"Well," says Dad. "That's why we're calling."

He pauses.

"You know we don't want to give you bad news on the phone. But we – well."

Mom cuts in on the extension. "We don't really have a choice."

"Mom?" says Dad. "Do you want to tell her?"

"No, no, Dad," she says. "You go ahead." Her voice sounds far away.

I should ask what's going on, but I can't speak. Someone is sick. Or dying. There's been an accident. A death? I should ask who – Sophie or Wes.

"Sophie's fine," says Dad, as though he's read my mind. "Sophie's just fine. Wes, too. They're fine."

"What is it then? Is it you, Dad? Mom? Are you okay?"

"It's your cousin Kalyna," says Dad. "Mary and Andy's girl."

What's wrong with Kalyna?

Dad clears his throat. "They found her this morning on the outskirts of Vegreville. Just south of the *pysanka.*"

Mom interrupts. "The big *pysanka* in Vegreville."

As if I don't know the *pysanka* that they're talking about.

"What do you mean *found* her? Who's *they?* Who found her?"

"The police," says Dad. "They think she must have wandered away from the house sometime last night. Mary didn't even know she was gone. You know Kalyna. She was always disappearing."

"What do you mean – *was?* Is she – are you saying that she's –"

Dad sighs. Mom is sniffling.

"Colleen," says Dad, "Kalyna didn't take a coat with her. God knows what she was thinking. God knows if she thinks – if she thought – at all. We're having a cold winter. Colder than usual. It's been getting down to minus fifteen, minus twenty at night. She must've gotten lost and disoriented, then hypothermia set in. She just curled up on the ground and went to sleep."

I can hear Mom blowing her nose in the background before she hangs up the extension. Dad covers the receiver for a moment and there are muffled sounds, muffled voices.

While Dad tells me about the funeral arrangements, I see Kalyna sitting beside me on the piano bench in our living room, her head bobbing up and down, side to side, in perfect time with the music, and I see her in Dauphin, singing along as Corey plays his *tsymbaly*. She's crossing herself in the Szypenitz church while Father Zubritsky chants, and chasing after me in the Edmonton airport with her silly lei, to wish me a *Bon Voyage*. To say *Aloha*. I don't want to think about her dying alone. Shivering in a snowbank next to the giant *pysanka*, without a coat or blanket. I want to remember her like she was when she stayed with us. When Sister Maria held Kalyna in her arms, and rocked her to sleep.

I should be used to the feeling that washes over me. The nausea, the dizziness. I've been through it before, when Sister Maria died. I felt it earlier today, when Mrs. McBain told me that Rosa isn't coming back. After I've hung up the phone, Shelagh and Katja come up beside me, to walk me back to my cubie. I think they know that I've had some bad news because they put their arms around me as we make our way to my room. Maybe they've heard about Rosa, too. But they don't say a word, and I'm glad. I don't want to talk.

What I want is to go to sleep, and then wake up to discover

that Kalyna isn't gone. That Rosa is back in her cubie. That this whole day was just a bad dream.

But I can't sleep. It's still sweltering outside. We haven't had rain in months, and my cubie is like an oven. I think somehow that rain would make me feel better. It would make everything come to life again, in green and red and gold, and it would cool the air, and wash away the dust.

The rain would wash away my tears, too. Bathe the salt from my cheeks. Carry me far from here on a giant, gentle wave, all the way home.

The next flight from Manzini to Johannesburg leaves in the morning. If all goes well, I'll get on a plane to London at noon, then catch a direct flight from London to Edmonton. In two days, I should be back in St. Paul, in time for Kalyna's funeral.

Mrs. McBain says that, under the circumstances, the college can waive my final exam requirements. My grades over the past year have been excellent. They speak strongly enough for my academic performance. She'd like to have a copy of my Extended Essay before I leave, but I don't need to sit my exams.

I have Mrs. McBain to thank for arranging my last-minute flight. Mrs. McBain and Katja. After I spoke to Mom and Dad on the phone, Katja went straight to Mrs. McBain's house to tell her that I'd received some bad news. Then the two of them showed up at my cubie door, and sat on my bed with me, smoothing my hair while I cried, passing me fresh Kleenex.

For a while, I couldn't talk, and they didn't ask about the news from home. Eventually, though, I calmed down enough to explain. To tell them about my cousin Kalyna. Not just about her death, but about her life. I told them everything. How Kalyna used to be normal, and how she changed after her nervous breakdown. About the year she spent living in our house, all the hours I spent with her at the piano. Mrs. McBain and Katja nodded as they listened, taking turns rubbing my back. Katja held my hand the whole time, tightly, like she was never going to let go. And the words poured out of me. I was like a dam that had suddenly burst.

I told them about Sister Maria, hiccuping as I described the way she played the piano, and the numbers on her arm. I told them about the day that Sister Maria met Kalyna. The way she soothed my cousin by speaking to her in Ukrainian. And I told them about Sister Maria's funeral. How much I miss her. How I think about her every time I play the piano, every time I hear a piece of music. When I wake up in the morning, and before I go to sleep at night.

It never occurred to me that I could make it home for Kalyna's funeral. Mom and Dad didn't even ask. But Katja said that I should try, and Mrs. McBain drove me down the hill late in the afternoon, to her travel agent in Mbabane, to inquire about changing my ticket. It all happened so quickly, I hardly had time to take in what was happening. When we got back to campus, Mrs. McBain walked me back to the senior hostel. She left me with Katja while she went to see the headmaster about my final exams.

So I'm going home tomorrow. Just like that, I'm leaving Africa. I don't know how I'll get all my things packed in time.

One by one, though, the other scholarship girls appear at my cubie door, along with Thandiwe. They offer to help me take down my posters, fold my clothes. There isn't room for all of us in my room, so Katja sends them away with armloads of my belongings. She takes charge. Shelagh and Nikola are to wrap my knick-knacks in newspaper, all the stone carvings I picked up in the market, and the Swazi candles. Maria will put all of my books in boxes, which they'll mail to St. Paul after I've left. Hannah and Thandiwe are going to fill my hockey bags with clothes and shoes, bedding and camping gear. Whatever doesn't fit, they'll send by post.

Katja stays with me in my cubie. She says that she'll help me take down my posters, all of my photographs from home. The embryo drawings that Rosa gave me over the past few months. I tacked up her pictures everywhere – over my desk, above my bed, around my window.

We work in silence for a few minutes, our backs to one another. I lean over the desk, Katja kneels at my bed. Since Rosa was sent away, we've come to a kind of truce – though we've never actually discussed it. I'm not sure if this is the right time to talk to Katja about what's happened between us. I don't know if this is the right place. But I'm leaving tomorrow. I might not have another chance.

I speak slowly, and softly. "This means a lot to me. Everything you've done to help me. I don't know how to thank you."

I look over my shoulder at Katja. She keeps working, keeps her back to me.

"I wish we'd gotten off to a better start," I say, "at the beginning of the year. I wish things had been different."

Gradually, I work my way around my cubie, pulling down pictures as I go. Rosa's red and green Christmas embryo, surrounded by holly. Her cartoon drawing of a fluffy Easter embryo – a cross between a baby duck and a baby bunny – inside an Easter egg, popping its chubby cheeks out of a crack in the shell. She won't have another Christmas, or another Easter.

"You were right," I explain, "Ukrainians did a lot of terrible, awful things – during the war, before and after the war. They did kill people. They murdered Poles and Jews. I've known that for a long time. I just didn't want to admit it to you."

I'm shoulder to shoulder with Katja now. Both of us are kneeling on my bed, staring at the same wall as we take down the last of Rosa's pictures – a series of charcoal sketches, black on white. Embryos with blank expressions on their faces. Empty eye sockets. Of all the embryos Rosa gave me, these are my least favourite. I don't know if they're supposed to be young or old, male or female. They look half-finished to me, only half-formed. I've never understood them.

"I have nothing against Polish people. Really. I never have. I can't even remember anymore why I got so defensive with you, why it was so important that I prove you wrong. I'm sorry. If I could take it back – that piece of paper I gave you – I would."

We've finished with the pictures. My cubie is bare again. But Katja keeps her eyes on the wall in front of us, the wall beside my bed, while she reaches into her pocket.

She pulls out the notes that I made for her, from *Ukraine: A History*. The pages are dog-eared and covered in creases. They've been folded and refolded a dozen different ways.

"I've carried this around with me all year," she says. "This history lesson. More than a history lesson. It reminds me of how stubborn I can be, even when I'm wrong. History isn't so simple. I wanted to tell you. I stood outside your room many times. I tried to knock. I just couldn't. Then Rosa was sent away. It was my chance to show you what I couldn't say."

Katja turns to face me. She still can't say it. But I don't care. I'll say it for her.

"That we can be friends."

Katja nods.

Shelagh and Nikola appear at the doorway of my cubie, wondering if I have more knick-knacks that need to be wrapped. I pick up two carved wooden masks from the bottom of my closet, and the tiny figurines that I bought at Ngwenya Glass – a hippo, an elephant, a lion, a giraffe. The masks are for Sophie. She can put them up in her apartment. I bought the figurines for Wes.

I tell the girls that I can wrap these myself. I'm finished taking down the pictures from the walls of my cubie. I explain to them that I have nothing else to do – except finish my essay.

"How much is left?" Katja asks. "How long will it take you to finish?"

"An hour, maybe two."

I'll write a quick conclusion. Nothing fancy. Anything to get it done.

"Then for heaven's sake go *finish,*" she says. "Go down to the music room. We've got your cubie under control."

I shake my head. I feel bad, leaving the girls to finish my packing. And I don't want to face my essay.

"Imagine that Rosa is by your side, helping you."

When the tears start spilling down my cheeks again, Katja puts her arms around me. We hug for a long, long time.

"Think about your cousin. Don't push away your memories. Write for your old piano teacher, Sister Maria. Imagine how proud she would be to read your essay once it's completed."

The truth is, I'm not sure that Sister Maria would be proud. And I think that I knew it all along, deep down, the whole time I was working on my essay. Right from the start. Maybe that's why I haven't been able to write the conclusion. Sister Maria wouldn't be proud. Far from it. She'd be downright disappointed, just like Mrs. McBain. Sister Maria would say that my essay topic isn't challenging enough because folk songs are too simple, too easy. If she were here, if she had her way, I'd be writing about Ukrainian composers. Continuing with her work. It's what she wanted, the reason she left me her boxes of music.

And if Kalyna were here, sitting beside me at the piano in the music room? If Rosa were at the desk next to the stereo, her sketchbook open to a fresh page? They would tell me to carry on. Kalyna would be humming *"Tsyhanochka,"* and clapping her hands in time with the music. Rosa would be studying my title page, coming up with theories about how *pysanky* are just like folk songs: timeless, never changing artforms that are passed down over the centuries, repeated perfectly by each new generation.

But folk songs do change. That's the whole point of my essay. I don't know who wrote the songs, or what they sounded like when they were first performed. My oldest recordings are from the 1950s, so I'm not even sure how my grandparents sang them, if they sang them at all. Instruments changed when Ukrainian immigrants came to Canada. Over the years, their children dropped words to songs, and lots of Ukrainian dance bands translated songs into English. These days, they play folk music with synthesizers, electronic accordions, and electric guitars. They add rock and roll rhythms. I've heard folk songs played to samba beats, with Spanish guitar in the background. I've heard them played with saxophones and trumpets. I've heard them rapped.

Pysanky have changed too. How do I know that the designs I make are authentic? *Baba* never taught my mom. Our family learned how to make them by looking at a book, with electric *kistkas* that Mom bought at the Ukrainian Bookstore in Edmonton. And Rosa didn't even use the designs that I showed her. She drew embryos on her eggs. Of all people, she should know – she should have known – that *pysanky* are different each time you make them.

Flipping through my essay in the music room one last time, I finally see what my paper is missing. I've said everything there is to say about how Ukrainian folk music has evolved in Canada. My harmonic analyses are solid. With the recordings that I've collected, I make a clear case for the ways in which new instruments were introduced, and lyrics altered. But I don't explain why the changes took place, and I don't say whether it's a good or a bad thing that the songs are never the same. I have to make a decision. It's time for me to take a stand.

I just can't stay focused on my essay. I keep thinking about flying home, about what it will be like when I step off the plane in Edmonton. According to Mom and Dad, Kalyna's funeral is going to start early. Ten o'clock in the morning, at the Ukrainian Orthodox in Szypenitz, with Father Zubritsky presiding. My flight arrives at eight, and the drive to Szypenitz will take close to two hours. Which means that we'll make it just in time. I won't have much of a homecoming. A few quick hugs at the airport before we head off to the church.

The burial will follow the funeral service. Dad said that, a few years ago, Auntie Mary and Uncle Andy bought plots for themselves at Szypenitz. They prepaid all of their funeral expenses so that the family wouldn't have to worry about money when the time came. Kalyna is going to be buried next to her dad. One day, Auntie Mary will take her place beside her husband and child.

To take my mind off the funeral, I plunk a few notes on the piano. With my right hand, I play some of the songs from my Extended Essay. *Chervona rozha*, the red rose. *Oi u luzi chervona kalyna*, in the cranberry grove. Tears drop onto the piano keys. It's hopeless.

Poor Kalyna. The ground will be so cold. It isn't right that she's going to be buried in winter. Spring would be better, warmer. And I can't believe that Father Zubritsky is going to bury her. Is he still alive? I don't want him chanting at her grave – *hospode pomylo, hospode pomylo* – like a voice from the dead. Kalyna deserves a different funeral, a different farewell. Something brighter. She had enough darkness in her life.

Outside the music room doors, as I play *hospode pomylo* on the piano, a group of Swazi women gather to sweep out the practice rooms, dust the pianos. They're the same women who clean the hostels and do the students' laundry each week. When they work, they sing. I love to hear their voices. One woman always starts with a single line, then another responds, repeating the first woman's melody an octave higher. Then everyone joins in, singing in perfect, four-part harmony. Kalyna should have music like this at her funeral. Music that makes you want to dance and laugh. Music that makes you feel good.

Not *hospody pomylui,* or *vichnaia pam'iat.*

Quickly, before the cleaning ladies finish in the practice rooms, I grab some of the manuscript paper that Mrs. McBain keeps in the piano bench. Then I transcribe parts of the song that they're singing. It doesn't take long. I'm good at melodic dictation, we've been working on it all year. And it doesn't matter if I can't understand their words.

Because I'm going to change them.

I'm going to replace the African words with Father Zubritsky's words.

In fact, I'm going to change the melody of their song, too. I'll keep the basic, four-note motif, but I'll add on to it with parts of folk songs from my Extended Essay and the first few bars of *Vichnaia Pam'iat*. So that the new song – my song for Kalyna – will sound partly African and partly Ukrainian, with some Ukrainian words, and some English words. All of the minor chords from the Ukrainian music will have to go. I want it to be a song of celebration, not mourning. With an upbeat tempo.

I know that Father Zubritsky will never allow me to sing my song at Kalyna's funeral. But, then, I couldn't sing it anyway. The performance of the piece will require two voices, at least. Preferably four. Ideally, a whole choir of singers.

What matters is that I write it.

For now, I'll call it "Kalyna's Song," though I'm not writing it just for her. I'm writing it for Rosa, too, and for Sister Maria, and for me. When I've finished, I'll make it the conclusion to my essay. I can't think of a better way to complete it. Mrs. McBain will be pleased.

At dinnertime, I'm still writing. The cleaning ladies left the music wing an hour ago, but I still hear their voices in my head. I hear them singing my composition. Lifting it off the page, bringing it to life. And it's beautiful. Their voices give me shivers.

When Thandiwe comes to find me later in the evening – sent by Katja, to see how I'm doing – the song is almost finished. I want it to end the same way that it begins, with one voice singing a single melody line, a simple phrase – the original four-note motif. I think, though, that the final words should be different from any of the words in the rest of the song.

While I play the four notes for her, Thandiwe stands over my shoulder.

Then she glances through the sheets of manuscript paper that I've filled with my writing, making suggestions as she goes. *Hospody pomylui. Vichnaia pam'iat. Mnohaia lita.* None of them fits. They've all got too many syllables. And I need a new phrase, one that I haven't used before.

Thandiwe smiles. She has an idea.

"*Hamba Kahle,*" she says, counting the syllables on her fingers. *Ham-ba Kah-le.*

I like it. It's perfect. I'll keep it. Why didn't I think of it myself?

Hamba Kahle is how Swazi people say goodbye in their language.

Hamba Kahle.

Go well.

EPILOGUE

St. Paul
1992

The idea is mine: I choose to go. I want to visit the cemetery again. I want to eat on Kalyna's grave.

Someone from our family should be at *Provody* this year – it will be the second since Kalyna died, and none of us went to the first. Last spring, I was still in a tailspin, readjusting to living in Canada again. Mom and Dad were busy with school, getting the garden ready for planting. Sophie was moving back to St. Paul for the summer. Wes had graduation on his mind. All of the aunts and uncles gathered at Szypenitz, but we didn't join them. We didn't seem to have the time.

This year, when I overhear Mom talking to Auntie Mary on the phone about *Provody*, I decide that we need to make the time.

Dad says that he can't come along. He'd like to, sure, but it's the weekend and it's spring. There are rocks to be picked, fields to be cultivated and seeded. Sophie says that she would rather pick rocks on her hands and knees. She'd rather seed all of Dad's eighty acres by hand, churn up the soil with a rake and a hoe. Anything to avoid listening to the priest's voice for two and a half hours.

"Plus," says Sophie, "with the warm weather, the church will be like an oven."

Wes isn't even around to ask. Two weeks ago, his summer job started, which means that he's stuck seventy miles north of a university research station near Athabasca, studying frogs. This is a crucial time for his work. Most of the research data for his project is collected during a brief, ten-day period during which all frog eggs are miraculously transformed into living, gill-breathing, sperm-like swimmers. Wes is going to catch them and drop them into cages submerged in ponds; then he's going to add various species of minnows to the cages. For the rest of the summer, he's going to watch the effect of the fish on the tadpoles.

Only Mom agrees to come along with me to church. Reluctantly, at first. She hasn't been to *Provody* in years. I've never been.

The day before church, in the morning, I ask Mom if maybe we should bake *babkas* and *paskas,* and roast a ham. How do we prepare for *Provody*, exactly? If we start now, maybe we could make a few *pysanky* − simple designs, nothing fancy − or just dye a few eggs in solid colours.

Mom laughs at my suggestions.

"But aren't we supposed to bring Easter bread and Easter eggs to be blessed by the priest?"

"That's for Easter. For *Provody*, we bring whatever we like."

Mom decides to defrost a ring of moose *kolbasa* from the freezer, and a *kolach* left over from Christmas. She'll boil some eggs.

"Think of it as a picnic," says Mom.

"A picnic with the dead," says Sophie, humming the theme music from *The Twilight Zone*.

Early the next morning, while I get ready to go to church, Sophie hovers around me in the bathroom, asking what in the world has come over me.

"It's the most *morbid* tradition," she says.

I turn on the hair dryer.

"We never go to church," she says, raising her voice. "Hardly ever. Since when are you such a devout Ukrainian? It's all those boxes you're going through, isn't it?"

I turn off the hair dryer, try to close the bathroom door in Sophie's face.

"Are you going to become a nun, too?" she says, poking her head through the door.

"No," I say, gently pushing her away. No, I am not going to become a nun.

Sophie is only teasing me, of course. We've had long talks about the work that Sister Maria has done, and the work that remains to be done. For the past three or four months, on our weekends home from university, Sophie has been helping me go through Sister Maria's material. Sometimes Mom and Dad join in, and Wes, too, if he's around.

The easy part is sorting through the completed transcripts. We all sit together with a bottle of wine, organizing the music according to its original composers. The more difficult work lies ahead: transcribing the new material, trying to make sense of the bits and pieces that Sister Maria collected, and collecting further material from Europe. From what we can tell, Sister Maria was in contact with half a dozen musicologists and historians, some in France and Germany, some in Ukraine. I'm going to write letters to all of them, explaining that Sister Maria passed away, and that I'm picking up where she left off.

Sophie says that there's a Master's thesis for me in all of this. A year ago, she started her Master's degree – in sociology – so she know what's required. I'm not sure if I want to follow in her footsteps. I just finished my first year at the university in Edmonton, and I'm trying not to think too far ahead. I have enough on my plate these days.

Next week, I start my summer job at the Boys' and Girls' Club in town. I'm going to be help run their Youth Drop-In Centre on main street. It's a place where kids can hang out during the day, or in the evening – troubled kids, mostly, whose parents can't afford day-care or babysitting. A lot of the children who go to the Centre are Native. My plan is to bring my guitar with me to work every day. I might even set up guitar lessons for some of the older children.

In my free time, I want to keep working on Sister Maria's

project – not just collecting the Ukrainian composers' music, but learning how to play it, too. Lately, I've been spending hours at the piano, poring over the songs that Sister Maria and I were working on before she died, studying new material that we didn't have a chance to look at together. Sometimes I have trouble tearing myself away from Sister Maria's music. It's like I'm making up for lost time.

On the weekends, I hardly move from the piano. If I get tired of playing, I turn to my own composing. I pick up melodies and harmonic structures from the Ukrainian composers' pieces – parts of their songs that I can't get out of my head – and then I incorporate them into my songs. I'm majoring in composition at the university, so a lot of the work that I do will help me in my classes. I don't have to do any courses in performance or beginner theory anymore. Most of my classes are in composition, and I choose my professors carefully. No more Dr. Kalman, no more Dr. Pohorecky. But university is different this time around because, for the first time in my life, I'm doing something that's more important than courses and exams. I don't care what my professors say about my work. It's what I think – what I feel – that matters.

When I'm sitting at the piano, filling manuscript paper with my ideas, I'm like Thandiwe, singing on the stage of the assembly hall at Waterford. I think that I know her secret now. She doesn't think about the audience when she sings. She doesn't worry about impressing anyone. Thandiwe sends her voice like an arrow right back into her own heart so that every time she sings it's as though she dies and she's born again, in the same moment.

I think about Thandiwe all the time. I haven't forgotten her songs. I'll never forget the sound of her voice.

But when I'm at the piano, composing, I think about Sister Maria, too, and Rosa, and Kalyna.

I'm going to *Provody* to remember them, the three women I've lost.

Sophie doesn't understand, but I don't really mind. I'm not

sure how to explain to her that *Provody* isn't a morbid tradition.
That it isn't morbid at all. Visiting the graves of loved ones, bringing flowers and food. What could be more beautiful? It's not just
a way to remember the dead, either. It's more than that. It's sitting,
and talking, and eating with them. It's like saying that they've never
really left us. Or that they've left us, but they aren't really gone.

M om and I leave home at nine, which gives us plenty of time
to get to Szypenitz. *Provody* starts at ten. The drive takes
forty minutes, more or less. We take a big basket of food along
with us, in the back seat, plus an embroidered tablecloth to spread
over Kalyna's grave.

I've got a bouquet of roses in my lap. I picked them up in St.
Paul yesterday, at the new flower shop – a place called Re-in-
Carnations – on the east side of town. Carla Senko arranged the
bouquet for me. She's been working at the shop since it opened,
right before Christmas. We had a long talk while she cut the stems
of the roses, and fussed with the baby's breath. I think it's fitting
that Carla works at Re-in-Carnations. She looks good – much
better than she did the last time I saw her, at the Rodeo Beerfest
after our graduation. Things are looking up for her. She's got a
good job, her own apartment, a new car. Before I left the flower
shop, she asked me about Africa – if I liked it there, how long I've
been back, what I'm up to these days. When I told her about my
job at the Boys' and Girls' Club, she said that the flower shop could
donate some plants to the Youth Drop-In Centre, to add a bit of
life to the place. I think the plants are a great idea. I'm going to
stop by again in a few weeks to work out the details.

As Mom and I pass through St. Paul, heading west down main
street, we talk about all the changes that have taken place in town
since I left for Swaziland, and since I left again for Edmonton. A
dozen new four-by-fours roar past us. The parking lot at the Co-
Op Mall is full of vehicles. Peavey Mart has doubled in size. The oil

patch is booming, so there's lots of activity in the streets. We have a Dairy Queen now, and a Subway restaurant. There's talk, apparently, of a McDonald's opening in the fall.

Mom says the town is growing, moving forward. It's full of new faces. Local businesses are doing well for the first time in years. She thinks that the changes are all for the better.

I'm not sure that I agree.

Near the centre of town, on the convent lawn beside the Catholic church – between the cathedral and the new francophone school, *École du Sommet* – there's a Century 21 sign. The convent is closed up, For Sale. When I ask Mom what's happened to the nuns, she tells me that all of the remaining Sisters of Assumption have moved east to convents in Montreal. The Bishop has erected an enormous sign in front of the church – a billboard, really – with a photograph of a young, pregnant girl and a photograph of a fetus, and the words, *Love Them Both*. North of town, the Bishop's new retirement residence is nearly complete, triple-car garage and all.

So much has changed. The Donald Hotel has new owners, and they've renovated the building inside and out. They've put up new fiberglass siding and new cedar shingles; new paint on the doors; a new sign above the door of the bar. On the new sign, Daisy Duck is lifting a mug of frothy beer to her bill; Donald Duck is passed out at her webbed feet.

The old bingo hall has been given a facelift, its corrugated iron walls painted blue and white. Beside the bingo hall, there's a posh new spa outlet that sells indoor and outdoor jacuzzi tubs and whirlpool baths. A new RCMP detachment – all brick and glass – is under construction in the empty lot next to the Rec. Centre. The Lebanese Burger Baron has burnt to the ground. Al's Topline Tackle has become Sunshine Video; since Mr. Wong passed away, the Boston Café has become UFO Pizza.

And, after twenty-five years, the UFO Landing Pad has finally found a UFO. This year, to commemorate Canada's 125th birthday, the Town of St. Paul has decided to put up a new building next to the Landing Pad. It's tall and oblong-shaped with an enormous, glowing green dome and hundreds of flashing yellow lights. Rumour has it that there are several rooms inside, and a sort of cockpit inside the dome. The UFO is going to double as a TIC. Tourist Information Centre.

A part of me is glad to see that St. Paul is getting bigger and more prosperous. There are new *Welcome to St. Paul* signs on both sides of town announcing that our population has grown to 6,000; that St. Paul is a "People Kind of Place." On each new sign, a local artist has painted a red voyageur sash intertwined with the ribbons of a woman's red-poppied headpiece, all superimposed on a drawing of a teepee perched on the UFO Landing Pad. Words have been painted below the picture. *Bienvenue, Tawow, Biᴛᴀemo.*

Deep down, though – beneath the surface – some things haven't changed. A group of hitchhikers huddle on the shoulder of the highway just west of town. Three older Native men, looking for a ride to Saddle Lake. As we drive past them, they don't bother to stick out their thumbs. They can see that we're white. They know that we won't stop. A few miles down the road, we pass another hitchhiker. He looks away as we pass by.

Driving through Saddle Lake, I think about the *Welcome to St. Paul* signs, and the words painted on them. *Bienvenue, Tawow, Biᴛᴀemo. Tawow* must be the Cree word for "welcome." I didn't know that. How do you say "hello" in Cree? I lived in Swaziland for one year, and I know how to say "hello" in SiSwati. I lived in St. Paul for eighteen years. What is the Cree word for "hello"?

Maybe I'm still in a tailspin after all – just like I was when I got home from Swaziland – because when Mom asks me what I'm thinking about, midway to Szypenitz, as we're approaching the bridge at Duvernay, I'm not sure how to answer. I'm thinking about how familiar this road is to me, and how strange; about how easy – and how hard – it would be to keep on driving, past Duvernay, past the old Szypenitz Hall, past the church, and into the horizon. There was a time when I wanted to run away from all of this. There are still times when I want to run – back to Africa, or to some other corner of the globe where everything is new, and anything seems possible. But I'm tied to this part of the world. I know it now. My family is here, my history, my roots. My future is here, too. I want to stop at Szypenitz, and stay a while. There are so many things that I don't know yet about this place, so much that I still have to learn.

I tell Mom that I'm thinking about the countryside. It looks different to me. As different as St. Paul, with its new storefronts, and its new restaurants, and its new UFO. The fields looks greener, somehow. The roads seem wider.

I try to explain how everything has changed, shifted. Grown.

Mom raises her eyebrows.

"I didn't know that I'd raised such a philosopher," she says, grinning. Szypenitz church is in view now. "Maybe you should think about taking some courses in –"

She slams on the brake, and gasps.

"Oh *dear,*" says Mom, slowly pulling up to the gates.

The churchyard is empty.

"Where is everyone?" I ask.

Mom's face turns red. "It's been so long – *so* long – since I've been to *Provody.* Ten o'clock. It always starts at ten. Look at your watch, Colleen. What time is it?"

Ten to ten.

I've never seen my mother so flustered. She apologizes a half-dozen times, fumbling through possible explanations of what might have happened. We've got the wrong day. The wrong time? There's a new priest, she's heard, now that Father Zubritsky has retired. Father Zubritsky always held *Provody* services the Sunday after Easter at ten o'clock. Maybe the new priest does things differently. Maybe he holds *Provody* here two Sundays after Easter, or three. She should have double-checked with one of her sisters. Just to make sure. She should have called.

We wait half an hour for the priest to drive up to the church yard, for other cars to arrive.

"Why didn't I call?" says Mom. "What does it take to pick up the phone and call?" She shakes her head, tears come to her eyes. "You were looking forward to this, I know. I know you were, Colleen. This was important."

That's when I grab Mom's hand, and I squeeze.

"We don't need a priest. We don't need other people. We can have our own *Provody*."

Mom doesn't look convinced. She keeps searching the road for signs of other cars, other people.

"Come on. We didn't come all this way just to turn around and go home again. Let's eat! Just the three of us, you and me and Kalyna."

But there are others with us in the cemetery as Mom and I spread the embroidered cloth over Kalyna's grave. As we set out the bread, the meat, and the eggs, as we lean the roses against her gravestone, I feel their presence, as real as if they were sitting beside us.

I'm not mourning for them, though. I'm lifting my glass with them, and laughing with them. I'm telling them that spring has arrived here, at home, in the most remarkable way, touching everything in its wake. The snow has all receded and melted, the ice is gone from the lakes. The days are long now, and getting longer. Of course, some of the back roads are dotted with potholes and lined with deep, muddy ruts. But the roads will dry, and the ditches will be green again, soon – green, gold, bright pink, deep red. There will be sweetgrass, and brown-eyed Susans, and highbush cranberry, and wild, wild roses.

Rosa, I think, could see this all for herself, if she wanted to, only she's pretending that she doesn't hear me as she peels the shell of her boiled egg.

Sister Maria sees it all, of course. She takes everything in, and smiles. But this place isn't her home. She's never really been at home here.

And Kalyna is humming to herself, rocking back and forth with her knees pulled up to her chest. She's cocking her head sideways, squinting to keep the sun out of her eyes, and she hears everything I say about the arrival of spring. She just doesn't care to talk about it. Kalyna wants to know my name, instead, and she wants me to sing for her.

Mom and I talk over lunch about how relieved we are, really, to have missed the long church service – the up down, up down; the incense; the *hospody pomylui* from the choir loft. We say that it's just as well we came early. And we decide that we should do this again next year, the same way, skipping the service altogether.

The rain starts to fall as Mom and I are finishing our lunch. A few random sprinkles at first, then big, wet droplets. We quickly wrap up our food in the embroidered cloth – the shards of eggshell, the half-ring of *kolbasa*. The roses we leave on Kalyna's grave and the braided bread, the *kolach,* we leave for the birds. By the time we reach the car, the rain is coming down in sheets. One long, heavy downpour. We decide to wait awhile in the car – for the rain to peter out a bit – and then we'll head for home.

"It rains like this in Swaziland," I say, watching water collect in puddles on the shoulder of the road in front of us. "They get terrible electrical storms, thunder, lightning."

"When you were there?" Mom turns up the heat in the car. "I don't remember you writing about storms, in your letters."

I explain that, because of the drought, I never experienced a big storm in Swaziland. We hardly had any rain.

"Would you have told me if you had?"

I don't know what she means.

"I was such a basket case before you left. I always wondered if you were on guard in your letters. If you were – I don't know. Careful not to tell me anything bad, so that I wouldn't worry. You never wrote about feeling homesick or lonely."

Mom pauses.

"I was too hard on you before you left. I didn't do things right. All that business with *Baba* and *Gido.* I'm sorry."

In the year and a half since I've been home, Mom and I have

talked a lot about Swaziland. We've talked about my school work and my teachers; about my friends. She's seen photos of Rosa and Siya, and she knows what happened at the end of the year. But neither of us has ever talked about my decision to go to Swaziland. How hard she tried to convince me not to go.

"I'll never forgive myself," she says, shaking her head.

The rain makes the sound of a drum against the hood of the car.

"Will you forgive *me?*" I ask.

Mom turns to face me. There are tears in her eyes.

"I didn't want to hurt you," I say. "I didn't mean to. Maybe I should have done things differently. If I'd explained why I wanted to go – why I needed to go – or if I'd spent more time with you before I left."

"I was scared."

"I know."

"I thought that I'd lose you."

"You haven't."

The rain keeps falling, and the windows of the car are fogged up now. I wipe the inside of the windshield with the edge of my sleeve so that we can look out onto the churchyard and the highway.

"The problem is that I couldn't have put it into words then why I had to leave. Even now, I'm not sure if I can. I didn't feel like I belonged here. I thought that if I went away – if I went far away, to some other part of the world – I'd become a different person, and I'd finally fit in. I never realized how hard it would be to live in a new place. How hard it would be to make new friends. Of course I was homesick. Lots of nights I wanted to pack up and go home. Especially in the beginning. But I needed to feel lonely. I needed to know what it's like to be on my own. I changed a lot in Swaziland. In some ways, I *did* become a different person. The important thing, though, is that I came home. Because I figured out, in the end, that this is the place where I belong. Here. In this part of the world."

I take a deep breath after I've finished talking. Slowly, the rain begins to subside. Mom and I stare out the window. Neither of us says a word.

And then, as she puts the car in gear, Mom says, "Yes."

"Yes, what?"

We ease out of the churchyard and onto the highway heading east.

"Yes, I forgive you."

Mom smiles. She turns on the windshield wipers, I turn on the radio.

I forgive her too. She knows. I don't even need to say it.

On the way home, we listen to the radio and to the steady beat of the rain against the windshield of the car. Mom is thinking about what she'll make for supper, maybe, or her lesson plans for the next school day. I'm thinking about the new instrumental piece that I've been working on, two pianos, four hands.

When a commercial comes onto the radio, though, ten minutes outside of St. Paul, Mom turns down the volume, then smacks the heel of her hand against the steering wheel of the car.

"Sing for me," she says.

"What?"

"Sing for me. I haven't heard you sing in so long. Sing something for me. Anything."

I pause for a moment, thinking back to all of the songs that I've performed over the years. *"Ave Maria,"* the song that I tried to sing at Sister Maria's funeral, but couldn't get through. "Grandpa." The song that I should never have sung at the Rodeo Beerfest after my high school graduation. And *"Tsyhanochka."* How many times have I sung *"Tsyhanochka"*? Too many to count. My little gypsy, my girl with the twinkling eyes: it's time to retire you once and for all.

I settle on the song that I wrote in Africa, the day before I left. But I can't sing it alone.

"You have to sing with me," I say, stopping after the first few bars.

"I don't know it. It's not a Ukrainian song, is it?"

"In a way."

Slowly, line by line, I teach her the song. I sing a phrase, and she repeats it. Then we sing the phrase together. We go through each line and each phrase until we can sing the entire song in harmony from beginning to end. It occurs to me that I sound a lot like Mom when I sing. In fact, we have the same voice.

And so, on the last stretch of road to St. Paul, we sing to each other, and for each other, in time with the windshield wipers, to the rhythm of the falling rain. All the way home we sing, until our voices are hoarse, and the sky is blue again.

Acknowledgments

I wish to thank the following people who read and commented on early drafts of this book: Jodie Sinnema, Kate Baer, Colleen Greer, Colleen and Darren Caharel, Steve Doak, Wendy Foster, and, especially, Tobi Kozakewich. Michael Baer helped me remember details about Swaziland that I had forgotten, and portions of the narrative were inspired by Barbie Wright's art. Special thanks to Greg Hollingshead, Geoffrey Ursell, and Barbara Sapergia who gave me invaluable editorial advice along the way.

I could not have written this novel without the love and support of my family, Gloria, Marshall, Jana, and Chad Grekul, and Jacqueline Pollard. My husband Patrick was, and is, a saint for putting up with my characters and me, and for never giving up on any of us. Thank you all from the bottom of my heart.

about the author

Lisa Grekul grew up in northern Alberta, worked as a musician, and attended school in Swaziland. She received a creative writing award while at the University of Alberta, and a doctoral fellowship from the Social Sciences and Humanities Research Council of Canada.

She is currently completing her Ph.D. in English at the University of British Columbia in Vancouver. *Kalyna's Song* is her first novel.

An international anthology of excellent stories by Ukrainian writers

TWO LANDS: NEW VISIONS
Stories from Canada and Ukraine

Edited by Janice Kulyk Keefer and Solomea Pavlychko

ISBN: 1-55050-134-8

"A great way to introduce Ukrainian writers to Canadians."
— WINNIPEG FREE PRESS

COTEAU BOOKS
WWW.COTEAUBOOKS.COM